Smoke, and Steel

and Steel

Newcastle 1640

a novel

by Harry Child

Tyne Bridge Publishing

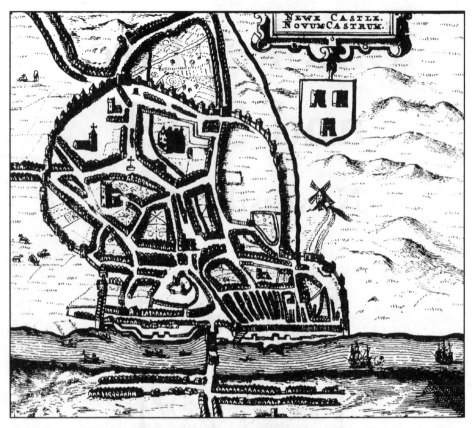

Newcastle in the early 17th century.

Smoke, Fire and Steel

Acknowledgments:

Tyne Bridge Publishing would like to thank Ann Caddel and Vanessa Histon for their help in the editing of this book, and the Local Studies Section, Newcastle Libraries & Information Service, for help in research.

The cover illustration is from W. Gray's *Chorographia, or a Survey of Newcastle upon Tyne*, 1649, republished and illustrated by Joseph Crawhall, 1884.

The map of Newcastle is Hermaniddes, 1610.

Both illustrations are from the collections of Newcastle Libraries, Local Studies Section.

Published by City of Newcastle upon Tyne
Education & Libraries Directorate
Newcastle Libraries & Information Service
Tyne Bridge Publishing
2001

www.newcastle.gov.uk/tynebridgepublishing

Cataloguing-in-Publication Data: a catalogue record for this book is available from the British Library.

ISBN: 1857951166

Printed by Athenaeum Press, Gateshead.

Chapter 1

A Shields Landing

Wednesday, August 12th 1640

'Easy there, damn you ...' By then I was nearly choking with rage. 'You clumsy Scots bastards, harm that beast, and I'll put my steel through you!'

Below me, on the *Mary of Leith*'s main deck, the sailors had already stripped the hatch and were rigging the heavy lifting tackle ready to hoist my mare out of the ship's hold. With luck, they would set her down safely on the quayside at South Shields. In an effort to keep my temper, I turned away and gazed down river again, over the choppy waters at the mouth of the river Tyne and out to where the North Sea was settling, sullen and grey, after a week-long storm that had kept us at sea off the Northumbrian coast.

A seagull wheeling low over the mizzenmast gave me a mocking, raucous cry and a splatter of green-white droppings fell on the cracked planking at my feet.

For a man coming home after close to nine years service overseas, I was in a rare ill mood with myself. Dark thoughts welled up inside me. I could feel them seething, a black brew of bile and spleen, anger and melancholy.

'Your beastie and your baggage safe on shore at the Shields, North or South, as the wind best holds, Captain Ellyot.'

I had heard the *Mary of Leith*'s master limp up behind me but I had chosen to ignore him. The man's endless whining after what he was pleased to call 'expenses additional' irritated me more than my patience could bear. In addition to the passage money we had agreed on at Christiansand, the cheapjack had weazled other money from me – near enough twice a day – during the two weeks' voyage. Coppers for lamp oil to light my way to tend my mare in the hold; more for firewood to boil up a mash for the beast's comfort; silver for a slop of rough pickling vinegar to bathe her hooves. The sum he had taken had been small enough, but the damnable, greasy, oblique way he had of mentioning his damned expenses additional – larding them between civil conversation – had brought me close to taking him by his skinny throat and pitching him overside. I let him wait while I struggled with my anger.

In the hope of finding some distraction, I looked out across the river to the Northumberland side. Nothing had changed. The coal fires burning under the iron salt pans at the water's edge blazed bright in the gusting wind. Long streamers of dirty smoke swept out low over the water to soil the clean white spindrift as it hurried in over the sands. I turned on him without warning and spoke sharply:

'*When* she is safely set on shore, Skipper,' I reminded him of the precise terms of our agreement. 'I think your men will be a while yet.' The storm had put much of the *Mary*'s gear in sorry need of repair.

'We're uncommon short-handed this trip ...' Captain Harvey whined in his throat, like a dog when a bone is held out of reach. I came as near to a smile as I had in a week. He might well complain to me about his lack of crew. I'd had a hand in that. We had been delayed in Christiansand for three weeks. The tale had been that there was a Dunkirk privateer loose with a twenty-gun ship along the Norway coast. So I passed the time playing at Novem with the *Mary*'s mate, one of your raw boned Dundee men with uncommonly long arms and a head for drink that was remarkable even for a Scot. Enough to say that at an inopportune moment the quicksilver with which he had loaded his dice had popped out on to the table with a fair pile of my small coin in front of him at the time. The rogue had snatched out his knife, and I in my turn had fetched him a grand backhand swing with a stoneware tankard and broken his jaw for him. I had feared that my putting down the ship's mate would bring me into danger from the rest of the crew, but the rogue was a bully, free with his fists, and much feared. Two of his cronies came at me with their long dirks, but a pistol shot into the deck close to their bare feet had filled their toes with splinters, and civil direction with the muzzle of my second pistol had sent the pair dropping overside to scamper all soil-a-breeks through the shallows back to Christiansand. The whoreson of a mate now lay at my feet, stretched out and groaning, in the polecat's hutch that served the *Mary* for a stern cabin, his jaw bound up tight in a scold's bridle of spun yarns. It is my opinion, lately much reinforced, that the Scots are for the most part a greedy, mean, and rapacious nation. Though when they have been hard drilled, they make an infantry second to none. No man who had seen the Whitecoat regiment at Wittstock could say other than that.

When the *Mary*'s skipper's slow wits had at last grasped that there would be no more money until he had truly fulfilled the whole of our bargain, he took himself off, yelping at his sailors to hasten their work. I watched him go and it came into my mind that it would be a prudent thing to check the seals and the stitching of the seams in my baggage.

I dressed with care. After so long away a man should look well for his homecoming. My new buff-leather jerkin fitted me handsomely when I had drawn it at the waist with a wide sash of dark blue silk. The effect was indeed pleasing. My mouth formed itself into a prideful smirk, as I bent to peep at my face in the bottom of a copper pan polished up to serve as a mirror. A single white hair in my beard caught my attention and I frowned sourly, then snorted with a sudden disgust at myself. 'Lord God Jehovah, man, where you've been these last years, you're lucky to have kept a head on your shoulders at all – and you have the gall to frown at a white hair!' Nevertheless, I bent closer to the little pool of burnished metal to see the other reminders of youth that had gone for good. My eyes were still the same clear blue-grey, but there were wrinkles at their corners – small to be sure – but there nonetheless, and the skin over my cheeks had tightened under the tan and the windburn to give me a gaunt look. I snorted again. Winter is long in Sweden. How else should I look? A chance turn of my head brought me a reflection that reminded of the days when I had tried to make the most of a distant likeness to his Majesty Gustav Adolphus. Who had not? Gustavus, The Lion of the North, my king ... I had wagered everything on the fortunes of Gustav – and after years of victory I – we – had lost at Lutzow... well, the whole damned world knows what happened at Lutzow.

Nothing had been the same after that battle. In the years since the King had been killed the spirit of the Swedish army had changed. Our will, *his* will, had faltered. The implacable military machine created by Gustav ground on, but without his organising genius, his apostolic boot-up-the-arse to dithering officers and sly courtiers, the thing had lost direction. The Swedes had won Lutzow. They were still winning battles for the Protestant cause, but already their discipline was not the same and their zeal was lost. My own folly lay in ignoring the signs, perhaps choosing to ignore them. Under the King, we foreigners had been esteemed. We, the English, the Dutch, the Huguenot French, and I suppose even the Scots, had taken all our knowledge and skills to that backward nation in the far misty North and those skills allowed Gustav to field an army which was the most feared in all Europe. We had been favoured, at first. Advancement had depended upon cities taken and battles won so a man could rise through ability and bravery, regardless of origin. Then, slowly, the ugly pettiness had crept in, initially in small things – like the even-handedness with which good rations were tempered with poor. Then it had been declared that promotions for foreigners were to be halted. So I came away.

In the end, I think I had done better than many who had stayed on, in the hope that some new campaign would restore them to favour. Yet, as I made ready to step ashore on to the quay at Shields, the whole of my worldly goods made a little enough pile to show for my years of service.

I had been allowed to keep my personal weapons and, remarkably, my wages had been paid, more or less in full. In my saddle bag there was a captain's commission, cancelled, which would give me the rank of gentleman. I also had a testimonial thick with black wax seals set with the signatures of two senior officers who had hardly been close to gunpowder in their lives. I had drawn new clothing from the quarter-master only a few weeks before – horsehide boots that would last me ten years, a new buff leather jerkin, and a heavy woollen cloak trimmed with wolverine fur – such things matter to a seasoned campaigner. The rest was my own, the small change of booty; things bought cheap and held on to when other soldiers had sold theirs for the price of a drink. There was a fine Augsburg clock that kept time to the minute, all stripped down to its parts and packed in wool, a fine set of seven blued steel razors with amber handles, and a few books, kept, I confess, for their rich bindings. These were the things I had fancied I would need for my new life as yeoman farmer in a peaceful England.

A whinnying squeal of fear brought me bounding out on deck. My mare was at last being swayed up out of the hold and high overhead. The seamen hauling on the heavy tackle had rested, leaving the mare aloft and swinging freely.

'Have a care ... By God!' I had opened my mouth and began again to damn the *Mary*'s crew for their carelessness in leaving the mare where she was. I stopped abruptly for I realised it was my own shouting that had startled the poor beast and caused her to struggle in her canvas slings, setting her to turn in the wind. The sailors started to haul again, but now they seemed not to be able to raise the mare so much as an inch higher as the tackle resisted their strength. Anxiously I scanned through the tangle of makeshift rigging overhead for the one thing that could destroy one of my main hopes for the future. If, somewhere in the crazy web of ropes and canvas overhead, a single pulley block had jammed, the mare was as good as dead. I had sailed aboard vessels carrying horses before and knew it was beyond the strength – and, most likely, the skill – of the *Mary*'s ragged sea-vagrants to free a living animal from the trammel of ropes and set it down safely. If all else failed, a man would go aloft with a well-honed knife and cut the mare's throat. I made up my mind that, if it came to it, I myself would climb up and settle the business. The *Mary*'s crew, I reflected wryly, would then have more than a few days surfeit on the dark, sweet tasting horse-flesh. For me it would be no more than another dream gone sour.

There was a sharp crack overhead. and the mare dropped bodily in her slings. It happened so suddenly that, for a second, I thought the whole cat's cradle of ropes had given way. She stopped, her hooves lashing out at the empty air and her big eyes rolling to show blue-white. The jerk of the tackle coming free sent a juddering vibration through the *Mary of Leith*'s tired spars bringing screeches of alarm and the thump of tumbling bodies up from the hold. Then it was over as the yard swung outboard with a rush, creaking under the weight. It was checked, steadied, and at last the mare was lowered briskly on to the cobblestones of Shields Quay.

I relaxed and let out my breath slowly. The mare and my ambition were spared. It occurred to me only at that moment that I had not given the mare a name. From the first time I clapped eyes on her she had been simply 'the mare', a rare piece of unlooked-for good fortune. I had settled with our regimental paymaster, a gobble-snot of a Gotlander, for a written order allowing me to draw a horse from the royal stockade. Knowing the quality of beast that the order would get me, I had agreed, though that had been only for the sake of getting something. At best I had hoped to sell whatever I drew to a glue boiler for a few crowns.

She was among a big herd of half-broken remounts brought down from Nykoping and earmarked for the heavy cavalry. I think that I may claim to know as much about horses as any man in the Army and she caught my eye and my hunger for a future straight away. She stood out. Her rich dark brown coat was shining with high condition. The width and height of her shoulder, the look of intelligence about her magnificent head – everything about her had made her stand out among the rough beasts in the stockade. I had to own her. The next officer who happened along would, nay could, do no other than come to the same conclusion.

And I got her. For half an anker of Hamburg schnapps, the regimental farrier exercised his *legerdemain* and transferred the mare from one stockade to another; and hence to me. By what means of book-keeping he would account for the exchange of the broken winded bag o' bones that I had been meant to draw, was his business, but she was mine.

Yet the cream of the jest was to come. For two pounds of Roanoake tobacco the same sergeant had the mare served by the new colonel's own stallion, a real destrier, a horse bred to carry a man in plate armour at the gallop. If that mounting took, and from the hang of that stallion, I should be surprised if it did not, then, come July of 1641, I would be the owner of not one, but two, splendid animals.

I left Karlskrona next morning at first light and set out riding westward to the border with Norway and the nearest port for England.

A deep sniff gurgled behind me, and the scrape of horny feet on deck planks that always set my teeth on edge warned me of the return of the *Mary*'s skipper.

'There's a need for me to warp m' ship out aways intae midstream, Captain Ellyot. The tide in this river runs verra low at this season and the *Mary*'s heavy laden. She's like to take harm if she settle wi' oot a sufficiency o' water under her keel. So if …'

'You have indeed done all we agreed upon, Master Harvey – my baggage, my beast, and presently myself, set safe on shore …' I took out my purse. 'And a more comfortable passage, with more gentle companions, I could not have wished for.'

My sarcasm was wasted and there was no profit to be had out of delaying longer. My mare was on the quay, saddled and loaded with my scanty baggage. Slowly I began to count out the balance of my passage money into the skipper's waiting hand. It was a bitter shame to have to pay out so many of my sound silver pieces, every one of them un-clipped and fresh from the royal Mint at Uppsala, to a greedy Leith crack-louse like Harvey. But there was no help for it since I had no less worthy coin to give. He took the Swedish money with a greed unseemly even in a Protestant. With Scots money debased far below any other in Europe there would, I knew, be a tidy profit in the deal for him.

'And now a drop of good usquebaugh for aa' your braw laddies, Skipper!' Suddenly I raised my voice in a recruiting sergeant's shout of rollicking bravado. 'A measure o' the very best for every man aboard! Here's tae a heid the like o' a twenty - gallon piss-pot fit tae burst … Master Harvey, I'll look to you to see that it's aa' hand-somely done!'

My counterfeit of the Low Scots tongue wanted something, but it served its turn. I had taken the man completely aback. Harvey goggled his watery eyes at me, first with disbelief and then with a wince of dismay, as I spun four bright new crown pieces twinkling into the air, before catching them adroitly and placing just one of them with slow deliberation into the fellow's open hand.

There could hardly have been a sailor aboard who was not sure beyond any meas-ure of doubt that a whole shower of silver had been crammed into Harvey's bulging purse, and then stuffed away into his dirty plaid. I laughed full in his face.

'That, my bold Alexander, is a return on your miserly boiled kale and your stink-ing fat mutton; and, most particularly, on your damnable expenses add-eesh-onal.' Already the scarecrow crew were crowding aft for their share of the fancied bounty. 'And to crown your morning, Skipper, I would say that you are about to be boarded by pirates.' I pointed to the quayside.

There was a harsh yell and a fusillade of hearty abuse in the dialect that I had heard little of for so long. Two old men, each carrying a rusty halberd and what chari-ty might allow was once some manner of town livery, charged across the quay towards the *Mary*'s gangway. A third fellow, a skinny longshanked youth, who, from his tattered black gown and the brass-bound ledger he hugged, was some manner of a clerk, scuttled after them. It would take a sharper fellow than any Leith skipper to get the better of a Shields man in the matter of port dues. I stepped ashore in England for the first time in nine years.

The fishing village of South Shields was much as I remembered it, save that it looked more busy than it had a right to be. I allowed the mare her head to carry me up the steep slope to the first houses. She picked her way up through the rubbish-strewn vennels that twisted between the tarred walls of the fishermen's cottages. In the lanes, busy with folk, I came upon a crowd cheering on two lads, swine drunk the pair o' them, who wrestled their way to the edge of the Mill Dam and tumbled together head-first into the dark water.

Shields holding a holiday? I was puzzled. A market day? No – that was not likely, that much I knew. The Newcastle merchants would never relax the monopoly that their royal charter gave them. I had never seen the Shields men openly defy the law no matter how much they resented it, yet hardly a house or cottage was without a hastily set up booth of planks on upturned barrels before its door. A look at the crowd gave me a swift answer – sealskin caps, knitted bonnets thrummed through with coloured wool-strands, half-slop breeches, wide as kegs – these men were seamen. The sheltered waters of the Narrows would be packed the whole width of the Tyne's channel with storm bound vessels, for the most part colliers, deep laden with coals for London and Bristol. The same storm that had kept me at sea had pent the ships into the Tyne. A week of bad weather had seen their provisions eaten, or gone rotten and upward of five hundred men and lads would be hungry and demanding strong ale and stronger spirits. A wagon full of Newcastle doxies, screeching and cackling at some joke of their own, was turning on to the square of churned turf that served as village green. The whores had followed the weather-bound sailors down the river to catch the stranded trade.

As I rode on to the green, I was taken by a strong fancy for a bite of something fresh and a pot of ale, but a look at the way the crowd was milling and beginning to cluster into tight groups made me curb my appetite.

The gale had brought a windfall to the folk of Shields. The trade would be brisk, but there would be a cost before the day was out. The sailors' money would soon run out and sailors denied credit would riot. It were better, I decided, that I waited for my ale and my cut of roast beef.

Gently, I urged the mare through the crowd, taking care to give no man offence, and ready to calm the shy beast if she took fright. Outside one of the makeshift boozing kens I saw a whore, grossly fat, her face flushed with the drink, dancing a lolloping jig to a wild tune played out by a piper. Her coloured skirts tossed high at every ungainly turn to show a spot-mottled rump and a belly that wobbled like unclean dough. When she saw me riding high above the crowd she cracked her paint with a broad smile and gave me a wink that was the very soul of lewdness. I grinned back and swept off my hat to her with a flourish that set half the drunken sailors around her cheering. They opened their swaying ranks to me with a show of good humour. A gentle touch of my spurs to the mare's flanks took me clear of the crowd and out on to the track that would take me to Newcastle.

The blind man playing the small pipes had been the first soul that I had recognised since I stepped ashore. Not too much could have changed if Blind Davy Turnbull still worked his bellows and chantered his bagpipes, no whit improved for another nine years of practice up and down Tyneside. He was no more blind than myself. It took less than half an eye to see that the rogue's lids were stuck half closed with a dab of poacher's birdlime. Even as I watched, I saw him give a wink and the poke of a finger in my direction.

I found myself again falling into melancholy – a raddled old harlot and a counterfeit blind piper – a fit welcome home for an old soldier.

I had gone less than half a mile when the thud of hooves coming on fast behind me made me turn in the saddle. The track was narrow so I reined in and pulled the mare gently to the side. On this day John Ellyot would give way readily enough to a man in a hurry. As he galloped past, I had time to see that the horse was good, too good, I thought, for the rider, a tavern idler, from his battered hat and shabby cloak. Yet I could not help but notice that he sat his horse like no village bravo, and that he was drunk.

I patted my mare's neck and waited, for it occurred to me that I could be witness to a horse thieving. I looked back along the road track to see if there was any pursuit, having already made up my mind that nothing would make me risk my mare in hard riding after some gallows-damned horse lifter. Yet I knew there was something amiss. Not even a tavern knight spurs a horse bloody for his pleasure.

It was almost as though the fellow did what I willed him to do. He reined up, hard and cruel, and sat there for a moment. Even at that distance, there was no mistaking the leer on the fellow's face as the bastard watched me! Then he cut at his mount with his whip, wrenched the poor beast's head around savagely and galloped off along the Newcastle road.

'One day, my friend,' I whispered to myself, 'you'll mount a horse that has a spirit as mean as your own ... and that beast will snap your stupid neck!' I sat back in the saddle and watched until he was out of sight.

Chapter 2

The Musketeer

The ill-humour dogging me was no more than the effects of three weeks eating victuals steeped in brine since Noah sailed his Ark. The voyage had dragged on too long, and I had been shabbily done by, it was true. What soldier had not? I had looked for better, having done good service and fought in five savage campaigns. All were past and gone now, gambles at best, and the final accounting not near as bad as I had at first reckoned.

I followed the track that skirted the great mudflats about Jarrow. The ground was hard and the wind blowing full into the back of my military cloak, so I made good progress.

My reckoning of things improved as I thought about it. I had a whole body, not so much as a finger lost, no scars worth speaking of, nor had I brought any pox home with me – for which God truly be thanked. I had close to thirty pounds worth of Swedish crowns about me, and, stitched into the waist of my breeks, there were letters of credit drawn on a reliable Amsterdam merchant house that, even after discounting, would be worth almost another hundred pounds in English coin. It was no great fortune to be sure – not the bucket of gold Maximillians that I had once looked for, but better men than I had returned home with less, and above all else there was the land.

Each year, sometimes more than once, I had sent home the surplus of my pay and what small booty I had won, as letters of credit, entrusted to Tyne or Wear bound skippers. My brother Luke had used the money to get the freehold of the little farm above Scotswood, the holding that our father and grandfather had worked as tenants. Slowly as the years passed, we had added small fields and parcels of land round about, enough to say that we owned enough land now to keep the two of us and any families we might have, without any need of strife between us.

It was thinking about land and the fine draught animals that I would breed from my precious mare, that did much to clear away my ill-thoughts, so that by the time I had passed by Hebburn village I realised that I had been whistling like a lad a' courting as I rode along.

The cry sent my mare into a skittish canter. I had been caught unaware, deep in my calculations of the rate of natural increase of fine horses. I reined up sharply and listened. Over the soughing of the wind in the bushes, I heard a man curse.

A little way ahead the track dipped steeply into a valley, a dene as we call them in the North. Again there was another snarling curse. Below me, in a thicket of hawthorn in the dene bottom, a man was crashing about like a wild boar. My hand crossed to my sword. The instinct that had brought me out alive from a dozen ambushes among the forests and marshes of Germany and Poland took command of me.

I watched and listened for some time, turning the mare slowly around so that I could see all about me. Then making sure that I kept open ground between myself and any bushes that might offer cover to footpads, I urged the mare into the dene.

As a precaution I drew one of the long pistols from the sadly unmatched brace of snaphaunces at my saddlebow and started to prime it. The ear-splitting crack of a good handpiece fired off at close quarters would do more to frighten off a gang of hedge thieves than any amount of sword waving. The pistol I had levelled was charged with nine swan shot. That is a gunner's load, well suited to stem any screaming rush of troops.

He was a brown bear of a man, no giant, but uncommonly broad of build, his chest like a firkin cask. Unaware that I was watching, he charged through a clump of whin, stumbled, pitched forward heavily and lay still with his face in the turf. I cocked my snaphaunce.

It was no great puzzle to see the cause of his torment. Head and hands were gripped cruelly between the closed beams of a common pillory. He had escaped, carrying off his prison with him, the hinged jaws of the pillory's crossbeam wrenched from the stanchion post.

Satisfied, for the moment, that he was no decoy, I allowed my pistol to drop to the crook of my arm and looked him over with a professional eye. An old slash, a wide score of white scar tissue, ran in a long curve from his forehead to his cheekbone and went on to hide itself in his matted beard. It was a face with which to frighten bairns. At some time, this fellow had faced cavalry. That cut had come from above, from a stroke delivered from horseback and the wonder was, that it had not taken his head off!

His body told other tales. Along his side there was another rippling scar that marked the passage of a deep ploughing musket ball. Under the tatters of his shirt I could count more of the small change of battles, the rough peck of stitches and the dark ridges left by the surgeon's searing irons.

He grunted, contorted his body, kicked the heels of his much-cobbled boots into the soft earth and used the impact to heave his bulk up into a sitting position. He looked at me for a few seconds, grimacing with pain, then, unable to hold his purchase longer he fell back again.

I backed the mare away a little and sat at my ease in the saddle, watching as he rose, this time with a better balance, and grinned at me through strong white teeth.

'Well soldier,' I said. 'It looks as though the constables picked up what the Provost Marshal's men dropped. Stealing the seat from a three-hole privy is a felony, my man; if you're taken in possession of that, then it's hanging for sure!'

The foundation of blue shoddy holding together the patches of his baggy breeches and the tasselled garters tied below the knee, told me his profession. I was looking at a musketeer.

I could also guess the cause of his plight. A discharged soldier with no licence to beg was more than likely to be seized as a sturdy vagabond by any magistrate who had the constables to arrest him. The pillory and the lash were there to keep such men away from towns and villages altogether.

'If y'r Honour could see his way clear to lettin' me out o' this Devil's gin-trap?' The words were strangled off and trailed away to a string of blasphemies as he toppled backwards. He tried again. This time, he managed to rest one end of the beam on the ground, sawing it back and forth to make a furrow that would help him hold his stance, but the effort was wasted; whichever way he turned, he was still as helpless as a trussed fowl. The beam skidded, he fell back heavily and for a moment lay still. I could see that he was close to exhaustion. His great chest heaved up and down slowly and his face was white with agony.

'And if y'r Excellency can't see his way clear ...' There was a pause while he struggled once more to sit up for long enough to look me in the face, 'then may the good God fester your bowels, y' whoreson bastard – may the Italian pox eat your nose off!' He went on and on, the sheer effort serving to keep him balanced upright.

Left as he was, the poor bastard would strangle. That pillory had not been built to hold such a broad body. The sharp edges of the timber had chafed a collar of raw flesh around his neck and his wrists were held so tightly that his swollen hands had turned purple, yet the whole devilish device was held tight closed by nothing more than a twist of iron wire passed through a cheap hasp.

Without a word, I drew my sword. At the skir of the blade leaving its scabbard the soldier stiffened. I leant forward in the saddle and put the point into the wire. A turn of my wrist had it loose, the heavy timbers fell apart easily.

For a long moment he lay there, then he sat up, grinning hard, but his face had gone suddenly white from the pain of his swollen hands.

'Thank'e ... Captain,' he said quietly. Then he jumped to his feet, turned his back and I waited while he stood, waist deep in the steam of his long held piss, the changing set of his shoulders showing the easement he enjoyed.

'Well then, Musketeer, have you a name?' My inclination was to ride on at once, but curiosity held me for a moment. But for the grace of God, it could well have been myself standing there. I owed it to Fate not to ride off straight away.

I knew I had made a mistake when he looked up at me and cocked his head on one side.

'In Germany, when I was in the service of the Elector of Saxony, I was on the muster rolls as Jacob Grantus. In the service of His Highness, the Prince Archbishop of Cologne, I was Wilhelm Schukte – there have been others. Here, I am, as I was when I left, Will Blacket.'

I shook my head at him, slowly. Two months before, this man would have put a musket ball into me, or I could have touched off a cannon shot that would have torn him into a bloody bundle of guts and splintered bone. I was looking down at the enemy.

'You have the look of a man with a talent for getting himself into mischief, Jacob Grantus, Wilhelm Schukte … or what you will.'

He spread his hands and looked at them. Though the wrists were raw, the swelling was already going down. The pain had to be severe, but he hardly showed it.

'As the good Lord is my witness, Captain, I went into a tavern on the road out of Hartlepool and called for a pot of ale …'

I held up a hand for him to cease. I could predict the rest of his tale.

'I'll take your story as told, soldier. For myself, I've done with wars, soldiers and all their works for good and all, and my advice to you is to do the same, as soon as ever you're able. Forget that you ever wore a uniform coat. Find work, if you can. Stoop low and talk small until you're placed.' I pointed down to the tasselled garters of green silk that bound his galligaskins below the knees – a foot soldier's finery. 'And get rid of those! They might as well sound a roll o' drums. Steal yourself a suit of sober clothes and weave a sober tale to go with it. Unless you have folk or friends hereabouts, your best hope is to seek work with a foreigner. There are Dutchmen in Newcastle, come to set up a glassworks. Seek them out. Hang about the workings until you know who to ask and what tale best to tell.' It was sound enough advice to give, and like most advice, cheap. Then I saw his eyes go towards my saddlebag and knew what had drawn his gaze. There was a canteen tied to my saddlebow. The morning I had left Karlskrona, I had filled it with good Swedish akvavit and had had no cause to touch it since. I unwound the strap and held the big flask out to him. He grabbed it, took a mouthful, and carefully spat the fierce spirit on to the torn skin around his wrists. The sight made me suck in my breath. Even good royal issue akvavit is no soothing salve for raw skin. His action moved me to nod him into taking another couple of swigs from the canteen.

'Remember, Will Blacket, get yourself into service,' I said when he handed me back the canteen. 'Where there's no war, there's the power of justices and magistrates and the pillory and the whip for wandering, masterless men.'

'You wouldn't be wantin' an officer's servant yourself, Captain?' It was a forlorn hope and I sensed that it cost him much to ask. I didn't look down at him.

'No, Will. I've done with all that. I'm away home to be a farmer, and God knows there'll be no work for a body servant where I'm bound.'

It was not my inclination to do so, but I found that I had put my hand into my belt, my fingers closing on a fat silver crown piece. I had spun it to him before my prudence had time to stop me. He caught it neatly.

'God bless y'r Honour!' He said the words in thick German and like the fool I was, I could not ride off before I had swung up my sword blade in mock salute.

Chapter 3

Freelances on the Road

My meeting with a rogue, whose fortunes had been so much worse than mine, should have made me appreciate my own luck. It didn't and I knew it! I was still plagued by a sense of caution beyond all reason. That tense eve-o'-battle feeling gnawed at me, dull but deep, like the phantom pain of an amputated limb. I'd had the same such feelings on the morning I had taken a firewood detail into the forest and come back to find that Pulkowitz's cavalry had attacked our camp and slaughtered every man. Now I was on my guard for footpads of the common sort, mangy hang-dogs too fearful, I hoped, to attack a well armed, mounted man. I rode on, spurring the mare a little. A pale sun broke through the wind-wracked cloud scudding over-head, allowing a splash of brightness to spill over the north bank of the Tyne. I saw – just for an instant – the gilded weathervanes and the great lantern of the church of St Nicholas and the red roofs of the houses, all safe behind the town's walls. It felt like a welcome to me and I think I eased my guard because of it.

There were four of them, four horsemen, standing in my way and waiting for me. They sat back against the high cantles of their saddles, seeming to be at rest, showing all the easy arrogance of cavalrymen. Freelances, Condotteri, Soldiers o' Price, call them what you will. There will just about be time, before they cut your throat, burn you alive, or, if they need diversion, crush your private parts in their pistol locks while they bid you sing a merry song. In Pomerania, the peasants swore that there were free-lances who could not be harmed except by a silver bullet. At Arneburg, I had heard the screams of their prisoners come clear across the Elbe – a whole day and a night of it. There was no mistaking those parti-coloured clothes, the slashes lined with rich stuffs and the rows of tiny gold buttons, the knots and favours of bright silk – gaudy fairings to give a festive air to their butchery.

'Well met, good comrade! What cheer? Whither bound?' The accent was a thick south German, I guessed Swabian, but the English words were clear enough, and their tone was too hearty for my liking. Wolves do not coo like doves.

I reined in with a sharpness that brought a little snuffle of protest from the mare.

The leading freelance saluted after his fashion. 'We are troopers of Von Berlicht's Company, hired by his Majesty, King Charles, to garrison his castle of ...' He waved a gauntleted hand over his shoulder and laughed, 'Newcastle.'

I saluted in turn and gave each man a civil glance.

'Our captain sent us out this morning to find farmers with fodder to sell.' He laughed again and shook his head ruefully. 'A damned hard detail it has been.' He held up a fist and made a hard grasping motion. 'Tight!' They all laughed and I found myself laughing with them.

'Provisions are scarce hereabouts and costly beyond belief. All day in these damned hills and hardly a wisp of hay to be had at any fair price.'

I listened carefully while I nodded in supposed sympathy, but I was alert, waiting for word of command in German that would signal their move against me. I watched their faces, letting my gaze drift from one to another. Could I be wrong? I was in England now, within a mile or two of home and friends. I looked again. The old man, a deep-salted veteran had said nothing, but the magnificence of his gear and trimmings showed his rank in the bloody brotherhood and the success he had enjoyed. The youngster who spoke English so well, aped the old man with cheaper finery. Perhaps he was a little nervous. The other two riders had to be mere troopers, even among freelances, slab faces and piss-pool eyes, waiting for orders. Had I been too ready to damn? Was I some frightened farmer creeping home from market?

Freelance. It was a pretty distinction for me to make since I had been only a little removed from the same thing scarce a month before. It was, I fancied, entirely possible that they *were* in the King's service. Ink on a royal muster-roll washes away more sins than Jordan water. If they were King's troopers, then before the Law they were in better standing than I was and I would need to be careful. It is no light matter to draw a weapon on royal servants. It was that knowledge more than anything else that was keeping my hand away from my sword hilt.

It was the unconscious licking of a lower lip by the youngest freelance that broke my indecision. I had seen that nervous moistening flick of the tongue before. The last time was in a tavern in Stralsund, and the next thing I had seen on that occasion was my own blood spurting through my fingers from a stomach wound that nearly did for me. The young one would make the move, but that would be a feint. Their captain would make the first thrust. My hesitation had already allowed the youngster to edge closer. The old captain was beginning to move, while contriving to make it look as though it was no more than the restlessness of his horse. I knew. The lip-licker would say something to divert my attention – then the two flank men would close. There would be a feint from one side and a swift lunge from the other blades – these fellows wanted no pistol shots to be heard so close to the town.

I reckoned that I had a dozen heartbeats to live. I spent three of them stilling a spasm of panic. Then I bellowed like a goaded bull and went at the bastards. I snatched a pistol from its holster, presented and pulled the trigger, watching the hammer fall and knowing that I had a slow eye's blink to centre my aim on the nearest freelance before the priming reached the charge. I heard the dull crunch – no flash, no loud crack, nothing. The flint was flawed. It had struck the steel and shattered into grey flakes. A pistol that has misfired is a danger to its master. Angrily I flung it – butt first – into the face of the freelance to my left causing him to rein back so sharply that his mount reared and almost threw him.

I am an old hand at close fighting on horseback. There's no call here for fancy blade play or volleyed fire. Instead, there is a mortal need for plenty of hard sweating, grunting, slash and stab work with any weapon that comes to hand – and all that backed with the Devil's own cunning.

I took the young freelance with my remaining pistol shot. It was my guess that he had thrust himself forward for the glory of it. I put the mare into a caracole that fetched her back cruelly on to her haunches and fired from the protection of the beast's neck. The charge of swan-shot took the lad handsomely below his oxter as he stood full erect in his stirrups, his arm raised high to slash down at me. The force threw him backwards and he rolled clean out of the saddle, arse-over-tip, screaming like a lassie!

Well begun! The freelances paused in their attack and exchanged glances. For a lone horseman I had done them more hurt than they had perhaps been paid for. This Ellyot's lad was no clodhopper of a cattle dealer.

They came on and I spurred to meet them. There was no help for it; had I turned and tried to flee, they would have overtaken me within a dozen yards and slashed me into crow's bait.

Ahead of me, the track widened where the farm carts had swerved to avoid a slough-pond left by a clay digging. The open space was wide enough for three riders abreast, or room for one man to swing a long blade. On one side of the track there was a dry stone wall. For perhaps twenty paces on the other side, the track had crumbled away to a steep sided drop to the black filth of the slough. This was the killing ground.

I saw that if I was to have a lame dog's chance of staying alive, I had to gain an inside position, my left flank guarded by the wall and my sword arm free to play. Above all I had to be where no rider could get past to come against me from the rear.

The old freelance realised my tactic and trotted his horse forward to cut me off. This was a craftsman killer – indentures served under the best masters in Europe and entered into the full mystery of his guild. Every motion of his limber body was aimed at bringing me to fear and confusion. The best of his work was done before we had even struck steel. The studied dropping of the reins and the drawing of his sword, swiftly as though by sleight-of-hand, were all a part of his craft.

He favoured a light sword and he held a dagger ready drawn in his left hand, the *main-gauche* of a generation or more ago. An old fashioned weapon need be no less deadly than a new. I had my long bladed old bitch of a Scaviola, a King's issue weapon and heavy to swing, but we were used to each other and I had dressed the edge carefully that very morning.

Frightened men commonly leer. I felt the muscles in my face twitch and twist up into an ugly rictus. I was afraid, but that would go, along with the sick empty feeling in the guts and the too hard grip I was keeping on the hilt of my sword. All would vanish the instant our blades clashed.

He did cut me off. Guiding his mount with his knees in the Magyar fashion, the whoreson wove his beast's head from side to side until at the right opening he dug in his heels to send his mount shouldering its way between my mare and the wall. I cursed myself. While I had been tugging at the reins like a village daftie riding on his hobbyhorse, the freelance had gained the advantage.

A few words of heavy beast-snarl German tossed carelessly over his shoulder to his comrades made them laugh. He crossed his blades before his face and planted a smacking kiss on the steel.

It was a deliberate and unholy perversion of a chivalrous salute. Then the hell-fiend cleared his throat and hawked at me through the cross. The wetness of the still warm phlegm hanging in the hairs of my beard sent me into a red fury. I could no more help my actions than an open barrel of powder could withstand a glowing coal.

We exchanged a dozen cuts, hard and fast and not one of them to be found in any manual-of-arms. The clash and scrape of our blades rang out sharply over the nervous blowing and snorting of our horses and the irregular thud of their hooves as we struggled for place.

He was as good as any I had met. His posturing had deadly substance to it. We had been to the same bloody school and we both knew it. Acknowledgement of that, came as a half breath's pause and a twisted exchange of grins.

We went at it again. At the end of a second vicious passage I had a small dagger nick on the inside of my sword forearm, but he was breathing hard, sniffing the air up his flared nostrils in short wheezing gasps. The glitter had gone from his pale blue eyes, its place taken by the watchful look of a man who concedes to himself that this time he might not win. The chill in my own guts eased and the roaring in my ears was muted. It was my turn to give him the grin through clenched teeth.

I thought I had him. Our blades crossed and locked at their guards. I felt the strength in his thin arms, watched for the flicker of intention that would warn me where he would aim the point of his dagger. His hand feinted at my stomach – but his eyes had already warned me to guard my throat. I caught his hand in mid strike and gripped it hard. My thumb found his and forced it back with all my strength. The dagger dropped free and fell between us.

On foot, I would have jerked his sword from his hand with a sharp upward lift, the cross quillons of my sword locked in his. I remembered the trick before my muscles could serve me false. As I pulled away, he would lean hard back in his saddle. A spur prick to his horse's flanks and I would be drawn out, off balance, over-reached. Somewhere, he would have another dagger – hidden where it would come easily to hand.

For a few seconds we grappled close. His breath was rank, like a dog that has been at carrion and his sweat had a bitter staleness to it. Close-to, I was amazed to see just how old this dog was, a few stumps of teeth decayed black and a face seamed and creased deep with wrinkles, every line traced out with ingrained dirt like the crazing on an old pot. And I saw too that there was a fine ripe pox blossom, like a rotten cherry, festering away at the corner of his mouth.

We were turning. He urged his horse's head around and I knew that I would be forced to turn with him. If I held on, he would soon have me turned far enough for his comrades to cut in at me. I disengaged and the old master too, had had enough of fighting alone. As he called for his men to come and help him, I glanced to see if they would obey, a bad mistake which almost cost me my life. The old devil went for me again with a flurry of slashing strokes, cursing like a madman, his lips foaming with spittle. Yet even when he was in a frenzy there was still purpose and trickery to it. Little by little, he forced me to turn again, to expose my flank to a rush from his men.

I have always had distaste for making a horse suffer, but here my need was desperate. I freed my right foot from its stirrup and raked the rowel of my spur hard along the flank of the freelance's horse. The poor beast sprang aside with a scream and distinctly, I heard the freelance's thighbone crack as the full weight of his pain-maddened horse crushed him against the wall.

The old bastard had courage, that much I'll give him! With his horse bucking under him and his smashed leg hanging useless, he swung a slicing blow a me. I took it the only way I could, presenting to the blurred arc of bright steel the thick metal at the base of my own blade and, trusting to the stout hide of my gauntlets to save my hands, I blocked the stroke quarterstaff fashion.

The shock of it jarred me to the shoulder – but it finished the business. He had perhaps just one eyeblink to see that his blade had snapped off clean. I gave him no more time, but drew my arm back and split him breastbone to bellybutton! The old bag-o-turds opened up like a rotten sack, his intestines bulging and spilling through his fine jacket like live eels. Jesu! I had never felt so glad, so God Almighty triumphant about letting the ghost out of a man. There would be no guilt after this one, no vomiting in a ditch. Damn my sinful soul for it, but my heart was swelling in my chest with pure unsanctified pride as I turned on my remaining attackers before the old sod's corpse had hit the ground.

It may have been that the look on my face was enough to pluck the hearts out of them. I heard myself yelling Swedish battle cries, laughing loud and bawling snatches of stern Protestant hymns. I think that I should shortly have seen the pair of them away, but it was not to be.

There was the sharp crack of a pistol. One of the freelances grunted and clapped a hand to his shoulder. The other rider looked past me, his jaw dropping in astonishment. Then they had both broken away and were galloping for their lives down the road towards Gateshead and the old bridge over the Tyne.

My ally was tall, I think over six feet, his face florid, a man who liked his wine. He wore a fine pair of mustachios, in the French fashion, twisted at the ends and waxed. Big though he was, his suit of mulberry velvet hung loosely about his frame, as though it had not been made for him, while at the same time the bagginess of his clothes contrasted with the strained tightness of the soft leather boots he wore. I looked hard into the face for some sign of emotion. When one gentleman has just come to the aid of another, they might both be expected to have a word or two to say. This man said nothing, though he was nervous for I saw the tremor in his fingers as he began to reload his pistol. He was deft and skillful, plainly he had been drilled to the task. The thought came to me that perhaps this had been the man's first true passage-of-arms and that he had been struck a little dumb by the experience. That is often the case.

I dismounted stiffly, the knocks and bruises taken unheeding during the fight just beginning to make themselves felt. The deep nick in my forearm had started to throb painfully.

'You have my thanks, Sir ... I was hard pressed when you happened by.' I sought for something to say that was civil and seemly as I led my mare by her bridle and walked towards him.

The corpses of the two freelances that I had killed lay where they had fallen. Their horses, such as they were, were undoubtedly mine, and I was beginning to entertain hopes that I would find a trifle or two about the bodies that would give me some recompense for all my trouble. Only a canting hypocrite would have thought to do otherwise. Was I to leave hard won booty to be picked up by the next carter or cowherd that passed that way?

For a moment, I had feared that my new ally would seek a share, but soon it was clear to me that he had taken the encounter for an adventure or an exercise-at-arms, for his eyes were fever bright.

I was bending over the corpse of the old captain of freelances, when I heard the double snick of pistol locks being cocked. I looked up in time to see the devil's snarl on the stranger's face – lit up by the flash as he fired.

Chapter 4

Bruised, not Broken

It was pitch dark. My fingers scrabbled frantically among dust and rubble. I was lying on a rough stone slab, stark naked, and the stone beneath me was getting hotter than I could bear. Heat struck up to scorch my bare backside. I put out a hand into the sulphur stinking blackness and felt the shimmer of more fierce heat. When I tried to raise myself, my heels grazed on sharp gritstone and there was tightness to my skin that was like the pull of a healing wound. With a jolt like a hangman's drop, I remembered.

The flux of horror spun slowly in my brain, steadied itself at last and then, out of that terrifying whirl of images a single memory resolved itself. This, surely, was the hellfire promised me when I had been a little laddie of eight or nine and standing with my father on the village green at Benwell. A ranting preacher with the Spirit full on him had, as it had seemed to a child, looked at me alone out of the crowd of laughing, ale-flushed lads and lasses dancing at the harvest home. His accusing finger had fixed on me as with a haunting look of utter assurance. He had delivered to me the certain promise of inescapable Damnation.

There was flutter of sound close by, like a multitude of candles being blown out. A dazzling seam of fire, flickering yellow and white, lapped up and down a long crack in the wall. I threw up an arm to cover my face, hearing myself whimper. After a moment, I turned my arm into the light. Sweet Jesu! My skin had turned grey, leprous, and when I moved, the very flesh cracked, big flakes of it dropping away. I opened my mouth to call on the Almighty for deliverance. My frantic wail came out as a parched rattle.

'Here y' are, Captain ... take a swig o' this.'

A tarpaulin was flung aside, letting the pale morning sunlight into a narrow passage of broken stone and packed earth. It was the musketeer, Will Blacket, standing beside me, smiling cheerfully and holding out a quart sized leather jack. I sat up, dripping with sweat, grabbed the hide bottle and drank like a madman.

'You said I should get myself into service again, Captain, as sharp as I liked. Well, I reckon I pulled myself a master o' sorts out of a brick burner's clay pit.'

'Where in hell am I?' I heard my own croak and knew that it sounded like an old man on his deathbed, but I swung my legs out-over and tried to stand up. A bolt of agony – bone deep – seared across my chest. Pain sent me swaying on my feet. I gagged at the sick feeling that welled up inside me then Will Blacket grabbed my arm and helped me to sit down on a rough bench. He found a filthy blanket somewhere and draped it across my shoulders.

'Drink some more of this and maybe take a bite o' something.' He held up the leather jack to my mouth. The cool ale was rough yeasty stuff and full of floaters but I drank deeply and almost at once I began to feel better.

'This here is a brick yard, a mile or so outside o' Gateshead. You're safe enough. The gaffer is an old soldier and a sometime comrade o' mine. I was on my way here anyway to seek him out. So when I pulled you out of that clay pit, I lugged you along. I couldn't think of anything else at the time.'

'Tell me what happened, soldier …' I grabbed his arm hard. 'Tell me everything you saw.'

Blacket handed me a flat cake of bread with a slab of cheese folded into it. I took it and bit into it ravenously. Wheaten bread, by God! After so many years on the dark, sour rye bread of the Swedish service I had almost forgotten what white bread tasted like.

'The main body o' the tale you know well enough, 'ceptin' that I came up with you by chance the second time. You followed the road along the river while I cut straight across the fields, wishin' to keep out o' folks' way, like …' Blacket looked at me and gave me a short nod of approval. 'That was a very creditable piece of work, Captain. Freelances is hard chewin', even one to one; but you saw two of the pig-buggerin' bastards away and had every look of doin' the same service for the other two, when that big fellow in velvet turned traitor.'

Now I remembered, vividly. I had straightened and stood up. The pistol ball had struck me high, above the chest but below the Adam's apple. The impact had knocked me over backwards and I had fallen, spread-eagled out on to the stinking mud of the clay pit. My struggles had only made me sink deeper into the filthy slough. I had watched the man dismount and walk slowly over to the edge of the pit where I could see his face looking at me as though I were a louse found in his shirt as he fired again.

The pistol ball had struck me full in the body! Why, then, was I not dead? My hand strayed to the place. Blacket chuckled when he saw and handed me a crescent shaped piece of steel: my gorget, the small piece of armour that I had kept back as a vanity when I had sold my war gear at Karlskrona. At the battle of Lutzow, a Swedish duke had snatched it from the neck of a dead lieutenant and hurled it at me. I had been too deaf from the concussion of the big cannon to hear what he said but I had understood. That had been the day I had become a commissioned officer. The curved gorget had deflected the ball, the impact shearing away one of the three gilt crowns embossed on the surface of the steel, leaving a bright smear of lead. There was also a mark to match the outer rim of the metal, bruised into the flesh from collarbone to collarbone. My noticing it had made it bloody painful.

'You've had the Devil's own luck about you, Captain. Maybe you inherited it from the freelances you killed.'

Will Blacket opened his hand and I saw it held a single pistol ball of small calibre, no bigger than a robin's egg. I took it. It was still a sphere, unflattened by impact. I looked into his scarred face, not understanding.

'All I know is that it fell out of your cloak this mornin'. His smile made his scar even more prominent. 'As I said, Captain … the Devil's own luck!'

I began to understand. I had indeed had the luck of the Devil. It was an old argument among gunners that a wet hide or a thick blanket would, if hung loose, stop a musket ball in flight. I had seen the trial made: the answer is that sometimes it is so, and sometimes, not. For me, this time, it had been so, and I was properly grateful.

My musketeer handed me the ale again before he went on with his story.

'Well, when your friend in the tight boots had, as he thought, finished you off, he tried to drag the two stiffs alongside o' you, but the old bastard's guts had spilled out steamin' like new turds on the road. Our squire didn't savour that, so he dropped him where he lay.' Will Blacket laughed. 'Nor was he best suited wi' the smell comin' off the old'un, so he tried the other, the lad. Well ... when I saw that pickin's like that were a-goin' to be chucked into the mud, I stirred myself. Not lookin' to be cut down for a witness, I set to makin' the bushes shake and shoutin' here an' there like I was more than one man. That did it. He mounted up, drove the freelances' nags off up the fellside and he was off.'

'What about my mare?' I asked quickly.

'Oh, he grabbed the bridle sharp enough and led her off at the gallop. He followed the same line o' march as the other two – makin' for the Tyne Bridge.'

I put my head in hands and cursed long and hard. Will Blacket went on, heedless

'So first off, I dragged you out o' the boghole. That was some job – your boots were full of water and your cloak was thick with mud. Anyways, I got you on firm ground, took the pickin's from the stiffs and got you down here. That was yesterday. You've been like a man dead since then.'

'I'm grateful to you, Blacket.' I said looking at him straight. 'And I'm under obligation to you ... I owe you my life, soldier.'

Blacket came, I guessed, as near to blushing as he was ever likely to do and then grinned all over his scarred face.

'Well, Captain, if you would give some thought to the notion of my takin' regular service wi' you, I'd account the score between us settled. That and more. I was close to dead when you loosed me from that damned pillory; you would ha' gone under that mud in no time if I had left you where you were ... which is quits.'

'Quits it is then, though I know of men who would have stripped me along with the rest and gone on their way satisfied that they had done enough by leaving me my life.'

I laughed. It was the old mixture, a fine sense of the ludicrous mixed in with the bitter gall of disappointment. The effort of laughing sent a new shock of pain through my neck and chest.

'I'm stark naked, I've like as not got a smashed collarbone, or worse. I'm caked head to foot with dried filth and I haven't a penny's piece to bless myself with. So

why in God's name, soldier, do you want to take a servant's place with me? Saul's
bleeding fundament, man, but you're fit enough, you could be drawing your seven
pence a day in any army in Europe.'

The old soldier gave me a knowing look. 'Just as you could be drawin' your two
shillin's, Captain?'

He shook his head slowly. 'Last winter I lost too many comrades, good lads all,
inside a week. I've seen mates of mine, all once stout raging fellows, afraid of nothing, now draggin' their bodies round on stumps and kicked out of the way like dogs. I
was in my own country a day and a half when I was clapped in the jugs and promised
the lash on the morrow for bein' a beggar ... Eee—nough, Captain!'

Blacket took the leather bottle and swigged at the ale.

'I went for a camp-striker and baggage lad at Antwerp in sixteen hundred and
eighteen – run off a Blyth brig to escape starvation and buggery. That gives me better
than twenty-two years service and it makes me, as far as I can reckon, past forty years
o' age. This far along I've found the sense to want to eat some decent vittles regular,
to sleep under a roof most nights, and when I come to die, I want to be wrapped in a
linen shroud and lowered gently into a proper hole dug in the ground – one that I
don't have to be sharin' wi' three or four hundred other poor sods.'

Blacket looked me in the face, as straight and as level as a man might. 'Take me
on, Captain. In return I'll give you good service. I can trim your beard and cut your
hair, dress a wound and set most broken bones, tell good coin from bad, mark a cheat
at cards or dice, find fire and provisions where another man would starve ... and
watch your back in a fight. What do you say, Captain? Am I on the strength?'

I needed little thought to decide. A man like Will Blacket might serve me well if
my new life was to go on in the same fashion that it had begun.

I offered him my hand. 'You are on indeed, Will Blacket. I take you on ... to rise
if I rise, fall if I fall. You'll get paid when I have money to pay you. If these last hours
are a guide, I think that I am in sore need of a good man to watch my back for me,
and, perhaps, both our fortunes will thrive on the partnership.'

As a servant, Will Blacket wanted something in appearance, though in the time
since I had freed him from the pillory he had found a shirt of coarse grey flannel that

was clean enough to have come off some goodwife's clothesline. Nonetheless, he had made me no false promises and it was with a little look of satisfaction that he produced a half keg of clean water and began to chase the chill off by dropping heated stones into it. When I had soused the caked mud off myself, I was able to inspect my injuries. Cleared of dirt the wound looked worse than it really was. There was bad bruising that would go all the colours of a regimental banner in a day or so, and the flesh was cut deep in places. But Will assured me that there was no break in my collar bone, having mercifully tested it while I was unconscious. Then I sat still while he combed the filth out of my hair and beard. His work on my clothes was little short of miraculous.

'Baked them as hard as ration biscuits and then battered the dried clarts clean out of them,' he explained, and to be fair I would have to say that they seemed to have taken no great harm from Will's ministrations.

A search along the waistband of my breeks reassured me that at least I still had my letter of credit,wrapped well in oiled silk so that it would have taken no harm from the wet.

'Not in such bad fettle as you had thought, eh, Captain?'

Will helped me dress and when he had done, he looked me up and down with the eye of a general's valet. It occurred to me that the old soldier was so apt at his work that he might well have been an officer's, or gentleman's, servant before. I thought about asking him, but decided against it. After all, the man had saved my life, and likely he would tell me if and when he wanted to.

He shook his head over the big bundles. 'Lawful booty, Sir, though to tell the truth, I've had more from loot from an alms-house privy. Damn me, but I would like to have caught those two nags.'

He had reason to complain for the sum of the booty he had collected came to little enough. All the fine stuff of the freelances' gaudy finery was spoiled. Where my sword had not slashed the thickly embroidered fabrics, the death spasm of the men's bowels had fouled the once-rich garments beyond the help of lye soap or fuller's earth. Nonetheless, Will went through every stitch once more with the sharp point of a knife, stopping every so often to show me a place where something had been sewn into hiding and then cut out. At last, he was satisfied that there was nothing left of value in the stinking clothes – only a hoodie crow would get closer pickings from a corpse than a musketeer. Will thrust the bundle into a vent hole that led into the flames of the brick kiln.

In the end we had three very sorry piles, some pieces of jewellery, a few weapons, and a little money. The jewels, such as they were, lay clustered on a stained satin handkerchief. There was a fat ring of good red gold, set with a small ruby, another silver ring with a shabby garnet, a short length of gold chain, thick and weighty, but of such a lean alloy that I doubted it was worth more than a few shillings, a silver crucifix missing two of the six turquoise lozenges that it had once carried, and lastly there was a soapstone charm in the form of a woman coupling with a beast-headed man. Will looked at it carefully for a moment, then looked at me. Without a word I nodded. He spat on the thing and flung it far into the flames of the kiln.

The only other thing was a small printed Latin Testament. For a moment, I thought that he was going to pitch it into the flames as well, but suddenly he muttered something that I could not catch and thrust the little book into his jerkin. War had taught me to leave well enough alone there too.

Our weapons muster looked to be better. There was one fine steel hunting knife of the best Milan work which had clearly caught Will's fancy. I picked it up, spun it for balance, and offered him the hilt. He tucked it into his belt without a word.

Surprisingly the sword that had belonged to the young freelance was a better weapon than I ever hoped to own. With a plain-chiselled steel hilt and guard, the blade had the running wolf of Solingen incised into the blade and even better, the initials of the maker had been added under the town's mark. Only the best weapons are signed in this way. I slid the blade back into its worn scabbard with a warm feeling of increased security.

'I'll guess one thing, Captain. These lads had been on short rations for a long time. When I stripped them there wasn't hardly the pickin's o' a fat rat on either one of them – and there's this.'

Will Blacket scratched his head for a moment. 'No offence, Captain, but they must have been damned hard up for work when they took you on. Look here ... five shillin's straight, from the young'un, ten from the old'un, say the other two 'lances had five apiece. If they had taken the usual half on account and had half coming when the job was done, why then that's two pound and ten shillings all told.' The old musketeer's face split into a grin that brought his facial scar into hideous prominence.

'How does it sit with you, Captain, to know that some bugger has thought it worth his while to put all o' fifty shillin's on your head!'

Chapter 5

Betrayed at Benwell

At Will Blacket's urging, I rested and slept for two days. He had predicted that I would feel worse before I felt better and he was right. My left collarbone and my chest ached with the bruising they had taken and I grew feverish. The small cut in my forearm swelled and showed angry red. I woke once and found that my wounds had been thickly poulticed with sphagnum moss and bound with clean linen. Men talked outside the kiln. I heard the scrape of shovels and the sound of wheelbarrows being trundled about, but so far as I knew no one looked in on me.

It was growing dark, at the end of the third day, when I saw Will again. There was a look of pride on his face. He was carrying a sack which he began to empty out one bundle at a time.

'Not a soul knows me in Newcastle, Captain, so while you slept I went across the bridge to see what I might see ... so to speak.' He opened a parcel and held out a piece of smoked ox-tongue for me to smell, and I realised I was ravenous.

'Your four freelances were on the muster rolls at the Castle.' He cut a slice of tongue, put it on to a coarse earthenware plate and handed it to me. 'Were, I say, because they aren't now. Forty men o' what they call the Swabian Company were paid off and rode south three days ago. Rumour has it that they're on their way to York.' He shook his head slowly. 'This country is no good for free companies. King's pay is all very well, but to really prosper your real, red-raw freelance needs plenty o' good fat peasants to plunder.' He found a pepper pot in his sack and offered it to me.

I began to wonder how he had come by all the good things he had fetched from his visit to the town – a man who was a competent military servant might have some dubious skills in settled life. Nonetheless I sprinkled the coarse pepper freely over the ox-tongue and bit into it hungrily.

'Where did you get all that?' I pointed to the pile of booty and fixed him with a questioning eye. Will had only shirt and breeks to his name when we had first met. I could hardly complain if the man tried to better his lot any way he could. It occurred to me that now he was my own servant I had to find him two suits of clothes a year. He gave me a look of injured innocence – in a musketeer, the mark of sure guilt.

'Every scrap a lawful purchase, Captain!' Will was enjoying himself. 'If there's one place in this world where a fellow can dispose of loot or stolen property, it's in a garrison stores. That is if you're willing to take payment in kind.'

I nodded, for that is nothing less than the simple truth.

'So I went to the Castle yard and looked out the quartermaster,' Will continued. 'He was Christian enough to allow me to dispose of the odd pieces of our takin's from the freelances.' He held up a foot and shook it. The broken boots he had worn were gone and in their place he had on a pair of new King's issue boots and stout knitted stockings. The tasselled garters were still there.

'And while we bargained for this and that, I asked the good sergeant the odd question about the comin's and goin's around the Castle.' He found a clot of dried apricots in one of his bundles and broke off a handful for me. 'It seems, Captain, that there were ten men of Von Berlicht's company missing when the troop rode south.'

He poured me a glass of red wine from a glass demijohn. 'Four o' those are going back to Germany. I had that from one of them myself on the quayside not an hour ago.' He licked his lips. 'We know where two are … and one other was wounded. That leaves three men who might give us trouble if we meet. Though I think not.'

I thought not too. The attack on me was bought-work, a business deal. The man who had betrayed his own hired killers was much more likely to be a target now.

'Nonetheless, Will, I think that we'll play canny. We'll not go into Newcastle town at all for a while.' I moved and a spasm of pain told me that I should be foolish to try going anywhere for a day or two. 'As soon as I can walk, we'll go up-river to Dunston or thereabouts. When the tide is low the river is easily fordable. That brings us near my home. We'll be safe there, among friends.'

'Beggin' y'r Honour's pardon but by y'r leave we will be ridin'. I went to the beast pound at the Felling and paid a shillin' to claim the pair o' them.'

'By God, but you're a damned good soldier, Will Blacket!' It was all I could say. I was delighted, 'Well done!'

I took a drink of wine. Suddenly it tasted very good.

'So we'll be able to find our friend in mulberry velvet. I want my own mare back, Will. She's all the future I have.'

At first light two days later, we rode two miles up river on the south bank and forded the Tyne above Dunston, by way of King's Meadow and Clarence Island.

When the river is low in summer, the islands are little more than water meadows. In the season they are set with salmon traps, but they divide the river into narrow channels so that when the tide is low, a man who knows the way can cross with the water reaching no higher than his horse's fetlocks.

My heart began to race as we rode up the bank towards the farm. I had in my head every acre of land that my money had helped to buy. Luke was no real hand with letters, but he could limn out a sketch map very prettily and he had sent me three or four of them over the years, though that was not the same as looking at the land and trying to judge how many cattle or horses it would feed. A pride I had not known before surged through me, swelling as I rode. I had heard men speak of pride in land before, 'Your own dunghill to crow upon!' was what they had said, but never had I felt it in my bone's marrow the way I did at that moment.

The house looked the same from far off, but as I rode up to it I could see that every window was now fully glazed, and there was a new barn and stable about which my brother had written to me.

'The place looks uncommonly quiet ...' Will was the first to murmur that thought but it had already been worrying me. The only sign of life was a flock of geese under the charge of a wee lassie, moving high up on the hillside above the house. I tried to work out what day of the week it was. Surely it could not be the Sabbath.

We dismounted before the front door and tied up our horses. The silence was even more uncanny. No farm is quiet on a working day. I listened. The only sound was the wind gusting down the Tyne valley. I opened my mouth to hail, but the words would-n't come. I had expected my brother to meet me at the run.

'Best cock and prime a pistol, Captain – I can feel my nape hairs a-liftin',' Will warned me softly.

I turned, frowning. 'I've come home, Will Blacket. There'll be no call for pistols here.' Yet I felt he was right. One failed ambush did not mean that there could not be another. I pictured my brother being held inside the house while the hired killers lay in waiting.

'Luke!' I bellowed. 'Luke Ellyot!' My shouts echoed and were still. I looked about, half expecting to see my brother come out of the door, or turn a corner and come at me with his familiar lumbering run. Though he would look a little older, being three years my senior, he would still be broad shouldered, and open faced. His kindly smile had always drawn the bairns to him. Where was he? In the barn? A difficult calving would keep him there, heedless of time. Or was he indoors and gritting his teeth over the scanty accounts he was forced to keep?

Will got down from his horse and stepped up to the closed front door. That it *was* closed was strange in itself. He knocked loudly twice, and then twice again. There was no answer, yet I sensed that there were people in the house.

Then, from somewhere by the stable yard, there was a call, a man's voice, high-pitched, and fearful, and almost at once the harsh scratch of claws on stones. I had never seen dogs of such a size. They turned the corner, bunching, tumbling over one another in their rush towards us. There were three of them – mastiffs, brindled, black and brown, with pale liver patches that formed a mask about the eyes.

As they came at us, the slaver stringing white from their muzzles, the lead dog leaped at Will. Reared up high, its forepaws stretched, the beast stood taller than the man by a head, but astonishingly, Will began to snarl and bark at the animal like a madman, grinning widely, his teeth bared through his beard. He rushed the mastiff and I heard the clash as the animal's jaws shut, but Will hugged the beast tight to him and tucked his head into its neck to escape the terrible bite. Reaching up, gripping the hound's muzzle, his grin widened to a terrible mirthless smile. He held the beast's mouth fast shut with one hand, while with the other he punched the long dirk up under its brisket. I watched Will's elbow move in quick, hard-driven jerks as he sliced into the dog's guts. The mastiff sagged, fell sideways and turned on its back, already dead.

The other two mastiffs came at me. I cut at them both with my sword edge and they backed away snarling. I knew the danger if I tried to thrust at them with the point. Attacking one dog would only offer an opening for the other to reach me. My third or fourth slash drew blood from one dog's shoulder. It leaped at me, its jaws clenching on the blade of my sword. As it worried at the honed edge, bright blood from its lacerated mouth spattered over my face and clothes. I booted it back just as the other mastiff lunged and I staggered as its forepaws hit my chest. The iron ribs of my sword-guard held before my face parried the ravening jaws. I swung the animal around in a half circle, then there was a howl like a banshee in Hell and the weight of it was gone. Will Blacket had kicked the beast in the ballocks from behind! Then he came in on my flank and gripped the animal. It yelped as he hoisted it, its paws kicking in empty air. Then I heard its ribs and backbone crunch as he knelt hard, pulling its forelegs apart with all his strength.

The dog that had bitten on my blade stood in a pool of its blood, panting, seeming to see nothing. Will Blacket held out a hand for my sword. There was a swish and a thud and the cut took the beast high on the back of the neck. The head was still attached to the body, but only just.

Will shook his head and laughed as he recovered his dirk and wiped it on the brindled hide. 'There's nothing stupider than a dog, Captain. You can take 'em in two ways: you can let the buggers put fear into you so bad that you just stand there and piss yourself while they eat you alive, or, you can tell yourself that weight for weight a dog is smaller than a man and that in any case all it's got is its teeth.' He sheathed his blade. 'I learned the dog-knacker's trade when I served the Bishop of Maintz. The Spanishers sold him a pack of slave-hunting mastiffs from Cuba to use as war dogs.'

A toss of the head and contempt on the old soldier's face finished his story for him.

'There's nothing for you men here!' came a cry. I looked up and saw a man leaning out of an open window. He was trying to put on a bold face but his pallor showed that he was badly frightened.

'His Excellency, Captain Ellyot of the Swedish Royal Guard has come … You'll be hurryin' down to make the gentleman welcome!'

Will's bawled out summons sent the man backing away from the window, but I could hear loud whispering and a short scuffle in the room. Then the bolts were drawn and the door swung open a crack.

I knew the face of the maid who looked out at us. She had been only a wee lassie driving the geese the last time that I had seen her.

'Well then, Bessie Carver, are we to be welcomed into my father's house or d'ye mean to keep us standing on the step like tinkers?' The lass was hard put to know what to do. At first sight of me her young face lit up with welcome, yet almost at once she looked afraid.

Recovering her composure she smoothed her apron with her hands, saying, 'Aah'm to tell you that the mistress is feelin' poorly and cannot be receivin' visitors … today.'

It was the look on the girl's face that started my laughter, but the idea of such a message from a house where we had just been set on by a pack of mastiffs loosed a guffaw from me that would not be mastered.

'Well, Bessie …' I said softly, determined not to vent my anger on a servant girl, 'you know me to be Jack Ellyot?' I waited until she had nodded her head. 'Then I may tell you, my pet-lamb, that I'll not be barred from this house by the orders of any man alive.' I gave the door a gentle shove and the lass gave way to me, lowering her eyes and dropping a little courtesy.

They were gathered at the foot of the stairs. The man's face was familiar, but I could put no certain name to him. Before he spoke he looked about him as though expecting help from some quarter.

'I'm Matthew Stobbs …' He paused, his expression building to an outburst of spluttering bravado but I looked at him blankly, his nerve failed him and he moved aside.

I remembered the maids well enough, but the woman, hardly more than a girl, was a stranger to me. There was no doubt she was the mistress of the house. Even had she not worn my mother's keys at her waist, the richness of her dress told all. Money is not so free in the North that many women can afford to wear a gown of Venetian velvet during a working day. I thought she had a fey look about her, like the painted face on a Paris doll, being very white skinned, seemingly naturally so, with curiously narrow green eyes. Those green eyes looked at me, but the expression on her face was like that of a child play-acting, imperious, over-done, like court manners learned or copied.

'You must be my brother's wife.' I said as I stepped towards her to kiss her, as is our custom. She shrank from me for an instant and as suddenly smiled, childlike. Overcoming her fear, I felt her lips on my face, fleeting and cold.

'Poor Luke ...' she said, her voice soft and distant. Giving a little shudder she hugged herself against a sudden, imaginary draught and bit her lip as though to keep some deep secret.

'Poor Luke?' A wave of icy apprehension passed through me, and I cried, 'Where is my brother?' I knew well enough – but I asked, hoping that I was wrong. The room became unreal, strange. Absently I picked out the changes, the Flemish curtains and a wall tapestry, much new pewter, a carpet, a carved chest – things that would be brought to a new household for the making of another generation.

I had no words from the girl, only the stance of her body told me. Her hands stretched out as though to embrace me, then were snatched back again. Tears welling up and spilling down her cheeks, she retreated back into herself and found no comfort there.

I turned without warning and took the maid's arms into my hands, 'Bessie Carver, your mother and mine were friends from being girls. Now you stand there and you tell me where my brother Luke is ...'

I stared into her face and would not let her turn away. She looked down and whispered, 'Master Luke is dead.'

Chapter 6

Poor Addled Margaret

'He was thrown from his horse and broke his neck. Just after Christmas that was.'

'That's enough girl! Shut your poxy bloody gob!' said Stobbs roughly as he stepped out towards us. He was clearly frightened of Bessie Carver letting slip something to me, yet he was also afraid to silence her by uttering threats in my presence. I saw his fists clench and watched the tremor of his arm muscles. I knew then, that if he had dared, he would have silenced the girl with a blow.

So I took the offensive and hit him, my fist catching him under the jaw, knocking him flat on to his backside. And as I had known he would, Stobbs turned over and feigned unconsciousness. The blow cost me a spasm of sharp pain from my wound, but I didn't begrudge it. I turned back to the maid who was looking on, wide-eyed.

'Don't be afraid now, tell me all, Bessie ...' I began, but to no avail. She still gawped at Stobbs with a look of horrified dismay on her face, so I let her go.

My thoughts were racing. By any measure of decency, I should have been weeping for my dead brother, but I could not mourn now, I had to keep my wits about me, their edges honed keen.

A man's wife inherited his possessions, so this girl who stood squinting down at the man on the floor now owned half of the farm. The thought struck me that Luke might have had a will made out, a proper lawyer's will, but it was unlikely. Every farmer, for miles around, would have known that Luke and I shared the little farm, just as every neighbour would have noted us increasing our holdings almost every year for the last seven years. It seemed a churlish thing to have to mention my share of the farm, but I had to know.

'So, sister-in-law, it seems as though we shall have a half share each in this property...' I waited to see her reaction, but the face had become even more like that of a French doll. 'Though perhaps you would wish to have the advice of an attorney, and have him present when we talk?' Ashamed of myself, I stopped.

'I cannot see why that should be necessary, brother-in-law, my dear husband's witnessed testament was most clear on the point,' she said, her voice sounding more distant than ever. It came as less of a shock to me than it might, merely adding the fine detail to the pistol ball fired at me on the road from Shields. 'Master Stobbs is my tenant here now!' she cried, pointing at Stobbs again and again as though she were accusing him. Then without warning she became wild eyed and excited. Testily, she beat down the maids' hands as they tried to calm her, then with a sharp loss of patience she fetched one of them a ringing slap across the face. Plainly they were much afraid of her, but they both persisted gently until they had her hands held. Suddenly she seemed to tire utterly of her struggling and fell on the neck of the maid she had struck, sobbing.

I looked at Stobbs who by then had picked himself up from the flagstones and was eyeing me with a look on his face that told me that he just might spring forward to attack. While he looked at me in that fashion, I knew I was safe.

'Tenant?' I said blankly.

'Tenant ...' she said loftily. 'In ...' She remembered the term with a half giggle of delight, 'fee-simple, to be renewed annually at pleasure.' The maidservants had coaxed her as far as the foot of the staircase, when she turned again as though to deliver an afterthought. Her voice became high pitched and querulous, again that of a child imitating its elders. 'Matthew Stobbs! Did I not tell you to whip this fellow off. Do it at once, or you may yet find yourself turned out!'

Stobbs opened his mouth to answer then shut it again with an almost audible snap while my sister-in-law shook herself free of her maids and swept up the stairs with great haughtiness.

When she had gone, I looked at Matthew Stobbs. If you want the truth from a man, knocking him flat on his arse at first meeting is not always the way to get it, but Stobbs had a wounded pride to salve, and in his efforts to show what a bold rogue he was he rushed to tell me all he knew.

'She may be addled i' the head, but by God, Ellyot, she's right enough in what she says. She's Margaret Bronsard. The House of Bronsard has become a great power in the town, aye, and in the County as well, these last years. Master Nicholas Bronsard has been at Court three times to my knowledge. He has dined at His Majesty's own table.'

The way the jack swelled when he spoke of his patron's greatness told me that he drew some pride and hope of advancement himself from his acquaintance with this Nicholas. I asked him delicately: 'And have you yourself dined with this Nicholas Bronsard?'

'I have been at his table ...' Stobbs' answer was framed with a betraying precision, '... more than once,' and he straightened his shoulders as though to affirm the truth to himself. He looked at me directly and added, 'Those who stand well with the House of Bronsard have flourished.' Stobbs clearly felt himself to one of these.

'So you'll be a murderer, and a thief as well, Mattie Stobbs, like your master!' I hissed.

He changed colour, gawping and choking in his efforts to gasp a denial. Grabbing him by the front of his jerkin, I drew him towards me and said through gritted teeth, 'Listen well to me, you poxy midden-rat. I own a full half of this farm and all that goes with it. I was my brother's partner. I can show proper title to my half in any court o' law, and in due course, I shall do so. So hold tight to the money you save for your rent next quarter – for you will have to pay half of it to me!' I threw him from me.

Even a turd-hoarder like Stobbs could be abused hard enough to loosen his caution from his pride. He bared his teeth and snarled at me, his voice shrill with vehemence.

'You're shent and broken, John Ellyot! For all your fine schoolin' and bein' apprenticed as Merchant Venturer to daft Ralphie Carr ...' Stobbs almost gagged in his eagerness to give vent to his sneering triumph. 'You ran off for a soldier, and that's all you still are ... the wastrel son of a tenant farmer ... whatever else ye may think yourself!'

If Stobbs had gone on I might have felled him again. There was more truth in what he was shouting than I could bear to hear aloud. His words were doing no more than adding flesh to my own thoughts, but he stopped short as he saw Will Blacket standing in the doorway.

From the whimsical look on Will's face I could see that he had something to show. He said nothing, but raised a bushy eyebrow at me and stood aside. He was holding the bridle of my Swedish mare.

My spirits leapt as I strode outside to pat and stroke the fine animal.

Stobbs' truculence left him like spit off a hot iron. The man dissolved into shaking anxiety, his thin lower lip quivering like a maid's about to weep.

'You'll not be taking Master Nicholas's new mare!' he pleaded, his voice a whine of terrified dismay. 'He laid out twelve pound for it only yesterday. He charged me to …'

Words failed him. Certainly he was desperate enough to try and attack again. He stepped forward, but after an instant of hesitation he thought better of it and stopped. Truly, whoever this Master Nicholas was, Stobbs was mortally afraid of him.

'I found the Captain's mount hidden in the byre,' said Will, coming stiffly to attention, his new boots stamping down on to the flagstones of the floor as he reported. His use of the military mode of address was for Stobbs' benefit and for want of anything better I acted on his cue.

'Well, Master Stobbs, this changes everything. I hope that you have an answer for yourself. The holding of stolen property is nearly as much a felony is the theft itself. This beast has the three-crown brand of the Swedish army on it. And I have an honest bill of sale declaring the animal to be mine. It was stolen by highway robbery and attempted murder on Gateshead Fell. We have more than seven witnesses, all good Gateshead burgesses, ready to swear their testimony in court.'

I paused, fearing that I had embroidered too heavily. Stobbs gawped at me and then gave me a look of half disbelief, but a half only.

'No matter,' I snapped briefly, 'we'll see what answers you have to make when you stand before the court at Durham. The crime was committed on yon side of the Tyne so you'll have to give account of yourself in the Bishop's domains.'

The nail was in, but not hammered home. Doubt – the merest flicker of it –

showed as a twitch at the corner of Stobbs' mouth. He was a fearful man, whose loyalty, as far as I judged it, would go no further than his greed, his fear, or what he felt was the strength of his master's protection. It was an inspired shot. The rivalry between the bishops of Durham and the town of Newcastle was bitter and of long standing. In Stobbs' mind he would not be able to see himself getting the false weighted trial he might expect his masters to arrange for him in Newcastle. I guessed that this Nicholas Bronsard would not be able to help him once the Tyne was crossed and he was into the County Palatine. Will Blacket drove the nail home.

'Hang the bastard now, Your Excellency!' he roared. I almost laughed. Blacket, a comic figure in his ragged breeks and rough sheepskins was standing to rigid attention and contriving, as old soldiers do, to speak without allowing his mouth to move at all.

'With Your Honour's leave I'll call up three or four lads from our company,' he added, looking sideways at Stobbs. 'A red hot pistol barrel up this knave's arsehole will get the names of his accomplices.'

'Be silent, Sergeant!' I barked at Blacket. 'I'll have none of that here. Good God man, d'y think we're in Germany?'

I turned my back on Stobbs and looked away across the Tyne valley towards Whickham and then up to Ryton and the closely wooded land that lay along the banks of the Tyne and the Derwent. My mother had loved that view. I swung round as though I had arrived at a decision.

'Master Stobbs will be given a chance to turn King's evidence against this ... Nicholas?'

It was too much. If Stobbs had been going to tell me anything, the mention of that name struck him dumb. He just stood where he was, gasping, like a man afflicted with a binding stutter.

'Secure the prisoner for now ...' I snapped. It was all I could think of. Will snatched Stobbs' whip from his belt and quickly bound the wretched man's wrists together behind him. 'We'll take this buffoon with us, Will. The men can have their pleasure with him ... We owe them some sport.'

Stobbs goggled at us in disbelief. Now I think he was ready to believe anything I said. His legs buckled under him and he hit the floor with a crash and this time there was no doubt. Stobbs had fainted.

Will Blacket looked at me, and waited. For a few seconds I stood still, then I laughed, but not with joy – there was an edge to the sound that was strange to my own ears.

'Will, for all our ranting ways, it looks as though we've been routed by a half company of poxy lawyers.' I sat down heavily on the worn whinstone mounting block that was set against the doorway of the house … my house! I banged my fist hard against the stone, hard enough to hurt my hand and set my bruises throbbing again. I was so weary.

'What would you do in my place, Soldier?' It was a daft question, asked in bitter jest without the hope of a sensible answer.

'Well, Captain, since, as y' say, this is something of a retreat… what our officers used to call to call a trifling reverse …' here he screwed up his mangled face like a man wrestling with some weighty problem, pushed a broad thumb across a nostril and winked at me, ' … do what any honest soldiers would do on a retreat – set torch to this place to deny it to the enemy – round up the stock and drive it off for what it will fetch at the Reiver's Market.' He paused. 'Then, Captain, there's the womenfolk.' He hitched up his breeks and looked around, his expression taking on a flush of honest lust. 'There's one of them maids back there that's got the sort of purse-lipped, never-had-it face that I can't abide,' his voice deepened to a growl. 'She's like to be a tight as a pair o' new-issued boots. She'll squeak a bit on first tryin', but never mind, I've the horn about me to put a smile on her frosty face …'

'Enough, Blacket!' I barked back. 'That's a rascal's way. I mean to employ the same sort of guile as this Bronsard has used to get his hands on this place. I mean to have my due from him, and by God I mean to make the bastard smart for his trouble.'

'Well then …' he said, reaching for his knife, 'permission to skin the dogs, Captain? Dog's hide makes supple leather. Any glover in Newcastle will pay five shillin' a hide, and that's a good day's pay for the pair of us.'

I searched the farm buildings from end to end. Something in me needed to know what I had been robbed of. I found my saddle and one of the two leather trunks that carried my belongings piled in a corner of the barn. I was still searching for the other trunk when Will Blacket's warning whistle made me pause. It came again; this time more urgent.

'Riders, Captain ...' he said, pointing up the hillside. The party was far off and I knew that it might yet turn, heading for the west, but then they topped a fold in the ground. There was no doubt now, they were riding down towards us. There were five riders, coming downhill at the canter. Ten minutes would see them on us. I motioned for Will to mount up. There was a small task I had yet to perform. I grabbed the hind leg of one of the skinned dogs and, dragging the dripping carcass into the house, left a bloody trail across the floor.

Stobbs was still lying where he had fallen, feigning dead, but when I dropped the dog flesh dripping raw and still warm across his face, he spluttered and spat into staring life again.

'Listen to me Matthew Stobbs.' I whispered, my voice silky as I gripped his hair and rove at it until his lips spread back baring his teeth, 'do you truly believe me to be a man o' violence?' He nodded, then nodded again more vigorously. 'That is good, Matthew. That is *very* good, because I want you to know, that if any harm comes to the maid Bessie Carver, in any way... in any way what-so-ever. I shall return to this place and do to you what I have done to your dogs ... That you may truly believe.'

As I walked away he nodded, and kept on nodding. The riders were close when I climbed into the saddle.

'Let's away Will, for now. You're right, I think, we'll need to find our own lawyers for this work so we'll ride into Newcastle. I have an uncle there who will know as much of this business as any man.'

Chapter 7

Into Newcastle Town

We came into the town by the Pandon Gate. I had thought it wiser to ride a round-about way, skirting the town walls and coming in on the eastern side. We pushed our way through the gateway among the hundreds of carts crowding in with fresh provisions for the markets. The half dozen pikemen on guard were alert enough. My hand dropped casually to the hilt of my sword and twice I looked back over my shoulder, at the gate we had just passed through. The watchmen spread themselves across the cobbled inner courtyard so that no more than a single cart or horseman could pass the piquet without being looked at closely. I exchanged warning looks with Will Blacket. Then I saw a dressed fowl being offered and accepted, with as straight a face as could be wished on both sides. We had come on the guard's toll-day. The pikeman who had stood in my path was already reaching out to the cart that followed behind me to grab his booty. We were noticed for sure, but sight of the burnished steel gorget at my throat and my leather jerkin seemed to be passport enough to allow me to pass untaxed. Will Blacket too, ragged though he was, sat in his saddle as straight and as proud as one of Wallenstein's cavalry troopers. I fancy that we were taken for garrison troops and allowed to enter unhindered.

Newcastle had changed little enough in nine years. As we rode up the old Pilgrim's street I saw that the row of ancient wooden houses that I knew well had been torn down and replaced by fine mansions built of Dutch brick. For a few folk, at least, there looked to be more money in the town than there had been when I left.

Ralph Carr's printing shop, however, was far from being the way I recalled it. The coal smoke had been allowed to get the upper-hand and had caked its black grime over the once yellow stucco. The timber beams had not had their dressing of Dantzig tar for years either. Uncle Ralph had always kept his shop as clean and as bright as could be. The great ship's lantern with its gilded copper dolphins that was the shop's sign was still hanging over the door but its curved glass panes had been smashed. My boots crunched on shards of broken crystal as I mounted the stairs from the street.

The inside was no better. As a lad I had never been happier than when I had been allowed to help in the print shop. I went through the door with my eyes half shut, breathing deeply to take in the smells of new paper and calf leather, glue size and above all the magical scent of printer's ink that Ralph made to a secret recipe from the soot of burnt whale oil. Instead my nose wrinkled at the reek of spilled beer, stale urine, and bitter cold. The house had that damp chill about it that told me that there hadn't been a fire in the grate for weeks. I reached up for the rope pull of a ship's bell that had always hung above the counter, only to find it gone.

'Service to y' ... M' master?' mumbled the fat youth who came rolling out of the back shop, still wiping the grease from his mouth. He was wearing the ink-stained apron of a printer – and, damn me, but it was the full apron of a master printer at that. One look at the half vacant, half cunning leer on his slab-sided face was enough to persuade me that the fellow hadn't the wit to blow his nose unaided much less set a page of type.

'Fetch me Master Ralph Carr,' I said quietly. The young man was no shop-hand, standing there with his hands on his hips and his thick lower lip curled outward, stupidly truculent, waiting for me to speak again. No man who has served from being an apprentice would have stood before a customer in such fashion. I could guess little of him, but his manner put me on my guard. My uncle would never have tolerated such a lout in the front shop. I chose my new character quickly. I was dressed as a soldier, but a soldier of what kind? 'Tell your master that Major Kreutze of the Castle garrison is here to see him.' It was a start. The freelances had been Germans. It was likely that there would be other Germans in the garrison so I affected the thick accent that I had heard some of our prisoners speak.

'I wish for some broadsheets to be printed. His Majesty has need of some good strong fellows to serve him.' I gave him a thin smile and looked him up and down in the man-hunting way of recruiting officers. The creature was too stupid even to be alarmed. He narrowed his little eyes for a moment, looking at me hard, as though he was trying to gather enough thought to answer me. While he looked, I raised the counter-leaf and strode into the shop.

The printing press had been stripped out and taken away. Without Great Simeon's eight feet height to tower over the centre of the room the very soul of the place was destroyed. That printing press had been Ralph Carr's life. I remembered the way my mother had worried when he had gone all the way to Antwerp himself to bring the giant machine home safely.

'Where is Master Ralph Carr? I have business with him … King's business!' Now I made my voice boom out as I would on the great parade ground at Uppsala, trying to shock some kind of answer from the fellow. I had more than I bargained for. The stupid look on his face gave way to an ill-natured smirk. 'Carr's gone away … fled … overseas.' The smirk turned to a gloat. It was as much as I could do not to raise my fist to him.

'Hold y'r havering tongue, Eckie!' The sharp crack of a warning cut across the shop and silenced the fool; the look on his face turned to guilt and his meaty shoulders sagged.

'Now, Sir, mayhap I can help you, though I fear that if it's printing you want done … you're a week or two behind the fair.'

She was bonny. I don't mean just that she was good to look at – many Northern lasses are that. No, she was truly comely. With a swift grace she stepped across the room into a patch of pale sunlight, holding herself straight but without stiffness. The face was fine-boned, strong, yet womanly, and she was affecting a strict manner that I sensed was not her own.

Caution told me that my counterfeit German accent would not long deceive this young woman. The eyes that were quizzing me so intently were an uncommon grey, dark with curious large jet flecks around the iris, and lustrous and wide without the use of belladonna.They were too keen, perhaps, for my comfort.

We assessed each other with the same quick scanning gaze, hidden under the same pleasant half-smile. I could not tell how much she had heard of what I had already said. To be safe I changed my story a little.

'I have ridden through from Durham to seek the services of Master Ralph Carr.

The Governor of Durham Castle has need of some recruiting broadsheets, and I am given to believe that the printer here has a fine cunning flourish with words.' I treated her to a knowing smile, and added, 'He has a name for being able to charm plough-boys into joining the King's service.'

I raised my eyebrows at her and waited for a reply. If she didn't believe me she was damnably well skilled at hiding the fact. She spread her hands in regret. This girl knew the way to serve a customer. The stance was right, the manner was there, yet that manner also had authority. It is not much our way in England to have women in authority, but in Germany and in the Netherlands it is not at all uncommon to find that a woman is sole mistress of a workshop and all its business, even a member of a Guild. I rummaged through my memory but though there was something familiar in her face, a family likeness perhaps, I could not recall it. She was, I guessed, twenty, not much more. She would have been a little maid when I had left for Sweden, yet the impression that I had known her once was strong in me.

'This shop has forfeited its licence to print,' she said.

I forced a twist at the corner of my mouth. Rarely did a printer lose his licence. Where he did, it was almost always because he had been tempted by the rich rewards to be made and set his press to printing out lewd tales illustrated with obscene engravings. I have seen hundreds such. Ralph Carr had said that a man might print whatever filth he wished just so long as it were in Latin, but I knew that it was something he would never have done himself.

The dark grey eyes widened and then narrowed for a moment. Clearly she had both the wit and the knowledge to catch the cause of my amusement.

'Ah! Not so …' Her lips pursed and her face took on a serious cast, 'Ralph Carr was accused of having printed certain seditious pamphlets, of uttering scurrilous attacks against His Majesty,' she explained, pausing to see how I was taking the news. 'There is a warrant issued for his arrest. I may tell you that he left this shop as the Town Watch was marching up to his door, three weeks ago today. 'Tis said that he sailed for Antwerp.'

'And took his great press and his type with him,' I added ironically as I looked at her. She was about to say something but stopped before a word escaped and merely nodded. Clearly she was as troubled about the fate of Ralph Carr as I was myself. I could not show my feelings, nor could I safely ask any more questions about a man I was not supposed to know. My uncle was a notorious Free-thinker. But he held all factions in equal contempt, and I knew for certain that he was too canny an old fox to be taken up for printing seditious pamphlets.

I shrugged and asked, 'Are there are other printers in this town?'

She smiled softly and nodded. 'Few so skilled as Master Carr ... but if you pass down to the Stockbridge and look for the sign of the Red Boggart, Will Keenlyside will get your bills set and printed in a day or two.'

'The Red Boggart?' I queried, feigning ignorance of the hideous red and black painted sign – once a ship's figurehead – which I knew as well as any man in the town.

'It's a ...' Throwing back the hood of her cloak, she put her thumbs to her forehead and waggled her fingers. When I still simulated ignorance, she crossed those wondrous eyes and thrust out her tongue. I laughed. When she looked like a little girl at play, she was indeed a beauty.

'And whom shall I say sent me?'

'Tell Will Keenlyside that Aphra Thornton sent you.' I doffed my hat, sweeping it across my chest as I bowed low, the way that I had seen the French Ambassador's followers do it in Stockholm. Aphra Thornton courtesied low, returning the mockery in full measure.

'And a good day to you...' There was a long pause. 'Captain John Ellyot!'

I was halfway down the stairs to the street when I heard her last words and the soft laughter that followed me. I had taken another two paces before the meaning of what she had said struck me. Before I had reached the top of the stairs again the door had been slammed and the heavy bolt shot home, but even through the thick planks of that door, I heard her laughter.

She knew me; she knew my name; she knew me as a returned soldier. That I had made a fool of myself with my play-acting over the printing of bills was neither here nor there now. Aphra ... sweet Aphra! I knew that a man with the troubles I had about me had no need to add more to his burden, but still ...

Will Blacket was not with the horses. A lad, ragged and caked with coal dust and street mud was holding the bridles while he wolfed down a hawker's pie.

'I was to tell you, Sir, that Master Will has gone about chasin' a hare.' He shrank back between the horses as though he expected his message to earn him a clout. I nodded gravely. This encouraged him to go on. 'He sends his respects and says that if you were to wait at the Three Crescents he will report to you there … when he's catched his hare.'

I gave the lad the price of another pie and took the bridles from him. Will must have had cause to run off, but I knew enough of the man already to realise that only patience would reveal his reasons.

The Three Crescents was no inn for gentlemen. During the daylight hours, it offered a meeting place for horse dealers and wool buyers from the county. Its tap-room was wide and the floor well sanded. I discovered that the ale was good and the tobacco not only very good but also suspiciously cheap. It would do until my affairs were in better order. I chaffered with the landlord's wife for a room on the first floor, and feed and stabling for the horses. The room had a box bed of the kind favoured by the Scots with a space under it where Will could sleep.

I found Will standing in the doorway scanning the taproom when I came downstairs. He had been running, but he looked happy enough.

'I followed the booby,' he said. I must have looked puzzled, for he added, 'the fat lad in the printer's shop. He came out of the side lane with a look o' happy mischief on his face and chantin' your name and description to himself as though he was daft. Daft Eckie they call him, though just how daft, depends upon the weather, I'm told.'

I knew that I should have little sense out of Will until I had bought him a drink, so I signalled for two tankards of best ale.

'I followed him down the bank to the quayside,' he continued. 'He went like a homing bee to a merchant's counting house.' I waited while Will took another thirsty draught from his tankard. 'Bronsard is the name you seek …'

'Bronsard?' The name of my new in-laws again. 'Brownsword!' It came up from memory with a rush. 'There used to be a family called Brownsword, in the corn trade,' I cried.

'That may well be so, Captain, but these people are called Bronsard now and as our friend at your farm said, they have become damned powerful in this town now.' Will looked at me over the rim of his tankard. 'And this Bronsard knows that you are alive and abroad in the town.' Will paused, 'Also, Captain, I've had sight o' the man who shot you.'

I looked at him directly: 'Go on,' I said in almost a whisper, 'did you get a name?'

Will winked slyly at me. 'That treacherous bastard's name is Bone – Mouncey Bone.' He touched his nose with a finger. 'But this time he had shed his velvet suit and he was wearin' a red sash and a lacquered breastplate! It seems that our friend is known as Sergeant Bone of Harrison's troop.'

'You're sure of this, Will?' He nodded.

'I just happened to see the bastard as he rode up to the countin' house. I had to look twice but it was him. All I had to do was point him out to the next garrison soldier walking by and ask the name.' Will cocked his head on one side.

'But the main news is that Daft Eckie was running to blatherskite his news of your coming to Master Nicholas Bronsard, who, by the way, is soon to be dubbed a knight by the King himself. I was told by an old wifie sellin' old clothes on the Sandgate, so it must be true.'

'And how did you learn that I was known?' I asked.

My rogue of a servant smiled his scoundrel's innocent smile. For all that he had found himself a respectable pair of townsman's black breeks since last I had seen him, he still looked every inch a sergeant of musketeers.

'Why, God bless Your Honour, I went up to the poor hapless fellow and asked him fair and civil why he looked so sad and put down.' Will would have his own way of recounting a tale, and it would be the better for being told in his own way. He looked into his tankard. I waved for two more pints.

'Well, I saw him go into Bronsard's house, so I stood as close to the street window as I could, feigning drunk and ready to vomit like. There wasn't a lot to hear clearly, except that Bronsard and Bone were shoutin' at each other like fishwives for a long time. Then Sergeant Bone came out and rode off south across the bridge at full gallop.'

I nodded. It was my guess that he was going to take a close look at a certain slough pit. 'And then?'

'And then our friend Eckie comes out lookin' as forlorn as a sutler who's taken a bad florin.' He tilted back his tankard and finished his drink. 'Always pay your spies. Even when they bring nothing of worth, always show appreciation and pay a little on account. It seems that Eckie's news quite drove any thought of payin' the poor lad out Sir Nicholas-to-be's mind. The poor fat bugger was close to blubberin' when he came out again. So I goes up to him and greets him, comradely like, and invites him to take a drink wi' me. It seems that wor Eckie was given leave to lodge in the printin' shop. He was told that if a man came askin' after Ralphie Carr, a tall man, a fair man wi' a beard, in the dress of a soldier – a man called John Ellyot – he was to run and report on that as fast as his legs would carry him. That was two weeks since. It seems that Bronsard forgot to stand down his watch when he thought that they'd killed you. We might have moved about the town in safety for a while longer if he had.'

He gave me a wicked grin, and continued, 'That intelligence cost the privy purse one shillin' and four pence for a pint of piss that was claimed to be Canary wine.'

'Well done, Will. You've earned your rations today, soldier,' I said.

The Three Crescents served an ordinary, but the smell drifting into the taproom was that from fat mutton. Sheepshead broth is a fine dish on a winter's day – for a poor man who can afford nothing else! I thought we deserved better.

I had Will repeat the story, slowly and in fine detail, as we each chewed a handsome serving of roasted beef brisket straight from the spit, at an eating house up in the town by Black Friars. It was the first fresh meat I had eaten since I had landed.

'I want to see this Bronsard,' I said, picking a shred of the juicy beef from between my teeth, 'today!'

Will shrugged. 'If you've a mind, Captain, but it might be a prudent thing to cast off your officer's sash and that buff leather jerkin, and perhaps you should leave off your sword. Without those you might well be taken for a hard-riding cattle-dealer or a buyer of wool. There can't be too many Redesdale buyers who wear a real ostrich plume in their bonnets.'

It was good advice. When I entered the Bronsard counting house I did indeed look a lot less of a soldier and more of a travelling merchant than I might have hoped. I had a sound business reason to be there, for my letters of credit, which I had sewn into my breeches before I had left Karlskrona, now lay in my pocket. Nothing, I told myself, could be more innocent than a merchant travelling around the northern counties wishing to have a letter of credit discounted at a well-known house of business.

The sight of a large bill drawn on the House of Steeksma in Amsterdam was a charm powerful enough to have me taken straightway to the table of Nicholas Bronsard himself. Some sign must have passed between the clerk and his master because I was greeted handsomely, more so than my appearance might have warranted.

The head of the House of Bronsard was, at first sight, a warm and cheery fellow, though his handshake was hard and cool. He waved me to a fine padded chair before his table and steepled his fingers under his chin to let me know that he was ready to do business. I handed him the letter at which he seemed merely to glance. It was as though he was more interested in myself. I had expected something different. The usual money-changer's trick is to begin a transaction by giving out a moaning tale about how bad trade is and how he has heard that the fortunes of the house that had issued the letter of credit are in doubt. There was none of that. He didn't even go through the merchant's ritual of having the client wait while the bill itself was examined in a hundred ways.

The few minutes that he took to scan the paper *did* give me a chance to look at him closely. He was, I supposed, not much short of forty, wearing a black taffeta overgown, somewhat like a lawyer's garb, but when he reached for his quill a fold shifted and the brilliant sheen of brocade showed. On one finger he had a heavy gold ring set with a large topaz large enough to interfere with his writing when it slipped. As he entered the transaction in his day book, he paused and looked up at me suddenly and our eyes met. They were ordinary brown eyes with neither fire nor steel to them. He bent to his writing again, and I waited while he wrote and caught the sound as he buzzed a hymn tune softly through his nose.

All trades have their tricks. In Sweden I had much to do with the prize agents, the so-called merchants who bought the booty that soldiers brought home from Germany and Poland. It was the custom in the offices of the prize agents always to have much gold coin in plain sight and it was also the practice to get drink into a client as soon as possible. Here a pile of gold coins lay stacked on an embroidered cloth spread across Bronsard's table, not a piece of it less than a Spanish gold onza. The money glowed against the blue silk, yet I knew it was as much for show as the white lead on a whore's face. If I sat before this table a year hence the self same coins would be lying there. It was bait.

'This is a sound bill, Master ...?' He left the question hanging and, by God, I almost said my name.

'Bell, Jonathan Bell of Otterburn ... Originally. Though I've since served he House of Ferens for twelve year ... Hull, d'y know?' I grinned. 'Now I scratch for myself, where I may.'

It was as polite a way of telling him to mind his own business as I knew. That was, as I judged, what any north countryman would have said and what Bronsard would have expected.

'I can discount at six per cent.' He was already reaching below his table into a cash box.

Had I not been so greatly concerned with other things, I might not have been so pleased with such a discount. I had paid forty-two pounds worth of Swedish crowns for a letter of credit with a face value of forty pounds English. A sheet of paper is much safer to carry than coin, but Bronsard would take two pounds and eight shilling for himself from the face value of the note before he handed me the gold. It was no trick now to see how money multiplied for him and his kind.

There was a tinge of amusement on his well-fleshed face as he watched me put the gold in five or more places about my clothes.

'Have you a mind to lay out, say, twenty of those pounds, in an interest in an enterprise to do with a cargo of tin?' he asked in a voice fruity and sonorous, like that of a good singer. 'I can guarantee a return of nine percent at least in three months – by Michaelmas at latest.'

He reached behind him for a stoneware bottle and two glasses. 'I would value your opinion on this Geneva. I have a cargo of the stuff expected any day. Take a glass and tell me.'

No man in my supposed business would turn down a free drink so I allowed the brightness of furtive pleasure to light up my face and took the glass. It was good, so far as any man in his right senses can say that any gin is good – it was good enough to get blind, legless drunk on. And he had poured almost a gill of the clear spirit for me.

I tossed off the drink as easily as I was able. Then I shook my head and tried to look sullen.

'Horses are my interest. Horses that I can send ...' I cut myself off as though I was in danger of being indiscrete, then started again, 'I am up to buy good strong horses, for the ploughing.'

Nicholas Bronsard was not the man I thought him to be if he could not guess that what I was suggesting was gun horses for export abroad. He would know the price of a good English draught animal in North Europe better than most.

For an instant I thought he would rise to the bait. If he offered me my own mare I would have him, but the moment passed and I could feel the fumes of his damned Geneva gin rising to my head. I looked around the room.

It is said that much can be told about a man by the surroundings he creates for himself. Counting houses are not places where people often have occasion for laughter or even for smiles. Beyond Bronsard's table four clerks worked at ledgers without raising their heads or passing a word to one another. Every man was clad in grey woollen cloth, from the same bolt, I would swear. Again I knew my man. Bronsard liked to own his servants, body and soul. I rose to my feet, the slight sway in my stance not all simulated. I think on another day I might have had much more of his persuasive attentions, but now, it was clear that he was preoccupied. I hoped it was with John Ellyot's return from the dead.

'I do thank you, Sir Nich ... Master Bronsard ...' The slip of the tongue was almost accidental, but it had no less effect for that. The frown that had begun to crease Nicholas Bronsard's brow unfolded itself and was transformed into a warm smile. He stood and thrust out his hand.

'And thank *you*, Master Bell... You'll remember what I said about the venturing of twenty pounds ... I hope that we can be of service to you again on other occasions.'

My capacity for play-acting fled from me as I walked across the counting house floor. I pulled my hat down half over my eyes and gathered my cloak about me as I strode over quickly to the door. It was as well that I did. Even on short acquaintance there was no mistaking the whingeing wet voice of Matthew Stobbs.

My plan was quickly made: I would crack him under the jaw as he entered and run, but a sideways glance at the man as he came into the room, told me that I had little to fear that he would raise any alarm. The last time that I had seen a wretch who looked as Stobbs did, was when I had seen a captured spy being fitted with the thumbscrews. Matthew Stobbs was looking across at Nicholas Bronsard as a rabbit looks at a stoat.

'There wasn't anything I could do, Master Nicholas ... there was eight or nine of them all armed troopers ...'

The fear in me turned to softly grim laughter as I went to find Will Blacket. It would do me no harm to have Bronsard suppose that I had a party of riders under my command.

Chapter 8

Breaking and Entering

'This lad here is Dougie Pigg, Captain.' I looked up to see Will Blacket standing over me. I had eaten a good meal in the taproom of the Three Crescents and sat enjoying a pipe of tobacco. The ragged little man standing at Will's side looked frightened. His pale blue eyes darted back and forth across the room, looking now at the door that led out to the street, now towards the curtain that covered the back way out of the tavern.

'Dougie's a ruffler, Captain, and by all accounts a middlin' fair one – that is, when he isn't sweepin' folk's chimneys,' said Will, grinning. Pigg twitched nervously as Will put an arm around his shoulder, all comradely, to stop him from bolting.

I swung my boots up on to the table and drew slowly on my clay, allowing the smoke of good Virginia to trickle from the corner of my mouth. It is always as well to look comfortable when you are dealing with a nervous fellow. And spurred boots do lend a man a certain authority.

'Are you truly a good thief, Dougie?' I asked, peering at him, much as a man might look at a doubtful cut of beef. Pigg still looked fearful enough to run, so I poured a pot of strong ale from my jug for him and held it out. Damn me, if he didn't look over his shoulder twice before he took the pot in both hands, and he had that gill of ale down his gullet before I had raised my own pot to my lips!

Will continued to catalogue Pigg's abilities. 'Our Dougie's a grand man at dancin' on the pantiles ... He was only ever caught the once. And then there was a mite of doubt about the business that time.'

He winked and pulled Pigg's grey woollen bonnet off to one side. The man's right ear had been bored through the gristle – a shilling's piece could have been passed through the hole. The housebreaker gave me his shifty little smile, looked over his shoulder again and pulled his bonnet back into place. I recalled that I had once had a man in my siege-train who claimed to have been the Master Thief of Lubeck. Both his lugs had been burned through.

'Well now, Master Pigg ... I am indeed glad to know that we are dealing with a fellow who knows his trade: as it happens I need a master not a journeyman for the business I intend to do.'

Pigg gave me a lopsided look that was too innocent to be honest. He was not nearly as stupid as he was pretending. I gave him back half a smile, and raised one eyebrow. Then I straightened my face and shot him a look as grim as that of a hangman's apprentice. The pale eyes fell. I motioned to him to take the bench opposite. Will squeezed in next to him to wedge him hard against the wall.

'I'll come directly to the matter I've in mind, Dougie. I need your help in a bit o' roof dancin'.' As I knew he would do, Pigg at once twisted his head to try to look over his shoulder. 'There's a place I need to take a look at ... without interruptions. It may even turn out that I want a few things lifted.'

I paused and stared hard into Pigg's eyes. The man was incapable of looking a fellow creature directly in the face for more than a second or two at a space.

'Or, it may well turn out that I want things so arranged that only the Almighty would ever know that we've been there at all ... ' Pigg screwed up his face. He was puzzled. I went on, 'In either case your own back will be well covered.'

Will broke in, 'Tell me Dougie ... what would you reckon to get for a good night's work in the Town?' He had spoken, clearly, but I would swear that I had not seen his lips move. 'After you've paid off your inside man and countin' only what you pick up from the stallin' ken.'

I was surprised to learn that a even a petty thief like Pigg would go a receiver. Felony looked to be as well organised a business in Newcastle as it was elsewhere in Europe.

Pigg hesitated. 'Ten poun's ... ' Will roared with exaggerated laughter and banged his tankard down on to the boards. His outburst had been loud enough to make even the incurious drinkers of the Three Crescents turn their heads towards our booth. He sat back and began to slap Pigg between the shoulder blades with a force that shook the little thief to the very bones.

'Listen to me ... y' shite gobblin' little get,' his musketeer's voice hissed out through his teeth like a long blade leaving its scabbard, 'try that wi' the Captain and aal take pleasure in howkin' the livin' pluck out of your scabby carcass.' The point of Blacket's dirk came up between the edge of the bench and Pigg's belly. Without seeming even to look at what his blade was doing he snicked a horn button off the thief's greasy jerkin.

'Why I'm sure that our Dougie was only havin' a wee bit of a joke with us, Will.' I smiled benevolently across at Pigg. He looked relieved.

'I was thinking more of ... ' I moved my arm across the boards of the table as though to move the ale jug and opened my hand to show three gold coins. 'That is the price.' I said quietly. 'I've added an extra piece so that you can leave the town for a week or so once the job is done.' I let the thief look at the money for a few seconds before I closed my fist. 'Well?' I levelled a gaze and waited.

'One piece now?' Pigg's eyes followed my hand as I withdrew the money. The greed in his look was almost comical. I feinted the roll of a single coin across the table. As Pigg's arm shot out to snatch what wasn't there Will Blacket jabbed him under the ribs causing him to wheeze.

'Y' can trust me, Captain!' Pigg got out his assurance hastily. 'You can trust Dougie Pigg.'

'Why man, Dougie, I'll be sure to ask the Sheriff the next time I'm taking a glass of Canary with him at the Tolbooth ... '

This time, the thief saw the humour. 'But you'll have to tell me where and when, Captain – there'll be arrangements to make, gear to sort.'

'We'll have need of your craft tonight, Dougie Pigg. The time will be well after midnight. From what I've seen, it seems to me that it will be roof work ... with perhaps a window to be opened ... very quietly.' I stopped, wondering if I had not already told the thief too much.

Pigg nodded. He looked to be thinking hard. 'Where?' He flinched as Blacket hitched along the bench towards him again. 'Aaah mean ... if y' could give me some notion of where. Maybe I already know a servant who will let us in – quiet like.' Pigg smirked. 'That would be easier for you … seein' as you're not used to the game.'

I nodded. There might well be some sense in Pigg's suggestion. If a servant in one of the nearby houses could be induced to leave a door open, then the task of getting into Bronsard's house would be a lot easier.

'I'll go so far as to say somewhere between Low Bridge and the Side.'

That had been an error – plain to see as Pigg's face paled under its grime.

'Jesus an' Joseph! Them's all hostmen's houses. Hangin's certain sure if we're took. There's few ever robbed them careful bastards and not been caught. Folk say there's ways they have of askin' and finin' out … ' The man was clearly terrified.

'The hour the business is over, I'll pay your passage to Edinburgh or Hull and see you safe on board a vessel … ' Pigg was already shaking his head vigorously. 'That's a pity. Dougie, it truly is.' I turned quietly to Will, who had been making sheep's eyes at a big-breasted serving lassie. 'Skewer the little bastard's guts to the settle, and we'll away … I hear tell that you can always hire a good thief across in Gateshead.'

'Aah'll do it!' Pigg gasped, his eyes bulging.

'Landlord! Two ordinaries for these good fellows.' I grinned across at Pigg. 'We must always feed the troops to keep them in good heart!' Then quietly I spoke again. 'D' ye take on? True and steadfast?' I wanted his bond.

'Aye … aa'll tak' on … true!' A hand like a rat's paw stretched across the bench. We struck palms, but Pigg was still holding out his hand.

Will signalled wildly against it, but still I gave the rogue one of the promised gold pieces. He stood up to go, but Will laughed out loud again and thrust at him so hard with his hip that Pigg slid bodily along the bench and lay with the breath knocked out of him.

I held up a finger and wagged it slowly at him while he struggled to suck back his wheeze.

'Best you stay here with Master … ?' I waited for Will to catch on and grin. 'Sergeant Zoetvinger …' Will smirked. He was about to add some filthiness of his own but I cut him off. 'Yes,' I purred softly. 'You keep him company, my good sergeant, see him kept safe until … until I call for his services.' Then to Pigg, 'Sit y'quiet, Dougie!'

The potboy arrived with two brown glazed bowls loaded with neck o' mutton and boiled cabbage. The food swam in its own grease, but Pigg went at his like a starving hound at broth.

'Feed him, but keep him close and sober, Will.' I watched Pigg ply his pewter spoon for a few seconds before I put on my hat and cloak and stepped out into the lane.

For an hour or more I strolled slowly among the crowds of folk along the quay-side, taking in everything I saw. Time and time again I stopped and made certain that I was not being followed. I took a pot of beer at three or four of the waterside taverns, and as I walked about, I bought a few odds and ends of this and that, fat Sicily raisins, and a bag of new landed almonds. I also greatly enjoyed a Valencia orange that cost me a tenth of what I would have paid in Sweden, but always I kept the big house on the Side in view, and constantly my glance went up to the dormer window in the roof. If I were to learn anything of value, it would only be found in Nicholas Bronsard's private chamber.

The sight of a woman and child leaving the house next door to Bronsard's counting house made me pause. The little girl had clearly been fitted with new spectacle glasses. The child's delight was plain and heartwarming to see. I climbed the creaking stairway all the way to the topmost floor and stood before a board painted with white lettering announcing that Master Petrus Peale, late of Parfet Lane, London sold spectacles, sea-glasses, telescopes, mirrors, instruments and Opticks of all kinds.

Had I had the time I might well have spent an hour looking over the young man's stock of wonders, and also casting an eye over his lively young wife, who had a look to her that I did not mistake. Instead, I announced that I had need of a good pocket spyglass and allowed him to show me the dozen or so he had laid out. Looking around me while he prattled, I saw that I was in a shop, not a workshop. At night all of the stock would be packed into the big leather chests I could see piled near the door. Most probably it would be carried away to the young couple's lodgings for the night. That would serve me well enough.

The view from the top floor, out over the river, was indeed impressive. With the aid of a trim speculum metal telescope I picked up from the array offered for me to try, there was much to be seen both up and down the river and coming into the town from the south across the Tyne Bridge.

Then I had luck, when a Bedlington farmer clumped heavy-footed up the stairs and demanded to be fitted with spectacles, in an accent that so rolled its r's that the shopman begged leave to place me in the hands of his pretty young wife while he attended to him.

I was glad enough to be left with the dark-eyed lass hovering close at my elbow and singing the praises of her husband's wares. Set into the wall at the back of the shop there was an unglazed shutter, through which I could scan the roofs and yards of all the houses along the Side. It did not take me long to pick out a route.

Ground space for building is scarce between the steep rock face under the Baillie Gate and the river's edge. The yards behind the houses were small, but each was protected by its wall of rough mortared stone. One yapping watchdog in any of them, I knew, would rouse the street.

Bronsard's house was secure indeed. To get to it from the ground, I should have needed to trespass across the yards of two other dwellings, but the pantiled roof beneath the shutter where I was standing led almost directly to the neighbouring house. This had to be the way, dangerous but not impossible, leastways for a determined man led by a master thief.

I bought the little spyglass I had been using. It seemed a justifiable expense.

The town's clocks were striking out two in the morning when the three of us set out. The plan was simple enough. Dougie Pigg made short work of the iron locks on the street door. With his quill ready primed with neat's foot oil he blew into the keyhole to ease the mechanism. He had his own set of pick wires to lift the lock's wards. It was the work of a moment.

We left Will Blacket outside, across the street to keep watch. I had foreseen that his heavy tread alone would have made every stair in the house creak and I had more than a fancy that no roof would have borne the big musketeer's weight!

There were undoubtedly folk asleep in that house, but we heard nothing of them; and as we crept upstairs past the silent landings, it seemed that they too were inclined to hear nothing of us!

The door to the spectacle fitter's room had been left open. It was as I had expected. Save for a couple of tables and a few chairs the room was now bare.

Shifty eyed and a stench at large, Dougie Pigg may have been, but he knew his trade. In the darkness he became a different man. He closed the doors behind us and silently allowed the bar to drop. Then he tied open the shutter that let out on to the rooftops. I followed his way, footstep on to footstep across the tiles. Until I was half a dozen paces out along the ridge of the roof it simply did not occur to me to be frightened at all. Then a tile shifted and began to slide as my unsteady footstep came on to it and I froze stiff, a young recruit again, and hearing the first whisper of a cannon ball. It was almost as though Pigg had been expecting it to happen. Walking silently on soft hide shoes he came back and lay down with his body straddling the ridge of the roof. He held the heavy pantile and signed that I was to walk on. There was a rime of white dew like frost on the tiles around me, and the chill trickle of sweat between my shirt linen and my back was every bit as cold.

In sunny daylight the distance across the roofs had seemed small. Now in the dark it yawned before us, but in the end we were there. We lay alongside the dormer window on the roof of the Bronsard house. About us the town's clocks were striking three, and twice we had to flatten ourselves low as light from swinging lanterns cast tall shadows of the Town Watch wavering against the fronts of the houses across the street. Each time, we waited until the steady beat of the Watch's single drum had gone from our hearing.

The dormer window proved easy to open. Every trade has its proper tools. Pigg took out a short bladed knife with its point ground flat and began to prise open the strips of lead that held the little lozenges of green glass in place. I could only watch and listen. All about me there were a hundred sounds, the wind whistling softly as it found its way in under the pantiles, the gentle groan as the great oak timbers of the roof moved. With my ear resting against the window's wooden frame I fancied that I could even hear the folk inside stirring in their beds. Suddenly, there was a loud thump.

Pigg stiffened and took his hand away from the glass. Someone was inside the room. I heard the creak of the sneck as a cupboard door was closed, then, distinctly, there was the muffled scrape of footsteps. We lay there helpless.

Whoever it was, looked to be as stealthy in his work as we were, that much was plain. For a moment I saw the glimmer of a tallow dip. Then all Hell was loosed! A crimson flash lit up Pigg's face and a vicious double crack made the roof shudder under me as the whole window casement exploded outward, spewing shattered glass fragments out on to the pantiles to fall tinkling down on to the cobbles far below.

Chapter 9

Setting a Trap

I flattened my body against the chill pantiles of the roof and waited, thinking of what reasonable defence I might offer at my trial. There was nothing else to do.

Through the whole building grew the din of a household roused. I heard footsteps clattering on stairs and cries and doors banging. A pot dropped and shattered. A woman shrieked and began a lament that was suddenly cut off. Bronsard's mellow voice boomed back and forth, ordering his people back to their beds.

I heard the door open and saw a bright light fall across the window sill. The tread across the boards of the floor was measured, unhurried. There was the muted scrape of something heavy being dragged and the waft of a heavy cloth like a blanket being spread, then a sweep of shadow as the door closed, the scrape and clack of a key in a heavy lock and silence – save, I could swear to it, the soft gurgle of Nicholas Bronsard laughing. It was only then, that I saw Pigg was already a dozen yards away, walking upright and fast, along the ridge tiles.

'Pi …!' I choked on the half syllable before it could escape. My teeth clamped shut, but still my curses came through, 'You whoreson! As God is my witness I'll hamstring you.' My anger was wasted. Pigg had gone.

Sometimes a prudent man in low fortune should cut his losses and wait for better times. That was what I thought for the half hour that I clung shivering to the pantiles of the Bronsard house under silvery bright moonlight. Then my wits returned. If I fell from the roof I would break my neck. If I waited until daylight I would be seen and taken and have my neck stretched at the Gallowgate.

Getting into the dormer window proved a lot easier than I could have hoped. My fingers sought out the fragments of broken glass on the window sill and I stowed them in my pockets, clearing a way into the room. I think the loudest sound I made was the mighty sigh that escaped from my lips when my feet landed safely on the floor inside the window.

The sharp, rotten onion smell of newly fired gunpowder still hung on the air. I breathed it in slowly. It is a strange thing, but the smell of burnt powder served to calm me.

The man's form lay framed in a bright patch of moonlight. Bronsard had draped a blanket over most of the body, but I recognised the hat with the sadly bedraggled scrap of a hat plume lying beside the corpse.

It was one of the freelances and he looked as though he had been flung across the chamber. His body had been thrown against the window casement and rebounded.

I found a rushlight and was able to coax a flame from the last embers in the fireplace. Shielding the tiny flame with my hand, I began to look around. Blood was spattered everywhere. A clot of brains and hair fouled the fine moulding of the stucco panel above the fireplace. One shot had lifted the fellow's brainpan cleanly from his head like the top of an egg; the other had sheared away the lower jawbone, leaving a hideous grin of jaggedly broken teeth. Black spots of unburnt gunpowder pocked the blue-white of the staring eyeballs.

The cause of the freelance's destruction was easy to find. For him to have been hurled across the room he would need to have been standing or crouching over the stout iron chest that stood against the wall. That the chest was fixed by chains to great ringbolts screwed into the wall timbers was itself a clever temptation.

I stooped and sniffed. The blast had come from the chest. There was a tell-tale ghost mark of a powder flash seared white around the lock. Lifting the stiff lid, I heard the click of a strong spring and the short skirring sound of a knurled wheel. A bright shower of sparks lit the room for split second and I cringed. I had guessed aright – Bronsard's coffer was fitted with some infernal machine. I knew of such devices by repute: some threw a dagger, or shot a crossbow quarrel. I had even heard tell of a Milanese lock that threw out a cloud of poisonous dust. This toy was of the most wondrously fine Nuremberg work. It mounted a brace of heavy calibre barrels, larger than any pistol. A cunning mechanism of blued steel levers and springs set itself to cock and fire the lock mechanism just as the lid was raised to three-quarters open.

Well, the device was harmless now, so I looked for the treasure that was worth getting killed for, and I found the bait. A wooden bowl full of coins lay on top of the papers piled up inside the chest. I picked up a heavy gold piece, a rose noble of the time of Henry VII. I smiled in the darkness.

The open bowl of money had served to capture the freelance's attention. At least the poor bastard had died with a gleam in his eye.

'A mouse in the trap lets his brothers feast without fear.' The words of the old Swedish proverb drifted softly from my lips and I smiled as I began to pick up the heavy coins one at a time from the bowl and stow them carefully about my clothes.

Papers and parchments almost filled the chest. I lifted out the bundles carefully and laid them out on the floor. Most of the stuff was drafted out in Latin or lawyers' French, but doubtless for his convenience, Bronsard had attached to each document a gloss in English that gave an outline of its essentials.

I was amazed at the extent of the man's interests. Some holdings were in his own name but many others were held in the names of other men in the family. Every deed of ownership wove through them back to him. That he was a hostman, a member of the clique of merchants who controlled the sale and export of coal from the Tyne, I had assumed without thinking, but it was clear that Bronsard owned or had powerful shares in a score or more of coal mines as well as the deeds or mortgages to houses in every ward of the town. He traded in wool, in hides, in Gateshead millstones, and Shields lime. Within the last month he had paid in gold for a new merchant vessel. The thought came to me that I could injure Bronsard grievously if I simply set fire to the piled papers, but I stayed my hand. That was not the way that I would be revenged upon Nicholas Bronsard. Burnt papers could be written anew and no doubt there would be copies elsewhere, in places safer than any iron chest.

A seal, much larger than usual, caught my attention. It was too elaborate to be that of any merchant's house, but even though I held the purple wax close to the flame of my rushlight I could not make out more than a word or two of the lettering. The seal had been pressed into the wax too hurriedly and the imprint had run smooth again.

Within five minutes of undoing the bundle and beginning to read, I knew the thing that Nicholas Bronsard wanted more than anything else on this earth.

He hungered after coat-armour. Bronsard the merchant wanted to be Sir Nicholas Bronsard, knight. The letters were a part of a long correspondence between Bronsard and several courtiers. There was much mention of 'respectful gifts' and of 'benevolences'. I could also guess at the reason for the records of long loans of handsome sums at minute rates of interest made to the same courtiers, but they were loans only. Our would-be Sir Nicholas was no gullible bumpkin and he would only pay for value received, when it was received.

I read on until the rushlight became short. My understanding of the politics of my own country was poor, having been overseas for so long, but I was able to divine that Bronsard was playing a cautious double game between those he referred to as the 'King's loyal servants' and at least two other factions.

In the way that such things seem to fall out, I found the papers to do with my farm came almost last of all. Everything was together in a stout envelope marked with the name of the property, as neat as any lawyer's work. I read for a long time.

The clocks chimed across the rooftops and the muted thump of the watch's drumbeat came and went. To an untrained eye there looked to be nothing that might be disputed in a court. Certainly nothing that could be won in any court in Newcastle. The farm and all the stock – the list was more extensive than I had thought – had indeed passed to Margaret Ellyot as lawful wedded wife of my brother. The details were but the small change of lawyer's work.

'Y're shent …Y'damn-fool soldier!' The words came out before I could stop them, and sounded like a parade ground shout. My hand went to the hilt of my sword and only then did I remember that my blade was in its scabbard, hanging at the head of my bed in the Three Crescents. No one stirred. I put the envelope back into the chest. There was no reason for me to keep it.

It was my nose rather than my eyes that led me to a bundle of letters that had been folded into a soft wallet of Muscovy leather. By the last spluttering flare of the rushlight I read enough to make me bite my lip.

Written words can be read in different was ways, but here the meaning could be only one thing. Nicholas Bronsard bore an unnatural passion for his niece, Margaret. There was no doubt about it. Here were more than a dozen letters from the girl, all written in a large childish hand. True, it was only one side of a conversation, but there was scant need to hear Bronsard's part. It was plain enough that the bastard had had his way with the glaikie lass. She had not been willing, the first time and I felt my anger rise. Margaret Bronsard, Margaret Ellyot I should say, was too daft a creature to be at all discrete in the choice of words she used. I sat with my back against the wall and read on.

Now I'll own to have sniggered with the rest of the company when jests about incest have been told, but it becomes a different matter indeed when the business concerns your own kin, and it is a hard thing to learn that your own dead brother has been cuckolded within a month of his wedding day. The last letter spoke of a visit to the farm at night. She was begging Bronsard not to come again. The lass was fey and silly – I could better understand the cause now – but she was a woman and had been a decent creature until Nicholas Bronsard had corrupted her. It was not in me to think well of my sister-in-law, but at least now I could spare her my hatred. My sigh sounded loudly in the silence of the attic room.

I made my mind up. Nicholas Bronsard would not die, at least not cleanly. A devious man himself, I would destroy him by devious means, though I could not even begin to think how I might bring it about – that was the promise I made myself.

Meanwhile, I would be no proper gunner if did not pay the bastard Bronsard something on account. He would raise the lid of his coffer thinking that it was safe, that the charges had been spent on the freelance. My smile was grim. Bronsard had been thoughtful: a little copper powder flask, still more than half full, and a bullet bag hung by a thong inside the lid of the chest. I spilled four perfectly cast lead globes into the palm of my hand and held them there for a moment before I let them roll off among the papers. No siege gun was ever loaded as carefully as I re-loaded that mantrap. I cleared the touchholes and primed the pans with the fine gunpowder, tapping the sable dust home with my forefinger so that there would be small chance of a misfire. I was liberal handed with the main charge. The powder flask was much lighter when I had done. For wads I tore corners from Bronsard's correspondence with the Court of St James and chewed the thick paper until it was soft, the iron gall from the ink setting my teeth on edge. When all was done to my nicest satisfaction, I set the mechanism and lowered the coffer lid until I heard a pleasing double click.

The soft pad of bare feet past the door, a fart and a groan, followed by a man's voice swearing quietly caught me unawares. It was still dark outside and the moon was lost in cloud. For a moment, I was attacked by the fear that I would not be able to make my way back across the rooftops, but my footing on the dew wet tiles held long enough for me to grasp the ridge and pull myself up. Then I walked upright, not with the sure tread of Dougie Pigg, but well enough to see me back to the spectacle-seller's shop with no more mishap than a soaking with my own sweat.

Will Blacket was waiting for me in the dark of an entry across the way. He handed me a leather bottle with a couple of mouthfuls of raw Geneva left in it and said nothing until I had handed back the empty flask.

'Did y' find what it was you were seekin', Captain?' he asked.

He grinned at me as I nodded and pummelled his shoulder with with my balled fist. 'I'm obliged to you, Will, most men would have run,' I said quietly. The old soldier grunted something indistinct and looked sheepish. 'Did that cowardly whoreson, Pigg, happen to pass your way?' I could not bear the thief any venomous ill-will. I doubt that the firing of gunpowder was something he met with often in ruffler's work. But it was certain that we were lost if he was put to any hard questioning.

My servant said nothing but he rubbed at his long scar with his thumb.

'Well?' I asked again, impatiently. I was tired and failed to read the sign. He aimed his forefinger at a big midden heap piled against a wall. The hill of human and animal ordure steamed a white mist after being disturbed with the wooden shovel that stood upright in it.

'Desertion in the face o' the enemy ...' Will Blacket intoned dryly. 'The bastard was in too much of a panic to know what hit him. Don't worry about him, Captain. That waster broke his faith wi' me – it was me brought him to you – and he played you false. Let him bake in there like a goose in an oven till the turn o' the year. Newcastle folk never shift a midden 'til it's good an' ripe!'

Chapter 10

The Stank Tower

My strategy had been right, but it was plain that I had still made one fatal error. They seized me as I stepped out from the lamplight in the Three Crescents' taproom into the dark of the street. I should have known. Having slept late and spent the day in idleness, I had given the enemy time to manoeuvre. It was useless to curse myself now.

The little company from the Town Watch knew its trade. Hard hands gripped me and my sword was lifted from its scabbard in what seemed like a single motion. A watchman's half-pike was levelled at my throat.

'John Ellyot, you are herewith taken up. In the King's name I arrest you for theft. You offered to sell these jewels to Master George Dodds ten minutes ago. He has sworn that against you. I have just taken the said jewels from inside your coat. These men are witness.' He spilled a cloth bag into his palm, to show a handful of bright baubles, a necklace of misshapen pearls and a broken amethyst brooch. But I glared at the fishhook that was fixed to the bag itself.

No pickpocket could work for long in the taproom of the Three Crescents, but someone had contrived to put the corrupt evidence on to my person. I had felt nothing. Nobody had bumped into me while I had been in the inn. Then I recalled that I had taken a hand of cards and sat at the bench for half an hour. The skirts of my coat had hung free and the rogue had simply lifted the flap and hooked the little bag with the handful of cheap jewels in it on to the cloth of my coat. I had been caught by the oldest trick, but the man who had spoken against me had to be a gentleman. That was worrying for this was no casual taking up of a stranger on false charges.

It had to be Bronsard's work, yet I could see no way that Nicholas Bronsard could have connected me with the work done in his counting house – save want of an alternative. I had been a fool to stay inside the town at all.

'You will be brought up to appear before the magistrates at the Tollbooth ...' The litany went on, word perfect, uttered a hundred or more times before, but the man in helmet and breastplate was not of the Town Watch, being far too well dressed for that office and too young. Whoever and whatever he was, surely he was not in Bronsard's service.

'Where is this perjuring bastard, Dodds?' I demanded. There would be no profit in knowing, but I was angry. A gentle touch to the throat with the point of the half-pike, and a broken toothed smile that was as coy as a maiden's, told me who was to lay the false evidence against me.

'Best come easy!' Those last three words were the Watch's cry in every town. A man might struggle, but that made for hard work, and one of the company might take injury in the course of the business. I was being offered a choice. I nodded my head, and as I did so I caught sight of Will Blacket standing at the front of a small crowd of onlookers. He gave me no sign.

They took me to the Stank Tower, one of the towers along the town wall. There, I knew I would rot until the magistrates met on Monday. Being marched through the town streets under close arrest, even after dark, gives a man a strange, helpless, hopeless feeling, a hollowness in the guts. But my captors seemed to bear me no especial ill-will. The man who had betrayed me was inclined to talk, as though he was making the false somehow real by telling me of it. The jewels were the property of a lady, he explained cheerfully, who lived near the village of Jesmond. They had been stolen two days before when someone – me – had broken into the house. I had been found in possession of the stolen property. He did not utter the obvious conclusion to the syllogism.

It was clear, too, that I had been expected at the Stank Tower. For certain I was not one of the mob of miscreants whom I could hear, stirring behind the inner door. It seemed I was a special prisoner. That might bode better for me than I had a right to expect – or much worse.

My little company of town cut-throats and perjurers stayed and took a supper of kippered herring and flat cake. To be fair, the youngster in half-armour gave me a pot of the poor sappy ale they were drinking, and a cake of bread with half a herring in it. I drank the ale gratefully and put the bread away for later, but I had no need of the smoked fish that would bring on a raging thirst during the night when there would be no drink handy. A lad came into the tower swinging an iron basket filled with glowing charcoal, a bunch of chains slung over his shoulder. I saw why my guard had stayed. They wanted me safe bound before they could leave.

There was a curiously long silence when a tall man wearing a cowhide apron over his clothes appeared in the doorway. One of the watch hurried towards him with pot of ale and a share of their supper. He took the ale, but his eye was clearly upon me. He smiled and looked at me keenly.

'Just you be puttin' your boot up here, bonny lad. This won't take but a minute of your time, and if you hold still it'll not cause you any hurt.' He treated me to a friendly smile as he went down on his knees and took a grip on one of my ankles.

As he promised, the work of clapping a prisoner into manacles and leg irons took almost no time at all. A hinged circlet of rusty iron was clamped hard around my boot, then the tall man tonged a slug of iron, red hot from the brazier and dropped it neatly into place. Half a dozen blows with a hammer served to mushroom the end of the still glowing slug into a stout rivet. There was hissing sound and a little cloud of steam as the lad dashed a dipper of water over the joint. The other leg and my wrists were served in the same deft fashion and the whole tangle of ironware was rivetted to a stout ring set into the stones of the wall. The town was full of good fellows who knew their trades well that night.

'There y'are, m'master, if you can get yourself free o' the bilboes that I clap on to you, why then, you're welcome indeed,' and he laughed hollowly, like a tomb being opened.

With me well secured in my irons there was no reason for the watchmen to stay longer. They drank up the town's issue of watered small-beer and made for the door.

I had two guards, and like all the gaol-wards I had ever seen, they were both short on soap and had dull wits for everything save the keeping of their prisoners. They were playing at nine-men's-mumble or some such board game at a table set up just inside the door. The old man had but two teeth in his lower jaw and cataract on one eye. The younger I had heard called Cuthie. I thought it would be useful to talk with them, if only to form some idea of what manner of fellows they were. I still had five pounds out of the money for my letter of credit stowed in my clothes, though I doubted that so small as sum would be sufficient to bribe them to let me escape. Perhaps for a gold piece, one of them might take a message to Will Blacket. If my manservant could search out Master Dodds and cut out his perjuring tongue all might be well with me yet. I spoke aloud. 'The bugger was uncommonly civil about the business.'

My observation was interrupted sharply by a snort from under a pile of dirty straw heaped against the bars of the inner lock-up and a gurgling, bitter laugh.

'Civil! Aye … ah suppose that might be. He damned well ought to be civil. That was Big Geordie Errin'ton. He's the town's hangman! Them fine boots o' yours will fall to him when you swing, so he doesn't want you sellin' them for drink before he gets them!' The laughter rose up and echoed around the damp stones of the Stank Tower.

My two guards took no notice of me. Twice I tried to get them to talk to me. The second time, I offered to send out for a flagon of ale. The old man ignored me and Cuthie looked for moment as though he was going to rise to my offer, but something the old man said beneath his breath made the young gaoler settle back on to his stool again. I forced myself into a fitful sleep. My body was exhausted and if there was to be any other end to my case but the choking rope at Gallowgate, a week come Monday, I needed to have my full wits about me. I had seen the numbed stupidity of condemned men, often enough, not to allow myself to be driven to exhaustion. A church clock struck midnight before I dozed off.

I was woken sharply by the goaler's gasping shout, 'Why, man, the bitch is mother naked! Dancing in the street like a madwoman … Wheee heh, y'bugger!'

I saw the two men's backs as they struggled to get a space to look through the iron bars in the wicket of the gaol door. For the moment young Cuthbert had the view, but he was being forced aside by the old man. I managed to get to my feet and frog-hop across to the door before I was pulled up short by my tether chain. I had the merest glance. Outside, through the wicket, I saw a woman, without shred of shift or petticoat to cover herself, dancing. A sudden brightness of moonlight caught the pale skin of her turning flanks, full breasts, and the dark triangle between her thighs. She was singing, softly, seemingly unaware that she was being watched. On her face there was a slack, half drunken smile that invited lust.

'Here, you, gallows bait!' I was grabbed by my chains and hurled back on to my straw, but young Cuthie was too eager to get back to his place to take much notice of me. Now the old man had his face wedged firmly at the port and was holding on so that for a few moments the two men struggled hard. I heard Cuthie try appealing to his mate for fair play when he found that the oldster could not be forced aside.

I sat in my straw – alert. There are many strange things to be seen in the world, but naked women do not dance in the streets at past two in the morning, even on a warm August night and they certainly do not do it in Newcastle-upon-the-Tyne. I had not long to wait.

'Errrr ... Now cover y'self and be away home wi' ye.' The old man's voice said one thing but the shortness of his breath suggested another.

Cuthie was at least more honest. 'Come in here an' get a warm, m' hinny ... there's a good fire and a drop of spirit,' he wheedled as he snatched the key-ring from its hook and moved for the door.

A whisper of old man's caution, 'Now mind, Cuthie!' was ignored. I heard the woman's singing low and throaty just outside. There was a witching note in it, old as Sin. I had heard just such songs sung in the forests of North Germany.

Now I was sure I had friends outside. Young Cuthie opened the wicket door in the gate a fraction and reached out. The woman's song became more distant, floating away, then it returned. The gaoler reached out further, hissing with frustration. I think the old man realised what was happening before I did. He gave a warning shout, but it was too late. Young Cuthie stuck his neck out like an inquisitive chicken, a loop of hide went round the fellow's neck and he was jerked headlong out through the wicket in the gaol door. I heard the crack of hard wood on skullbone. The old gaoler threw up his hands and flung himself at the fall-bar to secure the door. I thrust out my feet and tripped him, but I was too clumsy and too late. The bar had swung down and the wicket-gate was tight shut. There was a sudden quiet. The old man ran back and forth, muttering to himself. I edged myself forward, towards him. My tether chain was not long enough to reach the bar that held the door, but I thought that if I could get my hands on the old man I could at least stop his noise until the gaol door was forced. Then a chain clinked against the door, and without warning, great blows from a sledgehammer struck against the timbers, shaking the main door and bringing down the dust from the roof beams. The old gaoler stood back from the door, a look of triumph on his face. Then I knew for certain what the men outside were about and I gathered up my chains and dived away for the corner, pressing myself down against the flagstones of the floor and covering my head with my arms. Now I could hear the splutter of the fuse. The hammer blows had been the spiking of a petard, an iron pot filled with gunpowder, against the tower door.

The blast was tremendous, like being punched between the shoulders. I felt the backs of my hands seared by the flash and I choked on the sulphur-reeking smoke.

The oak beams of the great door were wrenched out, hinges, lintel, beams and forged iron bars. A cloud of mortar dust billowed down into the room. I raised my head as the bright orange flare of a torch lit the cell, held up so high that the cobwebs fizzled in the flame. I blinked in the light, seeing only a tall shape in a cloak and a broad-brimmed hat. Then I heard the woman's voice, the naked dancer for sure, but now there was no magic in her tone.

'For Christ's sake give's me clothes an' me money and let me be away home tae m' bed!' There was a coarse laugh and the sound of a hearty slap on naked flesh.

'Ellyot!' More torches glowed in the haze of flying dust. Perhaps I was not out of danger. There was a fair chance that Bronsard had sent his own freelances to kill me in the confusion of a gaolbreaking. I gathered up what slack there was in my chain and backed against the wall. I would not go tamely.

'Get that crowbar in here, now!' commanded a voice. The accent was of the North but not of Tyneside. I would remember it. 'Prise that chain free from the wall ... Look sharp!'

A man wearing leather jerkin and breeches staggered into the cell carrying a great iron bar with a curve at one end. He rammed the end of the bar into the stout iron ring that secured my chains to the tower walls and leaned hard against it. The ring warped and the metal parted allowing my tethering chain to fall free. Manacles still gripped my wrists and the leg irons still hobbled me like a horse, but I could move. I gathered up my chains and tried to stand.

The man in the cloak held out a hand and I was pulled to my feet. I could smell the salt-sea smell wafting off the woollen cloth of his cloak.

'Did they mangle you? You can walk?' I nodded and he chuckled. 'Then your luck has held for you. Master Nicholas Bronsard sits waiting for you now, to be fetched to him at the Heber Tower. They say that he has a way with him when he deals with a man who has given him offence, and you're the fellow who rigged his coffer to blow up in his face!' He sucked in his breath hard between his teeth. 'By Gobs but you're a lucky laddie this night, John Ellyot.'

A flask of hammered silver was put into my hand. I took a good pull at it. The liquor was kummel.

'Now where does a man get a taste for carraway liquor like this? Poland?' I snapped my fingers. 'Courland!' There was another chuckle but no answer in words.

Other business was being transacted around us. There was a cry and a jangle of heavy keys, then the inner doors of the gaol were open and figures like rag bundles were being helped out into the street. I heard a Lowland Scots curse and heard the thud of a bare foot as a Jock took revenge on still form of young Cuthbert. The old man lay in a corner, groaning, and covered with his own blood.

The wafting stench that the prisoners threw off as they were hurried past forced me to twist my face in disgust. My rescuer laughed and lifted my arm to my nose. Already, I had begun to have the same foul smell on me.

As I was led to the door, the cloaked man turned and hurled his flaming torch back among the prisoners' bedstraw. I watched it flare up, a yellow flame at the heart of a dense pall of grey smoke that writhed as it spread. The rats came out, black rats scampering from under the smoke. Someone touched my shoulder. It was Will Blacket, grinning a wondrous scar-faced grin that was made more frightening by the dancing light of the flames. He helped me to hop-stagger out to a two-wheeled cart whose driver threw back a canvas to show a coffin lashed to the cart. He gave me a wink and a mocking little bow. Will Blacket picked me up like a truss of straw and laid me into the corpse-box. That was the second time it occurred to me to have misgivings about the intentions of my rescuers. Even with Will's presence there, I still had an uneasy feeling in my bones as I stowed myself with my chains and flinched as the coffin nails were hammered home an inch from my face.

I had thought that it would not be difficult for me to tell where I was taken. We set off down a bank and took a corner so fast that I was pushed hard against the rough timber of the coffin, then I lost all track of both direction and time. The cart slowed and I heard the clatter of the horse's hooves on paved road and then the soft thump they made on packed earth. I knew that we had not left the town because I had not heard the echoing rumble that always sounded when a cart passed out under a gateway. Then I thought that I was deceived by my senses. The coffin began to sway and swing. I could hear men grunt and curse softly, then all was still again.

I was afloat. From the sound and the curious side-to-side motion, I knew that the boat was being sculled with a single oar.

'Are you still alive, Master Ellyot?' The sharp rap on the coffin lid startled me.

'Near enough, I thank you, Mistress Thornton.'

My voice was thrown back at me from the nailed-down planks only a finger's length from my face. It was becoming close and airless in the coffin. 'Have we far to go? It is becoming a mite stuffy inside this death chest.'

'Strange indeed, Master Ellyot ... We have never had such a complaint before.'

The girl was laughing at me and I knew it. But before I had time to become angry, an edge of metal came between the planks and there was a sharp screech as the coffin nails came free. Cool air, damp and smelling of the river wafted across my face. I drew a deep breath and looked up at the bright stars.

She offered no help as I forced my way out of the coffin and sat on the thwart of the little foy-boat. We were afloat for a while, drifting upstream with the incoming tide, the girl standing in the sternsheets of the little boat. Even in a rough woollen dress with a dark plaid wrapped around her shoulders, Aphra Thornton was indeed a striking young woman. She worked the oar skilfully, her lithe body twisting gently as she sculled the boat up river. Twice, I caught her looking carefully at me, and more than twice our eyes met. In the half dark, I could not see her face fully, but I sensed rather than saw that there was a mocking half smile in her gaze.

I had thought that we would put in ashore somewhere on the south bank of the Tyne but I was wrong. We were under one of the arches of the Tyne Bridge. Aphra Thornton had chosen her time well. Only at slack water was it easy to make a landing on one of the bridge's stone piers. But why were we putting ashore on the bridge at all?

It is no easy business to scramble from the thwart of a small boat out on to stonework, greasy with moss and river filth. It is perilous when you are clutching an armful of chains. I made my jump and landed, tottering, on the slime. But when I looked around, the foy-boat and Aphra Thornton, had gone. My swearing echoed back from the arch overhead.

'Whisht! Are y' soft i' the heed? Why don't y' call out the Watch and have done wi' it!' Someone grabbed my coat and turned me about. A hand pushed my head down so that it could pass under the lintel of the tiny doorway, then I was forced hard upwards by a shoulder set against my backside. It was only then, that I recalled that years before I had seen coals being taken from keelboats up into the cellars of the houses that stood on the Tyne Bridge.

I stood in the dark and tried to sort out my chains. A lantern shield flapped and there was light. My companion was, as we say in the North, the height of six-penny-worth of copper, and as sour-faced a runt as could be imagined. He shook his head at me and his mouth narrowed in stern disapproval.

'Kneel!' His voice had a bite to it that I did not like at all. I felt my chin rise up and my shoulders go back, but he merely went on impatiently, 'Kneel now, m' man, or go chained for the rest of your time on this Earth. I've no fancies in the matter m'self but there's a wee anvil at your feet and it'll not stand liftin'.'

I knelt. My small friend was a blacksmith. As he placed my foot against the anvil, the smell of hot iron and the sweat of horses came off him. For all his small stature, he was skillful. On only one of the rivets that secured my irons did it need more than a single blow of the hammer to the cold chisel to shear away the rivet head and let the gyves open up. I had been manacled for no more than a few hours but I gained an uncommon pleasure from rubbing my wrists.

'Ma' fee will be tuppence ...' I think that I must have gaped at him as he held out a hand. I fumbled in my clothes for money. I never knew what coin I gave him.

The room reminded me of the great cabin of a large merchant ship. I had been led through the darkness to heavy curtains and through them into the bright candlelight of a room whose window overlooked the river. I stood on a floor covered by a rich red and blue Turkey carpet. There was a desk of dark wood and a high backed chair, a bookcase filled with many well-worn books.

'Sit down, Captain Ellyot ...' said a voice whose tone was gentle, scholarly. I turned and saw the neatest creature that I had ever clapped eyes upon. The shaven face was golden in the light, the sea-grey eyes were strangely bright. His hair was iron grey, cut into a fringe, but not cropped like a soldier's locks, rather it was barbered with care. He was dressed entirely in black. His coat was of the finest black broadcloth, with plain buttons of Whitby jet that glistened with tiny points of white light. Only at his neck was the black a little relieved by a collar of starched snowy linen, thinly edged with fine Brussels lace.

He looked at me with a level gaze. I was suddenly reminded of one of the fanatical Protestant chaplains that went wherever the Swedish armies campaigned. Those eyes had a spirit in them, I could see it flickering behind them, but whether it was a spirit of good or of evil, I did not know.

'I tell you fair, Captain Ellyot, that I may not use the name I was baptised with. Few men know that, but will Sylvanus Webster do for now? It is the name that those who know me hereabouts use.'

I bowed a little. 'Sylvanus Webster is as good as any other name.' We shook hands. The grip was cold – it was like grasping a stone.

He came directly to the point and I was glad that he did.

'You are in my debt ...' There was no hardness in the statement. It was simply that, a statement of fact.

I could only answer, 'If you were the cause of my being broken out of the Stank Tower... then I do indeed stand in your debt. There is little doubt that I would be hanged on the evidence against me.' The urge to address him as Reverend came and went again, quickly, 'Unless of course, you were also the cause of my being arrested on false charges in the first place.'

There was no anger, no sign that the suggestion had offended the man at all. He smiled like a scholar detecting some humorous innuendo in a Latin phrase.

'No, Sir, we do God's work and that is sufficient to prohibit our employing the devices of the Enemy.' He took up a quill and waved it at me. 'That you were taken was due in great measure to your own lack of wits. It was a bold thing you did in climbing into Nicholas Bronsard's house, but in the event it has proved to be less than prudent. Always remember, Captain Ellyot, that a man who will conspire with you, will conspire against you. The man Pigg had an accomplice. Did you not notice a woman hanging on his heels when your manservant brought him to you at the Three Crescents? No? Then it was as well for you that we did ... Her name is Black Peggy. Whether she was ever in truth Mistress Pigg,' his shoulders shook a little at the thought, 'we know not. Enough to say that she was seen to go to the counting house of Nicholas Bronsard. There we can suppose that she was very civilly entertained, for all her ragged gown and bare feet. Fortunately for you, she was equally willing – for a small consideration – to tell me what she had told Nicholas Bronsard's clerk.'

Again he motioned me towards a chair. I sat down, and struggled to stop myself from rubbing at my wrists further.

'And the guard captain, the man who arrested me?'

I supposed that I might as well ask for the whole story.

'A friend.' The man who called himself Webster looked at me earnestly. 'Should you meet up with that young man, then you owe him your thanks. Bronsard had ordered that you be taken to the Heber Tower. Our friend risked his own future well-being to have you taken instead to the Stank. He arrested you minutes before another company of men were to have come to the Three Crescents to call upon you.' I under-stood perfectly.

Webster frowned suddenly and waved his hands before him to indicate that we needed to talk of other things.

'I will tell you that I have had much trouble in my efforts to find you, John Ellyot. Do you know that my agents missed you by less than half an hour at Karlskrona?'

Chapter 11

Sylvanus Webster

'**K**arlskrona?' I asked. I had left that town less than a month before, and already it seemed a lifetime ago. Mention of the name brought a feeling akin to nostalgia to my mind. Captains of artillery are as common as fleas in Sweden, and they do not rank high in such towns, but I had enjoyed comfortable quarters, all the akvavit I cared to drink, and all the tobacco I could smoke.

'Yes … My agents had been seeking you for some time. Indeed, as I said, they visited your lodgings a bare half hour after you had left,' replied Sylvanus Webster, the merest wraith of a smile passing across his stern face. 'You told the landlord that you were bound north to Stockholm to take up an appointment at the Royal Arsenal.' The smile disappeared. 'That traveller's tale cost my agents dear in hard riding and time. You had, of course, gone to the nearest border … Good! I am pleased that you can be a man of especial prudence, even in everyday matters, when the need arises.'

It was my turn to smile. I had told this tale to the landlord of my inn because he was a great gossip, and I knew that news of my supposed good fortune would get to the ears of a couple of stupid but, alas, well-connected Swedish officers whose arrogant ways had been of some annoyance to me.

'Colonel Von Starhemberg speaks uncommonly well of your abilities,' he said as he finished reading the top sheet of the pile of papers on the table before him, raising his eyes exactly in time to meet my own as the last syllable of that hated name left his lips. It was too late for me to disguise my reaction to it.

'The Colonel is very gracious,' I muttered. It was all I could think of to say. If there was a man whom I had cause to despise, and, even at a hundred leagues distance, to fear, it was Simeon Augustus Von Starhemberg, a fiend in human form. I began to wonder if this neat man in black broadcloth, with his clean, well-kept hands and the smell of washball soap about him might not be kin to Von Starhemberg. The Colonel had kept two terrified valets busy, day and night, looking after his wardrobe of Paris-tailored clothes.

'But tell me now,' Webster continued while I waited, interested, but apprehensive, as he framed his question. 'What of the ship *Hedwiga*?'

I had seen it coming. I suspected that he knew the story well enough without asking. 'There is little enough to tell ...' I replied.

'But that little ... Captain Ellyot.' The voice was soft but he raised his head in a way that suggested that it would be better if I told the story. It occurred to me that, had a man asked the same question in the taproom of an inn, in broad daylight, I might have shrugged, told the tale, and taken a glass of wine without worrying, but the man I was sitting before now had contrived my escape from prison and conjured me out of Newcastle. I was about to hear the full price of my freedom.

I sat back for a moment, screwing shut my eyes, and decided that it would be as well to tell him the whole story. A sullen morning light was beginning show through the window behind Webster's chair when I had finished.

'And so it is true that you raised the great ordnance ... You *did* recover big guns from the bottom of the Gulf of Bothnia, from a depth of forty feet under the sea?'

'Assuredly,' I said quietly. 'Twenty-three bronze cannon-royal, along with a great quantity of iron shot and much of the gunner's gear ... and all done in the Finnish winter.'

It also occurred to me to tell him of the hundred and twenty prisoners of war and convicts who had died of the cold and the poor food, but I did not.

'And you used a ...' he shuffled through his papers, '... a diving bell?' His look had turned to one of genuine admiration. 'You descended into the depths of the sea and brought forth the King's great ordnance?' His reverent tone made it sound as though he was reading from the Testament. His shoulders gave a sudden shudder.

'That is so ...' involuntarily my voice was almost a whisper.

He got up and stood with his back to me, looking down at the river.

'Could you make another diving bell?' he asked.

'Master Webster – you mean would I be willing to go down in a diving bell?' I wanted him to come to the point. Even though I was free of the chains I had been wearing, I knew that I was Webster's captive. 'I have the knowledge to direct craftsmen as to how such a thing should be made, and I am able to instruct men into how to work it,' I added reluctantly.

Suddenly I wanted to deny that I had any knowledge of diving bells. I saw the dark green water as the bell was lowered into the freezing Baltic. I felt again the shock of the icy cold, even through many pairs of greased woollen stockings, as the sea-water rose inside the bell, the choking grip of terror when the bell tilted, spilling some of the precious air trapped within it – but I had survived, and after a month the work became a commonplace. Sometimes, it was almost easy. Often, the cannon were found to lie right and all I had to do was tie on the lifting hawsers. It was the poor devils above, who hauled on the ropes to raise the massive weight of bronze cannon up through the dark waters who suffered, in the blizzards and the killing frosts.

'Am I to take it, Master Webster, that you have some enterprise in mind, or in hand? You need to raise something from the sea?' I allowed myself to ask boldly. By God, if this were true, this time I would have my full due from the game and be cheated by no man.

'Say, rather, that I have need of a diving bell, and all that is needful to go with it, and that for the moment is all,' Webster replied, the ghost of a smile flickering. 'In my work I find that what a man does not know, he cannot be made to tell.'

'But I need to know,' I insisted. 'Unless you tell me, how can I know how big a bell to construct, how great a weight is to be raised, and from what depth. How many men will be needed?' It was plain to see that the truly practical elements of the business had been of little concern to Webster. Political men seldom *do* trouble themselves about such matters, but in the business of diving bells I was master. 'There are things that I must know before I can say whether the enterprise is even possible.'

Webster shook his head slowly. 'I can tell you no more than I have done ... except that the problem has, in the most general of terms, been set before a most-learned philosopher of Amsterdam. The task is possible, and, indeed, is perhaps not so difficult a business as that which you carried out in Finland.' He looked down at his papers again. 'At least you will not have to break through a foot of ice before you lower your diving bell.'

I thought quickly. The work Webster was offering me – whatever it was – would at least give me a breathing space. I was as close to being outlawed from Newcastle as made no difference, and as a felon, I had no chance of proving my claim to my half of the farm. I had hidden almost all of my money in my room at the Three Crescents, which would keep for long enough, for I had made a good hiding place. Will Blacket would have had the wit to take the mare to a safe place. Webster would give me at least a month of his protection, and money into the bargain. It was as though he had read my thoughts.

'You will doubtless want to know what your reward will be for undertaking this enterprise?'

I nodded, and now it was my turn to smile. 'I own a scarce skill, and this is likely to be a dangerous business. That itself is worth something more than a soldier's pay.'

Webster was watching me carefully. I sensed that he was not interested in how much I might ask for, but rather what else I might want. I hesitated for a moment.

'Four shillings a day, and provisions for myself and my man-servant.' I replied, looking at him directly. 'Good wholesome provisions, sufficient in quantity.' There was no doubt in my mind that I was bound for sea and I wanted no more of the food I had endured aboard the *Mary of Leith*. 'And...'

I got no further. Webster held up the palm of his hand towards me.

'There will be neither prize nor shares in this enterprise. There cannot be,' he said.

I was puzzled. Even the Swedish Royal Commissioners had paid me a few silver crowns for each gun raised from the *Hedwiga's* hull.

'If you are successful, if this business comes out well, then there will be much that I can do for you; much that I could not do for you ... if it does not.' He leaned forward and wagged a finger at me, slowly. It was the sort of conundrum that I had half expected from Webster. There would be truth in it, but nothing like the whole truth.

He went on, 'If this enterprise is successful, then Nicholas Bronsard will be dis-comforted – sorely so, perhaps even destroyed, which should be more than agreeable to you. If his power in the town of Newcastle is weakened, then I shall have friends there who will be able to have all charges against you disproven. You should then be able to claim your share of your family's farm. It is a mere possession to Nicholas Bronsard and he will need much money very soon and I dare say you will be able to buy out your sister-in-law's half of the land without too much trouble – that would be the prudent man's way.' Some further jest, it seemed, had occurred to him for he smiled slightly as he looked out on the pale morning sunlight dancing brightly on the river as the fog lifted.

'In this England of ours, John Ellyot, the days when one man could win a dispute over land with the edge of his sword are almost gone. You must change, as we all must, for England is due great changes. That is something that greedy men like Nicholas Bronsard and his friends must learn.' His smile widened. 'Do this work for us John ... ' then he gave a short bark of a laugh. 'Help us school these ... gluttons!'

I understood little, but the offer he made was all I had. I was not so stiff-necked a fool as not to see that. I offered Sylvanus Webster my hand and he took it in a grip like iron.

'Now,' he said briskly, 'I must leave this matter to simmer and boil for a few days so I leave you in the hands of my proxy. That person can tell you less than I have done for she knows less than I do. All I can say is follow the instructions that shall be given you, and suffer the small pains to which you will be put without demur or complaint.'

Webster looked down and began to gather up his papers. I caught a glimpse of letters penned in a scholarly hand and some rough sketches, but there was nothing I could see that gave me any inkling about his plans.

'Goodbye, Captain Ellyot. We will meet again in a few days,' he said, standing up. As he came from behind his desk, I saw that he leaned more heavily on one leg than the other.

'If you will wait here for a short while, I will send my servant to you. He will find you something to break your fast upon,' his mouth wrinkled a little, 'and I dare say he will wish to begin work upon your transformation.'

After he left, I suppose that I must have fallen into a doze in my chair, but I woke with a start to find myself staring full into the face of the broken-toothed bastard who had betrayed me at the Three Crescents. I yelled mightily and leapt up at him.

'Hold! Stay your hand, Captain,' said Will Blacket, who I now saw was looking at me over Aphra Thornton's shoulder. 'By rights you could say that you owe Master George Dodds your life. If he hadn't warned Mistress Thornton that you were to be arrested ... there would have been no rescue for you and you'd be swingin' now.'

'But the bastard put the evidence upon me and then false-swore my life away!' I rejoined.

'George is a friend, Captain. The guard that arrested you wasn't sent by Bronsard and I'd say that you owe him your thanks for his quick wits.'

I gave George Dodds a little bow and got back a wink, and a grin that came through the filthiest set of teeth that I had ever seen in a man's mouth.

'So you have spoken with Master Webster, and has he told you what is needed?' asked Aphra Thornton, sitting down at the table. Her face was drawn and tired, but she was no less a beauty for that.

'I have agreed to take service with Master Webster in the matter of ...' but I got no further for Aphra held up her hand and put a finger to her lips.

'In the matter of which you spoke,' she said. 'The fewer that know of this business, the less our chances of being discovered.

'As you say, Mistress Thornton, but I was told to place myself at the disposal of Master Webster's proxy. I have been here since last night and ...'

'And this is where you should be,' Aphra replied. 'There are hundreds of men out looking for you at this moment. Sir Joseph Astley has been asked to loan three troops of horse from the Castle garrison to search the countryside for you. There are men as far away as Morpeth and Hexham, with orders to shoot you and any other of the escaped prisoners on sight. You are worth ten pounds in gold to whoever gives the information that leads to your being taken and that is a great sum for a poor man to resist, Master Ellyot. There are many men with no other work to feed their bairns who now find employment in searching for you. Believe me, you are safer in this house than you would be almost anywhere else on Tyneside.'

I spread my hands, looked across the table at her, and sighed, 'It seems that I am in your hands completely, Mistress Thornton.'

'That you are, Master Ellyot – that you most decidedly are.' A small dimple of amusement appeared on her chin and those wonderful dark grey eyes sparkled mischievously for a moment. 'If John Ellyot is such prized quarry, then John Ellyot had better disappear, as though the fairies had taken him,' she said, regarding me in a way that I did not much care for. 'For the second time today you will owe Master George Dodds your life.' The dimple appeared again and I knew that her amusement was to be at my cost. 'For not only is Master Dodds a loyal member of the Town Watch for the Westgate Ward, but he is also a master barber and the leader of his guild. You could not ask to be in better hands,' she gave a little laugh, 'and it is in those hands that I leave you now.'

Will Blacket pushed his way into the room carrying a tub of steaming water. He was followed by George Dodds who was now wearing a white linen apron and cap and carrying a red leather bag. I had not much liked the look of Dodds as a member of the Town Watch; I think that I liked him only a little better as a master barber.

'Ah!' he said, and nothing more. He looked at me then looked at Will, and damn me if Will didn't grin at him.

'Orders is ...' Will said slowly, 'that you have your hair cropped short ... and the beard.' I nodded. It was a bit late in the year to be having a crop, but I was not inclined to argue. I lay back and waved Dodds on.

I would have to give the rascal that truly I did not feel a thing until it was too late. He went to work upon my hair with a pair of steel shears, the steady clip-clip sound close to my ears lulling me so that I closed my eyes. The long hair at the back of my head was soon gone and Dodds began on the sides. The trimming of my beard began with the same stealth, so that when he started lathering me I said nothing. I heard him strop a razor, then I heard Will chortle.

It was too late. Dodds had shaved away one side of my beard and then gone on upward in the same bold sweep to bare my scalp. I sat up, sending the master barber scampering backwards with his razor held high.

'Orders is, Captain, that you are to be shorn as bald as a drumhead,' Will coughed into his hand. 'Down to the very skull!' He handed me a silver mug with some brandy in it and settled the barber's linen drape around me again. 'An' I would have to say that you do look sort o' different, already.'

I damned Will, and George Dodds, roundly but I had to admit to myself that if there is a way to change a man's appearance so that even his friends might have trouble in recognising him, then shearing him bald and barefaced would certainly have done the trick. However, I had not quite bargained for the thorough job of work that was done to me. It took a long time and there was much lathering and re-lathering – but in the end, Dodds had done. My skull was as pale as a well-plucked chicken, and my face was almost the same.

When I saw myself in the mirror Dodds held up for me, I gasped, and then I groaned aloud.

'Good!' exclaimed Aphra Thornton, bustling into the room. I put a hand up to cover my naked scalp and sank down in the chair cursing under my breath.

She pulled my hand away roughly. 'A shearing is a sight better than a hanging, Sir!' she whispered into my ear, and I could smell the faint verbena perfume that was in her hair. She waved Dodds and Will out of the room and stood before me, inspecting me. 'First, I shall stop you from looking like a freshly plucked fowl,' she said, opening a glass vial and spilling some dark spiritous liquor on to a scrap of rag. Then she began to rub the soaked rag hard across my naked scalp and freshly shaved face. The stuff burned and stung like the very devil, but when she finished and held up the mirror I had to admit that I no longer had the look of a chicken about me. Indeed, I looked as though baldness was my natural state. My skin had been stained a pale yellow as if I had been sunburned, and in the morning light it did look natural enough. It had been all of eight years since I had seen myself beardless, and the effect was strange – but not unpleasing. The eyes looking back at me from the mirror were my own, but the rest seemed the face of a stranger.

'Well enough,' said Aphra, holding the looking glass to the side of my face to throw more light, 'but you should have more of the look of a Hollander about you.' She took up a little razor and shaved away the edges of my eyebrows, giving me the appearance of a slight slant to my eyes. 'Stick a pipe in that mouth and we have a Rotterdamer to the very life,' she said, clapping her hands in satisfaction.

Will brought new clothes and dressed me with all the care of a general's body servant. I thrust my arms into the sleeves of a fine lawn shirt and allowed Will to tie the strings of the wide lace-edged collar. He held out Dutch-cut breeches of dark blue velvet for me to step into, and produced a jacket of matching cloth. Without a full-length mirror there was no way that I could see the whole of myself, but what I could see looked uncommonly fine. For certain, a man would have to look long and hard to see anything of John Ellyot in the foreigner who was being fabricated, but the work was not yet done. I stepped into shoes decorated with cloth rosettes all of five inches across, and with crimson heels that added almost an inch to my height. Aphra reached up to slip a pair of green tinted spectacles with square lenses on to my nose. That truly did add the final garnish.

'Well that's quite a transformation, Master Ellyot ...' she said, her face clouding a little. 'It remains to be seen if we've done enough to keep you from harm.' Almost absently, Aphra ran a cool hand down my face. I reached for it but before I could touch it she had drawn it away quickly and turned her head from me.

'Now,' she said softly, 'there is someone else who wishes to speak with you.'

Chapter 12

Mistress Thornton

We stepped into a large room, ablaze with light. Not only was the early morning sun pouring in through an open shutter, but there was a candelabrum with a dozen wax candles still lit in it, there was a bright fire in the hearth, and more candles burned here and there about the room.

'I would not have you think that we practice such extravagance every day, John Ellyot, but I need the light to look closely at you.' One of the oldest women I had ever seen spoke from a high backed chair by the fireside. Still handsome, she was bright eyed and alert in a way that seemed to defy her age. Her silver hair, plaited and coiled around her head, was like a crown. No old crone kept in a shift and gown, this lady wore a full dress of heavy satin, gamboge in colour and laced with silver threads, bright as a summer day and fit to wear to the royal court.

She appeared to read my thoughts, 'Yes, young man, if I live another month I shall be eighty-four, but all you need to know is that my wits are as keen as yours, and that Master Webster has placed you in my care and under my direction.'

'Mistress Hannah Thornton!' I bowed with my hand across my breast. The name had come to mind in an instant though it had been twelve or more years since I had heard my mother speak of the woman, but even then she had been known as Old Hannah. The Thornton family had been important in Newcastle for as long as any man could remember, yet the realisation that I had agreed to put myself under the command of a woman, even one as ancient as this, came as a great shock to me.

'You're Stella Carr's laddie,' she said, as though I were a little lad standing before her, and I supposed that, to her, I was. 'You have the Ellyots' long bones and that gives you a handsome height. Have you your mother's good sense?' she asked. Before I could think of an answer she snorted with impatience, 'I'm told that you are quick witted. Well, for the work that I have in mind for you over the next few weeks, you will have need to be.'

Weeks? This was the first piece of information that I had gleaned. Whatever else, if the work was to take only two or three weeks that would not enable me to me to save more than a few pounds in English money, but for those few weeks at least, I would have people around me whose interest lay in keeping me from being killed.

'Aye, my great-grand-daughter has done you well,' she said, reaching forward and taking my sleeve. There was strength in her hand. 'You'll think nought at all about your cropping and dyeing in a day or two. You look uncommonly well with it – as stout a Rotterdam merchant as I've seen. But mind you keep that shaven scalp bare. I'll give you a wee bottle of the dye to keep your head the right colour. Now sit by me and I will tell you what work I have for you. But first ...' her ancient mind had swung to another idea. and her hands gripped my coat like an eager child seeking a gift, 'tell me what you did in that wretch Nick Bronsard's counting house three nights ago, that keeps him from the sight o' man, and sends his servants about the house on tip-toe.'

I told her the tale and everything that I had done. She had me describe twice, and in fine detail, how I had loaded the device in the chest lid with a blank charge of powder, smiling a long inward smile to herself, her eyes gleaming in the firelight. Then she shook her head.

'Stella Carr's laddie, you're soft in the heart as well as in the head. Had you loaded a couple of lead balls you would have saved yourself, and us, from last night's work, and this.' She looked into the fireplace. In the side-glance of the candlelight I could see where, in part at least, Aphra Thornton had inherited her looks. 'And perhaps you missed the chance to avenge the murder of Luke Ellyot.'

That struck me like a blow to the face and I made to stand up. The old woman's hand held me fast.

'I say *perhaps* ...' Hannah Thornton motioned for me to sit down again. 'There is no proof. But if I live another season I shall find out. Men die around Bronsard with an ease that is uncanny, even for these times. And stranger still, whenever a man dies unexpectedly, it is Master Bronsard who profits. For certain, he did a good day's work when your brother married his niece Margaret. He offloaded a lass that was addled in the head from childhood, like her mother before her, and he got his hands on some good pieces of land into the bargain.'

'All that I know well enough, Mistress Thornton,' I replied quietly, 'just as I know that Nicholas Bronsard set a band of freelances to waylay me along the road from Shields, and that he had me shot and left for dead.'

'Aye,' she said knowingly, 'I heard tell o' that. Had he known that you were the same John Ellyot who was the subject of the letters that have passed between Master Webster and ...' she paused, 'sundry other persons, I have no doubt that he would have hired a troop of horse to greet you. But as the John Ellyot you were then, you came as a mere annoyance, a bumpkin who stood between him and full possession of a pretty wee farm and some decent stock.' Hannah Thornton cackled with a sudden laughter then her slight frame shook as the laughter turned into a choking cough that took the breath from her.

'Grandmother ...' There was a sudden rustle of starched petticoats and the soft sound of rippling fabric as Aphra came hurrying across the room. I felt my nostrils twitch again at the scent of verbena and Florentine orris that came from the girl. 'You should not excite her so!' she exclaimed.

I accepted the look of disapproval without offering defence.

'Be still, lassie. Get me my physick,' said the old woman, forcefully enough and I sat back and watched as Aphra bustled about. She spilled something like dried beans into a small copper pan which she held to the glowing coals in the hearth and from the rich smell that began to pervade the room I knew at once that it was coffee. In Sweden the drink was becoming a costly passion with folk of all classes. She knelt at the hearth to empty the roasted coffee into a mortar and then she began to grind it. I sat back and pretended not to be interested at all while she fussed with flasks and papers of powders, but I looked down at her graceful figure. The snug-waisted dress that she wore covered her well, but a man can make much from little with his mind. Aphra Thornton's body was a good match for her face, and those eyes. I sensed that I was being watched and glanced up to see Hannah Thornton looking across at me, with a keen judging stare.

'One of my grandsons is a merchant with the English Company in the Levant. He sends me a good bag of the Arabian beans twice a year. I would have been dead years ago wi'out it,' she said.

Hannah took the bowl of hot drink from Aphra and laced it with a good dash from a white glazed flask. 'Usquebaugh ... The only decent thing ever to come out of Scotland.' She paused and looked at me directly as she drank her elixir. 'Did you truly believe in the Protestant cause when you were in the Swedish King's army?'

I laughed, embarrassed. It was not a question that one man asked another; nor one that called for an answer. But Hannah was an old lady and I could take no offence so I told her the truth.

'In all conscience, Mistress Thornton, it was never the same thing after the great battle of Nordlingen – and it became less with each new fight,' I sighed. 'I was sickened by the reek of spilled blood. I had come home to settle here and forget, and to breed good draught horses, but it seems that even that has been denied me.'

'Oh, if you serve me well you may do that yet. We have your mare – your man Will Blacket fetched it across the bridge an hour after you were arrested. The beast will be well cared for while you are about the business we have in mind, but you'd not wish to be seen riding so uncommon a mount in Newcastle these days. Leave all in my hands, John Ellyot, the work I have for you will be enough to keep you busy, mind and body, for some time to come. If we win in this enterprise you may live to breed good horses – if we don't, then neither horses nor anything else will matter to you.'

The news that the mare was safe, lifted my spirits. If I could retrieve the gold coins that I had taken from Bronsard's counting house I might yet ...

'Tomorrow you will land at Newcastle quayside,' Aphra Thornton's words cut across my plan.

'Newcastle!' I looked at her. 'I will land on the quay at ...?'

She nodded. 'Only in Newcastle can we find the craftsmen with the skill to make the diving bell and its gear, but we must have the thing built in parts. No one workshop must be able even to guess what it is that they are making. There are few secrets in a town like ours and a man who gets a large piece of work must get some credit for materials, but to get that he may have to explain what the work is. How long do you think it would be before the word was out that a man was building a diving bell to go under the sea – and how long after *that* before men whispered of the treasures that were to be brought up?'

'It has all the earmarks of a grand piece of swindling in it,' I replied. 'We could sell shares in the venture!' I exclaimed

Aphra Thornton raised her hands in horror before she realised that I had spoken in jest, blushed, tossed her head and went on, 'You will take on the guise of a solid Dutch merchant. There are two ships from Rotterdam in the river now. You speak good Dutch, do you not?' she said.

That was true enough. Dutch was the *lingua franca* among the officers of the Swedish army, especially in the artillery. There had been months at a time when I had not heard a word of English spoken, nor much missed it.

'Get some rest here for today,' she continued. 'Tonight when it gets dark we will take you down river. It has been arranged with our friends in the Low Countries for you to be taken aboard one of their ships. When the Hollanders arrive on the quay they will be met by the Mayor and members of the various guilds who wish to do business with them. You will be in a party that steps ashore at Newcastle quay tomorrow.'

I waited, for there was a hesitation in her voice that told me she was holding something back. 'You will be met by Nicholas Bronsard,' she said at last.

I sat back in my chair and looked at the two women. It was strange, but my hand went up to my smooth shaven poll.

'Aye, and eat a dinner with him at the Guildhall and take wine with him,' Aphra went on, her grey eyes sparkling with excitement. I must have looked doubtful.

'Yes, John Ellyot, all of that,' Hannah attacked from the other side, 'and play at cards, and carouse, and vomit, and drink again ... and lay the doxies they will doubtless put at your disposal. Do all of those things ...'

Aphra opened her mouth to say more but suddenly stopped and fell silent. Her cheeks flushed a little, but she put up her chin and gave her head a little toss. Hannah Thornton chuckled.

'But the lass is right, John. That's a valiant flea that dares eat his breakfast on the lip of a lion. You say that Nicholas Bronsard has seen you for only a moment or two. It's uncanny how much of a man's appearance is set by his hair and his beard and I doubt if either Bronsard or his hired killer gave much thought to the shape of your head. Keep the green spectacle glasses on and let it be known that you have an affliction of the sight. Your clothes were tailored in the Netherlands, some baggage will be landed for you and we've Dutch money for your pocket – nothing has been forgotten.'

'And does this Dutchman have a name?' I enquired.

'He has a name, and he has papers in his name and letters in his baggage,' Aphra confirmed, proud that she had accomplished the whole business herself.

Hannah nodded her head, and for a moment I thought that she was going to fall asleep, but then she spoke. 'The keystone in your new identity is that you will be seen by a hundred people stepping ashore at Newcastle quayside from a Netherlanders' ship in the company of Rotterdam merchants. Time and place will do even more than your shaven head and change of clothes. Nicholas Bronsard himself is to lead the company that greets the merchants and I have no doubt that you will have the chance to clasp hands with him.' She gave a low laugh that sounded like the beginnings of a growl. 'And if the chance comes, John Ellyot, you will be courteous. Shake the bastard's hand and give him a right hearty *Aangenaam te nemen*! A dour look ever suits a Dutchman in matters of business, so there'll be no absolute need to smile – but we can do without any dagger-thrusts.'

Hannah stopped and stared at me until I had nodded my head in assent, before continuing.

'If all comes out as planned, you will see the House of Bronsard broken ... broken into pieces. You may think that they have done you harm and I have no doubt that they have, but there are tens of honest folk between here and the Border who can claim as much, and worse. It is they, who will be helping you in a hundred small ways in the next few days. This business is a part of a larger struggle.'

'And when I have landed from the Dutch ship?' I asked.

'You will be met by a man called Ord, Sir Joseph Ord. You have been described to him in detail and he will seek you out. Greet him as though you were old friends, and talk to him in Dutch. There will be a short procession through the streets to the

Guildhall where you will all fill your guts at honest folk's cost. Go, sit and eat, but keep to ale for these civic feasts tend to run to a contest to see who has the hardest head for drink. Sir Joseph will lead you away once the drinking is fairly set-to.'

'And afterwards?' I prompted. Hannah poured a glass of clear spirit from a flask at her side and handed it to me. I raised the glass in salute to each of the women in turn and drank as she replied.

'Then you do the work you have undertaken.'

I heard the words but could not answer. The drink that the old woman had poured for me was not gin, nor was it akvavit. It was the rough spirit the that Dutch call Jenever, and the stuff that was searing my throat and bringing the tears to my eyes was indeed the roughest Jenever that I had ever tasted.

'Take a good swig of that before you shake hands with Bronsard, and then breathe it into his poxy face – 'twill make your disguise certain,' old Hannah cackled at my discomfort.

Aphra waited until I had swallowed and gasped a few times.

'You will advise Sir Joseph Ord as to what is needed to make a diving bell. He will give you a secret room to work in and provide you with paper and drafting materials. He must have drawings and lists of what will be needed, but, so far as you can, you should disguise the true nature of what you are about. Everything that you specify, will be found for you. You are to be sure that you miss nothing out.'

The treasure that I was to raise, no matter what it turned out to be, must be worth it. Newcastle burghers have a keen sense of profit and loss, and building a diving bell was going to be no cheap enterprise and now I had a good excuse to ask for more information about the affair.

'I cannot say what will be needed,' I warned Aphra, 'until I know the exact nature of the enterprise,' making my point by taking another cautious sip at my drink, and settling myself more deeply into my chair. I waited as the two women looked at each other.

'We are not free to tell you anything, Captain Ellyot,' Aphra replied softly while Hannah fidgeted and scowled at me. 'In this matter we are sworn to secrecy for Master Sylvanus Webster governs the enterprise. The secrets are his – surely he told you that?'

'But I must know certain things before I can design the bell. I need to know the depth I have to work at,' I insisted, looking across the firelight at Aphra, 'and the weight of what I am to bring up, even if just to say it is an impossible task to perform. I am the man to risk my life going down into the dark waters.'

'All of that has been judged elsewhere. You can only be told when you are safe at sea,' she replied but I sensed that Aphra wanted to tell me something, and I pressed her.

'You must tell me how deep I have to go, so that I can make a diving bell of sufficient size, and you must tell me the weight of what I must try to bring up.' I paused, watching her. 'Without knowing these two things I cannot begin work.'

Without a word the girl rose and went across the room to a chest. She turned away for a moment and I heard the rattle of a key. When she came back she was carrying a single sheet of thick paper and, silently, she handed it to me.

It was a sketch-map, with a few drawings and perhaps half a dozen measurements in fathoms. It could have shown anywhere, save for the two words written on a part of the map. One word was 'Wameses', the other was 'Skeney' but I recognised neither. I guessed they were place names, probably English or Lowland Scots, but nothing more than that occurred to me. I read the measurements again and again before handing the paper back to Aphra.

'Thank you.' The look I gave her as I handed the sheet back was that of a man who has bitten into an apple and found half a worm.

'Will that serve, Captain Ellyot?' she asked, looking at me intently.

'Serve to get me drowned? Aye, 'twill serve well enough for that.' Then I relented as the dark grey eyes held a sudden concern. 'With what I have learned from yon piece of paper, I can at least begin to work, but I tell you straight that I will need to know more before we set sail for this ... Wameses and Skeney.'

～

As the foy-boat sped down river on the falling tide I tried to talk with Will Blacket, but almost as soon as he opened his mouth, we were hurriedly waved to silence by Aphra. She pointed to the north bank of the Tyne where a wavering line of torches flamed in the darkness. Against the flare, I saw the silhouettes of men carrying weapons. The company advanced to surround a huddle of keelmen's huts along the shore and I heard a woman scream and men's angry shouts. The torches began to move more quickly, crowding in around one point and a crimson flash lit the water for an instant as the harsh crack of a firelock echoed between the river banks. As we pulled over to the Gateshead side there was a short trumpet blast, then a ragged cheer.

'That's another corpse for the Gallowgate gibbet – the Town Watch has earned its ale money tonight. That's the fourth poor devil they've taken, or shot out of hand,' said Will under his breath and then spat over the side of the boat. 'It's been like that all day, Captain. Drummers goin' around every ward in the town, and the Mayor's proclamation read out on St Nicholas's steps. Rewards are offered – up to ten pound. That's a rare old hornet's nest we've kicked over since we came into the town.'

'They're out after me!' I exclaimed, shocked. 'Why, Will? I hadn't even been brought before the magistrates.'

'What a man's done and what he's charged wi' doin' is no great matter o' difference, Captain. The cry is out that one John Ellyot, a common soldier newly returned from the Swedish service, did break sundry prisoners free of the town gaol and that he did murder two gaolers.'

I opened my mouth to protest but thought better of it. The two gaol guards had been hurt, but they were both still alive when last I had seen them. It was just empty vanity, but being called a common soldier stung me hard, though I knew that it made no odds – it was as bad to be hanged as a humble gunner as a captain.

'They'd both had their throats cut across when the guard found them this morning … so far as could be told,' Will continued. 'The bodies were well roasted by all accounts – it seems that the killers threw the poor buggers' bodies into the flames.'

I sat silent for a while, thinking hard. Had Sylvanus Webster's men done the killing? It hardly mattered now as being accused was as good as being found guilty, and a man fleeing a double charge of murder was not likely to argue too much about an offer of work that would take him elsewhere. By having the two gaolers' throats cut, Webster could have made a powerful lever for himself, one to persuade me to anything. A couple of killings was a mere pinch of spice to flavour the dish when breaking a man out of gaol.

I didn't want to believe that Aphra Thornton had a part in such business, yet why not? I asked myself. I had known some pretty faces who could put a well-honed blade across a man's weasand – aye, and do it with a laugh and a giggle. I looked to the stern of the boat where she sat, her face turned towards me but seeming preoccupied. She showed no emotion, except to bite her lip from time to time.

On the other hand, it could have been simple enough for Bronsard to have arranged to have the two gaolers murdered. Surely that was Nicholas Bronsard's style. With a cry of murder out against me, no charge I made against him would count for anything at all.

I was still pondering when the boat bumped against the strakes of the Dutch merchant ship, and I climbed the Jacob's ladder to get aboard.

Chapter 13

The Dutch Merchant

I landed at Newcastle quayside as Mijnheer Dirk ter Bruggencate, a merchant of Rotterdam. It was not a name I would have chosen for myself, but strangely it had a more apt feel to it than any of the Vans and Van ders that I might have been given. Certainly it was a name to suit any one of the proud fellows stepping ashore as the town's clocks struck ten, and a five-gun salute began to boom out from the Castle yard on the rock above.

I was thirteenth ashore, which was my own fault. I had counted the Dutchmen crossing the gangway to still my nerves, and the realisation that there were twelve merchants ahead of me was my reward. I took a deep breath and moved with the crowd to be welcomed by Sir Nicholas Cole and the representatives of the town's Company of Merchant Venturers.

We are still a backward tribe in the North, and I say that as a Newcastle man born and bred. There was hardly a garment among the hostmen on the quay that either fitted or matched. The stuffs were rich enough and had cost good money, but the tailors who had cut the cloth, and sent men out on to the common street wearing it, should have been gelded with their own shears for such work. My opinion was upheld when I heard one of the Dutch merchants snigger a soft, 'Al draagt een aap ...' and shared the smiles that his quip drew from his fellows. Indeed, as the Dutch say, an ape is still an ape even when it wears a silken gown, but I reminded myself that one of these apes in silk gowns had signed a warrant for my arrest and might still live to see me jig at a rope's end. The thought sobered me, though I knew that my disguise was about perfect. I matched the Dutchmen well. Aphra had draped a fine black woollen cloak around my shoulders before we set off down river to board the ship. I was holding an ebony stick and wearing a wide brimmed hat with three real ostrich plumes in it. I passed full muster with the other merchants and all I needed was a sword, but old Hannah had seen to it that I went without a blade.

I raised my head and clapped with the others after the speech of welcome had been read out, in English, by the Mayor. Looking around I saw there was a good crowd of townsfolk watching the ceremony, and easily enough I picked out those who had been paid a penny or two to cheer. Honest townsfolk were already moving away to get on with the day's work.

It was then that I caught sight of the anxious face of Matthew Stobbs in the crowd, but my tenant was not looking in my direction so I followed his gaze to where Nicholas Bronsard stood in the little cluster of dignitaries, waiting to shake the hand of each merchant. Even at twenty paces I could see that Master Nicholas was better dressed than his fellows, clad in russet silk and dark brown Milan velvet, every stitch of his clothes London sewn.

My hand went to where, on any ordinary day, I would have carried a sheathed dagger but I stopped myself halfway through the motion. Hannah Thornton's warning came back. She was right, the game was now a bigger business altogether than my need to put this stoat of a fellow under the ground. Besides, it would have been a poor return to the Dutch if one of their number suddenly killed a hostman.

The merchant in front of me was exchanging bows with Bronsard and I heard Bronsard utter a few halting words of Dutch. Even before I shook hands with him and looked into his face, I knew that my disguise would hold. I smiled at him, looking through the green lenses of my spectacles, bowed deeply and swept off my hat to reveal my shaven pate. My fast pattering at him in my gunner's Dutch brought a puzzled look to his face so I stopped and began to speak to him in English, with a strong Dutch accent. There had been a Haarlemer with us in Sweden who had spoken in that fashion. My counterfeiting pleased me, and the act kept a smile on my face.

I had learned more of local trade than most townsmen knew themselves, just by listening to the Dutchmen during the passage up river, so while I scanned Nicholas Bronsard carefully from head to toe, I made conversation with him, asking about the new finds of silver-bearing lead in Weardale. It was soon clear that he was not interested in what I was saying, and that welcoming Dutch merchants was a duty not to his taste. I wondered if it were my mischief with the wee craikie in the chest lid that was troubling him for the long scarf of cream coloured satin that he wore hid his neck, but there was no mistaking the blue-black pocks that marked his left jowl. Lard and brimstone salve will hide only so much.

Bronsard's eyes were everywhere except upon me. This was a day when Trade, as such, did not interest him. He half listened to me, nodding in agreement at the wrong times as I asked questions about the price of Gateshead millstones, giving me an offhand answer that betrayed that his knowledge of the trade was a poor as my own.

I might have bowed again and moved on to make my respects to the Mayor and the other dignitaries, but some demon inside me bade me stay. I spoke to him again, asking this time about bad state of the coal trade, and he could barely disguise his irritation.

There was a sudden ragged fanfare of trumpets and the assembly formed rough ranks as a company of kettledrummers and trumpeters, clad in a much mended livery of faded yellow and red, struck up a slow dirge. We followed them in solemn procession to the Guildhall.

It is not far from the quay to the great oak doors of the Guildhall, so I did not speak to Bronsard again, slowing my step, allowing him to walk a pace or two ahead. If he noticed me at all, he made no sign of it and I sat comfortably inside my new identity as Dirk ter Bruggencate, as it matured and hardened around me. Bronsard was clearly more intent upon the people that still thronged the wayside, looking everywhere, even glancing up at the windows of the tall houses that stood back from the quay.

We were almost at the Guildhall when I saw Mattie Stobbs push to the front of the crowd. He waved his hat two or three times, making figure-of-eight patterns in the air and then I saw elation, bright eyed triumph, sweep through Nicholas Bronsard.

The hostmen's clothes may have drawn a well-deserved smirk from their guests, but a dinner at the Guildhall in Newcastle was something to marvel at. The rich smell of a side of beef, roasted whole, wafted out at us as we entered the hall. Casks of wine and ale lay in their racks with the spigots already hammered home and serving men were hurriedly filling the great silver ale cans ready to rush to the tables. The

Guildhall doors shut behind us with a hollow boom and I found myself smiling again. The townsfolk could be allowed to cheer the procession, but sight of the feast laid out was another matter.

And feast it was. The hostmen were making their guests heartily welcome, though from what I had overheard of the Dutch merchants' talk, they would have need to for Newcastle's coal trade was in sore trouble. The Dutchmen had come to a buyer's market and they knew it well.

We sat at long tables with the light streaming down into the hall through the reds and blues of the stained glass in the great rose window. I accepted a wide linen napkin to save my clothes from the grease of the roast meats and set to with forty other men to stuff my guts at the town's expense.

Aphra had told me that I would be openly approached by Sir Joseph Ord, who would welcome me and offer me the hospitality of his house. Sir Joseph owned quarries where the famous Gateshead millstones were cut and I had deliberately expressed an interest in buying such millstones to Nicholas Bronsard. Everything was as promised, save that no Sir Joseph Ord had come to me. So I waited.

The feast would last for hours, but before it ended I must be met by somebody for without the protection of the merchant company around me I would stand out as a stranger and would be questioned. Aphra had mentioned that Sir Joseph lived in a house close by St Nicholas's churchyard so, if he did not come soon, I would have to slip out and make my own way there.

The noise in the hall had risen, the air heavy with the fumes of drink, and raucous laughter, Dutch as well as English, echoed up to the high rafters. A band had struck up a lively tune, two trumpeters playing at counterpoint to one another with wondrous skill and I found myself tapping my feet. I was not drunk but I had supped my fourth or fifth pot of ale. Looking down I saw that beating time to the music had made me slop drink over on to the table and that brought me to my senses.

Nicholas Bronsard had been sitting at table a few places below me and I had glanced at him with a drunken grin on my face. Just for an instant I had the idea that he was looking at me intently and perhaps he may have been, but it was through his drink. He had thrown back his head, poured wine down his throat and thrust out his goblet to a server for more.

The sight of one of the older Dutch merchants rising to his feet and holding his hand to his mouth gave me a chance to make my exit as he floundered drunkenly past me. He had eaten over much beef, drunk too much of the red wine of Burgundy from a quart pot, and he needed to vomit to make room for more gluttony. An old tapestry hung across one corner of the hall and I had seen feasters stagger behind it, coming out still fumbling at the broadfalls of their breeches.

I rose from the bench and began to steer the old merchant towards the latrine as a Dutch voice called out a snatch of an old proverb about wine drinking and I chorused back the rest of it. Laughter followed us as we staggered among the folds of the tapestry. There was a line of half-casks set out, already half full and beginning to reek. I held the old man steady while he spewed mightily, shook his head, undid his wide breeks and relieved himself on the floor. Then he sat down on the fouled stones and began to sing to himself. I dragged him clear and left him with his back against the wall.

'Mijnheer ter Bruggencate?' I jumped, shocked out of my ale haze. It was one of the grey-clad serving men. 'Sir Joseph sends his respects and asks that you come with me.' He had my cloak and stick in his hands.

It might have been a trap. Nicholas Bronsard could well have been a lot more cunning than I had given him credit for and I hesitated.

'Trust me ... Captain,' he said firmly.

~

Sir Joseph Ord's wrath sounded down the stairs of his house like the roar of a baited bull. The profanity would have made a dragoon blush as I heard the crash of a pot being smashed and the clatter of fleeing feet, hollow on the floorboards. My escort pointed up the stairs and turned to slip away.

Upstairs, I came upon an old man lying in a tester bed, his head bandaged, and a look on his face that I had seen many times before – he would not last the day. This surely could not be the man who had roared.

The owner of the voice now entered. 'The bastards! The filthy, Godless ... bastards! They came looking for me and they've murdered my steward!' he growled like a Tom o' Bedlam. His grey hair and beard stood on end, the bloodshot eyes glared, and he was filthy, broad smears of clay and earth besmirching his ancient clothes. I like the tang of horse dung as much as the next fellow, but Sir Joseph Ord stood in a veritable nimbus of smell. I could almost swear that he shimmered with the stench. When he saw me he stopped his ranting and stood there before the bed, dropping his voice to a whisper. 'But a cool head conquers all, old friend ... I know that you would have forgiven ... But by the living God, Esau Tait, I shall send those evil-doers to the Devil who waits for them, before this week is out.' The rage seemed to leave him. 'You'll be Captain Ellyot,' he said quietly and without turning around.

'Dirk ter Bruggencate ... Merchant Venturer of Rotterdam,' I reminded him softly.

'Aye ... to be sure!' He turned around. Sir Joseph had collected himself and held out a hard hand caked with dried earth. 'You will have patience with my rage for Esau and I were lads together. Ha!' He punched a fist into the palm of his hand, 'the bas- tards cannot even do a simple murder without killing the wrong old man. They thought Esau was me. They thought the man with the wheelbarrow was the gardener!' I waited. The old man wanted to talk, to tell someone what had happened.

'It may seem strange to you that a knight o' coat armour takes to gardening, but I have three good parcels of land along the banks of the Pandon Dene.' He frowned. 'Mark you, I grow no cabbages.' I nodded gravely to humour him as he went on. 'My gardening is for profit. I have close to a hundred white mulberry trees growing there, and by next year there will be enough leaves to feed silkworms.' He punched me in the arm and gave me a nod and a wink. 'Silk from Newcastle, eh!' He shook his head sharply. 'This morning I was taking a barrow load of manure up to my holding by the Barras Bridge. Esau was following me.' He was close to tears. 'Damn me, but I heard the hooves and moved aside. There were two of the bastards and at first I thought that they were just drunken cavalrymen from the garrison out to set the townsfolk a-flutter. I've done as much myself when I was young and knew no better. Then they grabbed Esau's arms and galloped off with him between them.' The old man drew a sleeve across his face leaving a dirty smear. 'Jesu ... but they flung the poor fellow headlong at a tree. I heard his skull crack – by the living God that is a terrible sound to hear.'

At that moment, I knew how my brother Luke had died.

'You will need to question a man called Matthew Stobbs,' I said quietly. It was strange, but I felt no hatred for Stobbs. Any court of law would call him an accomplice to a murder, plainly, but in his way he was as much a victim of the Bronsards as I had been. Even so, I could watch misfortune fall upon him without disquiet – him rather than me! Besides, I thought that Stobbs was one man who had seen me clearly, and might recognise me even through my disguise, so it was as well for me, too, that he disappear, and I told Sir Joseph all that I had seen outside the Guildhall.

'The pimp will be found,' was all he said, but his expression boded no good for Mattie Stobbs.

'Sir Joseph,' I asked, 'You do know how to ... put a question to a man?' The grim look told me that he did not – he wanted only to hurt. I looked at him until I saw that he understood my meaning, and he shook his head.

'Mattie Stobbs is one of Bronsard's things, Sir Joseph,' I continued, 'but he has been no more than a frightened pawn in this affair – yet that wretch knows more about their secret doings than we might suppose. He even knows more than he realises himself. Hot irons won't serve you nearly so well as having him chained up for three days, locked in cold darkness, underground, without a bite to eat or a word of human company.' I looked directly at the old man.

'Truly, Sir ... I do have a knowledge of such matters,' Sir Joseph nodded slowly.

'Then, when his spirit is at a low ebb,' I urged quietly, 'have someone whisper to him in the darkness. Let them give him a kind word and a cup of wine then leave him in the silence for another day and another night. Let fear and hunger purge both his soul and his body, then begin to ask your questions, and when he has been drained, begin to win him over. Turn him against the master who has abandoned him.'

'And that will make him tell me who the killers were?' There was a hunger in the question.

'Oh ... I would be surprised if Master Stobbs did not beg to tell you that much the moment you lay hands upon him. He will know that Bronsard won't let him live a day after you let him free.' I grinned wryly and raised an eyebrow. 'Could Bronsard ever believe a man turned free with not so much as a bruise on his body?' Understanding spread across the old man's face, and then it turned to a look of pure cunning.

'His rent for my protection will be the tales he can tell,' he said softly, but the gleam on his face faded. 'No! Neither Stobbs nor the two killers is sufficient return for the death of Esau Tate. We both know who is at the root of this business.' A slow nod of agreement passed between us.

'Aye, Mijnheer,' he continued, the light of battle in his face, 'Esau had sons. They have a right to expect certain things from me; and I've lads a-plenty that will serve me without question. There is also the matter of my honour.' For a moment it seemed as though the old man was jesting with me, then I saw that he was not. 'It would put a deal o' salve on my honour to send two of His Majesty's proud troopers to perdition before this week is out.' He placed a hand on my shoulder. 'Bear with me for an hour – two at most, then we will get down to this business of raising the cannon.'

Cannon! At last I knew something. 'A prudent man, Sir Joseph ...' I began. He cut off my warning with a short laugh and a wave of his hand.

'A prudent man, Captain, would stay in bed.' He looked at the still figure on the tester. 'You have become entangled in Mistress Thornton's skirts, this, however, is man's work!' He laughed loud. 'I tell you plain so that you can savour it. I mean to go to the Guildhall ... and a fine spectre at that feast shall I make!'

~

I followed Sir Joseph as he strode back down through the steep and narrow streets and into the great Guildhall. He had gone as he was, in his earth-stained clothes, his hair and beard on end. The only preparations he had made for his entry at the feast were a long bladed Ferrara sword hanging from a plain leather baldric and a brace of wheel-lock horse pistols stuck in his belt.

I stood back and kept myself out of sight as he strode into the noise and smoke of the hall. The roar of laughter and drunken shouts fell and then stopped altogether. A pewter pot dropped from a table and rolled across the stone floor spilling dark ale. The old knight had the hostmen's attention.

'You gentlemen all know me ... I am Joseph Ord, a freeman of this town born, *Sir* Joseph Ord, dubbed knight by Queen Elizabeth herself.' Drunken men began to nod their assent as they looked to one another for confirmation. The babble rose again as the matter was explained to the Dutch merchants. 'I come here on a matter of honour ... and a matter of Law ... to tell of a felony.' The soft hiss of talk rose and then as suddenly fell away. Sir Nicholas Cole, mayor of the town, rose unsteadily to his feet and stood resting his knuckles on the high table.

'We know you well, Sir Joseph.' He swayed a little. 'But I ask you if this is the time or the place for a matter of this kind. You must know that the town entertains ...' The mayor swept his arms out as though to embrace the hall.

'That I know well enough. And as you know, except for what has been done this day, I should have been here myself.' Sir Joseph stepped forward. 'I come here to accuse Nicholas Bronsard of setting men to do murder for money.' There were two heartbeats of dead silence, then the noise broke.

Sir Joseph let the roar of voices spend itself, before he continued.

'I will swear on Holy Scripture and by my honour as a knight that Nicholas Bronsard incited and paid two men to kill me. That they slew Master Esau Tait in my stead makes it no less a crime.' He shouted loud and clear so that his words were thrown back from the walls. 'I call upon Nicholas Bronsard to face me ... to face my accusation ... and to look upon the corpse of Esau Tait.'

Those who had seen Bronsard in the hall began to look at the bench where he had been sitting. It was not empty. There was a Dutchman slumped over the table with his cheek in a pool of spilt wine, but there was no sight of Nicholas Bronsard.

'You see that Master Nicholas is no longer here, Sir Joseph.' The mayor was not so drunk that he would allow anyone to interrupt the feast. I could see that he wanted Sir Joseph Ord gone. 'It would be more fitting if you were to lay your accusation before the Coroner and then before the Justices.'

'I have done that ... Sir. Are not those gentlemen here today?'

I watched as the old man pointed along the benches to three or four different places. I could swear that the men sitting there sank down in their seats. 'But you are right, sir. My swearing alone will not sustain a charge of murder.' Again he looked around the Guildhall. 'Let the burgesses of the town fear not. All will be done properly. I shall have a witness, a man who has turned King's Evidence ... and before this day is done I will have the two murderers in chains ... Then we shall have the names of all the men who set them to their Devil's work!'

My first thought was that the old man had lost his wits. He had warned his enemies, *our* enemies – but as I scanned the faces along the tables I saw that the flush of
wine had gone from more than a few.

As we left the Guildhall, I saw three serving men armed with cudgels close in
towards us. Sir Joseph pulled at my arm. 'Take no heed – those men are mine. They
are to see that we are not followed.'

We climbed the steep cobbled street between the overhanging gables of the houses, Sir Joseph breaking the silence, 'You may have missed my meaning in that hall,
but the men concerned did not. I have just declared war upon the royal faction in the
town.' He turned to me and smiled. 'If it had not been today, it would have been
tomorrow. Mostly this town is for the King.'

I must have looked surprised, for he went on, 'The reason for that is not hard to
see. His Majesty gets two shilling pieces in tax money for every chauldron of coal
shipped out of the Tyne. That comes to a tidy sum in ready coin each year, but two
shillings a chauldron is a fleabite compared to the sums that are made by the
Newcastle merchants and coal-owners. It is, shall we say, a comfortable arrangement.'

'And the ... Parliament ... faction?' I queried, having heard only snatches of
information about the state of politics in England in the few weeks before I had left
Sweden. 'Where does it stand in Newcastle?'

Sir Joseph did not answer for a moment. He stopped and looked at me. 'The
Parliament also needs the wealth of Newcastle.' He glanced back down the hill and
across the drifting coal smoke lying low over the river. 'There is a war coming, I can
feel it in my bones. I pray that I am mistaken, but I know that I am not. War will
come to Newcastle, there can be no escape from that. Both sides will try to secure
Newcastle's coals – if only to deny it to the other.'

'And are the King's men also Papists?' I asked because I knew that Newcastle
had long been a town where recusant families, who did not attend the Anglican
churches, were common enough. Though I must say that, by-and-large, our folk minded their own business in matters of religion.

'Some,' he replied with a sadness in the smile he gave me. 'My own brother is a

Catholic and is for the King. I have friends of a lifetime, good honest men, who will serve Charles Stuart if they are called. But, like me, they pray that they are not called.' The sadness on Sir Joseph's face returned to a tight-lipped grimness.

It was in my mind to tell Sir Joseph of the papers that I had read in Nicholas Bronsard's counting house, but I could feel myself being drawn into taking sides in a quarrel that was not mine. It was nothing to me that Bronsard was a King's man. He had arranged to have my brother murdered, and that was my business and my quarrel with him. Sylvanus Webster had rescued me from the Stank Tower, and for that I had offered to raise cannon from the sea for him. Beyond that I would not think.

'You had a brother, Captain Ellyot ...'

'Luke Ellyot ... of Benwell,' I answered.

Sir Joseph nodded. 'I did not put the two names together at first. So this is blood feud for you too. More so, I think. Esau Tate was my servant and my friend, but he was no blood kin.'

I sighed without being able to help myself. I had done more than my share of killing. I was only a hairsbreadth further from damnation than the men who had killed Luke, but I heard myself say, 'Yes, a blood feud!' with a force that took me by surprise.

'Then you have honour of place in this business, and I think that you have the guile to carry out what needs to be done without bringing the town about our ears. Let Master Webster's affairs wait a day or so, they'll take no harm from it.' He looked at me as he softly said, 'Let my fellows find this Stobbs, then we shall know where to lay hands upon the two horsemen who killed your brother.'

'If any of the three are still alive. I've seen how Bronsard treats tools for which he has no more use!'

I half hoped that was exactly what Nicholas Bronsard would have done, and then I knew that the execution of the two assassins was something I needed to finish for myself. Though I did not know the men, I knew what they had done was a matter of business. Almost certainly they would have held no malice against Luke. He had been a piece of work, a job to be paid for and the money they got would have been spent on wine and whores the same night, the killing forgotten. I had served with many such men and not scorned to drink with them, yet I knew, too, that if I came upon the assassins I would kill them both. For me, likewise, it would be a simple matter of business, family business.

This would be a mere down payment. Justice's loaded scales would not be truly level until Bronsard had paid, and knew the full consequences of his actions – it could be a stab in the back in a dark alley, a pistol shot, or poison in a tankard. My mind played long on the ways that one man might kill another.

Chapter 14

A Little Revenge

'**M**aster Webster will be much angered when he hears of this!' exclaimed Aphra Thornton as she stood in the long gallery of Sir Joseph Ord's house, hands on hips and a look of sweet anger on her face. 'What devil-inspired daftness overtook you, Sir? I can think only that you were stricken by some temporary loss of your mind. Truly we must hope that Master Webster will think so too ...'

She moved towards the old man, her skirts swishing like a tigress's tail as she continued to rail at him. 'Already the story runs through the town like wildfire! Sir Joseph Ord has challenged the House of Bronsard. He has sworn to destroy the royal faction. He has marched into the Guildhall swinging a sword and called down damnation upon the hostmen!'

Aphra's breasts rose and fell as she took breath, and once again I noticed the fine body under that dress of plain grey with its wide collar of snowy lace.

I should have taken more care, for Mistress Aphra saw that I was stealing a look at her and she rounded on me with anger.

'You ... Sir Dutchman! You are let free for two hours and I find you in the thick of this business. Have *you* no sense either? The work you have to do here has been made doubly plain to you. You have just one task to carry out in this town. It was for that, and only that, we saved you from the gallows.' She looked at me, those wondrous grey eyes of hers fiery with intensity. 'Our cause has desperate need of your skills, Captain Ellyot. Two good men have already died in this venture, died ... under torture, at Berwick. If *you* are killed, then we have all failed and all our strivings will be wasted.' She tossed her head of a sudden. 'It would be a pitiful outcome indeed, if you contrived to get yourself taken captive, because you meddled in a matter that did not concern you.'

It was time to put a stop to her ranting. 'Hold your peace!' I exclaimed, 'Everything you say is true.'

Aphra's pretty mouth closed almost with a snap and I took the advantage before she had time to speak again. 'Events change cases – Nicholas Bronsard tried to have Sir Joseph murdered this morning. His steward was killed by mistake. So I think Sir Joseph was wise when he bearded Nicholas Bronsard and his friends in the Guildhall. At least it will give them something to think about and allow us more time.' I stood up and walked across the gallery until I faced her. Mistress Aphra Thornton was no small maid. I thought I would look down at her, but I did so by only a very little.

'The two matters are now intertwined, Mistress Thornton. You say that the murder is no business of mine, but I say that it is. The men who killed Sir Joseph's steward also murdered Luke, my brother. Bronsard paid for both murders to be done and when he fled the Guildhall this morning he showed his guilt to the whole town. Even his friends on the Council will hesitate to be openly associated with him now. All we have to do is to find Matthew Stobbs. He was privy to the killing. The man will be able to tell us who the hired murderers are, and we have not so very far to look, for Sir Joseph is almost certain that the killers were garrison troopers. Once we find those men, they will name Nicholas Bronsard, and I promise you that the House of Bronsard will be brought low!'

Sir Joseph was slowly nodding his agreement.

'Simpletons!' Her voice cut back at the pair of us. 'Do you both think that Nicholas Bronsard has been cowering in a closet while you, my bold bravos, strut about the town like drunken Scots? D'you fancy that his cunning brain has been idle?'

The derision in her voice was real enough, yet the way that she put her hands on to her hips and tilted up her chin made me catch my breath.

'We will be lucky if this Stobbs you speak of, is not already a neatly snipped thread,' she went on, her pale fingers scissoring in the air. 'And if he is not floating in the Tyne with his throat slashed, then there will be a half dozen gentlemen-perjurers ready to take the Testament in their hands and make a liar out of him. In Newcastle the royal faction has the courts in its pocket. Bronsard is the King's man.' She turned away. 'I would have thought that your own experience would have taught you that much …' She looked again at Sir Joseph. 'Is that not so?'

The old knight looked for a moment as though he would deny it. He puffed up his cheeks and raised his shoulders, then he subsided and nodded reluctantly.

Aphra drove her point home, 'And as for trying to get the governor of a royal castle to hand over any of his troopers to the Justices on the oaths of townsmen … If any of our people lays hand upon men wearing a King's coat, then Bronsard would be the first to call it armed rebellion. The troopers doubtless *are* the murderers – but we can do nothing about it, nothing at all … for now.'

The girl stood by the casement window looking down into the street.

I looked at Aphra's face in profile. She missed – by a very little – being beautiful. Her mouth was a little too wide and her nose a mite snub, and I think that the few freckles that clustered around that nose must have caused her much annoyance. I smiled.

Below us, in the street, I could hear the rumble of iron-rimmed cart wheels and the calls of shopmen. Somewhere in the house, a door banged, and a waft of smoke-tainted town air blew in through the window. Aphra turned to face us again.

'The sole accuser and the only witness to the crime is Sir Joseph himself. Do either of you think that Bronsard will stop because he failed at one attempt?'

She stood for a moment looking at us, there was no need for her to say more. I would have to confess that the idea that Bronsard would try to murder Sir Joseph again had not entered my mind, but it would allow him to solve many problems. If the look I had seen on some of the faces in the Guildhall had been a measure of their liking for Sir Joseph, there would be no great inquiry into how the old man died.

'You would seem to be right, lady,' Sir Joseph said, subdued and shaking his head, his back to the fireplace. 'Tell us what you think we should do, my dear, and Mijnheer ter Bruggencate and I will strive to do it.'

The use of my assumed name made me look at him. He stood with his shoulders bowed and his hands clasped behind his back. He had changed his clothes since we had come from the Guildhall and wore yellow stockings, slack and wrinkled, that showed his skinny old man's legs, and with the padding and slashes of his long out-of-mode coat and britches of faded red plush, he looked like an aged cockerel that had been too long spared the pot. Then I saw the mischief that sparked in Sir Joseph's pale blue eyes as he addressed her.

'Tell us, I say, lady ... and your wish shall be to us as sacred as the Queen's bidding.'

I was astonished as Aphra dimpled demurely, curtseying low to the old man, looking up at him and smiling like a little girl. She rose, and looked first at him and then at me before speaking.

'That is good, sirs,' she said, her hands folded before her almost as though she was at prayer. 'Then you will both understand that neither of you should be abroad on the streets by day or night, unless there is a pressing need. Where there is such a need, neither of you will go out without an escort of strong serving men ... but, I pray you, men armed only with staves.' She paused and I knew that she was waiting to see how Sir Joseph was taking her instructions. The old man pursed his lips and nodded in what might have passed for agreement, though he said nothing. Aphra smiled softly and bowed her head slightly.

'After all, gentlemen,' she went on quietly, 'Master Webster has informed us that he expects the making of the diving bell, and all its gear, to occupy a day less than Creation itself: no more than six days. We have letters which tell that he is to return to the North and Sir Joseph knows better than most men that Master Webster is not to be delayed, nor thwarted ... nor for long hindered.'

There was no doubting that the name of Webster carried weight with the old man. 'The plans for the diving bell are already well in hand,' he said, and he looked up at the decorated stucco of the ceiling. 'I will be giving orders to some dozen craftsmen this afternoon.' He pointed a finger in my direction, 'Captain Ellyot has already limned out handsome drawings and we shall soon have the device made.' I pursed my lips and slowly inclined my head as though to confirm what he said.

'I shall complete the drawings this evening. So far as I am able.' I asserted soberly, compounding the old man's lie, but not without a qualm. 'The main parts of the bell will then depend upon the speed with which Sir Joseph's craftsmen can work.'

I spoke with confidence, shuttle-cocking the business neatly back to the knight and catching him almost off his guard. With good craftsmen working together it had been possible to build a bell and all the hoisting gear in ten days, but that had been in a Swedish royal dockyard, with master craftsmen working with a will. No such thing was possible in Newcastle for, even without our need for secrecy, I knew that it was a solemn Guild rule that no craftsman in one trade would allow himself to be over-looked by a journeyman of another while he worked. It was not for nothing that trades were known as the Mysteries. For a moment I thought that Aphra was going to ask more searching questions and so did Sir Joseph. He snatched at a brass handbell and made it clang until a manservant appeared with a bottle of wine, and a large majolica plate piled high with almond and fig fancies.

'Well then, we'll drink a toast to the success of this enterprise,' he said, a bit too quickly, looking at Aphra and then at me. 'And perhaps to other ventures that follow.' I drank to the first, but resolved that there should be no further ventures.

'I also carry a message to Captain Ellyot from my grandmother,' said Aphra looking at me over the rim of her wine glass. 'She means to send your servant, Will Blacket, back to you. She has a well-founded fear that he will get at least two of her maidservants with child, if he is allowed to stay a day longer in Gateshead.'

'Aye, Will is a good man,' I replied, then realised that she would probably misunderstand my words. 'If my guise as a Rotterdam merchant stands, then Will will pass as my servant.' I was not at all sure that this was so, but Will's presence on this side of the river would give me the service of his quick wits, and an extra blade to guard my back. The only man who could identify Will for certain as my companion was Matthew Stobbs, but whichever way affairs went, I thought it unlikely that Stobbs would have either the chance, or indeed the mind, to point a dirty finger at Will.

'Though I doubt he will suffer to have his head shaved,' I added, grinning ruefully and patting my bald head.

I was rewarded with the nearest to a smile that I had seen from Aphra since she had arrived at Sir Joseph's house.

She seemed a strange girl to me, but I had to allow that my experience of women during the years I had been overseas had indeed been limited, though plentiful to be sure. There are soldiers' women – good women, girls with hearts kinder than respectable town wives could ever dream of. Twice in Pomerania I might have frozen to death but for a swig of brandy and the share of a blanket by a fire with a regimental slut, but their lives and their ways must bend to the needs of war and so, I suppose, the mark of their trade is branded on to them. I wondered how the proud Mistress Thornton would respond if I were to open my courtship the way we were used to on campaign, with a brazen stare and bold wink, and a pinch to the rump. My thoughts must have shown briefly on my face, because her voice cut frostily into my reverie.

'So I can assure Master Webster that you will be ready to begin his work no later than a week from today?'

I allowed my smile to spread. 'You may assure Master Webster that if the bell is not ready inside six days ...' I looked directly across the gallery room at her, 'I shall be as disappointed as he is.'

I paused to give her a chance to see that I stood in no fear of Webster, before I spoke again. 'But I have another message for Sylvanus Webster. Tell him that I have still to be told plainly what I must know if I am to go beyond making drawings for the bell. I need to know how many men will stand ready to haul the bell and all its weights up from the sea and I need to know the size of the ship which will bear the bell and all its lifting gear. Unless I am informed, I can promise you nothing ... nothing at all.'

She flounced. Aphra Thornton, the hard woman of business, stood aside for a split second allowing the young girl to show. 'But ...' Her pretty mouth opened as though with shock.

'But now,' I cut in, 'I must ask your pardon and leave you. A full day and most of a night's draughting work is still to do.' I said forcefully, catching Sir Joseph's eye, and just in time the old man caught on to my intention.

'Aye ... to be sure,' he agreed, 'we must return to our limning-out and our calculations.' Aphra stood for a moment, uncertain, then she looked hard at us both. I put my hand across my heart and bowed slowly to her. When I looked up she had gone.

'Y'have taken a fancy to that one, so you have ...' murmured Sir Joseph, warming his backside at the fire and rocking on his heels. 'But have a care, I have known her since she was in swaddles and she has the Thornton spirit. She's not a lass that can be won with poems and posies.' His chuckle rumbled in his chest. 'Half a dozen young men of the best families in the County have found that to their dismay. She has rough handled many a heart, has Mistress Aphra Thornton.'

'I regret that I can afford that maid no time to handle my heart, Sir Joseph. Until this enterprise is complete, my body and soul belong to Master Sylvanus Webster, for it is my habit to keep faith on a bargain, but the moment this enterprise is ended, I shall quit this privyhole of a town. There is still a deal of good pickings to be had in Europe, if a man cares little which side he fights on.' It was wild talk, but it served to still the old man's needling.

'Your brother had drawn together a fair holding of land and stock,' Sir Joseph responded, glancing my way. 'It would seem a pity that Bronsard should get all so easily.' I waited. There was something on the old man's mind. 'The land is of course now the property o' daft Margaret, so no matter what becomes of Bronsard, that much is denied to you.'

'I have a fair claim to half of the land!' I protested.

Sir Joseph smiled softly. 'So you do still care. That is good.' He moved closer. 'Master Ellyot, I have served our cause for more years than I care to think. I have served it with my gold and my sword, and given it my loyalty. I have not questioned, I have obeyed, but in the matter of Esau Tate's murder, I cannot stay my hand.'

The old man's voice had fallen almost to a whisper, but I had seen that look on a man's face before. Old as he was, Joseph Ord had a blood thirst rising in him.

'Even if it cost me my immortal soul, I shall see the men who murdered Esau Tate lying in their own guts.' He put his hands to my coat, gripping the cloth hard like a man drowning. 'I have no great long time to live John Ellyot and with Esau Tate unavenged, my days will be a torment to me. Without restoring my honour in this matter I will fret myself into the grave.' The look on his face had become wild, suddenly older, yet I could sense that there was still a raging fire within him.

I envied him for it, for he felt the way that I should have.

'You wish me to help you kill the two men who murdered your steward?' I asked, ashamed. The sour gall of my brother's death had been eating into me. My prudence had kept it smothered for four days. It had seemed that the right thing to do was to run away and hope to fight another day, and I had told myself that to take on Bronsard in open fight was a fool's challenge, but now the old man's blood thirst took hold of me. With or without malice, those two King's troopers had taken my own brother and hurled him to his death against the trunk of a great tree.

'Do this for me, John Ellyot, do this and I will do much for you,' pleaded Sir Joseph, an old man once more. I fought the temptation, and as I did so I writhed inside as one part of me called the other part a coward. A dozen scenes of how I might kill came to me: dagger thrust or sword slash, pistol shot or the sudden jerk of a silken garrotte, but no matter how I killed, I knew that once that work was done I should have to flee fast and far. I set my mouth and forced myself to shake my head.

'I too want to feel my blade in those bastards' tripes, Sir Joseph, but Mistress Thornton is right ... for now. Even trying to take revenge on those two troopers would do nothing except let Bronsard call us traitors, and that would surely put paid to any enterprise with diving bells ...' I forced a half-smile, 'which would not please Master Sylvanus Webster at all.'

I watched his mood change as the madness faded.

'I must look at their faces,' the old man said in almost a whisper. 'I need to make certain that they are indeed the men who killed Esau.' He balled both fists and raised them before his face. 'I want to be sure that when I look at their cold corpses, I shall see the men who rode us down in the Pandon Dene this morning.'

I draughted no plans for a diving bell that day. I sat in a chair in the gallery room and listened to the loud slow tick of a brass clock while Sir Joseph paced his gallery slow-ly, waiting for news. Every thief and huckster, every pimp and whore in the town, knew what was wanted. The knight's description of the killers brought us two names, the first of which I anticipated before Sir Joseph was able to utter a full syllable of the name – Bone, Sergeant Mouncey Bone. I saw again the face lit by the pistol flash as he fired down at me. The second name was new – Dawkes, Trooper Skelley Dawkes. As I already knew, they were men of the Castle garrison, and both had been spending freely among the low boozing dens and bawdy houses along the Skinner Burn. But that was as far as it went, for it seemed that the two men had vanished.

'What one rich man's gold might do, another rich man's gold might as easily undo.' The words came unbidden to my mouth. It was quite possible that Nicholas Bronsard had snuffed out his own hirelings.

'No …' Sir Joseph said quietly, 'there is little chance of that. My news is that Nick Bronsard has gone from the town by the West Gate and that he went at the gallop.'

~

We left Sir Joseph's house by way of his wine cellar. There was need, for the same three or four idle-seeming fellows had been seen skulking at the front of the house and by the yards at the back all day. We went down the stairs and among the casks. A well-concealed door opened and the dank smell of the river blew strongly up the tunnel. We walked a few dozen yards down the abandoned drift mine and climbed worn stone steps up into the cellar of another house further down the street. I should not have been surprised, for the town is riddled with old coal workings.

We went to the Skinner Burn, where boozing dens and cheap bawdy houses line the steep banks down to the water's edge. Every yard of it was ablaze with the flare of torches. It was the most likely place to find garrison troops with pay to spend. We were able to look into every likely booth and kennel without attracting more than a glance, for a dark cloak and a hat pulled well down, meant no more down the Skinnerburn than a couple of townsmen abroad at night seeking their pleasure. And King's coats we found a-plenty. There were places that soldiers had made their own, shops that served soldiers' drink, and booths that offered soldiers' whores. We peered through the smoke of torches and the fug of tobacco, mingled with the press of yelling men and their doxies among the blood and feathers at the cockfights, and overlooked many a game of cards or dice. Sir Joseph glanced about keenly, and from time to time he spoke to this man or that woman, but the answer was always a shake of the head.

At last we found a drunken trooper, sitting alone. A half mutchkin of brandy pushed across the boards without a word was greeting enough.

'We are looking for two comrades o' yours.' I waited until he had taken a drink from the pot and his gaze had focussed. 'Bone and Dawkes. They swore they'd meet us here and we've been waitin' these two hours.'

He made a sucking sound through blackened teeth and a cross-eyed leer of conspiracy came to his face. 'A matter o' work was it you were lookin' for?' He thrust a finger up a nostril and peered at what he had hooked out. 'Sergeant Bone ... Sergeant Mouncey Bone ... got his red sash last Easter.' The cross-eyed smile waxed fat. 'A-risin' fast is Mouncey Bone.' He flicked the snot from his finger end. 'Three years to sergeant!' The look of drunken incredulity was real enough. 'And Skelley Dawkes likely to do the same!'

Another drink bought us the information that neither man had been seen at the Baillie Gate headquarters for two days. Nor, he added, with a vigorous shaking of his head, was either man lodged in the Hole. 'That I knows for sure, 'cause I just got out!' He broke into a guffaw of laughter that suggested to me that we had wasted the price of the drink, yet I waited. Something told me that this man had something still to tell us.

'In my time, it took seven or more years for a man even to think about gettin' a sergeant's red sash,' I said, 'and then only when there was hard campaigning, to blow a gap in the ranks for a good man.' I plied him with soldiers' patter for a few minutes and he nodded, then there came to him a little space of lucidity. His smile was like a crooked sunbeam.

'Ha! Now I know what it is you're after ...' His pot hit the bench and splashed its dregs. 'An' I tell you now that you've missed your issue o' rations! You're too late! Bone and Dawkes 'as already filled their roll. They've got a company o' the hardest-bitten, hairy-arsed bastards as ever ransacked a house ... all ready and stood-to-arms up at ...' The fellow's eyes went curiously out of focus as he fought the drink. For a moment he looked as though he was seeing something that puzzled him greatly. Then he slumped forward, his forehead hitting the table with a loud crack. That was all the talk we would have with him, but we had news enough!

Chapter 15

The Night Attack

'So they think they'll come into the house by way of the cellars, do they! Well there are plenty of tunnels under this town and the swine may not find it so easy to get out again.' Sir Joseph clapped a hand on my shoulder. 'See you, John, this time Nick Bronsard has slipped on his own shit! This is no longer one old man's struggle. In such matters I can call on all my neighbours to come to our aid. Ancient custom must prevail – attack upon one house in the town is an attack upon all. I can muster the menfolk of a dozen households.' There was a wicked relish in his laughter. 'And no court will question our actions.'

I knew that the ground upon which Newcastle stood was riddled with coal mines, some abandoned for hundreds of years, many still working, even within the town walls themselves. The small passage that had allowed us to leave the house unseen was more extensive than I had thought. The arm of an old drift mine ran a-flank of the cellars of Sir Joseph Ord's house and connected with his neighbours' premises. To the servants, the old mines were a fact of life. Sometimes they gave a house extra space to keep coals and winter fodder; sometimes they allowed discrete, though far from secret, ways of coming and going.

'See,' Sir Joseph drew lines in spilled wine on the table, 'they may enter at any one of six or seven places, but before they can come into my cellar, they must pass here and here.' His fist closed with a snatch. 'No matter what befalls, once they are inside my house, they will find their way out barred fast and only Hell to flee to.'

The prospect of a fight seemed to take years from the old man.

'Would it not be better to attack them in the tunnel? A fight within your house could cause a deal of damage,' I suggested. It had seemed to me that the old man was more interested in the fight itself than the outcome of it, but he put a finger on the tip of his fat nose and tapped slowly.

'You may know the conduct of wars in foreign lands, Captain, but I have lived in this town for more than sixty years. We have our ways here. Think you this is the first time that we have faced gangs of looters, Scots, and ransackers?' He poured me more wine. 'They must enter the house itself. That puts them in the wrong before the law, and us in the right – no matter who they are! Can a man see a King's coat in the dark? But you're right when you say that there will be damage. Amen to that. It will be well worth it – this is one expense I will gladly bear myself.' There was much grim pleasure in his words. 'But I'm no fool. The bairns and most of the maidservants have already been sent to neighbours. Everything of value has been locked away, and we have laid in a good stock of cobblestones on the landings. Smashed skulls will be uncommonly easy come by this night.'

~

They came at about two in the morning, and we had good warning of their coming. A lad, his young face bright with excitement, came running softly down the tunnel and climbed out into the cellar. He had needed only to point the direction.

I had never thought of household servants as fighters, but these men, and some women as well, armed only with household tools and blackthorn clubs, stood-to-arms like seasoned pikemen.

I drew my sword, but Sir Joseph shook his head and motioned for me to sheath it. 'Leave this to folk who know how to manage things,' he whispered softly. 'We must keep our steel for Bone and his crony.' It amazed me that he could suppose for one minute that he was a match for either man, yet I did as he bid me – though I drew a pistol and cocked it.

The cellar door had been barred, but the beam had been left so that the point of a dagger forced through a crack in the door timbers would lift it. I was aware that there were more than a dozen of Sir Joseph's lads lying in wait behind piled barrels and bales. I could sense that they were there, even though they were well hidden. I fancied I could hear them breathe. The beam securing the cellar door creaked, then it began to lift. It fell with a thump on to the flagstones.

There was a deep silence, and I heard the faintest scrape of a boot as a man shifted position, and the slow angry sniff beside me as Sir Joseph glared in that direction.

Then the door from the tunnel swung open with a shrill creak. There was a faint flicker of light as an arm lifted a candle lantern and set it down without a sound. I felt the still air in the cellar stir with the draught from the tunnel. The human rats climbed out nimbly enough. In the pale light of the lantern I counted nine tall shadows.

Our people had been given stern orders about what was to be done. I had heard Sir Joseph bang his fist on the table as he hammered home his commands. The ransackers were to be allowed to begin their pillaging before they were attacked. Above all, no man who entered the house to loot should be allowed to get away.

So we let them enter, and they padded softly across the cellar and up and into the wide kitchen above. When each man is for himself there is no discipline – they left no rearguard behind them to cover a retreat. Inside a few seconds the entire pack of them had gone above with nothing to tell of their passage but the reek of their unwashed bodies.

Sounds of movement creaked and groaned in the darkness and shuttered lanterns were uncovered. In the soft light I saw men grimace at one another, nervously. Then the bedlam above stairs began. A body came headlong down the timber stairs with a crash. If he were not already dead, then the force with which he hit the stone wall opposite the bottom of the stairs must surely have knocked the life from him. A glance at the dirty bare feet showed that he was a raider. One of the serving men dragged the corpse aside.

The urge run up the stairs and join in the fight was strong, but it had been agreed, if the real purpose of the raid was to cover another attempt to murder Sir Joseph, then he was to be guarded by not less than six armed men at all times. A bang shook the house as someone fired off a fowling piece and Sir Joseph waved three more men up the stairs.

It was a trap sprung to perfection. In less than ten minutes the raiders had been battered out of existence, the house was bright with candlelight, and loud with the sharp edged, brittle laughter of men and women freshly relieved of a great fear.

I counted the dead men all laid out like a catch of rats on the cellar floor. There were eight bodies – but I had counted nine entering the house. Somehow one man had managed to escape. Dead men make sorry sights, and these rogues had been poor enough when they lived, as choice a bunch of gallows bait as I had ever seen. One corpse showed the scars of nostrils slit no earlier than a month before. One had a hook-hand, though it not served him well, for there was no blood on the steel. I tried to see the ways they had been killed. One man's right arm was almost blown off by the shot from the fowling piece, and had bled to death. Two had their skulls stove in from being struck, I guessed, as they charged up the stairs against a hail of cobblestones. The remainder were dead of thrust wounds, more stabs and gashes than were needed simply to kill. I could guess why, for green troops need to be sure that an enemy is truly dead.

'This does not account for Sergeant Bone,' I said. I had looked at the bodies with care. Trooper Dawkes was there. He had been easy to find, in spite of the rags he was wearing, and the fact that his skull had been smashed. His was the only one of the corpses that had been feeding on King's beef. All the others were rat-kin, hardly a picking of fat on any of them. I looked down at Dawkes's body and in my mind the scales of justice levelled a little. Dawkes had been one of the men who had killed Luke Ellyot. Now he was dead. That was proper.

The raid had failed, but to me the victory left a hollow feeling. 'It will pay us not to lower our guard until they are all accounted for,' I said, speaking just to have something to say.

Sir Joseph scratched his head pensively for a moment.

'It will be dark for some hours yet. Perhaps they will come at us while they think we are still overcome by the ransacking,' I ventured. 'If they do that, they will find the Town Watch waiting for them...'

He smiled at me and raised a finger to pull down a lower eyelid. 'I have a lad ready to run to fetch the captain of the Town Watch. So, before the Watch arrives, you'd best get yourself to bed, for you are surely just a tired Dutchman who slept through the commotion.' He banged a fist lightly against my chest. 'All to be done in due form, John. The town coroner will see the bodies and a full enquiry will be held.' He thought for a moment. 'Though I think he will see it my way when I suggest that one of our esteemed visitors from the Netherlands should be spared the tiresome business of attending a coroner's court.'

In the excitement, I had clean forgotten that I was in Sir Joseph's house as the Rotterdam merchant, Dirk ter Bruggencate. His reminder made me feel naked and exposed to danger. For a moment, I feared that I might have been speaking English for everyone to hear. But when I thought about it I had spoken only to Sir Joseph, and a few words to Will Blacket. Still, I should keep to my disguise in future. If I were asked about the doings in the house that night, my answer would be that I had been wakened by the noise, but had seen nothing.

'The Council will not make so much of this night's business with Dutch merchants in the town. Tales of ransack and riot do not lend confidence to traders, and our merchants have a sore need to sell their coals.' Sir Joseph was almost thinking aloud, but I knew that he was probably right, and I was glad of it.

But I was not to be allowed to seek my bed. A few muttered words in Dutch from Will Blacket had me walking quietly to where he stood.

'We'd best get a torch, Captain. It may be just a draught blowin' up yon shaft, but I fancy that by my time o' life I ought to know the groan o' a wounded man.'

Will took a torch of flax-tow dipped in kitchen slush, and when it was well ablaze we went down the few steps that led to the mine. I cocked both of my pistols. For the first ten paces up the passageway I could hear only the echoing patter of water dripping down through cracks in the tunnel roof, and the soft splash of our boots as we walked, but then we heard the sound again, this time from behind us. We turned about. He was lying wedged into a long narrow crack in the sandstone. We had found the man who had shown the raiders the way into the house. It was Matthew Stobbs.

We rolled him out, and Will carried him up into the candlelit kitchen where we put him on to a tabletop. When a man has taken a blade through his rib cage and into his lungs, a soft bubbling sound comes each time he draws breath. I had heard it often enough to know that Stobbs had been stabbed in a lung. Will Blacket cut away jerkin and shirt. The wound was no more than a dark patch with a mouth of swollen red flesh around it. He held a candle close.

'Poniard ... looks like, Captain.' He touched the dark patch at the centre of the wound. His nail grated on something hard. 'It could be that he's been a lucky fellow,'

133

Will grinned at me across the candle flame. 'Or maybe not, if Sir Joseph hands him over to the Justices for hanging. Either way there's more than five fingers width of steel point wedged between his ribs. His chances of lasting the night are better if that comes out, and the wound is bound.'

I decided. Whatever manner of scoundrel Stobbs was, he had long been one of Bronsard's dish-lickers. There was a lot he could tell us.

'I think not, Will,' I said, with a smile. 'The fellow is, after all, our own prisoner! We'll have a surgeon sent for and get the steel out of him.'

'Aye, Captain ...' He bent over Stobbs. For a moment I though that he was sucking the wound, and then I realised that Will Blacket had gripped the broken-off point between his teeth and was slowly drawing it out of Stobbs' ribs. He spat, wiped the steel on his breeches, and held it to the candlelight. I saw him frown and then his wicked musketeer grimace grew and spread across his battered face.

'Seems, Captain, that Master Stobbs has had the honour to be stabbed by a gentleman!'

Chapter 16

Guns to be Raised

I threw down my draughting quill and stretched back in my chair. It was done. Bright sunlight poured in through the dormer window and felt hot on my face. Even on Aphra's reckoning I still had two days in which to list the multitude of other things that would be needed, but the hardest part was finished. I had almost forgotten the satisfaction that limning out set of plans and sketches could give. Three sheets of wondrously smooth and white French paper lay before me. My plans, traced out in dark lines of sepia ink, and carefully annotated with neat lines of script, offered the plainest directions I could devise for the making of a diving bell.

Sir Joseph had done me well in the way of drawing instruments. A navigator's ivory straight edge, and a pair of brass compasses made good working tools. From God knows where, he had also found for me a tiny pinch of cochineal beetles. Crushed and mixed with a little Allepo gum they had given me a few drops of brilliant red ink to illuminate the important instructions. On two dozen sheets of common grey paper I had drawn part-plans to be given to the craftsmen who would – I hoped unknowing – make the lesser parts for the bell. I felt the enterprise coming together.

'You have a fair hand and a gunner's eye, Captain.' Will Blacket looked approvingly over my shoulder and nodded. 'But now, if you'll put your work aside, I'll serve you with some uncommon fine vittles.'

A handsome cut of roast pork and crackling sizzled as Will forked it on to a heated plate, and garnished it with baked potatoes and a goodly pile of cabbage. I tasted the cabbage first, closing my eyes in pure pleasure. My body had been crying out for fresh vegetables.

While I set-to greedily, Will poured a tankard of beer, dark, hoppy and bitter, from a wooden pottle. Ale is much the same anywhere – but beer – I had almost forgotten the taste of English beer.

'Sir Joseph's ordered two pigs killed for a feast for the household and the servants of other houses who stood-to last night. There's enough black puddin' in the house to feed a regiment. And he's broached a cask of this strong beer.'

I looked up at Will, pleased to see his face. He had changed much in a few days. The wild look that he'd had when I first met him was almost gone. He'd had his hair and beard trimmed, though not by a barber, I thought. A woman's hand had held the shears. The pale scar down the side of his face was still apparent but it looked not half so bad now. Indeed it was a line a maidservant might shudder to draw her finger down – and yet I could well guess the look on the lass's face as she did so.

Somehow, too, he had come by a suit of decent clothes. The black broadcloth was plain stuff, but it was not nearly as coarse as the grey hodden or dun fustian a serving man would wear for his day's work, and it had been neatly altered to fit his broad shoulders. The breeches were cut wider than any common servant would dare to wear, and a plain linen collar at his neck gave him the look of at least an upper servant in a respectable house, or perhaps of a master-craftsmen with his own shop.

'You're doing uncommonly well for yourself,' I mocked, dryly. He sniffed and squinted at me sideways, then he drew back his shoulders.

'As the master rises – so goes the servant, Sir!'

Then he stamped to attention, shaking the floorboards. 'By your Honour's leave!' Now Will was mocking me. I looked down and saw that he had new garters tied below the knee. They were braided silk, of dark green, musketeer's green. I laughed. In time, he would become a servant worth keeping, as good a man, maybe, as ever served a colonel, but at that moment it was a great deal more comforting to me to be reminded that this bear of a fellow was still a musketeer and that he had twice saved my life.

'But you do well enough, Will?' I raised a questioning eye. I wanted to know what had gone on at Hannah Thornton's house after I had left it to become a counterfeit Dutchman.

He looked down at his jacket with just the glimmerings of pride in the set of his mouth, and smoothed the cloth with a caring hand. 'A gift from a widow, Captain. On account o' ... '

'Spare me the tale, Will,' I held up my hand and smiled, 'until I've the time to hear all the details.' I motioned for him to take a pot of beer and sit with me. 'But truly, Will, what news?' I asked quietly.

'The bodies ... eight of them ... gibbeted high at Gallowgate. Sir Joseph gets cheered in the street. There's to be no special enquiry into the matter. A farmhouse was ransacked at Gosforth a week ago, so folk in this town are only too glad that the bastards have all been caught and knacked for it.'

'And Matty Stobbs. He's still on this earth?'

Will shrugged. 'No way to know, Captain. He's gone.'

I looked at him sharply. 'Gone?' I felt no anger, for Matthew Stobbs had not figured largely in my plans, but I had thought that he might be persuaded to tell something of Bronsard's affairs.

'He's not dead, Captain, I mean that he's been taken away. Two serving men, big buggers by all accounts, came and carried him off ... and he was alive enough then, groanin' loud and a-callin' on God to save him. They heaved him on to a plank and away with him ... without so much as a by-your-leave.'

I spread my hands and looked at Will, quizzically, waiting for him to tell me more.

'None of the servants knows any more than I do, and Sir Joseph has been riding around the town on a white mare, taking the salute as it were, since early on.'

'Mystery within mystery, Will,' I commented, pushing away my meat plate and applying myself to a steaming dish of figgy duff, well splashed with a brandied sauce.

'I asked the new steward about it,' Will went on, 'and he said that it wasn't by Sir Joseph's order. He'd sworn to have Stobbs up before the Justices and hanged.'

He reached into his belt and pulled out the point of the poniard he had drawn from between Stobbs's ribs. Then he pulled a broken poniard from his belt and fitted the edges together. The match was perfect.

'Spanish work, Captain ... I found this in the cellar tunnel this morning. It's old, but of the best workmanship. Mind you, whoever bought it was robbed. That's a bodkin to wear for show, a popinjay's finery. No man with any sense would try to fight with it. See, the blade had been snapped off clean before and then finely brazed together so it was too weak – for which Stobbs should be eternally grateful.'

Will pointed to a band across the blade, where the dark blue on grey of the Damascene pattern in the steel was scored by a thin gold line that betrayed the mend.

He scratched his head. 'I could have sworn, Captain,' the words came cautiously, 'that I counted nine men come out of that tunnel that night.'

I nodded. 'I counted nine men too, Will, so we must suppose that there was another man ... and that he lost his nerve and fled back down the tunnel at the last minute.'

'And he stopped to put this skewer into Matthew Stobbs on the way home?'

'Or perhaps,' I speculated, half in idleness, 'Stobbs himself was the ninth man and he was stabbed by somebody waiting in the tunnel, for trying to flee. But there is no doubt in my mind that Stobbs had been sent as guide to the ransackers. Perhaps Bronsard had meant it to be Stobbs's last service to him.'

I thought for a moment. That only one of the two troopers had appeared troubled me, but there was no profit in thinking about that now. It may indeed have been that Bone had been lying in wait, ready to come into the house in the confusion of the ransack. I looked down at the broken poniard. No; an old weapon with a cobbled blade was not the weapon of a skilled assassin. Bone and Dawkes would be more likely to get a man drunk then throw him bodily though a high window, or crack his skull open before hurling him down a flight of stairs. There had always to be the chance that the death would be seen as an accident. In my experience, killers are as loath to change their manner of work as dog-stealers. The thin triangular blade that lay before me was no tool of theirs.

'Was Nick Bronsard himself, the ninth man? ' I wondered.

I stopped the thought short. There was no point in going on with it. Dawkes was dead, but my brother was still partly unavenged. I would settle that matter later – alone, and as my own affair. Cold vengeance tastes sweeter. For now, all my efforts had to be for Sylvanus Webster. I had fallen into the service of a powerful man – and a man who might become more powerful yet. I could persuade myself that I was halfway content with that. I could hope for no more. I would try my hardest to raise the guns that Sir Joseph had spoken of. Diving was a rare trade and I was as much master of it as of any. Success there would free me of any debt that I owed Webster, and I would think and make plans for my future when I was my own man again. If Webster's enterprise came to nothing, I would still find the means to bribe good respectable burgesses to clear my name of the charges against me, and then I would find a way to wrench my family's land out of the Bronsards' hands.

'D'ye reckon you can raise up those cannon?' The suddenness of Will Blacket's question did not catch me off guard. It was with some effort that I curbed my temper and instead merely looked across at him, raising an eyebrow.

'Of what guns do you speak, Will?'

'The guns that you are set to raise from a Scots wreck, lying between the Farne Islands, before the first week of September,' he replied as openly as you might please. Oddly, I found myself bitterly amused rather than angry. So much for Sylvanus Webster's hard preserved secrecy.

'I've often wondered how a man can hear so much with his ear pressed hard against a soft white breast. What else did the widow tell you, Will?' I asked.

The musketeer shrugged. 'I heard nothing from Meg, Captain. But the tale is common gossip in the servants' hall across at Mistress Hannah's house.'

I supposed that I should have expected it – the mistress striving for secrecy while her servants prattle. I paused while I thought what to do, for if the servants knew about something then all the world knew. Nicholas Bronsard would know, and what he knew all the Royal faction in Newcastle would know.

'And I was sworn to silence!' I muttered, through lips tight with anger. 'A grand ending to the enterprise … to raise the guns and find a King's man o' war standing by to seize them – and bring us into the Tyne hanging from the yardarm.'

Will saw that I was angry, but he did what any good soldier would do, and stayed silent. Perhaps he could see that my anger would fuel a plan. I stood up and looked out of the window, down over the choppy green waters of the Tyne.

There was more shipping in the river this morning. Then something happened which I took as an omen, and a bad omen at that. A cannon fired, a half-charge salute. I counted the following shots, feeling the shake of each blast through the soles of my boots, and hearing the rattle of the tiles over my head. Then, between the tarred sides of two deep-laden colliers drifting down on the tide, I glimpsed a brave blaze of colour. Banners and flags streamed out in the breeze and I saw the vermilion of the painted cannon muzzles, the band of blue round her hull, the gleam of gold leaf on her figurehead, and the ornately carved stern-castle. Already, there was a King's ship in the river.

'She's the *Endymion*, Captain,' said Will, and I sensed that he was pleased to anticipate my need to know about the warship. 'Thirty-eight guns ... commanded by a Captain Reece. She was off Tynemouth Castle yesterday morning so she must have come up river at first light. Rumour is that the King is coming to visit the North. Maybe that's why she's here.'

Will was probably right in his guess. No warship's commander would resist a chance to have his ship visited by the sovereign. Even in Sweden, I had heard of the money Charles had spent on his men o' war, and of the taxes he had levied to pay for them.

'Thirty-eight guns ...' I mused aloud. 'Powerful enough to blow a fleeing merchant vessel out of the water, with half a broadside.'

I sat down. It may indeed have been that the warship's visit was simple coincidence, but the tightness in my belly told me it was not so.

'Why is she here in Newcastle now? The King's visit is no more than a rumour,' I said, as much to myself as to Will. 'It's a two day's haul up the river from Tynemouth – that's a long way and hard work to come for water and coals. Is it not rather that His Majesty has need of a score or more stout fellows to serve him?'

'That's the fear, Captain. The talk in the markets is that the Council conjured up the warship to purge the town of what they call 'unruly and seditious elements', but the word along the quay is that there'll be no shore leave for the crew.' The laughter in Will's eyes spoke of some private memory of a similar occasion. 'Aa'm told that the last time a press-gang went ashore here, an officer had his skull smashed in, two sailors were killed, and the rest ha'nt been seen since.' Will's laugh turned to a low growl. 'Newcastle is a fair place for shelterin' a man who has run.'

I was still uneasy, fancying that I could feel a certain pattern to the fall of events. There were questions that needed to be answered and Sylvanus Webster was the man I needed to talk with. Guns to be raised in the Farne Islands? I supposed that it sounded reasonable enough. But there was something about the tale that had a faint reek of rotten herring to it. I tried to recollect what I knew of the Northumberland coast. The Farne Islands were indeed a dire hazard to shipping and many vessels had been wrecked there. An Armada wreck ... Spanish treasure? No! The thought died almost before it had risen. The Farnes lay virtually under the guns of both Lindisfarne and Dunstanburgh Castle. No vessel the size of an Armada galleon could ever have gone down unseen off that coast.

The more I thought about it the more improbable seemed even the few crumbs of the story that Aphra Thornton had let fall. Yet a man like Sylvanus Webster did not take the pains that he had taken over me without good purpose. There was something important afoot, but what?

With Will Blacket walking behind me, I went about the town's shops and workshops. We had devised a plan. The smaller pieces of work we ordered openly enough, paying a part of the cost and directing that the item be delivered to an address given me by Sir Joseph. The bell itself had to be made in one workshop, and, if it were possible, by one, or perhaps at most two, craftsmen.

We found what we needed at the far side of the Stockbridge, among the hovels of the poor Pandon ward of the town – a rheumy eyed old cooper working with just one apprentice, his grandson. The workshop was a poor sty of a place, no more than a heather-thatched lean-to set up against the wall of a bottle factory, but the few finished kegs that I examined were as fine as I had seen anywhere.

I gave the old fellow a drawing and questioned him to see that he understood what was required, but it was the grandson who took charge. The lad was eighteen at most, but he seemed to know his trade, and his tools were well cared-for. I maintained my disguise of a Dutch merchant, but I needed to explain exactly what was required, so I had to content myself with slow and carefully accented speech, taking care now and then to ask Will what this or that word was: 'Hoe heet dit in 't Engels?'

'I want this made in four days ... without fail,' I insisted.

The expected protest did not come. The young man nodded his head but he did not look up from scanning the drawings.

'This buoy, Master, you want it made from oak?'

'Buoy?' I blessed him. He had supplied me with a ready made explanation. Of course, the tall thimble shape was exactly like a channel buoy. 'Yes, I want it made of seasoned oak and well tarred, with pitch, within and without, like the ark that bore the infant Moses. I need a buoy that will stay afloat for three years without needing to be taken up.' His head dipped and came up slowly; his attention was still set hard upon my drawing.

'Yet you want the bottom of the buoy left open!'

That was something to which I had not given thought. I was still trying to conjure an explanation when Will saved me.

'That's not the bottom, lad, that's the top ... and it'll need to be opened and sealed again ... often, like.'

The slow wink that Will gave the lad was answered with a short gleam of understanding, and, I knew, a swift raising of the price.

'But four days means four days, lad. If the work isn't done, and well done, exactly as the drawing orders, by dark, three days from now, you will have lost your fee and be the owner of an arseless river buoy, because we shall have sailed for the Scheldt on that tide.'

I should not have marvelled at the old soldier's ability to spin a tale. Will talked on for a few minutes, hinting darkly at a tobacco smuggling ruse that fetched in bucketsful of money for a few clever mariners, and that this buoy might be but the first of many.

A double handful of English silver passed into the grandfather's shaking hands. I paid excessive. In part that was because I did not want the cooper to have to ask for credit when he laid in oak and iron for the work, but also, I knew, a man who gets paid a handsome half in advance would be more likely to believe Will's story of smuggling, and keep his mouth shut.

We returned to our solemn walk about the shops and booths of the town, a worthy Dutch merchant and his dignified manservant. I pointed at this or that with my stick and stood aside to let Will haggle in well-fractured English. He paid out in new silver from a fat leather purse, while swearing under his breath in the foulest Dutch and muttering that his master was truly the original prodigal son. There was method in it. A face and a guise, well-fixed in people's minds, would serve to drive out any chance recollection of John Ellyot. Besides, it was Sir Joseph Ord's good white money that I was sowing about the town. I had just afforded him the best night's excitement he had ever had, while burnishing bright his reputation in the town before his friends and enemies alike. And a man walking abroad in the guise of a wealthy merchant needed to keep up appearances. I spent freely, or perhaps little more than freely, but we did take precautions for a price on your head sharpens your wits. I was careful. Often I stopped to handle some piece of merchandise at a shop, seeming to dally, while Will, with a stiff unseeing look on his face, scanned the crowds for a man or woman who looked at us a little too long or too hard.

As an added precaution, we returned to Sir Joseph's house by devious ways about the town, at the end taking a short trip down river in a foy boat, ready to land at the Sandgate steps and walk home.

I had just paid off the foy boatman, and was about to step ashore when I paused, with one foot on the boat's gunnel. A serving man stood at the head of the steps, crushing his cap in his hands and turning his head to look behind him.

'Master Ellyot!' At mention of my name I stopped, one foot on the shore. The man was one of Sir Joseph Ord's fellows. He hurried down to the water's edge. 'My master says that you are not to come to the house …' He looked over his shoulder again, the tang of fear sharp on him. 'They're at the house … get away … '

A shout rang along the quayside, ahead of the crash of iron-shod boots. Will reacted first, whipping out a knife and thrusting it at the boatman.

'Move!' The order caught in his throat and came through his teeth as a vicious snarl. The fellow jumped to take up his sculling oar and fended off the boat, fumbling in his fear. Will grabbed the oar, put out an arm and pitched the wretch headlong over the bow.

A single heavy shot cracked out along quay, and I saw the white smoke. A musketeer had taken careful aim, his piece held steady in a fork.

There was an instant of dead silence, then the crowd along the wharf began to struggle. One women screamed and then another, and the hubbub of voices became louder. The man who had been sent to warn us had taken a ball clean through the body, and sprawled on the landing steps with his head and shoulders under the water.

'John Ellyot! You are under arrest. In the King's name!' The words rang across the widening gap of water like damnation from the pulpit. I saw an officer's helmet plume and sash at the front of the press of people. His company of musketeers was held back by the crowd of townsfolk along the quay, but one had forced his way to the front. He was kneeling down to take aim and I don't know whether it was by design or accident, but at that moment the crowd surged. The soldier was pitched headlong, still kneeling and clutching his heavy musket, off the quay's edge into the river.

It is strange how an event will change the humour of a crowd. The great splash brought a roar of laughter, and folk pressed forward to see. We had drifted off the shore perhaps twenty feet. Small boats were clustering in to drop passengers at the Sandgate steps. I took the oar from Will Blacket and began to scull the foy boat clear.

A ragged volley of musket shots rang out from the shore. My neck cringed into my shoulders as the bullets slashed whining past my body to rip into the water. I felt the little whip of wind and heard the buzz as a ball crossed close by my cheek, and a long splinter was torn from the boat's bow as though sliced away by the stroke of a broadaxe.

The crowd lining the quayside roared at this – now we offered better sport than a bull-baiting. I saw that the company of musketeers had at last forced a space in the mass of bodies and were resting their muskets to take aim.

I swear that we should both have been dead but for their captain's wish to have the volley fired off to the fall of his sword blade. His delay saved us. I heard the command to take aim, then the black bow of a keel boat drifted to meet us. Will Blacket reached out his hands to the keel's bow and dragged the foy boat around and into its shelter.

We had been given a half minute's grace. A second volley of musket balls threw up splashes around of the foy boat's stern, riving away more splinters, but we were protected by the bluff bows of the keelboat.

I sculled deeper into the shipping. We were still no more than four or five boatlengths from the shore, but we were now well among the craft rubbing and scraping to come alongside the quays. Boatmen looked at us in horror and tried to fend us off. I saw a space open between the shifting hulls and pulled for it, then suddenly we were in clear water. The midstream passage offered a narrow channel between the shipping traffic at either side of the river. A few dozen frantic twists of my wrists at the sculling oar had us across the fairway and put our bows between the hulls of two small merchant ships tied up on the Gateshead side.

'Jesu, Captain!' Will exclaimed, standing up in the boat, his teeth showing a dog's grin. 'I must be fated. There I was, less'n an hour ago, with a good soft billett and a young widow pantin' for m' body when ...' The splash of oars out in the stream silenced him. The troops had commandeered boats to search for us among the river traffic and now the crowd had started singing ribald songs as it swayed along the water's edge. Hundreds of townsfolk had left their work to line the quays, to shout and point, to taunt the musketeers who, burdened with helmet and half-armour, were leaping nervously between the moored vessels.

We waded along the south shore, sometimes thigh deep in the stinking mud. We kept the hulls of moored ships and keelboats between us and the north bank, moving cautiously until we found a place where we could climb ashore unseen. Then, without word or look passing between us, we ran.

Chapter 17

Fugitives

We did not run far, for a cluster of cottages and smallholdings along the river bank sheltered us from view of the north shore. We scrambled over garden walls and tore our way through hedges. Once we leaped over a gate and tumbled headlong into a flock of geese who raised an alarm fit to wake a dead man, but we were clear of the lane before anyone was roused. Then we found ourselves chased by a little dog, the mangy cur following us close, barking and snarling, until Will stopped and stared at it, and it padded silently away.

The land south of the river is mostly open field, breaking to bare fellside as the ground rises. That offered plenty of rough cover, but few places where two men could safely hide. We dropped down into a little burn and followed the course of water. Stooping low, we ran on until we reached the foot of Gateshead Fell. Before us, the open heath climbed, the fell patched with thickets of hawthorn, dense with summer greenery.

I looked behind. A furlong away a cart drawn by pair of white oxen came into sight, driving along the riverside road to Gateshead. Somewhere close-to, but out of sight, I heard a hawk screech, and the soft hum of a lure being whirled. I pointed at a dense thicket on the hillside and waited. Will looked for a moment and then nodded.

For perhaps two minutes we scrabbled our way up the open hillside, knowing that our silhouettes stood out stark against the skyline. Again I felt that cold tingling patch between the shoulder blades that comes when a man expects to hear a musket crack out behind him.

We reached the edge of the thicket and flung ourselves to the ground, crawling deep into the undergrowth. For a long time we were both silent, and I could hear myself panting and feel the hard thump of my heart in my chest. Fear makes a man do strange things, and I began to laugh. Were I to be hanged the next minute, I could not have stopped myself. I kept quiet enough, holding my sides and raising my knees into my stomach, but there was no stopping. It had happened once before, at the battle of Nordlingen, when a cannon shot had taken off the head of a fellow standing next to me. His name I could not recall, but I remembered every word of the filthy joke he had been telling me – so far as he had told it when the roundshot hit him.

Will looked at me for a moment, puzzled, but then his face creased too, and his white teeth showed. His great shoulders shook, and the fat tears began to roll down his cheeks.

'Well then, Captain, what's it to be?' he managed to say at last as our laughter subsided and we felt rested, and able to consider our plight.

I blew out my breath, and after a moment replied, 'To my mind, Will, it looks as though your own plan would serve us best. We can make our way south as soon as it's full dark and in three or four days we can be down to Hull. We've passage money to get us to somewhere between the Elbe and the Maas. We can sign regimental muster rolls and be back doing what we both know best inside a week. We may take our choice.' I bit my upper lip and pouted my lower in a parody of a Swedish colonel I had served under. 'You brave men will make your fortunes and gain honour and distinction … in the service of His Majesty … His Highness … His Eminence … His Holiness … or what you will.' Abruptly I shut my mouth.

I sensed, rather than heard – then I did hear it – the jingle of harness. The sound grew, the chink of iron overridden by the thump of hooves.

There were thirteen riders, the fresh brown lacquer on their half armour and helmets glistening in the sunlight. I took in the fine detail. The bold saffron and black bars on the padded sleeves of their jerkins showed up bravely; the young cornet o' horse at their head wore a silk scarf fluttering at his throat. There was no doubt that the troop had been newly accoutred, a rare enough event in any army. Most soldiers stripped their gear from corpses and wore that until it became too tattered to hold patches. New uniforms issued to garrison troops might mean that the Castle governor at Newcastle did indeed expect Charles Stuart to come to the North. Were I a spy, I thought, that news alone would have earned me a purse.

We lay low and watched the troopers. If the young cavalier riding so proudly at the head of his men even suspected where we were hiding, we would be taken, without a doubt. Thirteen horsemen could ring the thicket. Thirteen long swords were more than enough, and two runners offered a rare chance for sport. I've seen a fleeing peasant take a dozen terrible sword slashes from as many riders before loss of blood brought him down. I could feel their eyes scanning the place where we lay, before the officer gave a sharp command, and his troopers spread out. They began to quarter the level ground at the foot of the fell, cantering back and forth, searching, thrusting with their sword blades into bushes. I heard the soft whit as Will Blacket's dagger cleared its scabbard.

A jab in the air from the officer's whip sent a single horseman cantering up the bank towards where we lay.

'Let 'im get well inside the bushes. I'll bring 'im off.' Will's voice was less than a whisper but I heard every word. 'You mount up. I'll hold onto your stirrup and we'll away up the fell before the buggers realise it.'

We waited as the cavalryman put his horse at the bank. The beast was willing enough but its flailing hooves sent showers of stone and clay scattering as it fought for a footing. He tried twice. We were close enough to hear him swear at his mount and I could smell the horse's sweet breath and the wax on the trooper's gear. Will put out his dagger arm and poised himself to spring up.

The roar of laughter that followed the short whinnying squeal and the crash as horse and rider went over startled me. There was a short trumpet flourish followed by a rumble and clatter as the troop gathered and formed up. An order was shouted, and when I dared to look again, all I could see were the horses' rumps as the troopers galloped back towards the Tyne Bridge.

The noise that rumbled deep inside Will's chest might have been a sigh of relief, but it sounded like the growl of a wolf cheated of its prey. 'Uniforms, Captain ...' He spat contemptuously into the grass and put away his dagger. 'New uniforms, new gear, even down to new pennants and a silver trumpet. That's what saved us. Cavalrymen don't like gettin' their uniforms dirty.' Will was squinting at me. He was curious about something. 'You saw him, you recognised the bastard?'

I must have shown that I had not, and Will looked askance at me. 'The man on the black horse ...' It was only then that I realised that the rider who failed to reach us had been Bone, Sergeant Mouncey Bone.

We lay in the hawthorn thicket until it was almost dark. There was much coming and going along the road below us, but no more troops passed that way. Across the river, in Newcastle, the torches and lanterns outside the houses began to glow red in the smoky blue dusk. I listened to the town's clocks chime and ships' bells ring across the dark water. My mind began to run on everything that had happened in the last few days. I thought of my fight with the freelances and my first meeting with Mouncey Bone. My collarbone began to ache at the memory. For the first time I remembered that I had done nothing to find out what had become of my uncle Ralph. Now it was likely to be too late for that. The strangely wan face of my fey sister-in-law, Margaret, came into my thoughts. She was a Bronsard – yet I felt sorry for her. Then I snorted aloud at the realisation that if that poor glaikie creature was my sister-in-law then in like fashion I was myself kin to Bronsard. I had not thought of that before.

'We'll need some gear, Captain.' I had been deep in thought when Will Blacket woke with a start and sat up. From somewhere in his coat he pulled a flask and offered it to me. I took a swig of very passable brandy. 'And we had better find that mare of yours,' he added.

I had been thinking the same thing. It was just another broken shard of my dream, but one well worth picking up. The mare was a splendid animal. At sale it would fetch enough to pay for two shipboard passages, and leave enough over to see us through until we were drawing pay again.

'I would ... ' said Will hesitating. It was not the bold musketeer's way to hold back.

'Spit it out man ... ' I waved a hand and lifted an eyebrow at him. 'Say what it is you have to.'

For a moment he looked almost bashful. 'There's a woman, Meg, the widow I've mentioned ... ' He paused to see how I might be taking his words and I nodded him on. 'I promised to meet her tonight, and I was thinking that she would be able to tell us what state things lie in. Old Mistress Thornton will ha' learned o' the day's doin's.'

He paused again. 'We might be ridin' away from a battle that isn't lost … ' His wicked grin cheered me. 'Somethin's happened that has kicked the tripes out of our enterprise, but as long as we keep ourselves outside Newcastle's walls and on this side of the Tyne – and step very canny – the hue and cry won't stay hot for more than a day or two.'

Will looked at me expectantly. I knew that he had made himself at home in Hannah Thornton's house – and in a young widow's bed. I could understand his not wanting to leave his woman without a word. We were both old soldiers come home to look for a comfortable billet away from the wars. Thoughts of Aphra Thornton had flitted back and forth across my mind the whole of that afternoon. But so too did thoughts of the company of musketeers that had been turned out to hunt me down. They had opened fire with bare warning, and put a musket ball into a townsman on the public quay in a way that spoke Authority, powers way above those of the Town Watch.

Despite misgivings, we went, setting out in darkness, Will leading and I following through the moonlight, keeping him just in sight. We took a roundabout route, walking softly, and flanking houses and cottages as best we could until at last we came to the Pipewellgate at Gateshead.

The good burghers of Newcastle's neighbour town built no walls, doubtless reckoning that with Newcastle's walls and the width of the river Tyne between them and the Scots they were safe enough.

We entered the town and avoided the Watch easily. Will had arranged to meet his woman at the fountain where the big elmwood pipes carry the town's water down from the spring at the Pant Head.

I stood back in the shadows to let Will talk to his Meg alone. They spoke for a long time and the moon had set before he came back, but I begrudged them not at all.

'Jesu, Captain, what a day … ' He shook his head as though he could hardly believe what he had heard. 'We've lost a lot of men … or the truth is that we've lost a pair o' women. The bastards have taken up Mistress Aphra. She was arrested under King's warrant this morning and taken off in nought but her shift …' His voice fell. 'Dame Hannah got away by going down through her coal cellar and hailing a passing boat from the bridge pier. Then the old woman stood up in the boat shaking her fist at the bastards while the musket balls splashed around her.' I could see it. 'And then Sir Joseph Ord has fled the town. He's been ... ' Will sought to recollect the word. 'Attainted or some such.' He looked at me for help.

'Attaindered? Was that the word Will?' I watched his face as he thought. Then he nodded slowly.

'Aye ... attaindered, that's what my Meg said. What does that mean, Captain?'

'Attaindered means that you cease to exist in law at all, Will; it means that you have no rights and they take every scrap of property you and your family owns. It's one of the ways that a King has of beggaring a man he suspects of treason.'

I was hardly listening to Will's questions at all. My thoughts were running way ahead, and along many different tracks at once, all concerning the fate of Aphra. I had no doubts about the treatment that a woman, even a gentlewoman, would suffer when she was questioned in a matter of treason. I felt a spasm of rage rise up hot inside me; yet even as it rose, I knew that I could do nothing but throw away my life if I raised a hand, or took a step to help her.

'That's why there's twenty or so royal troopers billeted and makin' Liberty Hall in Sir Joseph's house.' Will's words interrupted my thoughts.

In Germany, we had billeted ourselves as we pleased, and behaved as we wanted, but I knew that more care had to be taken in England. A man of quite middling quality might take the commander of troops before the justices to claim recompense, even for such trifles as stolen chickens. Someone was uncommonly certain of his legal ground; or else had hard evidence of a crime against the King.

'Aye, Captain ... My Meg says that all was done by special order of the new King's Officer, a 'Commissioner' I think she called him.'

Will opened a cloth and handed me a thick slice of coarse barley bread and a slab of yellow cheese. The bread had been filled out with potato flour, and the cheese had more salt than was good for either it or me, but I hadn't eaten since morning and my guts were grateful to be filled again.

'King's Commissioner ... ' I had heard of the title before, in Sweden. I had never had to stand before such an official, but I had seen the blanched faces of officers who had swaggered in to testify before an enquiry into missing military stores, and they had been proud Swedish noblemen. No royal commissioner had anything to learn from the Holy Inquisition.

'At least Meg was able to tell us where your mare is kept, Captain. That gives us a head start, and maybe there'll be a nag for me to ride.' I could tell that Will was looking at me, trying to guess my intentions, as he went on. 'Best we quit this country for a season or two … ' There was more than half a question in his words. I had seen no more of his Meg than the flare of her red hair, but whether or not she was comely, there were obvious signs that he did not want to leave her.

I offered him no answer, for I had the same questions in my own mind. 'Where does Meg say the mare is being kept?' I asked instead.

My bones ached and I was tired. I knew too little about the happenings of the day to make a decision about a course of action. An outlying farm where Hannah Thornton's name carried weight could perhaps serve us well. We needed two or three days out of sight. A warrant for arrest would last for a hundred years, but my experience was that a hot pursuit soon cooled itself off.

'D'you know the village of Swalwell, Captain?'

I did, but only as distant smoke rising above trees. I had never been there though it lay directly across the valley from my family's farm, close to where the River Derwent joined the Tyne.

'Well, there's a farm about a half mile above the village. The farmer is said to have a rare way wi' horses, so that's where Mistress Thornton sent the mare.'

I sighed as I stooped to drink the sweet water that spurted from cracks in the wooden pipes.

It was no easy walk from Pipewellgate to Swalwell. The low land along the river was still swamped with floodwater, so we had to tramp a roundabout way that added some miles to our road. The village was silent as we walked through it, and turned up the hillside to find the farm.

Any pair of fellows who come on foot, knocking at the door of a lonely farm before full daylight, are likely to be met with a crossbow quarrel or a charge of bird-shot. The eastern sky was lightening with a false dawn when we got there, but on my reckoning there would not be a soul up and about for a full hour.

We moved into a little wood from where we could see the farm, and sat down to wait until we should see smoke from a fire, or a maid with a milking pail. I had dropped into a fitful sleep when Will's gentle tap brought me fully alert. There were riders coming up the lane and I dropped gently from the fallen log I had lain on and rolled quietly into its shelter.

There were four of them, and my first fear was that they were King's troopers, come to search the farm, but even in the grey of morning I could see that they were not garrison riders. All wore buff leather jerkins, and breastplates of half-armour, but beyond that each man wore no uniform.

Riders commonly laugh and talk, but there was no sound from these four; they rode warily, with a hand to the long pistols in their saddle holsters. As they halted before the farm, a door opened, and a lad ran out to guide them to the stables.

'Now there's a mystery, Captain,' Will said as he crawled across to where I lay. 'What are four Jock officers doin' here so early on a fine morning?'

'Scots?' I whispered. I had neither seen nor heard anything to identify the riders. Will gave a little chuckle.

'Trust me to pick out an officer by the way he sits a horse alone.' The grin widened. 'And who else but Scots would not have a piece of uniform gear the same between the four o' them ... save a blue bonnet?'

We waited. Candle light glowed and shifted briefly across a window, and was snuffed out. We saw the lad run out to the woodpile for an armful of logs, then later reappear with a milking stool and a bucket. Of the visitors, there was no sign.

'I think it best that we wait until it is full daylight before we make an approach. We can go back down the lane and come up openly making as much noise as we can.' I watched to see how Will took my suggestion.

'Four blue-bonnets comin' to a farmhouse this far south of the border ... at night. They are here on secret business, that much I can smell. They would not thank us for our presence here.' Will looked uneasy, as he continued. 'We can lie up here a while longer, but if those riders haven't gone by noon I think we should move. We can get some food down in Swalwell. It might be safer to send word up to the farm from the inn. Mistress Thornton's name would maybe clear a way for us.'

'Indeed it might, Captain Ellyot!' The voice was sharp and carried. We crouched down by the log. I put my head up and snatched a glance about. It was almost my last. The sharp crack of a light gun, and the hollow thunk as a musket ball lodged in the rotten timber no more than a hand's breadth from my head, made me press my body close to the leaf mould.

A man who knew my name was unlikely to shoot me out of hand, *and* there was something distinctly familiar about the voice.

'You have the advantage of me, Sir.' I called out.

'Indeed I do ... ' There was a hint of laughter in his reply. I was a little relieved – but only a little. There are men who delight in playing with their victims as a cat plays with a mouse. 'Indeed, I have had the advantage for a while now. Had I not recognised you, then I would have put a wee ball through your eye a quarter of an hour ago, but sight of you reminded me that I owe you three Swedish crowns.' He laughed. 'A crumb o' lead would prove a grand way of extinguishing a debt.'

'I forgive you the debt freely ... Lieutenant Alexander McLeish of the Seaton's Regiment.' His name came to me in a rush as I caught sight of him standing between the close forked twin trunks of an ash tree.

'Ach! John ... ' The regret sounded genuine. 'That's what comes of my having a Christian soul. I should have shot you anyway, you'd be dead now and none the wiser.'

I had spent a long Finnish winter playing cards with McLeish. He played recklessly, but he had studied for the Kirk, and his philosophical talk had been worth listening to – in small drams.

'You see the way of it is ... John, I am here under my commission. I have my orders.'

'Aye ... you were ever one for carrying out your orders.' I had expected to hear McLeish laugh at that. Instead, I caught the sharp click of the ratchet as he spanned back the spring of a wheelock. It was then that I saw that Will had vanished.

'So you mean to kill me?' The question was ridiculous. Alex McLeish would certainly shoot. I was as convinced of that as I was of anything, and yet the idea that I was about to be killed was beyond my belief. I had been as close to death before, often, and at those times I had known it. But now there was a feeling of unreality about the situation. I rose to my feet and looked to the place where McLeish stood and began to walk forward.

'Stand, I say!' he ordered me, with the merest tinge of hesitation in his voice. Now I could see the muzzle of the gun pointing out from between the twin trunks. It wavered – and then it steadied. I think that McLeish changed his mind at the same instant that Will Blacket charged. I saw him as a dark shape that rose from the ground and moved to come up behind McLeish. Had it not been for the vantage point he had chosen, the Scot would have turned easily and shot Will as he charged, but the whee-lock caught between the twin trunks as he tried to twist around. It gave just enough time and Will launched himself headlong.

The two men locked. McLeish gripped Will's wrists and was trying to loose the powerful fingers from his throttle. They fell to the ground struggling as I picked up the gun.

'Enough!' I shouted. Both men stiffened. Will looked up. There was a faint red glaze to the whites of his eyes. He shook his head sharply a couple of times and then, almost as an afterthought, he eased his grip on McLeish's neck.

'Yes ... Enough!' came the crisp order from behind us. 'We have, gentlemen, more to do with our time than to brawl like drunken soldiers.'

He sat his mare as straight-backed as a general at an imperial parade, the white linen bands at his neck stark against the solemn black of his coat, a grim yet half whimsical look on his face. We had found Sylvanus Webster, or rather, Sylvanus Webster had found us.

Chapter 18

A Fanatical Plot

Will Blacket had been right in his judgement of the riders. Their loud Scots talk hushed, and we were treated to surly looks when we walked into the kitchen. The soft creak of leather and the scrape of steel as all three readied themselves to clear their blades was not lost on me. The stamp of command was clearly on each of them. They were clearly officers. I bit off a smile when I saw that my servant had stiffened to attention in their presence.

'Gentlemen ... ' Sylvanus Webster walked over to the kitchen fireplace and stood rubbing his hands before the flames. 'You find yourselves together as strangers. Let me assure you – all – that the men here are loyal supporters of the same great cause.' He looked from face to face before he went on. 'That is as much as I feel it prudent to say. For the sake of secrecy I ask you to keep your talk to matters of polite interest ... as between gentlemen, and spare one another the burden of an exchange of names.' Webster glanced at McLeish, who was feeling the livid marks on his throat where Will had squeezed it. 'You, Lieutenant McLeish, knew Captain Ellyot when you were both in the Swedish service, so this is a fortunate re-union of old acquaintances. That is good.'

He paused long enough for the strength of the warning carried in his voice to be plain enough. He then continued, 'But since gentlemen must address one another in some civil fashion, let me give Captain Ellyot some names for these three officers.'

He stood in the middle of the kitchen, a hand on his chin while he thought. 'I have it.' His face lit with some old private joke, and he pointed in turn: 'Master Leith and Master Granton are apt names, but unrevealing.' The two riders he pointed to seemed to think so too. 'And Colonel ... Dundas.' The older man threw his head back and laughed quietly. Clearly they would not make me privy to the joke, but I knew that among the Covenanters the rank of colonel often signified that the man was also a nobleman, and that no mere kailyard laird.

'We understand, Master Webster,' he said in a soft clear voice. I guessed that he came from Aberdeen or thereabouts. 'We have ridden hard and far and need food and sleep. When we have restored ourselves we can complete our transaction here and be on our separate ways, with goodwill on all sides.'

'Colonel Dundas' looked older by ten or more years than his comrades, and his war gear looked well used. The face carried a few old scars; but the grey eyes were warm enough. I guessed that if I addressed myself to him in Swedish, he would answer readily. That he was leader was clear enough from the way that Alexander McLeish had evaded his glance. That young officer would have to find an explanation for the fact that my man Will had the fine wheelock rifle in his hands.

We exchanged bows and inspected one another. They all looked as though they had ridden far. As their clothes dried out in the heat of the kitchen the splashes of road filth began to show up clearly, and they had red rims to their eyelids that spoke of sore windburn and want of sleep. I took the gun from Will and offered it, two-handed, to Alexander McLeish.

'An understandable mistake, Alex ... and no harm done,' I said quietly.

If McLeish had wished to speak he was already too late. Before his lips could move, Colonel Dundas answered for him, a smile playing across his weatherbeaten face.

'Certainly, Captain Ellyot, no harm done, and this young gentleman is in your debt for a sound lesson in the proper care of his weapons.' The chuckle from the other two Scots released any trace of tension that had stood between us.

Plain bacon and soft wheaten bread had been laid out, with new ale to drink, and there was more than enough for two extra men. Room at the table was made for me and I allowed Will to serve me. I think that the Scots must have envied me my servant, for Will suddenly became the very paragon of an officer's man. He stopped the clanking smoke-jack turning before the fire, and without shame sliced me the best meat off the joint of bacon, and garnished a hot earthenware plate with neatly cut bread dipped in the drippings. Then he stood behind me with a white cloth laid over his arm while I ate. And while I ate, the Scots watched.

'A long silence is a terrible burden for a man to carry,' said Colonel Dundas, tapping the ash out of his long tobacco pipe as he stood up. 'So we will not be giving offence if we wish you … ' he paused and looked out of the window where a full bright day had broken, 'a guid nicht.'

Will relaxed as soon as the Scots had left, but he did not let up in his service. There was a kettle of hot water on the hob, and he found a razor, soap, and towels. He wasn't satisfied until he had me stripped to my shirt and had shaved me. I let him hover while I decided over my scalp where a golden fuzz like a three day's growth of beard had sprouted. John Ellyot had been the name I had been challenged by along the quayside at Newcastle. Mijnheer Ter Brugencate had served his purpose so I waved the razor away.

In spite of the cheer of a good breakfast and a close shave, my bones ached with tiredness, but I knew that I should not sleep before I had seen my mare. The farmer's lad led me out to a stone-built barn up the hillside, away from the farm proper. I could find no fault with the stabling. The mare looked well, her coat had a good healthy gloss and I saw that there were good brown beans in her feeding trough, and clean water in a tub. I was content – but sight of the beast brought the uncertainty of the plans I had cherished, like a knot of colic, into my guts.

'That is a fine animal you have there, Captain Ellyot.' I had not heard Webster come up behind me. 'She will foal next year?'

'Late in July,' I said wistfully, as I turned to look at him. 'Whether I am alive to see it or not.'

Webster raised his chin and looked hard at me for an instant, before turning his head to gaze out of the doorway and up the Tyne valley.

'We are squeezed tighter than we were at this time yesterday.' He stopped and listened attentively for a moment. I listened too, but heard nothing untoward. For Webster, listening was, I realised, no more than an ingrained habit.

'You made a bold escape from the quayside steps at Newcastle yesterday,' he went on, watching my face as I stared at him. 'I saw it all. I stood no more than a short musket shot from you. Indeed, it was I who put the toe of my boot into the fundament of that soldier and sent the poor fellow pitching headlong into the Tyne. So, you see, it was perhaps as well that I saw you. It had been in my mind to approach you, but I stayed back out of caution, or we might both have been taken.' He narrowed his eyes and squinted into the sun, just showing over the trees. 'You were betrayed ... we were *all* betrayed ... Sir Joseph Ord ... Mistress Thornton ... and myself ... ' His mouth twitched wryly. 'Yes, Captain Ellyot, I, myself, betrayed us all. I tried to dangle more strings than I had fingers for and I allowed Bronsard to slip from my sight for a few days. In that time messengers came from the Court of St James. Nicholas Bronsard is appointed special Commissioner, and charged with securing the King's safety, should he come to Newcastle.'

Webster's words explained much. Bronsard was using the power of the King's warrant to his own ends. Arrests, of no matter whom, would simply not be questioned. Clearly, Nicholas Bronsard could call upon royal troops from the Castle to help him exercise his commission. I knew only too well that he had already done that much, but it also explained the unsoldierly fashion of the search that the Castle cavalry had carried out the day before. No garrison commander would willingly bow to a knave of a town merchant, no matter what sheet of parchment he waved.

'And how long is Master Nicholas to be endowed with the King's favour?' I asked

'As I have it from a man who stood close to the Town Hall steps, when Master Bronsard read his commission for all the townsfolk to hear, he is to protect the King's person and dignity for so long as His Majesty shall remain within the bounds of the town of Newcastle.

'Then he anticipates his power,' I mused, 'for the King is surely not yet within the town ... and may not come at all. Charles Stuart delays at York. He has an army that is ill-equipped and has little stomach either to march or to fight. More than half of the wretches are pressed men. People think that he is in no hurry to travel through his Scottish realm, so it seems likely that the Scots will be spared having to use His Majesty's new hymn books, or bend to the power of the Lords Spiritual.'

Even in Sweden I had heard a little of the attempt to impose the English church style of worship onto the Scottish nation.

'A sheet of parchment is cheap at the price.' Webster looked hard at me. 'It gives Nicholas Bronsard leave to clear the streets and fill the lock-ups with the town's beggars and thieves … as well as those he sees as having slighted him, or perhaps owe the House of Bronsard money, and, lassies who secretly publish scurrilous broadsheets, uttering base calumnies against some of the town's most worshipful merchants.'

It had not occurred to me that Aphra had been involved in the spreading of the broadsheets. Women had no business in such matters. I cared about the lass, and I knew that I cared desperately what became of her.

'What will they do?' I asked, trying to look disinterested, even when the words caught in my throat. Webster was not deceived. 'As of this morning she has not been charged with any offence. Her name is on no calendar of the town Justices. I was in Newcastle last night to find that out. I came upon you only because I was returning from my enquiries. Aphra Thornton was arrested on the power of Bronsard's warrant alone. I think he will soon realise that he acted in haste.'

'But where is she … what are they …?' Webster's hand rested firmly on my shoulder. His gaze cut off my question in mid-sentence.

'I do not know where she is being held. I have men scouring the town and beyond. Don't concern yourself about Aphra Thornton. You have other duties now.'

There was no mistaking the direct order from a man who was used to having his commands obeyed to the letter. 'You will not interfere! Leave this business to those whom I have appointed. Know, John Ellyot, that the lass is very dear to me,' Webster's hand left my shoulder, 'but we all have our tasks assigned. Your business lies beneath the sea … and there only! You must strive to raise … '

'The guns?'

Webster did not so much as flutter an eyelid.

'Aye, Captain Ellyot, there are indeed guns to be lifted from the seabed. And I must make you concentrate on that.' Again the twitch of the lip that passed for a smile. 'And while I do that, Mistress Hannah Thornton has undertaken to secure the release of the girl, Aphra.'

'But the old woman … ' I began my protest.

'The old woman still owns her wits. No she-wolf ever sought her cub the way Mistress Hannah stalks that town. No alderman, no hostman will be allowed to rest easy until that lass is safe. Mistress Hannah will be winnowing out the dust from family skeletons. Grave cloths wrapping the shameful deeds of folk dead these fifty years are being readied for a brisk shake and a wafting in the frowsty air of the all town's closes and chares.'

I could well imagine what Hannah Thornton would do. It was a woman's way, but it was likely to be every bit as desperate as a fight with hard steel. The thought gave me no comfort. I wanted, I needed, to hack my way through Bronsard, meat and bone, to get to Aphra.

'You are not to concern yourself with what becomes of the girl. Let me be concerned for you. Unlike you, I am able to move about in the daylight. Bronsard now has a greater need than ever to take you, and that means that you are worth a deal more to them alive than dead.'

I was puzzled. 'A *greater* need? What greater need?'

'You left your drawings and suchlike in your room at Sir Joseph Ord's house, did you not?' There was no anger in Webster's tone, we might have been discussing a bag left behind at an inn. I nodded slowly. To tell the truth, I had not given the plans of the diving bell so much as a minute's thought since I had laid them aside the day before. 'Good!' Webster's response surprised me. 'Good ... very good ... most excellent, good.' He rubbed his hands together, his body poised as though he was about to begin a little caper of joy. There was a sudden brightness in his face. 'Ha!' The sound was almost a bark. Then, almost as though he was ashamed of the outburst, he shut his mouth and seemed to sink within his own thoughts for a while before saying, 'At last Divine Providence has afforded us a little of its light.'

'Master Webster,' I said, looking at him hard, 'I could wish that the same Divine Providence would show *me* the way, for it is certain that you have not. I have been cozened with fairy tales of sunken guns among the Farne Islands. Are there truly such guns?'

Webster pulled a bench from against the stable wall and sat down. It seemed that he had to hunt for words. He gave his fine head a short sharp shake as though to signify that he had made a decision.

'No; there were never any guns off the Farnes, but we have led everyone to think that that is where the guns are. We had charts expertly drawn, and allowed them to pass as a great secret from hand to hand, but they were an elaborate ruse. I have said before that what a man, or indeed a woman, does not know, they cannot be made to tell. Sir Joseph, Dame Hannah ... and even Aphra Thornton, all thought as you thought, but the guns are not within a half day's sail of the Farne Islands.'

'So that Mistress Thornton could be tortured into telling ... '

'Your carelessness with the plans for the diving bells has saved her from that at least. Bronsard will not take long to know what your plans and drawings mean. He will doubtless also have found the false maps which I gave to Sir Joseph Ord.'

I marvelled at the man. It seemed to me that he had garnished a ruse with the lives of his own people. Aphra could lawfully be put to torture and risk being crippled, just to keep Webster's make-believe secrets.

'So the lass stands to suffer the iron boot or the thumbscrews to save your worthless stories?' I asked, coldly.

He looked at me. For an instant I thought that he would be angry, but he sighed, and put his head in his hands. 'Master Webster, have you heard the crunch of a man's ankle bones as the wedges are given that last gentle tap?' he asked.

I bent and whispered softly to him, 'Aye ... '

His words were distant. 'And *I* have seen the blood spurt as a man's ears were sawn off. I have seen a woman's eyes threaten to bulge from their sockets as the cord was twisted. Three times I have heard the axe fall.' He looked up at me and I knew he was telling the truth. 'My body has suffered only a little,' he murmured as he pulled up the sleeve of his coat. The brown scars were faint but deep. At some time Webster had been manacled tight, and I guessed that he had been hung up in chains so that his own weight caused the iron to bite into his wrists. 'That only made my resolve stronger. There is no place for the sovereignty of earthly kings in these islands, north or south.'

His fanatic look returned. Webster's cause had taken hold of him again. He paused and took a handful of small silver coins from a bulging purse and held them out. There was a soft tinkle, as pieces spilled between my fingers onto the stone floor. They were silver groats, fourpenny pieces, the purse must have held several hundred of them. I held a single one of the coins to the sunlight coming in through the door. The coin was new, cleanly struck and unworn. All of the coins were newly minted. I handed them back to him.

'Charles Stuart's time is coming,' he said as he stooped and picked up one of the fallen silver pieces.' A king's head ... severed!' I watched the man, fascinated. In his fervour, he had gone from sane to almost mad, and back to sanity, in the space of just a minute. His eyes were bright and eager.

'There is an order of business which we must follow. No matter whose life is in jeopardy, that order will be followed.' His tone softened. 'Fortunately for your peace of mind, Captain Ellyot, this day will see a very great part of my task accomplished. Our Scots friends go back to the Border, laden with ... a bunch of the first ripe grapes from Canaan.'

I was in no state of mind to wrestle with passages from Scripture and I cared even less for secret correspondence between Master Webster and the Scottish Assembly, but it seemed that these things were intertwined. I waited for him to go on.

'Tonight will see the last load of silver handed over to the Scots.' He breathed deeply as though he had just set down a great weight. 'Every fortnight since March, I have weighed out small silver coin for them. I wonder that a housewife can break a shilling for change anywhere south of Lincoln after I have drawn so many coins from England these last months.'

I understood. Webster was paying the Scots a subsidy and small silver coin was pay for troops. An army on campaign might go a year without seeing a penny piece in pay, but no army would take the field without something paid on account. Certainly, no man would be fool enough to take a Scots army, officer or man, into the field unless he had the means to pay every soldier, cavalry, pikeman or musketeer, his due at the end of the first month.

'So the English are paying the Jocks to invade their country?' In spite of myself I laughed. 'It may cost you more than that to get them to go home.'

'Better the Scots than the devil-worshipper we have now.' Webster looked at me keenly. 'Think about it, Captain. You are now a traitor, a fugitive with a price upon your head, you are dispossessed of your land, and the lass you would have as your sweetheart is a prisoner – and every deed has been according to the law of the land.' He paused to let me reflect for a moment. 'But the day General Leslie's Scots enter Newcastle upon Tyne all of that will be changed. Instead of a traitor, you'll be a hero.' For a moment I thought that Webster was laughing at me. 'Your land will be in your hands again. Nicholas Bronsard will have fled the town. There will be no witnesses against you on any charge, no scrap of record of any charge ... and, all being well, you can court the Thornton lassie to your heart's content ... though of course I cannot vouch for hers.'

I saw that what Webster said was true, or perhaps that it could become true. Yet the idea that I was part of a conspiracy to bring a horde of bare-arsed Scots into my own town was an uncomfortable one.

'You don't like it?' Webster had been watching me closely. 'The Scots will be under strict military discipline every step of the way; for as long as they are in the North they will pay for everything that they take.'

My sudden laughter startled the mare. I laughed again, and cocked a disbelieving eye at Webster.

'Master Webster, do you think I am a bairn to be happy with such honey-tit tales? No army that ever marched conducted itself as you say the Scots will. You can have blood-soaked Provosts Marshal who are the very fiends from hell. You can hang a dozen of your own men a day, and still that will not stop rape and pillage. Armies cut a wide swathe, Master Webster. With twenty-thousand bellies to fill they can do no other. They strip the country as they pass across it. Do you think that the Border farmer cares whether the army is the King's or the Covenant's when his cattle are driven off?' It was plain to me that Webster had hardly thought of such matters. 'What of his wife and daughters ... raped, and raped again, and again?'

'General Leslie has agreed ... ' I had taken Webster aback.

I lifted a leg and stuck it out straight before me. 'Pull it, Master Webster. It is hung with silver hawkbells! Not even the wee crooked man himself can guarantee his men's conduct. Have you seen a line of infantry waver and break? No man cries 'run', but still an unspoken message, a contagion, passes down the line. The same thing happens when troops begin a massacre. I have seen it a dozen times.'

'There may be much in what you say, Captain Ellyot,' Webster replied, seemingly unmoved, 'but this enterprise is now well underway. We are committed; and so are you. The last of the subsidy money will be in Edinburgh within a few days. General Leslie's army will march into England soon enough.'

'And it will march upon London?' I knew well that the Scots could field at most thirty-thousand men. That was nowhere near enough to attempt the overthrow of Charles Stuart. 'Do you conspire with the Scots, Master Webster, to invade your own country?'

Webster had a ready answer.

'The Scots will attempt to occupy the town of Newcastle and perhaps Durham. The aim is to deny the King the revenue he is paid from Newcastle's coals.'

I think that Webster realised that he had said more than he meant to say, for he then pressed his lips together.

'And the Scots will take the entire revenues of Newcastle. They will sell the coals as though they belonged to themselves.' I heard myself snort with derision at the idea. 'Aye, Master Webster, General Leslie may not be able to read or write with any ease, but he knows that there is enough profit in the enterprise to have him keep his men in check while the Scottish nation fills its purse fat and tight with my town's money.'

I think the heat of my attack surprised Webster, but he did not defend himself. The slow shake of his head and the pursing of his thin lips conceded the case to me.

'I bow to your experience,' he said coldly, 'but none of it can concern you. You will go to Bishopwearmouth tonight,' Webster hesitated, 'that is where the guns are.'

I was more than astonished as Webster went on, 'You may as well know the story now, for events move too quickly and too powerfully for you to do anything to stop them.' He sighed, and suddenly looked utterly exhausted. 'Certain Norwich merchants wished to foster the Scots' cause. You will understand that they have common cause of religion with the Lowland Scots. They collected money, which they sent to Bruges. It was agreed that the gold was to be used to buy heavy ordnance for as you must know, the Scots were always short of cannon.'

Again Webster paused and listened. I could hear the breeze rustling the leaves and the steady sound of someone at work with a scythe. Caution was burned into the man's very bones.

'The munitions were loaded into three vessels. The ships set sail, roundabout courses but courses that would eventually fetch them to the port of Leith. Two cargoes arrived at Leith and the arms are with the Scots now, but the last ship, the *Gerda of Ems*, did not arrive. That was in February. We had thought that the ship had foundered in the great storm that had struck the North East coast while the ships were on passage, so we had to reconcile ourselves to the loss of cannon.'

Webster had risen and begun to pace the length of the stable. He put a hand out to the mare and patted her neck absently.

'The loss of those guns was a sore trial. Four bronze cannon royal ... great ship's ordnance.'

As he spoke I saw something akin to awe in Webster's face. Four cannon royal, perhaps the biggest single pieces of ordnance that could be moved on a wheeled gun-carriage. A single cannon royal could smash any town's walls with a few dozen shots. Fear of such giant pieces had been enough to make a town surrender its keys without resistance. Four of them would make a fearsome battery.

'But the ship did not sink in the open sea.' Webster had gone on with his tale while I had still been picturing the damage that the big guns could do, would do. 'The master attempted to run his ship into the mouth of the Wear. He was almost successful.' Sylvanus Webster put his fine hands together as though he was about to pray. 'The *Gerda of Ems* sank within a bowshot of the Wearmouth shore.'

Chapter 19

An Old Acquaintance

I was in better fettle when I left Swalwell than when I got there. Twelve hours' sleep in the sweet hay stored above my mare's stabling had taken the ache from my bones. Will brought me cold roast beef and dark crusted flat-cake, still warm from the oven. Washed down with farm-brewed beer the good vittles set me up. And somewhere he had found a leather jerkin to cover the mud caked rags of Dirk ter Bruggencate's Dutch finery. All in all, I ought to have been restored.

But none of these things eased my mind as they should. The thought of Aphra Thornton in the hands of Nicholas Bronsard haunted me, nagged at me along the blurred edges of my consciousness. I had wakened hoping that Sylvanus Webster would have news for me.

But Webster had left. The only souls that Will could find about the farm were the farmer's lad and a wall-eyed old biddie-wife, deaf as a post, who responded to questions with a cackle of laughter. Will questioned the lad with all his guile, and the offer of a silver sixpence. That proved to be an error, for the lad at once became suspicious of us and would say no more than that Doctor Webster was gone away and would not return for some days.

Doctor Webster! I found myself curiously unsurprised. A doctor? A doctor of Physick or of Theology? I guessed that Webster was a doctor of Religion. I had been right in my first impression. Strange, but what odds? I had learned a tiny crumb more about the man, but it did not help me at all. Then I asked the lad about the Scots. The answer was terse, sullen almost: 'Gone.' The lad was no more than twelve but clearly he had been taught to guard his tongue, and he kept his silence as he led out three sturdy fell ponies, mounted himself, and waited.

We rode out across the land between the Tyne and the Wear under a full moon.

Our way took us by twisting paths between high hedges and led us by no direct road. Yet I was not nearly so lost as I let the lad think as I allowed him to guide us. The broad lie of the land across Durham I knew well enough. First we struck south and east until we met the Wear below Penshaw Hill. Then we crossed to the south side and followed its course to the east.

We moved fast, and yet we were cautious. Once we had to turn away and go wide around the blazing watch fires of an encampment where there were more than a dozen pikemen set as sentries, and a line of tethered horses.

'Yon's a draft o' pressed men, Captain. The pikemen are there to see that no bugger runs off.' Will's whisper carried through the darkness. I could tell that he was amused. 'Them's no soldiers to face the Jocks with.'

I bent my head in agreement. The camp was set out in no sort of order, the men huddled together to make the best of the few blankets they shared. The flames of the watch fires were fed to give light. Will jerked his head in the direction of the sleeping men and grinned. He wanted to rouse the camp with a false alarm but I denied him with a wag of a finger. Troops being herded north to reinforce the Newcastle garrison. That would be a pointless cruelty to the poor devils. They would be roused soon enough, and the sight of them offered a little piece of intelligence for Webster's ears.

Daybreak found us within sight of the white limestone valley that had been sundered open where the Wear broke through to meet the sea. We had to heel our ponies' flanks to keep up with the lad guiding us. It was almost as if he had a fear of the sunrise.

At the top of the steep limestone cliffs we stopped. A wall of fog stood across our way. The small riverside towns of the two Wearmouths lay below us and I could smell the coal smoke rising up through the swirling sea fret. A church bell began to chime slowly; the steady distant thud of a shipwright's axe started up as a man began his day's work.

We reached Wearmouth, Bishopwearmouth, on the south bank of the river. But it would have been blind folly to have ridden downhill into the unseen town without some idea of what welcome we would find there. With the luck I had enjoyed recently, we were likely to find a troop of horse waiting for us in the market square with a noose at the ready. I sat for a moment, silent, with the steam from my pony's coat rising around me.

'What say, Captain?' Will rode up alongside me. 'An hour's wait won't hurt us ... and might save us a deal o' sorrow.'

'Very well Will, but you can go on foot and look over the ground.' I knew what the old soldier wanted to do. 'I'll kick my heels here for an hour or so.' The white scar on Will's face showed briefly as he gave a ferocious wink and a lopsided grin. He would enjoy himself.

'And what am I to look for, Captain?' He had slid down over his pony's rump and was standing at my saddle bow.

'Tall horses tied up before taverns, and the men who ride them. If you see even one man in a King's coat come away at once. Beyond that, use your wits.'

Will's broad frame was out of sight before he had taken a dozen strides into the fog. If all was well, he should be back within an hour. It was a proper precaution, no more.

The lad broke his silence, 'I'll need to take the ponies back, Captain.'

'Wait,' I answered. 'When Will returns, and if all is well, you shall have leave to go.'

'I have other work. The ponies are needed,' he replied. In the North we take no exception to being spoken to plainly.

'Other work?' I said pleasantly. 'Mast ... Doctor Webster spoke to me of no other work to be done today. And of no other work more important than you have done tonight. And I hope it will be my pleasure to tell him how well you have done that, when next I see him.'

The flattery took hold – just. The lad sat straight in the saddle. I looked at him squarely as though he was standing for inspection. It never fails. At heart all men love the game of soldiers. I held him with my gaze.

'But you were saying that there was other work to be done ... ' I spoke softly as though the matter were of little importance to me.

'I've to fetch the lady.'

My heart and spirit leapt together and then plunged. 'Mistress Thornton?' I asked, suddenly hard of breath. I had not caught him out. He was telling me because he wanted to.

'Aye ... '

'That would be young Mistress Thornton or ...?' Surely old Hannah would never ride a pony at her age.

'I know not, Sir,' he said brightly. 'If 'tis the young'un I get a halfpence, but if 'tis Mistress Hannah, why then I get a clip o' the lug and a silver sixpence.' Suddenly he was just a lad again.

'Take the ponies then, lad,' I said, dismounting stiffly. 'You will tell Doctor Webster how things fared here?' He nodded. 'And if it is indeed Mistress Aphra that you take the ponies for, you will remember me to her.' Again there was a short bob of the tousled head.

'And if it is Mistress Hannah?'

I laughed and flicked a shilling piece to towards him. His hand took it in the air, still spinning. 'Tell her she's to clip both your ears.'

I watched as he gathered up the two ponies' bridles and turned the beasts' heads back towards the way we had come.

Was Aphra free? I hoped so, yet I felt she was not. 'Nicholas Bronsard ... ' I whispered into the fog as though he were skulking there, 'if you have done that lassie harm, I promise that you will beg to die before I have done with you.'

I waited. Below me the two towns lay hidden in the thick sea fret. I stared into the swirling fog and tried to aid my memory of the place with my ears. Across on the north bank lay Monkwearmouth; below me, down the hill, was Bishopwearmouth. I heard the place begin to stir. Iron cart tires ground on cobblestones, street traders, abroad early, cried their wares, and cattle lowed. The fog became thinner as time passed and the sun began to burn it off the land, but it still carried the chill of the damp on it, and I shivered.

'A gentleman come from Swalwell?' The voice came at me out of the fog, clear and close, and I recognised it. 'Come on a matter o' ... fishing?' A stone crunched under the heel of a boot. He was standing at my side, a dark seacloak wrapped tight around a tall frame, and a broad hat pulled well down to hide his face. 'Will you fol-

low me, Captain? And I'd be obliged if you would keep silent until we get indoors.'
He stopped and half turned. 'We had two Newcastle spies in the town last night and
the lads have one still to run down.' Your style of speech has not the makk-it and
takk-it of Wearside, but your Newcastle tongue could get you noticed hereabouts these
days.' He walked on, seeming not to care whether I followed or not.

I was angry with myself as I followed him. I had heard little and seen nothing. I
had been standing there in a reverie, staring at the patterns that the swirl of the fog
brings before the eyes and could as easily have still stood there gawping while some
knave slipped a blade into my neck. Then I placed the voice – it was the man who had
broken me out of the Stank Tower and I sighed with relief, but I was still angry with
myself for being come upon so easily.

I followed him down into the town. Our way avoided both the High Street and the
Low as we kept to narrow paths. At one place we walked straight through a cottage
close to the waterside, my guide bowing handsomely to the young goodwife who was
frying a pan of whiting over a fire of seacoals. Twice we passed under the raised ribs
of ships being built along the riverside. The fog brightened to a pearly white. We
began to meet men with their bags of tools over their shoulders hurrying to their
work, but no one greeted us, which was a curious thing indeed, for I had always found
Wearsiders to be welcoming to strangers. We turned into Fish Street, passed through a
gate, crossed a yard littered with lobster pots and went into a house built of
unmortared stone, braced with great baulks of drift timber. The downstairs room stank
of tallow candles that had been allowed to burn with their wicks untrimmed.

'So, we meet at last in a Christian fashion, Captain Ellyot,' said a gruff voice.
'The last time, as I recall, we were a mite pressed and had no time for civilities. Allow
me to introduce myself. I am Ephraim Nellist, sometime shipmaster out of Hull.'

We had clasped hands heartily, and were grinning into one another's faces, when
the name came to me. I snapped my fingers, 'Stralsund! Ephraim Nellist of the ship
Korhaan?' I looked him, for the moment puzzled. The look on his face was that of a
man being praised more than he deserved. I would swear that the fellow was close to
blushing. 'But, man, you were blown up! I saw your ship disappear in a flash, sky
high! That was two years ago, two years gone February.' I remembered a grey Baltic

morning, suddenly torn asunder by a great sheeting flash of violet flame, a thunder-clap, and a pillar of black smoke rearing up slowly into the winter sky.

'Ah ... ' Nellist tilted his head on one side and cocked a wry eye at me. 'I was ashore when that mishap occurred. I'd spent the night with a pert young whore with more tricks to her than a Barbary she-ape.'

'And were you paid for the powder, Ephraim?'

At the time I had guessed that the blast had come from perhaps two tons of gun-powder – enough for the enterprise, but the *Korhaan* was a vessel of at least two hundred tons burthen. She could have carried that weight of powder if she'd carried an ounce. In the taverns and inns of Stralsund that winter there had been more men than me who had speculated on the matter.

'That ... ' he tapped a once broken nose, 'I'll tell you sometime when we're drunk, and when we've done with this business of Master Webster's.' Nellist winked at me and filled two glasses from a wicker-covered demijohn. Over the thick reek of the room, I smelled the same pungent carraway liqueur that Nellist had given me the night he had sprung me from the Stank Tower. He banged the cork home and tapped the demijohn. 'I was paid for ... certain work ... in demijohns of this stuff. And I still have more than twenty dozen of these great flasks to dispose of ... now, I could let you have some at an uncommon low price!'

'I thank you, Master Nellist, but as my present case stands ... ' He shrugged and we burst into laughter together.

'But for now we have other business.' He looked at me, the merriment in his face fading. 'How much do you know?'

I paused for a moment. 'Shall we say that I think I have guessed more than I have been told. I believe our master has let his partners see cards other than the hand he plays. It was some time ago that I guessed that Doctor Webster's hints about Armada guns sunk off the Farne Islands were a full shoal of red herrings.'

Ephraim Nellist coughed, then looked at me across the rim of a wineglass that caught a rainbow glance from a thin ray of light coming in through a crack in the shutters.

'In the interests of fair dealing, Captain Ellyot, I should confess now that the idea to spread such tales was my own.' His blue eyes twinkled. 'Is it not wondrous the way a cunningly seeded rumour of treasure sets a town by the heels! It loosens the hold men have on their wits. Though you will understand the notion was devised with intent to deceive the enemy, and not aimed at yourself.' He squinted at me, laughing. 'Besides which, as you say, it did not in the end lead you far astray.' He lifted the demijohn and topped up my glass with more of the clear oily kummel. It was no stuff to breakfast on, but I drank it.

'Sit and listen, and I'll tell you all.' Nellist took a fair gulp at his glass and softly belched out warm fumes of carraway. 'There are indeed four great guns, lying not five cable lengths from where we stand.' Nellist looked at me to see how I received the news and I nodded him to go on. 'They lie in no more than six fathoms. There may be some mud, but I don't think that it will be too deep. The harbour and its approaches have a clean bottom of white rock. So far as I was able to tell, the ship settled more or less on her port side. Her hold broke open and the main spars and timbers have been coming ashore since she foundered.'

'And you are sure of her position?' I had experience of sure and certain positions. It had once taken me twenty dives to find a wreck whose position was assured me by two master mariners.

'I was aboard the *Gerda of Ems* when she settled under me. I took three good clean bearings, one on the tower of St Peter's church. I can stamp my foot on the deck when we lie over her, and she'll be under my boot.'

'You were the master?' I regretted speaking. That was a question that I should not have asked directly and I was relieved when Nellist smiled and gave a little shrug.

'That trip, I was supernumerary.' Clearly, being in that position – an officer without shipboard duties – had pleased Nellist, for the word had rolled across his tongue. 'My care was the cargo not the navigation.' He paused and then looked at me, perhaps realising why I had asked. 'The *Gerda* was as well-handled as ever a ship was. It was uncommonly handsome seamanship to get her into this river at all in that storm.' I saw he was anxious to make that plain. 'The *Gerda* was an old hulk. She was laid down the year King Harry died. We needed to get into port and the captain took the risk, and failed. But I have never lost a cargo to the sea before. Say that I have my own reasons to want the cargo raised.'

'And my diving bell ... and the means of raising and lowering it?' It had seemed to me that all my labour in finding a craftsman to make the bell and the dozens of items that I had ordered two days before in Newcastle was lost.

'All you need will be here by tomorrow. All except the bell itself. That will take a day and a half longer, but it is promised.'

My mind scanned over all the things that would be needed. 'Everything?' It hardly seemed possible.

'It has been agreed.' He began to tick off the order of work on his fingers. 'You will go down into the water. You will fix strong hempen strops on to the guns. Then you will signal to be brought to the surface. The fetching up will be my concern.'

'But ... ' I was not protesting, but there was still much I needed to know.

'Leave the raising to me, Master Ellyot. I have my own trusted crew, and as many stout Wearside lads as I care to call upon. We have the heavy lifting blocks and tackle from one of Sir Joseph Ord's quarries. We have two keelboats lashed together, and stout sheerlegs ready to rig. Everything is ready. As I have said, all that is wanting now is the bell ... and yourself.'

Nellist clearly understood seaman's work. I knew well enough that the man was a rogue, perhaps a villain, yet I felt that he could be trusted to know his business when it came to it.

'I saw the King's warship, *Endymion*, in the Tyne yesterday,' I said. 'Suppose that she sails into the Wear one fine morning and catches us lifting a cannon royal from the sea?'

'And you down in your bell at the time.' The thought had obviously occurred to him too. I put my head back and looked at him squarely, but he laughed. Then he reached into his boot and took out a sheaf of papers. I opened the folded sheet he handed to me, and walked across to unlatch a shutter. Even as I blinked in the dazzling sunlight I could hardly fail to recognise the Palatine's lead seal and the formal: 'KNOW ALL MEN BY THESE PRESENTS ... ' in heavy black script at the head of the document. With ponderous words, much interleaved with Latin phrases, the deed gave permission for one George Lilburne to remove the wreck of the ship *Gerda of*

Ems from the entrance to the River Wear. The signature was that of Morton, Bishop of Durham. I was impressed.

'And George Lilburne is?' The name was in my memory somewhere but it would not come.

Nellist winked at me. 'A gentleman well-known on Wearside, and one who will soon be known even more widely. Enough to say that he is for our cause, and that his name carries a deal of weight hereabouts. You will find that folk act as though we were invisible. That is our best security. We are not seen – we are not spoken to, or of, either. Yet we have only to ask if we need anything.'

I handed Nellist back his paper, and he continued, 'Besides, Captain Ellyot, I have it from a good source that the frigate *Endymion* will sail tomorrow to join the rest of the King's fleet, which is cruising the Firth of Forth, in the hopes of frightening the folk of Edinburgh.'

'So by Friday?'

'Slack water is at about six o'clock in the morning on Friday. It will not be my fault if we don't have at least one gun raised and safe ashore by the end of that day. With good fortune we could be done before the Sabbath.'

'And then … Master Nellist … what then?'

I was more than surprised at Nellist's response. I had thought him a plain roguish fellow without any subtlety, so I was not ready for his reply.

'There will be war.' He spoke softly, but if he had been waiting for me to jump to my feet, he was disappointed, for there had been talk of little else among the Scots officers serving in Sweden. 'Our sovereign lord Charles Stuart rides too high. He is out of sympathy with his people. He treats with scorn some people who won't stand for it.'

I had heard it all before, but I listened to Nellist with show of attention as he continued. 'Most of all he has scorned the merchants and the farmers, and not content with that he has tried to force his bishops on to the Scots, along with an English episcopal style of prayerbook … Ach!' Nellist had sensed that he was telling me little that I had not heard elsewhere. He slapped at his thigh. 'The upshot is that the Scots will cross the border and try to take Newcastle. This will happen any day now – indeed as we speak, General Leslie's blue bonnets may well be on their way South.' I knew well enough that what Nellist was saying could easily be true. The thought of it sent a curious shudder of unease through me.

'Now we enter the realms of high perfidy.' Nellist gave a little laugh and shook his head slowly. 'Though you might think it strange that English men would wish to have one of their own English towns occupied by a horde of ravening Scots.' He laughed again, before going on. 'But the times are strange. The Scots are close to the men of the eastern shires in matters of religion. More than that, they have already taken up arms against the King ... and Charles Stuart has taken an army against his Scots subjects. You heard what happened at Berwick last year?' I had indeed heard how a royal army had marched across the border and been boldly faced down by Leslie's Scots. At Karlskrona one Scots officer had swelled with so much pride that he paid for the akvavit we were drinking while he told me about it.

'Well, the Scots are ready to fight the King ... now. The English are not ready, or in spirit they are ready, but they know that they are not prepared or trained. So we help where we may, and how we may. There's many a good merchant in the eastern counties who has willingly given a pound or two to help the Scots' cause.'

I had not meant to speak out but it came with a rush before I could moderate my tone, 'Aye, a pound is a small enough sum when you don't have those Scots bastards stripping your store cupboards and vomiting into your bedlinen!' I could not keep silent for I knew soldiers; I knew Scots soldiers. No man in his right mind could expect better of them, and yet it was strange that I should feel so now. Newcastle-upon-the-Tyne had been a sour spiteful old bitch of a town to me since I had come home.

'General Leslie has given solemn word that the citizens will be used with all civility, and every man's person and property will be respected,' came the reply.

Ephraim Nellist was not, I knew, a man to be taken in by such talk, yet, for all that, it seemed as though he himself believed the tale.

I tilted my head back and bawled up to the rafters. 'Let m' lift y'r clouts noo, Jeannie, an' we'll be wed at the kirk come Michaelmas!' The pitch of my voice echoed around us as I bit my lip and lifted my glass to Nellist. 'Enough, Ephraim, shall we agree to work together to raise what lies under the water ... whatever that may be. Let's get on with honest men's work and spare each other's tempers. Let true rascals prosper while they may.'

'Indeed,' cried Nellist, 'Let us do that, and do it with good heart ... But let me finish with my ...' he waved a hand in the air, 'exposition!' I sat back. There would be no work done until I had heard the man out.

'There has not been a war the like of the one which is being set in hand now.' A strange sincerity crept into Nellist's voice. 'We have both been in Germany – how long has the destruction lasted there? More than twenty years? And how many souls have been rent from their bodies? How many cities and towns levelled, gone?' I made no reply. We both had scenes of bloody horror in our minds to last for as long as we lived. 'Well this war will be different. There are those of us who will not allow the country to be riven apart in blood and flames. There will be battles. Armies will move, and men will be killed, but the better part of the fighting will be done by other means.' Nellist looked into his glass as though he were scrying an oracle. 'This war will be won, and lost, through and by gold. Charles Stuart has almost no money. He will have to call a parliament to raise money, but no parliament will vote him so much as one of his own brass shillings until he addresses himself to the long list of the people's grievances. And that, in his arrogance and stupidity, he will not do. He will wriggle, and he will half-promise, and wholly renege ... but it isn't in the man to bend. And because of that he stands to lose his throne, and perhaps worse. So the Scots are to be encouraged to take Newcastle, and keep for themselves all the revenues from all her coal, which will be sold uncommon cheap to the honest Norwich and London merchants. That pays Edinburgh off for the hire of their army while at the same time it denies His Majesty Charles Stuart the two shillings a chauldron for coal that he has been enjoying these last years.'

I laughed, but there was a sourness in it. 'By God Ephraim Nellist that's a better swindle than blasting an empty ship to hell after you've double sold the cargo.'

There was a silence between us as Nellist shifted in his seat. I heard him draw his breath softly high up into his head. He looked like a man who was trying to come to a decision, yet I saw too that he was struggling to keep his face straight.

177

'You'll not win me for your cause, Ephraim,' I said at last. 'I have soldiered across the north of Europe for nearly nine years, and come home to be robbed and left for dead the day I set foot ashore. Let men take warning. John Ellyot is to be his own man ... and a man for himself. A pox on all kings and governors! I tell you straight, Ephraim Nellist, that barring misfortune I shall not be one of the losers in this war of yours!'

Chapter 20

A Great Magic

Nellist roared the command, and almost in unison four anchors splashed into the green water. We lay inside the mouth of the River Wear and I stood aboard an unhandy-looking craft made up of two keelboat hulls, stripped of rigging and sail, lashed together with stout mast timbers. Sheerlegs, inverted Vs of stout spars, had been set up to meet over the ten foot span that lay between the twinned hulls. A single great pulley block, rove through with a rope of brown hemp as thick as a man's wrist, had been fixed to the apex of the sheerlegs so that it hung directly over the gap of open water. It was a gallows rigged to hang a giant, and that giant was a great thimble-shaped cask, all of eight feet high with its open-ended base suspended a few feet above the waves. It swung very like a great bell, as the hulls lifted on the swell.

'I think I may say, Captain Ellyot, that we have done everything we could so far,' said Ephraim Nellist, bowing to me. A muted cheer came from the dozen or so of his men who had conned the awkward vessel into position.

'Agreed, Captain Nellist,' I returned the courtesy. 'So it's time for Jack to earn his coppers!'

I could sense that every man of the crew was waiting. It struck me that they had that same tense, bright-eyed look that comes over a crowd when the public headsman raises his sword. It was not every day that they could watch a man go down to the seabed in a stockfish barrel.

I jumped over the keel's side and dropped on to the thwart of the foyboat that was the waiting-on tender and stood ready to climb under and up through the open end of the bell. I paused, and that was a mistake, for my chest began to heave like a bellows gone mad. Then I let the fear wash over me, willing it to drain away and leave me. That was how it always was.

It had been over a year since I had made a dive and that too had been for guns – a warship sunk alongside the harbour wall of a castle on the Gulf of Bothnia. It had been during the depths of a Finland winter. Today the sun burned hot and the sea was like pale blue silk.

I pretended to inspect the heavy garlands of cast lead weights hung around the bell to take her to the bottom. There was no faulting the work. Every piece was secure. I had no further excuses and stepped into the water, letting my head go under, gasping at the first shock of the cold. I felt the lambskin breeks and jerkin that I had thonged together soak and fill. I reached up, took hold of the wooden plank across the open end of the bell, and hauled myself up heavily.

Inside the diving bell the light glowed up green through the open end. My legs dangled down so that my feet splashed the surface of the water. I banged a fist against the thick oakwood staves that formed the bell's sides and the two men tending the foy boat handed me my tools under the space between the bottom edge of the bell and the water. I took hold of a long iron crowbar and an axe. A dozen other tools waited in the boat should I need them, but for now axe and crowbar should serve.

For a long moment I sat, taking deep breaths. There was a tap on the wood next to my hand: was I ready? My fist drummed in answer: ready – lower away! I heard the order repeated from the foy boat to the men holding the lowering rope.

The circle of green light below me came up to fill the mouth of the bell. My throat tightened. I fought the panic, the urge to struggle out of the bell into the open air. Then my feet and my bare calves were in the sea. My knees and thighs were under the water. I drew them up into the space of trapped air under the bell. John Ellyot was diving again.

The light at forty feet was good – better than ever I had known it to be in Finland. I crouched on my plank and looked down into the great lens of green light. Three or four chill pinpricks stung my neck and face. I knew what it was. The bell was as well built as I could have wished, but the sea was finding the tiny flaws in the seams and hard needles of water were being forced into the bell. Soon the wood would swell and the seams would close.

The bottom of the harbour mouth was clean enough. Flat rocks, rounded and glowing white through the green of the water lay nestled in soft mud, but I could see nothing of any wreck.

I let myself slide down from my plank. The sea was icy cold. A line from a little treatise, De Grijss's *The Whole Arte of Logick*, that I had read during that long Finnish winter, sprang into my mind: '"The Sea is Cold" is an exemplar of what men call a statement categorical.' When you are in the sea itself mere words lose their power to describe. To say that the clutch of the freezing cold water was like a steel claw tells nothing. It was high summer and I was in England, but I felt no difference between the cold of the Wear and the cold I felt when I was lowered down through a hole hacked in the Baltic ice along the Finnish coast.

I swam in a circle, came back to put my head up into the bell to take breath, and swam again. So much for Ephraim Nellist's bearings – we would have to move the keelboats to another place.

When you are possessed of a great magic, it does not do to make little of it before the mob. That was another thing I had learned in Sweden. I would not want Nellist and his crew, nor indeed Sylvanus Webster, to make light of my skills. If I were to keep their respect, I needed to preserve the mystery.

It would be prudent to stay beneath the waves for at least the time it would take a man to drown – twice over. I climbed back into the diving bell and sat on my plank, shivering, with my knees up under my chin.

We moved the boat three times that day, carrying the anchors away from the ship slung between two ship's boats, dropping them to the seabed, and then kedging the twin keels back and forth by main force of muscle hauling on rope.

Ephraim Nellist was much embarrassed. He strode about the deck, tight-lipped, his eyes darting here and there, keen to detect his men's smallest fault. And while he fretted and swore, I crouched close to a good driftwood fire set on a bed of sand down in the hold of one of the keels. Will Blacket had brought me a hot blanket to drape around my shoulders. For an hour after I had climbed heavily out of the water my body was as blue as a corpse. Even with Will's hot blanket and the fire. I could not stop my teeth chattering like dice in a pot.

Will handed me a black bottle. I was about to take a swig to kill the taste of salt water when there was a stir above us on deck. Nellist climbed down and squatted beside me. He was still in a bad humour, the set of his shoulders showed it; his lower lip pouted and the corners of his mouth had fallen almost comically. He had been so sure of himself. I patted his shoulder and handed him the bottle. He shook his head.

'I took the time to take careful bearings,' he said, talking to himself rather than to me. 'The ship was already settling under us but I took the time ... '

'Maybe ... ' I fell silent. It would be taken amiss if I offered advice on what was plainly a matter of seamanship. Gunners and navigators use similar calculations and instruments, but a shipmaster's pride is not the same as gunner's honour.

'We have moved the keels in three directions from the point we began at this morning.' I added, using a stick to scratch a cross of St Andrew into the sand and ashes at my feet. 'Kedge us out to the last corner, Ephraim. We'll try that. If the wreck isn't there we'll quit for today ... ' I forced a wry grin. 'Take heart, even if we have to dive over every inch of the Wear's mouth, it's not such a large expanse.' I spoke with more bravado than I felt. It would take a lot longer than I suggested to cover the whole river entrance.

But on the next dive I found something. I might well have missed it. At any other time of the year I am sure that I would not have seen the signs, but the river was low for want of rain, and the water was hardly clouded at all. The storm that had died the day I had landed at South Shields had been the last rough sea to strike the coast. The silt and mud had been given time to settle. We had been lucky.

It was my custom to swim out from the bell for about thirty feet before turning back to take air. I came up against a broken bulwark of oak planking twenty feet out on my second foray. There was no doubt that it was the *Gerda*. Her back had broken, so that the fore part of the ship had twisted to lie on its side; the after part was upright but it had broken so that the hulk had sloped down into deeper water. Storms had torn away much of her planking and all her masts and spars had gone.

I swam to the surface and waved. Our first need was a well-tarred bullock's bladder, blown up and tied to a strong line to buoy the site of the wreck.

I had earned a cheer but there was no sound from the keels. Will Blacket made a sign for me to swim alongside 'midships.

'Gi's your hands,' he hissed softly. I felt the grip and then I was hauled bodily out of the water. I rolled against the blessed heat of planking long baked under the sunshine. 'Keep still, Captain ... they seem to be riding on.'

I lay where I was. A scuffle and a scrape brought Ephraim Nellist crawling to me.

'Bastards! There's fifty King's troopers riding along the north shore.' Nellist handed me a small spyglass and I edged my way to a space between the sheerleg lashings and focussed.

I hardly needed the glass. A well turned out troop of horse is always a grand sight. The sun glinted on harness and armour; the greens and reds of sashes and ribbons danced in the heat haze. They had ridden round the headland, coming into sight along the north bank of the Wear without warning.

'So we'll have a fine garrison of His Majesty's horsemen in Wearmouth tonight.' I showed my teeth but could force little enough of a grin. Even cavalry officers would have the wit to see what we were about when we started to haul cannon from the water.

'No ... at least I think not. I'd have been told if the Castle intended to put troops into this town. Those rogues have been sent from Newcastle to be seen and make a show. Folk hereabouts make no secret of their loyalties. The aim is to let the good people of Wearside see the King's strength. Those troopers have been sent to show what might befall a disloyal town. If we are lucky, those troopers will drink their beer ration back in Newcastle tonight. If we are not ... why we must just bide our time.'

'Then we had best think about raising our guns in the darkness and be well away from this place before they can guess what we are doing.'

Nellist's thoughts had still been on the cavalry. He blinked once and stared at me. 'You have found ... ?'

I thrust out an arm and pointed a finger, jabbing at the place. 'She's there, or enough of her to hold the guns.'

'You've seen them?'

'Put the bell above that point tomorrow at daybreak and if the guns are there, I'll get a rope on them.'

But the appearance of the cavalry was not the only ill-omen. Ephraim Nellist had fixed lodgings for me at a tavern in Bishopwearmouth. Will Blacket rowed me to the south shore and we went back to find the Blue Anchor. All I wanted was a good dinner, a bottle of wine, and an early night, but the landlord met us in the street – a badly frightened man. We were not to go to the tavern, and we saw the reason when we came closer. Five well-groomed black horses were tethered to the common rail in front of the inn. I exchanged glances with Will, who gave me the ghost of a wink and made off towards the door. The landlord stood before me, wringing his apron hard between his hands and making nervous hops, shifting his weight from foot to foot.

'Calm yourself!' I saw that the fellow could only become more addled if I showed anger. 'Tell me what has happened.'

'They've taken over ma tavern ... ' His eyes were for all the world like a Baltic codfish's as he goggled up at me.

'When?' I asked quietly. 'How many troopers are in the town? What do they say they are here for?' I had to take hold of his skinny chin and grip his cheeks hard before he was calm enough to answer me.

The cavalry had galloped into town at eleven o' clock. They were not the same troops that we had seen along the north bank of the river. They had dismounted and stamped into the town's taverns demanding drink. The officers had billeted themselves on the homes of the local gentry and the better-off merchants. Even common troopers it seemed had been given license to make themselves at home where they could. The Blue Anchor had been an easy choice.

'And has there been resistance? Has anyone lifted a hand against them?'

The tavern-keeper opened his mouth to speak, then shut it again, shaking his head like a man with an ague.

'Good ... ' I kept my grip on his chin and looked hard into his face when I said it. 'Warn your neighbours that that is what the soldiers hope some man will do. Tell your friends to keep their daggers sheathed and their pikes hidden!' I shook him until he told me clearly that he understood what I was saying. I knew only too well what was afoot. Wearmouth was being baited. The slightest flicker of resistance would give the cavalry the excuse it needed for an orgy of looting. The severity of this rummaging would, I guessed, be as a fleabite compared to the way we had brought towns to heel in Germany. But it would be bad enough.

A pewter pot smashed through a window, and then another. There was a rumble of drunken laughter from within the tavern. The game was just beginning. They would drink the town dry and stuff themselves sick with the townsfolk's food. They would call for stock to be slaughtered to provide food for His Majesty's gallant troopers. Two or three days would see it done. There would be black eyes and bruises galore among the common folk – and in nine months time there would be a fine crop of bastards. I tried to stop a wry smile forming at the corner of my mouth. There was no mockery there; it was simply the irony of it all. It might as well have been the Scots in the town. What side a man served on when he broke your teeth with his musket butt and raped your wife and your daughter hardly mattered. The brutality that the people of Wearmouth would suffer in the next few days would not, I guessed, be unwelcome news to Sylvanus Webster. Suffering, so long as it is not too great to bear, gives folk zeal for a cause.

And I knew why it had been done. I had seen it before, often. When the paymaster's chests are empty and the troops begin to bellyache for their money, they have to be given something. The governor of His Majesty's Castle in Newcastle had as good as given the town's smaller neighbour to his troops as interest on their arrears of pay. That had been a short-sighted thing to do, for when the troops had ridden back to barracks they would leave behind a fine festering hatred against the King. Yet I wondered for how long these folk would cheer the Scots when they marched into the town.

The landlord of The Blue Anchor recovered his wits long enough to tell me to find my way to Blind Lane and find a bawdyhouse called the Danewife's.

A broken shard of red glass in a lantern was all the sign I needed that I was in the right place. I battered at the door with the heavy thirl pin and it was no surprise that it was skilfully carved in the form of a massive male member. I had to batter the door for a long time before a face thrust out of a window under the eaves. I was expected, that was plain, but no man rouses a whorehouse at that time of day without chance of getting a brimming pisspot spilled over his head for his trouble. At last, though, there was the clatter of iron-shod pattens on the stairs, and the double bars on the door were lifted.

'Aye?' She stood there, rouge and wrinkles, with her slack dugs swinging under a loose shift. That lassie's toenails could, I swear, have torn the bowels out of an ox.

'What business ha' ye here?' It was the growl of a wakened tigress. But it has been my experience that most whores respond to courtesy. I swung off my hat with all the gravity that I could muster.

'The landlord of the Blue Anchor told me that you might be inclined to offer the hospitality of your house to a gentleman and his servant.'

There is one beast on this earth with keener eyes than a Swedish drill corporal and that is a whore-mistress. I stood to let her scan me up and down.

'I have need of a room, Mistress … ' I got no further. She hooked a hand like a ham into my belt and jerked me in off the street.

'You must be the daftie what dooks doun in tae the water! Come away upstairs … sharp now. The swine will be here any minute.'

This was no Dane woman. Indeed I guessed that the house's name was as old as itself. The name of a good whorehouse is likely to last. But the building itself was as spacious a brothel as I had been in. I was pushed up three flights of steep wooden stairs, passing the open doors of rooms furnished with pallets of hay and sackcloth curtains. On a busy night the house could accommodate a rare trade.

I was housed with the pigeons under the heather thatching of the roof.

'Ye'll need to stay here until the bastards have a good skin full inside them … then y'll be able to wander where y' please. There's a bucket up there, so don't piss through the joists. Y'can amuse yersel keekin' doon through the ceilin' cloths.' The rouge cracked as she smiled at me through her few broken teeth. 'Y'll see sights y' never dreamed on!'

I doubted that. But I hauled up the ladder and shut myself into the dark.

The roof space over the brothel was as big as a barn. I waited until my eyes had become accustomed to the gloom. There was a hole where a sheaf of heather thatch had been carried away. A square of blue sky showed. I made for it, walking along the joists. My boots knocked caked pigeon dung off the timbers so that it pattered down on to the rotted cloths stretched below in place of a ceiling.

I had not long to wait. Far below the door banged and I heard the shrieks of false delight as troopers were welcomed. They were already more than half drunk. The house shook below me as the soldiers pushed their way in. If I knew anything of troopers they would have their women first, and that wouldn't take long. Then they would drink themselves into a coma. It was a mechanism that worked like a clock. I guessed that the town's Council would already have sent word that it would pay for the troopers' drink. The house's whores would give their services free. That would win the house a year's respite from being noticed at all by the Justices.

Troopers, drunk and well sated, were less likely to molest honest citizens. And with luck they would all leave afflicted of a fine red roaring dose of the French pox apiece. There was justice of a wild sort to it all.

I sat silent, up among the soft cooing of the pigeons, and I listened. Aye, and smelled as well. The smoke and stale reek of mutton tallow dips came up to me first, then the fumes of bad brandy and gin that must have dripped raw straight from the still copper into the bottles. Then after half an hour I heard a drunken giggle and the swish of skirts. There was a movement of shadows cast by a rushlight.

The lass knew her trade. She dallied longer and made more noise wheedling for a present for herself, than she feigned sobbing passion on the straw. She got her present – and she contrived to make the loon spill his handful of coins in the dark.

The hole in the heather thatching showed starlight when a stick knocked up at the trapdoor. I looked down into Ephraim Nellist's grinning face. 'Every man jack is snoring. Come on down.'

We moved through the house. It was like the morning after a battle. Men lay everywhere, arms and legs at all angles and in all manner of contorted positions. The figures snored and twitched among pots and bottles. A young whore gave us a gap-toothed smile as she looked up from her searching inside a trooper's breeks.

Will Blacket met us at the foot of the stairs. The man was a wonder. We had come into a town taken over by King's troops and he had walked among them, like Daniel among the lions. He was wearing a buff leather jerkin with a sergeant's crimson silk sash draped over the shoulder. A helmet of the Spanish fashion favoured in Queen Bess's time was balanced on the side of his head and he was carrying a halfpike as though it were a staff of office. It would have taken a sharp soldier to see that William

Blacket was other than a King's man.

It seemed that he had walked the town without a word of challenge; and if the bulging sack that lay at his feet was a sign, he had despoiled the Midianites on his own account. Will held the half-pike at the present and stamped his boots:

'Beg your honour's leave to report. Two troops o' Newcastle garrison cavalry in the town, and every man swine-arsed drunk ... Sah!'

Chapter 21

Cannon Royal

The good folk of Bishopwearmouth seemed to be keeping a second Sabbath – it would do them no good. The two Wearmouths might lie within the County Palatine and enjoy the protection of Bishop Morton, but not even he could grant them the protection of another Sunday. His Majesty's troopers would wake up with the taste of copper nails in their mouths. The gin that they had swilled the night before at the Danewife's had been raw stuff, fermented from spoiled grain and distilled no earlier than a week before. It was drink kept to sell to sailors, who knew no different. The clamour would be for a gill of brandy and water to ease splitting heads and queasy guts. And God help the man who was tardy in fetching it.

And I was right. The streets of Bishopwearmouth looked plague-swept. While we stopped to watch a black rat scurry across the road, a housewife in her shift crept out with her bucket to the midden steading. She saw us and scampered back indoors, her slops a-spill. No other soul was abroad. I guessed that when the true Sunday came the churches would be packed full and the hymns would be sung uncommon loud and the prayers would be most earnest.

But Ephraim Nellist cared nothing for the Sabbath, real or fancied. As he said, 'There's no Sundays at sea.' He had roused me early from my straw and blanket in a corner of one of the upper rooms in the brothel. Seeing the half dozen troopers and their whores, that I found lying around me snoring and twitching, when I was wakened, told me that I had chosen a sound hiding place for a man with a price on his head.

Our boots rang the quickstep march on the stones as we strode through the empty lanes that led down to the riverside. By the time the sun had been up half an hour Nellist had me and Will Blacket, and the sack of gear that Will had foraged, out to the anchored keelboats.

Even with a rumble in my guts for want of a bite to eat, it was still a beautiful morning. The sea shimmered as gold leaf does when it is blown upon – yet there was a brassy haze over the horizon. That sign boded no good for the weather to come. Nellist was looking at the sky inland, to the west. The Wear valley hid the far horizon but a bank of dirty grey cloud was already piling high and threatening. Sight of it made me aware that the morning breeze off the sea had fallen away. It would be a fine sunny day, but the air was already heavy.

'We may have until tomorrow; we may have less ... but I don't doubt that this fine weather will break soon,' said Nellist, dropping his voice so that only I could hear him. 'And I have more than a fancy that there will be blow.' He sampled the air deeply. 'Sniff at that! You can smell weather before you can see it.'

'The weather makes little odds to me,' I replied as he screwed up his face and sniffed again. 'I'll be under the water, Ephraim!'

Heavy rain might lessen the light getting down to the seabed, but I knew that I would manage to see what I needed to see. Better it rained and hid what we were doing from all sight. Besides that, I had had my doubts about the power of a bishop's letter in the face of an inquisitive King's officer. I wanted the work done, and done as soon as possible, so I could go on my way. Nellist looked at me, quizzically. 'Shall you find the guns today?' he enquired.

I winked and spat on my hand for luck. I had seen a Lapp shaman do the same thing when he had been asked a question for which he had no ready answer.

'If they are to be found ... ' I smiled at him sidelong, 'I offer Fortune no hostages.'

I did find the guns, and sooner than I had thought to. We had shifted the twinned keels twenty feet. I stripped and had Will Blacket lace me tightly into my sheepskins – a trick that I had learned when I was in Sweden. Even when a fleece is soaked with freezing sea water, sheepskin held tight against the skin soon warms up with the animal heat of a man's body. I may have looked like the Green Man o' the Forest, but with my loins girded and my bowels braced, and a wee lambskin cap laced under my chin like the goodwife's bonnet. I knew that I would be able to work a good deal longer than I could have hoped to do if I were stark naked.

On the first dive the crew lowered the bell too fast, perhaps because with the shifting of our position the depth of water under us was less than it had been before. I had tied a scrap of coloured rag around the hawser to warn them when to hold their lowering, but for all that the lower rim of the bell struck the bottom and threw up billowing clouds of fine mud. Dull green-grey light coming in from the bottom of the bell was blotted out, and I sat on my perch for a moment until the suspended silt had drifted away. Then I stood with both feet stuck down in the slime and lifted the bell bodily so that I could get out. Tilting the bell cost me dear in spilled air. I watched the huge silver bubbles rise up out of sight. The mishap meant that I would soon have to have the bell raised again to replenish the precious air. But the dive was not without profit. Through the green gloom I made out the long dark shape of the first of the cannon. It lay not ten feet away, still lashed athwart the *Gerda*'s bare ribs. My outstretched hands reached through the swirling fog of silt and gripped into the wrapping of heavy felted wool used to protect cannon when they were shipped. I tore away a double handful of the rotted stuff and my grip closed on metal. My fingers sought out the detail of ornate work cast into the bronze, some mythical sea creature with scales. Rope lashings parted easily when I sawed with my knife. Then I was able to tear away a sheet of felt, exposing the dolphins, the massive handles cast into the metal of the barrel so that the gun could be hoisted on to its carriage.

I saw too that the long barrel had been chained to a great iron staple hammered into the ship's rib-timbers. I should have expected that. No skipper would sail with the risk of having a heavy cannon break free at sea.

I had to swim to the surface and have Nellist's men raise the bell to replenish the air before I knew the worst of it. Two other guns were secured in like fashion further along in the *Gerda*'s hold. Of the fourth gun that Webster had spoken of there was no sign. And so far as I could see there were chains for only three cannon. It seemed that for once Doctor Webster had been mistaken.

I climbed inside the bell and sat for a moment. Three guns were better than no guns at all. Sylvanus Webster – and the Scots – would have to be content. If the fourth cannon were there at all it would be on the bottom, perhaps pinned under the keel. I put the need to think of it out of my mind. No man as cold as I had already become could think straight.

In three dives, with long rests to get the deadening chill out of my bones, I had loosed the first cannon from its chain. That I owed to luck rather than skill. In the way things fall, I had begun work at the wrong end of the gun. The chain was stapled tight fast. I had spent much time and used up my air trying to get the end of my crowbar under the big staple. Then I found that I had been trying to lever the wrong staple. I had swum to the far end of the cannon barrel to tug the line that would signal that I wanted the bell raised. It had been almost an idle jab I had made at the timber with my crowbar. The chisel end of the bar sank into the rotten wood. The staple came free at first wrench.

It was a long day, but by late afternoon my work was as good as done. Three massive cannon barrels lay fore and aft across the *Gerda*'s ribs. The first gun had taken longest to free, but the other two I had found were secured by wooden wedges bracing tight the slack in the chains. A ponderous slow battering with a blacksmith's sledgehammer that Nellist had to send ashore to borrow, had them cleared. All this would have been simple enough work to do on dry land, but in that cripplingly cold water the labour of even the simplest task was multiplied tenfold. I forced myself to swim around the three masses of dark bronze. They were indeed full cannon royal. But they were not new-cast pieces. The pattern was old-fashioned. Cannon founderers no longer moulded such ornament into pieces of ordnance. The modern style is for a plain gun. That they had been intended for sea service was clear from the ornament, the chase was indented with scales, and the muzzles were formed in the likeness of the gaping mouth of some sea-serpent. Perhaps they had been cast for a great warship like Charles Stuart's plaything, the *Royal Sovereign*. Nevertheless they would serve as well on land. Each would throw a granite ball, weighing perhaps forty-six pounds a distance of two miles; a cast iron roundshot would weigh closer to seventy pounds and would carry a mile or more further. But with either, one fair hit would shatter the gates of a town like Newcastle to kindling wood.

I swam the thirteen-foot length of one of the guns, feeling the bronze. The muzzle was closed tight with a carefully fitted oakwood plug; the touch hole had been sealed with melted tar. I would lay money that the bore had been filled with hot melted tallow to preserve it against corrosion. An hour's work would have the gun fit to load and fire.

There was no sign of the eight-inch gunstones, the white granite shot that the cannon fired; neither aboard the wrecked hull or lying on the bottom around her. Nor was there sign that carriages for the guns had been part of the cargo. But that was not my worry. It warmed the chill of the water a little to remind myself that I was free of service, that I ate no army's rations, and wore no King's coat. What happened to the three guns from the moment that they left the water was to be no concern of mine. I was no longer an artillery officer, I was a bell-diver – and I was that for not one moment more than need be.

And then I remembered that everything else I could find was diver's lawful booty. A man who dives for his pay alone is a fool. I took air from the bell and swam aft. Pickings from the *Gerda of Ems* were poor, uncommonly poor. I found a big pot made from riveted iron plates, and a meat cleaver, stuck deep in the chopping block in the galley. That aside, there wasn't so much as a brass farthing in coin to be found in any of the cabins. Clearly, the crew had had time to take their gear into the boats with them.

My preparations for lifting the guns had been the least difficult part of the work. I'd had one of Nellist's crew splice three slings, bands of rope, from lengths of new hemp cordage. I wrapped one of these around the barrel of each cannon once, crossed the loops through one another, and passed them out through the dolphins. That would let the weight of the cannon hang steady as it was hauled upward. Last, I took up the end of hawsers as they were lowered down from the surface and tied it with a bowline to the sling. A hearty jerk told the crew to take up the slack. That was it. I had made the necessary link between the cannon and the keelboats floating overhead. All that was left for Nellist's crew to do then was to pass the free end of the stout rope held aboard the keels through the pulley blocks rigged from the sheerlegs above. My work was done. It was Nellist's task to oversee the muscle power needed to lift seventy hundredweight of cast bronze out of the water.

But first they had to raise the bell and unship it, so that the hauling gear was free.

193

I had wondered what would be done with the bell and its gear, but now I was too tired to care. Enough truly was enough. I was weary to my bones and chilled to the marrow. Working short spells and resting long may have spared me pain, but I still felt the vice of cramp gripping at my stomach and legs. Will Blacket's kneading of my muscles gave me some ease but nonetheless I suffered much.

Nellist was pleased at the way the work had gone. He too was, I think, relieved of a burden. I could see it in the set of his shoulders and the swing of his walk as he paced the deck. He had even put on a fine shore-going coat of bottle green. Though he still cursed and swore at his men when they cheered him, there was no anger in it and they grinned back at his curses. Sailors are different from soldiers but it took little to see that the man held his lads in the palm of his hand.

And I gave the hauling crew a wee bonus. I threw the iron pot and the cleaver into to the common store, along with the chains that had been used to stow the cannon safely. They were diver's takings, and mine to give. I had bent a line to the ends of the chains and Nellist's crew had hauled them aboard. Three lengths, each more than seven fathoms of forged iron chain, would fetch a pound or two from any shipbuilder along the Wear. It is a good practice to keep the lads hauling your hawser well disposed towards you.

And my gift didn't displease Nellist. His pace quickened as he walked the few steps that the tiny afterdeck of the keel allowed. He was clearly a man with many thoughts buzzing in his head.

But there was something he was trying to hide. Nellist was being a little too hearty. He walked back and forth like a man pondering deeply on some scheme; or more like a player on the stage acting the part of a man deep in thought. I gave him his chance to speak when I winked to Will Blacket to busy himself and leave us alone.

'John!' Nellist's voice suddenly swelled with good fellowship. 'In the matter of pickings, like the pot that you fetched up for the lads … '

I smiled back at him brightly and waited. 'I think that there was another small piece of ordnance aboard the *Gerda*. It wasn't on the manifest of cargo but it strikes me that it might fetch us a pound or two.' He dropped his voice. 'I've a friend in Newcastle who will pay ready gold for such an item.'

'Aye?' I was as canny he was. I took up the white clay pipe well charged with dark Orinoke tobacco that Will had left at my side and sought a burning twig from the fire. As I filled my lungs with the calming smoke, I watched Nellist's response. He was a little disconcerted, but not much. I let him speak again.

'I recall that there was a mortar, a seven pounder, a wee thing, like they use to lob bombards over town walls. The *Gerda*'s master bought it for his private trading in Bruges.' Nellist's eyes had taken on a speculative look. And even that was as false as a quartermaster's scales. I felt, I knew, that he was broaching a matter that was of more importance to him than he wanted to show. Yet I was also aware that the plan he was making was somehow newly hatched.

'What is it that you have in mind, Ephraim?' I smiled so sweetly that he could hardly have failed to notice that I was suspicious. That set him back. He fidgeted, licking his lips and alternately frowning and smiling. It was the struggle between prudence and avarice working in him. I played with him a little.

'A mortar you say?' My frown matched his own. I shook my head slowly. 'I don't think so, Ephraim ... ' I set my jaw and looked pensive. 'That wreck has been sadly battered since she sank. The sea has left little enough for poor men to pick over. The *Gerda* has been stripped to her ribs and keel. I doubt I'll find any mortar there.'

I had gone too far. Nellist grunted a couple of words and strode away. I let him go. He would be back if there was anything of value concerned. I was the diver, and nothing would be fetched up from the wreck other than by me. I wondered what there might be aboard the sunken hulk that I might have missed, something that might yield some profit. The first thing that I had thought of was that the ship's own armament might be raised. That had been a sad disappointment. If there had been any cannon aboard the *Gerda* they had been jettisoned in the storm that sank her. My suspicion was that all she had carried for her own defence were Quaker guns, wooden logs painted in the semblance of cannon muzzles and pointed out of the ports for show.

I relit my pipe and waited. Nellist came back.

'And shall we raise the ordnance before dark today?' There was much that I had not been told and that had become less and less to my taste. A man likes to have his work valued at its full worth. And without my efforts enough heavy cannon to make the siege train for the Scottish army would have stayed on the bed of the Wear till Kingdom Come.

I had pondered over the problems that Nellist would have to solve if he was to get the cannon on to dry land. The guns would be useless until they were mounted on to their massive wheeled carriages and drawn away by six powerful gun-horses. We had not discussed, he had never said, how he meant to get the guns ashore – nor indeed what was to be done with them. I thought that a bigger boat, a merchant ship, would have to come alongside and take the guns aboard. Heavy cannon are a deal easier to shift by sea than land. But it might be the plan to put the three guns directly into the holds of one of the keelboats. One of the keels would be able to carry all of the guns. I closed my eyes and summoned up the table of scales that had been printed in the tattered little copy of Oost's *Handboek der Artillerie* that I had once owned. A cannon royal weighed eight thousand pounds. That was about seventy one hundredweights. I scratched a short calculation in the ashes. The three guns together weighed nearer eleven tons than ten. I knew that a full load for a Newcastle keelboat was twenty-one tons of coal. One of the keels would be just half-loaded if it was decided to carry the cannon away aboard her.

I had assumed that the cannon were to be handed over to the Scots. But when I thought back I realised that it was another trick of Sylvanus Webster's to let draw my own conclusions. I remembered the way I had been allowed to assume that the guns were in a wreck off the Farne Islands. It occurred to me that I had never been told directly where the guns were to go.

'The cannon will soon be off our hands.' I waited for him to say more but he turned away again. Was Nellist making game of me?

'A boat will come after dark tonight. If all goes well the cannon will have gone by morning.'

Suddenly Nellist looked at me directly.

'There was a great piece of silver aboard the *Gerda*. I saw it with my own eyes. I stood in the foundry when they poured fifty-six pounds weight of fine silver all molten into the mould. It was cast into the form of a small mortar bombard. I watched them break it out of the mouldbox and paint it with tar while it was still hot.'

'And I'll wager too, Ephraim, that you saw the thing being hoisted aboard the *Gerda* and you watched it with your own two eyes being lowered into the hold along with the cannon.'

Nellist needed no more goading to realise that he had been duped and double duped. Sylvanus Webster had found a way to keep Nellist keen. The prospect that he might somehow get his hands upon a great piece of silver had kept Ephraim Nellist loyal and hardworking. There was no doubt in my mind that the treasure had been sent to Scotland, but not in the *Gerda's* hold. I might have laughed aloud, but then I remembered in time that I hardly knew this man and that he might have taken laughter badly.

For a moment Nellist said nothing, but the change in the way he stood told me that my guess was right. Sylvanus Webster had kept his hand on Nellist, loose in the grip but still there, in everything that he had done. With me, Webster had, I believed, used his men to break me out of gaol. He had then counted upon my gratitude, and the fact that although I had been broken free, I was nonetheless a hunted man. And it had all worked. I wondered what other holds Webster had over Ephraim Nellist. Perhaps none, for suddenly the man's face twisted into a rueful smile:

'Ha! The old bastard has played the monkey catcher's trick upon me. He let me see him put a sweetmeat in a jar and he let me, as I thought, take a hold of it. And he knew that so long as I had my clenched paw upon it I would never let go!'

I judged it safe then to share in Nellist's laughter.

'But for all that, Ephraim, my work is done.' I said pointedly.' The guns are as good as raised.'

Ephraim Nellist chuckled softly. 'Your work is done, John Ellyot, when my work is done.' He wagged a finger at me. 'And my work is done when the cannon are put into the hands of General Leslie's artillery officers. That may be tomorrow. If the boat comes tonight and the cannon lift easy ... You do your one last dive and then – perhaps – you will be your own man again.'

The barb in the hook came as no surprise. I had been as certain as a man can be that there would be something, some other task, that remained to be done.

'My last dive?' I let the blue smoke trickle from the corner of my mouth while I gazed at him from behind a smile that I knew glittered like crushed glass. 'You mean the fourth gun? The mortar?'

'A small matter … '

'My pleasure and my honour to serve Y'r Lordship!' I flapped a hand before my face in mock courtesy. Then I had a flash of card player's insight. I knew that Ephraim Nellist was not convinced that there was no treasure aboard the wreck. My first thought had been that he had wanted to make a handy side profit from raising what he could from the *Gerda of Ems* while he still had the diving bell and the crew together. I had found little enough that was easily moveable on the wreck. But if her timbers could be raised they would saw up into much valuable oak. I could think of nothing else of value. But the business could take weeks, and the profits would share out thinly among so many men. I started to calculate what share of any prize I might haggle out of Nellist.

But no; all of that was too simple. The idea that Nellist was about some trickery of his own would not go away. I saw in my mind's eye again the column of smoke rising from the merchant ship off Stralsund. I liked Nellist. But I knew that he would rob me or anyone else he did business with because he was a rogue and couldn't help himself.

This last task, this small matter, was more important than any scavenging. How important I couldn't yet tell, but I was alerted to it. I would wait.

The boat came in from the sea as soon as it was fully dark. I heard the splash of oars and the soft bump of a bow against the keelboat's planks. There was a gruff exchange of few words then the keel began to sway gently as more than twenty pairs of bare feet moved. I heard the growl as pulley blocks moved and the change from soft growl to shrill squeal as the weight of a gun came on to the ropes. Then the hauling began. The rhythmic stamp-grunt-stamp of men putting their backs into bringing up more than three and a half tons of bronze sounded like some great machine at work. The swing of the bodies transferred itself to the planks of the deck causing the twin hulls to rock.

The guns came up slowly: an inch or two of hawser rope won with each heave: the tackle of pulley blocks served to purchase power at the price of slowness.

The boat was a ship's longboat. I was surprised. It would carry one of the cannon barrels but the burden would make it sit low in the water so that ... I wiped the thought from my mind. Once again I had been led to make my own wrong assumptions. I had been allowed to think that the intention was to take the guns away by sea. Not so! The words almost escaped aloud. That boat's bow was pointing up river. She was not being put to a dangerous sea passage round to the Tyne or up the coast to Blyth. I had thought that the Scots would send men and horses off from their line of march to take possession of the artillery. The guns would be taken up the Wear. It would make three trips during the night. Somewhere below the limit of the tidal water the three cannon would be landed to begin their journey ... to where?

The cannon broke the surface. I heard a murmur run along the double line of the crew. I had forgotten that the men were getting their first sight of the guns. Ephraim Nellist's growl stilled the noise. The sounds of the lifting gear, the creak of the sheer-legs and the ropes moving in the pulley sheaves changed as the big gun was lifted clear of the water. Progress became slower. Once the load seemed to have stuck. I sent Will Blacket up to help. He spat on his hands and went off with a swing to his stride.

The cannon royal was clear of the water by about four feet. There was a silence. In the dark I could see the clenched teeth of the men holding the load. The rank smell of fresh sweat soaking through long worn woollen cloth hung on the air. The longboat was pulled carefully between the keelboat hulls until it lay directly underneath the cannon.

There was a pause. I heard Nellist's voice, curiously gentle, give the order to lower away. The great gun settled almost imperceptibly down on to a cradle of willow withes laid in the bottom of the boat to receive it.

My guess had been correct. I stood and watched. Six oarsmen rowed without making a splash. They pulled up river, up the Wear, inland.

Chapter 22

A Hired Man Still

The white blade of lightning scored its way across the darkening sky. We blinked and then flinched as the double crack of thunder split the air around us. A storm had been threatening all day but the sudden break in the weather took us unawares. Rain, swollen drops, began to pock the oil smooth surface of the Wear. Circles on the water, like big trout rising, spread and merged. Then it came. The river smoked with white vapour as the raindrops danced on its surface. The heavy smell of the air changed, freshened, and cooled. I stood under the sailcloth rigged over the keel's hold and watched as five of Nellist's men struggled to pull the diving bell on board.

There was no need for caution now. The shoreline on either side of us lay invisible in the downpour. The lead weights were cut loose from the bell and thudded on to the boards. Then the bell itself was up-ended so that the narrow top of the thimble shape stood on the deck. A seaman stepped forward and raised the sledgehammer. It only took a few careful blows to slacken off the iron hoops that held the oaken staves together. The hoops slipped down and the whole thing collapsed like a bridge with the keystone blasted out. The diving bell had become a mere bundle of kindling wood.

'And where will the bell go?' I spoke to Ephraim Nellist without looking at him. His ill-temper was still strong. But the soft answer came from Sylvanus Webster himself!

'We shall certainly have other work for the device, Captain Ellyot.' He did not say the words but there was no mistaking the 'and hence for you!' his tone had implied. The voice was crisp. Webster was in good humour, almost in high spirits.

'It will be stored for us by friends in Wearmouth until we have need of it again.' I sensed a deliberate pause. He looked across at Ephraim Nellist. 'Is that not so Master Nellist?'

Webster's words were soft, silken almost, but Nellist could not have mistaken them. His first answer was a string of blasphemy hurled, seemingly, across at his crew working out in the pouring rain. Then he half turned and spoke softly: 'It shall be as you say, Master Webster.'

Nellist did not look at Webster. I knew that whatever plan he had attempted to gain my help with had failed. Ephraim Nellist was subdued, and I knew well that Dr. Webster's appearance on the keel was the cause of Nellist's plan being spiked. The longboat carrying the last of the cannon away up river had been barely out of our sight when Sylvanus Webster, as neat and dapper as ever in his fine broadcloth and lace edged linen collar, had put his buckled shoes quietly on to the keel's deck.

Nellist may have been able to hide his surprise but he could hardly suppress his anger. Clearly the ship-master was a man thwarted in some matter of importance. Webster knew it and he was amused.

'You have news of Mistress Hannah's grand-daughter, Master Webster?' My question was almost a whisper. I was overtaken by a sudden bashfulness, and I cursed myself for it. It was as if I were afraid even to speak Aphra Thornton's name aloud. Though if Webster noticed my discomfort he made no sign of it.

'No news, Captain Ellyot.' He looked at me, the same piercing look that he had levelled at me the first time that we had met. 'No news – that is, unless you are able to procure some news for us.' My response hung fire. What did Webster want of me now? If I allowed Webster to persuade me to go to Newcastle I was as good as a dead man already. No disguise would hide me. And yet I knew full well that if Newcastle were where Aphra Thornton was, I would go. It was no use telling myself that I was just badly smitten by the lass. I'd been that more than once, and yet I had always been able to force myself to follow the roll of the drums when the order to march away came. This time was different. I knew that there would be no riding away.

'Some news?' My mouth was dry. I hardly wanted to ask more for fear of what Sylvanus Webster might say. 'How could I get you news of Aphra Thornton? Has Mistress Hannah not been able to find her … ?'

'The girl is not in any of the town's lock-ups; she is not held at the Castle. No charge has been laid against her before any court in the town, civil or military.

Hannah Thornton has made certain of that herself. Nicholas Bronsard had Aphra Thornton arrested under his personal warrant as King's Commissioner. It seems that under his commission he is not obliged to bring a prisoner before any tribunal until he is pleased to do so ... Besides, who is to ask questions of him?'

'But she must be somewhere in Newcastle ... ' I had been confident that Hannah Thornton would by now have at least found out where her grand-daughter was being held captive ' ... or somewhere near the town.' I knew that it would be difficult, impossible even, to keep knowledge of Aphra's whereabouts a secret for long.

'Then she must be held in some place owned by Bronsard, some warehouse or store; perhaps somewhere owned by friends, folk beholden to the Bronsards or ... '

'Which could of course mean half of the families of note on the Tyneside.'

Webster did not even look at me when he spoke. He was watching Nellist's crew. The men still worked in the rain yet it had taken them no time at all to un-ship the sheerlegs and cut the lashings that held the two hulls together. The keelboats began to drift apart. Now only our anchor held us in place. Within minutes the other half of our makeshift craft had drifted up river on the tide and was lost in the downpour.

Will Blacket sniffed, long and loud, behind me. 'Which leaves us as orphans o' the storm! It'll piss down like this all night long,' he muttered, almost to himself, though I found myself grunting my agreement. He held a clean linen shirt for me to thrust my head and arms into. The warmed fabric, though well worn, was a cheer to me. Just where and how Will came by it I didn't ask. The same place, I supposed, as the mutton chop and barley that was stewing over the driftwood fire.

'So you still have work for me to do, Master Webster? Work which may concern Bronsard ... and which may yet bring news of Aphra Thornton?'

'I *do* have work for you!' Webster swung round. It was as though he had made a sudden decision and wanted something done as soon as could be.

'I have raised your guns.' I spoke to bring Webster up short. The fellow was clearly prepared to commandeer my services again without any thought for my own needs or wishes. He had had broken me out of the Stank Tower and now I had repaid the debt. The transaction was completed, so far as I was concerned. Though there had, I recalled, been mention of a few shillings a day in soldier's pay.

'True! The work was well done and took a deal less time than I had supposed.' Webster seemed to know what I was thinking. 'So now you are out of service and no doubt you seek employment.'

Touché! The man was right. I was free but that for the moment was all that I could claim. If I listened to my wits I would still run; I would still get as far away from Newcastle, from the North East of England altogether. A prudent man would force himself to forget Aphra Thornton. A sensible man, a man who wanted to keep a head on his shoulders would make for Hull and take the first ship to the Low Countries. There were merchants in The Hague who traded in soldiers the way other men trade in pigs and sheep. With luck I could be there in ten days; with halfway good fortune I could be on the muster rolls of an army inside two weeks. It was what I knew about; it was what I was good at.

'So you are likely to be off the Continent to seek service?' Sylvanus Webster truly did smile. I stood back a pace and allowed Will to hold my coat for me to slip my arms into. Will flicked over the coat with a brush.

'Very likely, Master Webster. Sergeant Blacket and I shall go to The Hague, to the House of Deaf Jacobus.' I twisted my mouth and smiled back at him a little, 'at the sign of the Golden Calf. I've heard tell that the agents of the Czar of Muscovy pay a handsome premium in gold for good gunners.'

'Why go so far?' Webster raised his chin and peered down his nose at me, like a merchant putting a value to a flawed diamond. 'We have a grand war here – just about to start. The pay for captains is all of two shillings and seven pence a day, and handsome victuals, lodgings, and a mount.' He gave the merest glance at Will. 'And of course an officer may keep a camp servant to see to his comfort.'

'Two shillings and seven pence, you say? Would that be English or Scots?' I knew that I would seldom have the chance to jest at Sylvanus Webster's expense.

'The Scots army will be being paid in English coin for so long as they garrison Newcastle.' Sylvanus Webster spoke in deadly earnest. 'General Leslie will cross the Tyne the day after tomorrow at Newburn, six or so miles above the town.'

I must have shown my disbelief. 'With him he will have more than thirty thousand men, good men. More than half of his officers are veterans of the Swedish service and a good many of the private men have seen service overseas.'

'And they will take Newcastle, the town with the strongest walls in all Europe?' I knew that what Webster was claiming was probably true, yet I felt impelled to offer him argument. The thought that thirty thousand bare-arsed Scotsmen should enter my own town caused a rare anger to rise up in me. Webster saw it and pressed his advantage.

'Consider,' he stepped closer to me. 'If you hold a commission issued by General Leslie and in the name of the Scottish Assembly, you can walk abroad in the town of Newcastle without fear of arrest.'

'Would you would have me, an Englishman born, swear allegiance to Scotland! You would have me strutting about the streets of Newcastle in the pay of those thieving bastards? Man, you must be daft!' Webster looked at me for a moment. The brim of his hat hid his face from the glow of the firelight.

'No ... I would not ... I would have you maintain allegiance to me and to the cause I serve. I offer you a chance to serve God, the Protestant Religion, and our English Parliament.'

I had been about to laugh. The King had not even called an English Parliament until the March of that year; and that had been the first for eleven years. But I held my face straight and waited.

'Serve me, John Ellyot, take the commission that I offer you, do my bidding for a year. I can promise you that by then you will bear the rank of major in a new English army, and that you will come into possession of a goodly estate, freehold and clear of any encumbrance whatever.'

Webster looked for a moment as though he was about to raise a hand. But his arm fell away and the fire in his gaze died down. 'I solemnly affirm that it will be so,' he said quietly.

'I will give you my answer tomorrow, Master Webster. Tonight I mean to dine well and sleep long, in a feather bed.' Webster's promise was not one to be taken lightly for I knew in my water that it had not been given lightly. Everything about this so-called Doctor Sylvanus Webster spoke of great affairs and power, and the doings of men who stood above the commonplace. He was a creature of court and chancery. He had a quality that reminded me of the scratch of goosequills and the sharp smell of newly poured sealing wax.

'Choose now ... ' It was a whisper but it cut right through me. I think that I almost agreed. It was in my mind that I should serve this man and his cause. But just in time, it seemed, my own will and wits recovered themselves. I did not speak, I looked at Sylvanus Webster straightly, and smiled, and allowed him to wait. Only when he had frowned and started to turn away did I answer.

'Three months!' I snatched back his attention. 'For three months I will serve you as well and as faithfully as I have done these last few days. After that we shall speak again. I'll take your two shillings and seven pennies a day. But you must pay Will Blacket here eighteen pence a day.' I waited until Webster had silently nodded his agreement.

'And you will need to provide us with a horse each, and arms ... and a small purse to cover our day-to-day expenses.'

Webster's handshake was hard and cold. 'Now ... ' The old precision had returned to his voice. 'First of all take this.' He handed me a scroll of paper with a scrap of red silk ribbon fixed to it. There was no mistaking the paper's importance. *By the Authority of the Assembly* ... The name John Ellyot had been limned-in along the line left blank for the purpose. Sylvanus Webster had handed me a commission made out in the rank of captain in the Scottish army.

There was no mistaking the ill-written signature. It was common knowledge that fine soldier though 'crooked wee Davie' was, his Excellency was close to illiterate. I saw that the paper was dated for a more than a month before and I snorted in derision.

'As for your horses and arms, your first task will provide you handsomely with both.'

I waited. I had had that answer many a dozen times from quartermasters when supplies were wanting.

'Cross to Bishopwearmouth and go to the tavern called the Mitre.' Webster looked over my shoulder at Will Blacket. 'Equip yourselves fully from among the troops you find there.' I fancied I heard Will Blacket's tongue lick out around his lips and I knew that if I turned I would see that he was grinning like a dog and showing his white teeth. 'Then I want you to deliver this letter to the Castle, to the Baillie Gate.' He held out a flat case of polished brown leather with a shoulder strap.

I took the case and turned it so that the flap was uppermost. There was no mistaking what he had given me. The C.R. and the royal arms woven in gold thread over a backing of crimson velvet. The scrolled embroidery of the initials for Carolus Rex.

Webster had given me something that was as good as the badge of a King's courier. The pouch would get me past any sentinel in the land; or else possession of it would get me hung, drawn, and bloodily quartered.

'Place that into the hands of a Major Salathiel Miniver. You will recognise him easily. Look for an officer who is as fat as the Gilsland Boar and who has the strangest nose that ever graced a Christian face. Miniver will not know you. Act as a trooper in all respects. If he asks, tell Major Miniver that you have ridden from Durham Town – that, you believe, the regular despatch horsemen had taken a fall and lies with a broken leg at Durham. You know no more. Say only that a cornet-of-horse, named Morteboys, gave you the despatch pouch and ordered you to take it to Newcastle at the gallop. And then, when he dismisses you, say to him that Mr Morteboys presents his complements and asks for 'news on that other matter'. If he gives you a note take it at once to Mistress Hannah Thornton.

'Mistress Thornton?' How was I to find her; the old woman was now as much a fugitive as I was myself. Sylvanus Webster must have divined the look on my face.

'Walk along Silver Street until you come to the shop of George Fenwick at the sign of the Bonny Rowan Tree. Go in and ask to be shown the new ivory chess set. That is all. Someone will take you to Hannah. By the time you get there she will have been told of your coming.'

I waited for more instructions but it was plain that Webster's orders were complete. His attention was elsewhere.

～

The Mitre shook to the rafters with the noise. A drink-slurred voice was bawling out the verses of 'So the Milkmaid says to the Curate, sez she … ', and at least a dozen others yelled out the chorus. The rhythmic stamp of the boots told us that the singers were troopers.

'We'll take our man as he takes a piss?' Will had brought the blackthorn cudgel ashore from the keel. He smacked it hard against his palm.

'But for God's sake wait until we can find a man tall enough. I want a coat and breeches, aye, and boots, that fit me – comfortably!'

The wall at the back of the Mitre had so much rubbish piled against it that getting into the yard was easy. And the dunghill from the landlord's pigs was high and ripe, and the yard was lit only by a slit of light from the still-room window.

Drunken troopers came and went, most to ease their bladders, some to spew and groan and stagger away back to drink again. I let four men go before I gauged that we had a man of the right size and girth. I nudged at Will Blacket's arm. He waited until the fellow had re-tied his breeches, then he stepped out of the shadow and fetched the unfortunate a sharp crack to the side of his head. I caught him by the arms before he had slumped into the pig dung. He was heavy. And he began to snore as we carried him away into the darkness.

When you rob a man it is better to strip him naked. A Christian has to find at least a rag to cover his nakedness before he can raise the alarm. Will tore the fellow's drawers and shirt into strips and set to trussing him up and tethering him to a bush.

The uniform was new enough and the gear in good order. I dressed as carefully as the want of light allowed. We were wanting a helmet however. Clubbing a drunken trooper is no great matter. Stealing a horse from the army is another business altogether. A cavalry troop guards its mounts well. The horses had been taken to the town's moor. And it did not take long for us to see that our chances of lifting a couple of beasts without rousing the guard were less than slim. There were four watch fires blazing bright. And the guards were sober.

There must have been an officer in charge of the six men because we could hear the challenge and the response, clear and loud, when guards met. Everything was being carried out in proper form and according to the manual. Each man carried a wheelock carbine, ready to loose off a shot. We watched the horses for a long time, hoping that perhaps the officer would stand down, and allow the men's vigilance to relax. It was beginning to get light.

Then Will Blacket nudged me and pointed. Beside one of the watch fires a trooper had filled one bucket with water from a barrel and another with grain from a new opened sack. Only an officer's servant would carry grain and water at that hour. We followed him.

Perhaps a hundred yards up a lane the fellow kicked open a door and went inside. We were in and out, and away, all inside ten minutes. Will Blacket's club hit the groom just as his lips were about to close on those of a young servant girl. She opened her mouth, then she saw Will standing there. Her eyes widened. Will put his mouth next to her ear and said something. The girl began to blush and then to smile.

The charger we found stalled there was a dappled grey. She was in high condition, full of fire. The beast snorted and stamped when I dropped the military saddle on to her back. I let Will play the valet on my uniform and accoutrements. He was satisfied only when he had found a helmet and laced the steel scaled cheek pieces firmly under my chin.

'Meet me in Newcastle, at Amen Corner by the church of St Nicholas ... I'll be there if I can, at the stroke of noon or at six o'clock in the evening; if you can't come yourself send word ... understood?' I handed him my purse. 'Good luck,' I said, 'good luck ... Sergeant Blacket!'

I was aware that a hue and cry could be raised at any moment but I had no mind to punish my newly-come-by horse. It was a fine powerful animal and it carried me easily. I headed west, following the track that had brought us to Wearside. But I crossed the river lower down, putting my horse into the water at South Hylton. At low tide it was less than belly deep and I forded the Wear without so much as wetting my boots. My choice of fording place was a lucky one. I had crossed the river obliquely, moving upstream, trying to find a place where my horse could get out of the water easily. My eye was caught by a pale blaze down the trunk of one of a half dozen ancient oak trees that grew close to the river's edge.

The tree had taken injury. A branch thicker than a fat man's wrist had been rent off. I think I smiled. I rode around the place, taking in the small pieces of evidence. There were places where the bark on the trees had been polished by hard friction, where thick ropes had been secured. There were the great hoof marks of plough-horses, printed deep in the soft mud and filled with water from last night's downpour.

Then I found the grooves made by the wheels of great wagons, all heavy laden. My three cannon had passed that way.

I took my time on the ride to Newcastle, flanking the North Road and keeping to higher ground. There was much traffic below me – carts and wagons, and driven cattle, and most moving to the South. I was not surprised. Northern folk have learned to be prudent. Newcastle was emptying. The wives and children of all who could afford to flee would go first. Their valuables would be hidden among bedding and carpets. What couldn't be carried would have been buried. That would be a most grievous folly. I found myself grinning. It would take more than a shovel full of earth to hide buried valuables from a Jock soldier. And if he couldn't find it himself, why then it was a wonder what crushing a man's knuckles in a musket lock would make him tell.

I had seen it all before, all over the north of Europe. Prices would fly to the sky overnight as farmers kept away from markets. Merchants would hoard their goods and raise their prices. Inside a week the town's poor people, the porters and water carriers, the day labourers and the washerwomen, and their bairns, would all begin to look gaunt about the face.

Newcastle looked the same – though even at a mile's distance I could sense the change. There were few ships moored at the quayside. It was a market day. I had expected to see crowds. Then I realised that it was the silence. The town should have had a buzz and a murmur that could be heard from far away. That had gone. Today my own Newcastle was hushed.

My horse's hooves clattered on the cobblestones of the yard in front of the Baillie Gate. My faith in the power of the royal cipher on the courier's pouch was not betrayed. I had passed into the town unchallenged and I rode by the pikemen guarding the Castle courtyard with no more than a glance. Even a humble trooper gains a shred of precedence when he carries despatches. I made my boots ring on the stones as I stamped my way up the narrow stairway to Major Miniver's room. There are Minivers in every army. I knew his kind at first sight. A gross body stuffed into a rich uniform; a swine in human guise, but always a cunning swine. Sylvanus Webster had not over-egged the pudding when he had spoken of Miniver's nose. The nose that the man had been born with had been big, and its having been broken and spread at some time had not decreased its shadow at all.

He was making entries against the names on a long muster role, and smiling as his quill scratched crosses against some. I stamped to attention before his table and presented the despatch pouch. He snapped his fingers twice but he did not look up from his work.

I handed him the pouch. But he made no move to open it.

'You have ridden from York, trooper?'

'From Durham, Sah!' I was a private soldier again. That meant that I offered no crumb of information beyond what I had been asked for. Miniver raised his chins and squinted at me. I knew how a humble trooper needed to look at a senior officer: look over the poxy bastard's right shoulder and at a point far in the distance. Never you, ever, look the whoremonger straight in the eyes. I recalled the leather face of old Joachim, the gunner who had given me that advice.

'Rider from York thrown when his mount stumbled, Sah! Mr Morteboys ordered me to Newcastle with the despatch, Sah!'

Mention of Cornet Morteboys's name was my *laisser passer*. Miniver breathed slowly and with a faint whistling wheeze deep down in his throat. The major was not a well man. Whatever the message I had carried from Sylvanus Webster was, the fat officer was clearly delighted to get it, and, I thought, somewhat relieved too. The pig's eyes narrowed as they scanned the half dozen lines of writing again and again. Then he sagged down in his chair, seemingly satisfied.

'Good ... Get out!'

'Mr Morteboys sends his complements and asks ... ' I screwed up my face as though struggling to remember, '... if Your Honour has any information on that other matter.' I saluted again and stood stiffly to attention.

There was a silence in the room. The sound of horses being led and the soft clank and jingle of harness passed by. Then I heard the even sequence of commands as a troop was brought into line and the men ordered to dismount. There was at least one troop sergeant in the garrison who knew his trade.

'As you were ... Wait!' Miniver picked up his quill and stroked his flattened nose with the feather end for a few seconds. Then he took up a scrap of used paper and glanced at the writing, scored through it and began to write. The message was short enough. He dipped his quill only once before he sifted sand over the wet ink. Chair and table creaked as Miniver fought his way to his feet. He went to the window and looked down into the courtyard. He stood there for a moment, wheezing and blowing softly.

'Your orders take you back to Durham at once, trooper?'

It was then that the bastard almost had me. I had opened my mouth and a smart 'Yessir!' was readied in my throat. It was the oldest trick.

'Sir ... No, Sir! Mount has a swellin' above a fetlock, Sir!' I lowered my voice. 'She belongs to Mr Morteboys, Sir. He was anxious to see that the despatches were delivered to you. Sir! I shall have to walk her back to Durham, Sir. Orders to return soonest ... Sah!'

I watched the greed on his fat face fade into disappointment. The mare was an officer's mount, there was no mistaking that. Just in time I had seen that Miniver had thought to commandeer it and send me back to Durham mounted on a trooper's hack.

He continued to peer down into the courtyard. I risked a step forward and a quick glance at the letter I had brought him. The few lines gave me a little to make guesses but not much. Even upside down, I could make out from the first few lines that it was an order summoning Major Salathiel Miniver to report himself to York. That too was an old trick. He was not the first officer who had contrived to get himself posted on the eve of battle. And I could understand his fear: a man of Miniver's weight and poor health would fare badly in a cavalry skirmish. Little wonder too that he had an eye out for a strong horse to carry his bulk.

I speculated. He was a quartermaster. He was in charge of provisions and supplies for the royal garrison. The richness of his clothes told me that, even if I could have overlooked the ledgers and rolls of paper lying about the room. I wondered what Sylvanus Webster would have to do with such a man. Then I almost forgot myself so far as to allow a grin to crease my face. I knew. Sylvanus Webster was saving one of his own creatures. He had arranged to get Major Miniver recalled to Headquarters at York – before the battle with the Scots. The pieces fell into place. The scheme had Webster's mark on it. One way to weaken a castle's defences was to buy its provisions and ammunition from a corrupt quartermaster. I guessed that Webster would see to it that Major Miniver would live to cheat the King again.

'Take this ... ' He spilled the sand off the paper, then he folded the scrap twice. 'Give it into the hands of Cornet Morteboys, and to nobody else. Y' hear?'

I saluted and reached for the despatch bag. 'Leave that! The case stays with me. Here put ... ' He stopped. 'Can you read, trooper?'

'Read, Sir? Me, Sir?' I sounded astonished and a little shocked. But Miniver had cut me off well before I could deny being a scholar. He thrust the little square of paper at me.

'Shut your hole and get out!'

I played my part flawlessly to the end. I saluted with a smart cavalryman's snap and a stamp of my boots that fetched a clink from my spurs. I turned for the door and there I was stopped in mid-stride. Mouncey Bone was already advancing across the room at me. His sword was in his hand.

Chapter 23

Into Battle

'Bone! What the Devil d'ye mean!' Major Miniver's splutter of anger saved my life. He was on his feet, his face like a ripe damson with rage at the intrusion. Bone looked aside, it was a mere flinch at Miniver's harsh yell. But it gave me time to step backwards and clear my sword. Bone came on. I parried two wild slashes, left then right, delivered with fury, but no great skill.

A man may learn to fight on horseback and remain a ploughboy when his feet are on the ground. Two more hacking strokes and a sudden lunge straight at my face had me dancing aside and backwards.

Two heavy men, stamping and grunting back and forth across the room, make a great deal of noise. My fear was that troopers passing under the arch of the Baillie Gate Tower would hear the clash of blades. The business had to be finished – and quickly. We stood for a few seconds, both of us breathing hard. Bone glared at me, his face twisting with fury. I knew better. Anger your opponent – keep calm yourself. I forced myself to incline my head in a mocking bow. He rose to that.

We went at it again. The swish and clang of blade on blade echoed back from bare limewashed walls. I watched Bone. It was plain that his skill at swordplay came mostly from looking at the woodcut pictures in a manual of arms. That momentary fancy almost got my skull smashed. Mouncey Bone may have had little enough of a *sentiment du fer* but he made up for his lack of blade sense with the full hand's breadth of height he had over me – that and his strong right arm. There was no room in this fight for *froise countered with sixte*; no flashing *remise* to carve a bloody but shallow scratch down a man's cheek and so to end a duel between gentlemen. This was stamp, slash, recover, and slash again. And the slightest fault in the other man's recovery opened his guard and offered the chance for a kill. We were evenly matched in our swords: they were of the same regimental issue: the long bladed Scaviola, forged to be swung or thrust with the weight of a charging horse behind it – and as much use for fine swordplay as kitchen pokers!

I swung low at the instant that Bone was raising his blade. The wavering th'wish sounded loud and lasted long, too long. He saw the stroke coming and jumped to avoid it. As his boots hit the floor planks again I flung myself forward. My helmet with its ridged crest hit him full in the face. I heard his teeth crunch. He should have fallen backwards with the full weight of my body thrown against him. He did not. Instead he stood there spitting teeth and blood. Few things touch upon a man's vanity so much as the sudden loss of his front teeth. Bone went red-eyed with rage. He leapt at me, attacking like a madman, slashing wildly, his blade lashing as though it weighed no more than a hazel wand. The closed room was hot. Dust raised by our movement danced in the thin beams of sunlight coming in through the mullioned windows. The warm reek of sweat and fear – half of it mine – hung heavy on the air. I stood my ground against the first storm of Bone's attack. Our blade edges scraped and clashed back and forth. The lime-plastered walls were scored where want of space had stopped our cuts and slashes. Chips of broken plaster littered the floor. The stamp and slide of our footwork crushed them to a pale powder that traced out ghostly tracks of our movements.

I had to give way. I let him back me across the room until I was against the far wall. Twice his blade scraped across my faceguard. Once he set my head ringing and blurred my sight as his sword struck home against my helmet. Bone's triumph came as an as animal snort through his nose and a toss of his head that spattered his warm blood over my face. Then I took my chance. I put a boot against the wall and got the leverage to push myself forward. Force of thrust overbore Bone, throwing him backwards. He tried a desperate downward slash as he staggered. His cavalry drill betrayed him. I took a short step backward. The point of his sword scored a line across the front of my breastplate. He had lost. I made the single cut as easily as though I were slashing at a turnip in the exercise yard. The first three inches of my blade tip took him across the throat. For once I had achieved the unhurried stroke of a master swordsman. My blade made a mournful sound and I could swear that I saw his blood spurt before my blade struck. Then for half an eyeblink I saw the pale circle of his windpipe cut across as cleanly as a butchered sheep's.

I stood clear, panting, and knowing that I was a little unsteady on my feet. Bone's breath soughed, out and in, once, through his severed throat as his blood bubbled down his chest. He stood, wide eyed, staring at me. Then he dropped to his knees and fell forward again, face down. I listened to the life going out of him.

There is always a pause after you have killed a man. I stood looking down at Bone. The sound of my heart thumping in my chest began to slow – the roaring in my ears was fading. I could smell the hot blood and the stench of his bowels. The scales of revenge for poor dead Luke Ellyot tilted up again.

The harsh click-a-click of a steel ratchet made me turn. All I could see was the top of Major Miniver's head, but I knew that sound well enough. His hands were trembling like those of a man with the ague but he was still spanning back the coiled spring of a wheelock pistol. Powder flask, ball, and wads lay spread on the table before him. I slipped my bloodied swordpoint in under his rolls of chin fat and when his head came up I reached forward and plucked the pistol from his shaking fingers.

'Major Miniver ... Consider!' My voice was soft, almost a whisper. He was boggling up at me. Sweat ran down his forehead and into his eyes, making him blink and screw up his face like a fat baby looking into bright light. 'Bone attacked you. The dog had attempted to rob the regimental pay chest. You stopped him.'

I reached down for Miniver's sword and drew it. The blade was Spanish. It was a finer weapon than ever came out of the Tower Armoury. 'We shall exchange blades.' I smiled again.' Mine own is a poor thing but it has the blood of glory fresh upon it.' Now I grinned into his face, showing my teeth and raising an eyebrow at him. I waited until he had shaken his jowls to show that he understood.

'Wipe a little of Bone's blood on you.' I touched the blade and smeared the darkening stickiness about Miniver's face and collar. 'A man who has gallantly cut down a thief can look his brother officers in the eye ... even if he has just been ordered away to York on the very eve of battle.' I let my lips curve upward to form a rictus that would not have disgraced a corpse. 'And Captain Bone doubtless has a fine powerful cavalry charger for which he no longer has need.'

Miniver needed no urging. Some plan of his own had already begun to dance behind his rheumy little eyes. His veined face wobbled as he stood up and struggled out from behind the table but there was no mistaking his determination. I give the fellow credit for making haste to garner as much as he could from an opportunity. He knelt beside Bone's corpse and when he stood up again he was well slathered with fast thickening blood.

I swept the pistol and ammunition from the table and put them into the courier's pouch. As I shut the door behind me, Major Salathiel Miniver was standing, with my sword in his hand, looking down at the corpse. Perhaps he was already half persuaded that he himself had indeed cut down Mouncey Bone.

I strode across the Castle Garth yard with all the swagger of a King's trooper walking out on furlough. My spurs jingled softly and I made show of pulling at the cuffs of my gauntlets. I knew that if I could maintain the show until I had ridden out through the gate, I would be clear. My horse stood where I had tethered it and never had a military saddle felt such a comfort under my backside.

'I say ... You there, Soldier!' I reined up and looked around.

'Sah!' I saluted smartly and set my horse's head towards the steps where he stood. The officer had just stepped out of what I took to be the garrison orderly room, and he stood there, one hand on his hip, slapping his soft leather boots with his riding whip. I dismounted quickly and stood to attention.

Again I remembered an old soldier's advice. Never you dare to look down on the bastards: it ain't wise for a trooper to sit up in the saddle when he speaks to an officer who's afoot. But this time I did venture to look him directly in the face.

'Ahhh ... ' He knew well enough what he wanted to say, but that throat sound was a habitual preface with younger officers. 'Where are you going at this moment, trooper?' He drawled the words slowly and with a curious drone sound coming from high in the back of his throat.

'Courier, Sah!' I dropped my hand down to the message pouch with its royal insignia. 'Returning to Durham Castle, Sah!' I lowered my voice a little. 'I have orders to return this charger to Mr Morteboys at garrison headquarters.' There would be no advantage, I decided, in mentioning the officer's lowly rank. And it had occurred to me that that particular cornet-of-horse might not even exist at all; he might be a mere thing out of Sylvanus Webster's imagination.

The pale brow wrinkled a little as though he were working on some weighty matter. I scanned him quickly. The lad could hardly be past eighteen. I doubt that he had held his commission for six months.

'Ahhh ... ' I stiffened and looked to my front. He stood there with enough jewels on his carcass to buy small farm. The pearl pendant dangling from his right ear was probably worth a hundred pounds or more. 'Well it is unlikely that your officer will be at Durham now. The Durham garrison has been ordered to come to Newcastle to reinforce us. So you had better join my troop for the present. We are to ride to some place called Newburn where we shall meet with the Scottish scum and destroy them.'

'Sah!' There was nothing else I could say. Already Miniver had begun to raise his alarm. But I comforted myself with the fancy that I could hear the prayer of thanks that some iron-faced Presbyterian pikeman would offer up to a vengeful and unforgiving Almighty when he ripped the pearl dangler from that youngster's lug.

All that afternoon I rankled at being caught and looked for an excuse or chance to get away into the town's streets. But with many a hundred fellows of the same mind we were well watched the whole time. The troop I been pressed into paraded before St Nicholas's steps to be blessed by a pale priest who stumbled through a benediction. Then we rode out. We went to battle without music. At our officers' commands we returned the three cheers of the assembled garrison, drawn up in ranks down the length of the Sandgate. And as ever the men who were not going to meet an enemy cheered us right heartily. Few townsfolk stood to watch us go.

We made our crossing of the narrow Tyne Bridge two abreast. Then we went at the slow gallop through a Gateshead that looked to be almost empty, and passed out by the Pipewellgate to march and ride towards the west. King's troops were strung out along the south bank of the Tyne for more than a mile. But it wasn't until we were clear of Newcastle that I realised that Lord Conway had split his army into two. I had expected that we would be about ten thousand of foot and three thousand of horse. Here we were just three thousand infantry and no more than fifteen hundred cavalry. My guts griped with dismay. It had been common knowledge in the streets that the

Scots army could not be less than thirty thousand strong. I was part of a forlorn hope. I turned in my saddle to look behind us. Jesu! never in all my years in the Swedish service had I seen such disorder. We had retreated in better order than this Royal army advanced. The infantry was pitiful to look at. The poor bastards were ill-shod and tinker-clad in bits and pieces of armour and equipment. There was no singing from those ranks.

We needed no guide to see us to Newburn. Scots watch fires burned bright in the misty blue of that Summer's night. The distant red sparks covered the hill of Heddon Law and then sprinkled, none so sparsely, down the darkening valley bottom to the village of Newburn.

There was to be no sleep that night. We arrived at the south side of the ford directly across the Tyne from Newburn. There was no sign of the Scots in the darkness across the water.

We were ordered to dismount and set to pull turfs to build breastworks to defend the river ford. A thousand men can pull a great deal of turf in five hours. By sunrise we had two breastworks built to bar the way up from the ford. One was close to the landing place and the other was raised a little way inland. Eight small cannon had been dragged from Newcastle. Four guns were mounted in each of the breastworks; though I could see that there was precious little ammunition for them.

By common consent rather than given orders, the work stopped when the church clock at Newburn on the Scots side of the river clanged out eight o' clock. Hundreds of men threw themselves down in the meadow grass to fall asleep.

I rode about the forward camp unchallenged. Here I was on no troop's muster rolls so I was known to none of the officers. Again the courier's pouch with its bright embroidery worked its magic for me. I thought I might cross to the north bank before the fighting started. I might have done that, but the tidal water stood high between the river banks. When the waters fell again the battle for the ford would begin.

I watched the ration carts arrive at Lord Conway's encampment up on the wooded hillside at Stella. My nose told me the three carts that arrived from Newcastle were loaded with fresh baked bread. They brought no fishes, so it would take a double miracle to feed our five thousand. I needed sleep more than food; but I drew rations and sat down at one of the fires to grill a scrap of salted belly pork. Then I found a place, rolled myself in my cloak and fell asleep smelling the sweet scent of the grass.

The first shot was fired late in the forenoon. I saw it happen. I had ridden down to the river to water my horse and fill my own flask. A man who neglects to do that before a fight is a fool. Scots cavalrymen were doing the same along the north bank. There was no offer of violence from either side. Then I saw a young Scots officer come out of one of the thatched houses. He stopped and put on a broad hat with a curling black ostrich feather in it. I let my horse drink while I watched. The Scot mounted up and rode his horse out into shallows. The heavy bang of a firelock from the top of our own breastworks echoed across the water. The Scot toppled out of the saddle. His horse went on drinking.

'T' bastard were lookin' at our defences.' The sentry was carefully reloading his matchlock. But there was a plaintive pitch, a note of excuse in his voice. White powder smoke from his shot hung heavy about where he stood marking his guilt. He got no praise for what had been a remarkable enough shot. His old sergeant said nothing but took out his pipe and spat on the ground.

The Scots returned fire before the echo of the shot had fully died away. A file of musketeers formed up along the river bank and loosed a volley across at us. Lead balls droned in over my head to thump into the turf of the breastworks.

A man screamed. Then the Scots cannon began to fire.

Their placement had been uncommonly clever. I saw the red flash and the ring of grey smoke that grew from its centre and drifted slowly outwards, widening as it went. But I could never have anticipated where it came from. The Scots had made use of the only point that overlooked the English defences at the ford. They had at least one cannon mounted on the tower of Newburn parish church. Then I realised exactly what manner of cannon they could mount in a church roof.

'Leather guns, by God!' So the Scots had brought more of their experience in Gustavus's wars home with them. The leather gun was no more than a thin-walled copper tube strengthened lengthwise with iron rods and the whole bound around with strips of horsehide. The pieces for the making of such a gun could well have been carried down from Scotland on men's shoulders. The Scots had indeed had a braw notion there!

The turf breastwork set up on our side of the river might have given good defence against musket fire for long enough, but plunging fire from cannon positioned so that they could shoot down into the defenders soon began to do damage that showed. And the men began to fret as their friends were killed around them and still no reinforcements were sent.

It was between three and four in the afternoon. The river level was falling fast. Newburn lies nearly fifteen miles from the sea, but the Tyne still rose and fell twice each day. And the Newburn crossing was only passable at low water.

They came on with a rush, their horses' hooves throwing fans of white water at either side. I reckoned that there were twenty-six horsemen in the vanguard, all well mounted, and they cheered like lads at play as they charged. Our four cannon in the breastworks at the ford fired off ragged blasts but I saw that none of the Scots horsemen had fallen. Perhaps our untrained gunners could not depress the muzzles of their cannon low enough to shoot into them. They came on. Then I looked around and saw why. Our English troops were running. A thousand or more of the blue bonneted Scots had rushed from cover to pour down the steep clay slopes of the north bank of the Tyne and splash into the shallow water.

They cheered, bagpipes squealed and droned, and their cannon kept up the bombardment. More shots from the leather guns screamed over the heads of the Scots, to throw up splashes of brown earth from the meadows where the English were now fleeing headlong and heedless.

For a moment it looked as though the retreat was general. I mounted up and was prepared to ride after my comrades. Then there was a trumpet call, short sharp blasts, rising and falling. English cavalry had formed up for a charge. They were coming up from the east, flanking the course of the river and bearing down on the fording place where the Scots, foot as well as horse, were already swarming ashore.

I would take my oath that what happened next could only have come about by bloody treachery. The front line of English horse were within a hundred yards of clashing with the Scots when the trumpet sounded again – this time it played the doleful notes that signalled the order to retreat. I bear witness. Never have I seen horses reined up and turned about so readily. The English were only too eager to obey that trumpet call. Yet there were a handful of men among them who kept their soldier's honour. And as ever, they were plain fellows, few of them were of the nobility. These were the horsemen of the rear-guard. They rode through their own fleeing ranks and charged the Scots, battering down the wall of wooden shields held up against them. For a moment it looked as though they would throw the Scots back from the ford. They were soon well set-to in the clash of brisk swordplay in the shallow waters. But it took no military genius to foretell the outcome. They were bold but too few. The rearguard cavalry were outnumbered and quickly overwhelmed, dragged out of the saddle by Scots pikemen.

It was done. The English horse took themselves off in a galloping mass up the hill towards the south. The foot soldiers just ran away, the way they had come, back towards Newcastle. Scots cavalry, led by the great General David Leslie himself, pursued the English horse but it was plain enough to me that the blue bonnets had orders not to give any hot chase. By five o'clock of that afternoon of the 28th of August 1640 the Scots had won an easy victory.

And it looked also to have been a cheap one: I counted twelve corpses left lying in the river. It was a strange feeling for me to see my own country's forces run off the field while I held in my pocket a captain's commission signed by the general of the enemy army. I rode inland along the south bank of the Tyne. I must have been the only man in the whole of the English force to ride in that direction for I saw not a soul. A mile or so up the river I came to the head of the tidal water and crossed easily. With my helmet slung from my saddle bow, and a piece of grey and black plaid that I had picked up draped over my shoulder, I reckoned not to be one wit out of place in the Scots camp. And so it was.

For all their valour that day, the Scots army at Newburn looked like crowd of Merry Andrews ready for a St Bartholomew's Fair. There was hardly a piece of uniform gear to be seen among them. Though it is strange to say that most of the men were Lowlanders, and decently breeched. I saw hardly a philibeg among them. And I wondered how the day would have gone if Lord Conway had known just how very few firelocks and how many archers there were in their ranks.

I rode among men drunk with joy if with nothing else. General Leslie's tent was easy to find. It stood at the centre of a great crowd of cheering soldiers. Yet I had neither a long wait nor trouble in being taken before the General. I found Alex McLeish close by, sitting on a stool before a surgeon's tent, having a handsomely laid-open cheek stitched. I handed him my flask and let him take a good pull on the last I had of Ephraim Nellist's kummel.

'That's rare scar you'll have to impress the lassies wi,' Alex.' I winked at the elderly surgeon who snipped off the ends of catgut. 'Will y' not fill the wound wi' a good pinch o' gunpowder and touch it off?' He took the flask from McLeish's hand, winked at me, took a gulp and spat a little of the spirit on to the new stitched wound. Just in time I put my hands to the young man's shoulders and held him down until the pain of the cauterising had died away.

'I have every expectation that I shall have such a grand possession, Captain Ellyot.' McLeish blinked and forced a wry smile.

I leaned forward and flicked a single bright tear from the corner of his eye. 'Aye, Alex ... but y'r mither'll weep sore when she sees her bairn!'

He smiled again and then winced as the curl of his lip pulled at his stitches.

'Did you see us? Did you see the College of Justice Troop charge across the river? Was it not ... grand?'

I made a face that he might have taken to mean that I did indeed think that the lawyers' troop o' horse had performed miracles. But I would be double-damned before I would say as much.

'I need to talk to General Leslie ... ' I pulled out my commission and put it under his nose. 'Master Webster wishes it.'

To my surprise McLeish laughed loud in spite of his gashed face. He wagged a finger at me. 'Say rather that you are here at General Leslie's bidding.' His fingers tapped the rolled paper of my commission. 'This sheet makes you ours, Johnnie Ellyot.' I felt my mouth pucker as though I had bitten into a crabapple. They can't help themselves. Give a Scot a hound's lick of authority and watch the bastard make the most of it. But I let him go on.

'Your Master Webster may be a powerful man in his own country but he is only the lad who fetches the subsidy money from the Norwich merchants.' Young McLeish set his shoulders back and threw out his chest. 'And after this day's work there'll be little enough need for us tae hae a siller-bringer. We have the wealth of the Newcastle coal trade gripped fast in our hands!'

It was a bitter draught for me to swallow but I knew McLeish was right. Ever hungry for money, the Scots had long wanted to get their hands on the gold and silver that the Tyne's coal would bring them. The English supporters of the Parliamentary cause were happy enough to deny the King the all-important wages that the northern coalfields had paid him – for the present at any rate. That the folk of Newcastle should have thirty thousand rat-eyed Scots looters billeted upon them seemed not to matter. That was a sour thought. And the Scottish army would be followed soon enough by hordes of Edinburgh merchants and their Writers-to-the-Signet as they called their lawyers. Who would dare then to take a Scot to law in Newcastle?

I thought I would have to kick my heels for many hours before I would be allowed to see David Leslie, but to my surprise I was standing before the 'wee crookit mannie' himself within minutes.

'Aaaah ... A' ken ye, laddie.' He looked up from the papers he had been struggling to read. It was common knowledge that the great general was no scholar. 'It would ha' been in Stralsund in '35 or '36 ... ' He looked at me, scanning me up and down before his piercing eyes came to rest on my face. I could sense the power and the sheer strength of will in the man. He was softly spoken and plain, but there was no mistaking his natural authority. I saluted, in the Swedish manner, and his wrinkles shaped themselves into a broad smile.

'Y'r a braw gunner as I recall?' I saluted again. 'An' ye've come home to fight for the Protestant cause?'

'I have come home, Excellence.' My tone said as much as the words. I was certain that it would be worse than useless to tell David Leslie anything but the truth. He looked at me again.

'Aye ... as ye say ... ' He understood and I knew that he understood. 'But ye've taken our commission now, Captain, have ye not?'

'I have a paper commission given under Your Excellence's hand. I had it from the man I know as Doctor Sylvanus Webster.' Only the literal truth, plainly spoken, would do for this man. 'I have given my word that I will serve Master Webster for three months. Then I have a mind to give up soldiering for all time.'

'Och, ye have, have ye?' The amusement was unfeigned. What I had said had touched the Scottish general's humour. His eyes twinkled for a moment. 'That is a common ambition among the English gentry these days.' We grinned at one another, for a moment as two professional soldiers.

He went on. 'Well, Captain Ellyot I do wish you heartily well in that worthy enterprise ... indeed I do that.' There was no mistaking the counterfeit gravity that he put into his voice. 'But keep our commission the whiles. I have a task for ye that will serve me well and will do much to please friend Webster.' I listened with extreme care. If I were asked to repeat my instructions back to him I was determined not to be found wanting. 'Bide here for an hour or two.' Again the eyes twinkled. 'Gie the English time tae clear the roads. Then ride tae Gateshead. Find the only cobbler's shop i' the toun ... the sole one if y' tak ma meanin' ... ' I thought it prudent to reward his Excellence's rare Scotch humour with a stupid grin. 'Seek out the cobbler ... ye'll ken the chiel by the red sark he wears. The man will answer tae the name o' Elias Grant. He's the man tae set ye tae work. Tell him that his cousin, John Martin o' Addiewell, was askin' after his health. Take instruction from him – he kens ma' will in certain ... nice matters.'

I waited to be given more detailed instruction but none came. Brevity in the giving of orders, it seemed, was the essence of high command. I might have stood there like a ninny yet, waiting to be dismissed, but for the entrance into the general's tent of a senior officer. I recognised him at once. It was the man to whom Sylvanus Webster had given the name Colonel Dundas. And he greeted me warmly.

'Ah! Captain Ellyot! Y'come in guid time it seems. In time to see the fruits o' your labours gathered in.' He looked at David Leslie for a nod of permission and then opened his clenched hand. The piece was still thick with tallow, pale grease with a sheepish stink to it, but there was no mistaking the coin. It was a double-ducat minted at Utrecht.

The fogging on the mirror in this enterprise suddenly cleared for me. The cannon royal that I had lifted from the bed of the Wear would indeed be important. Perhaps they would be vital to the way the campaign fell out. But nothing could match the gold now held in Scots' hands. Just the rumour that next month's pay was already in the paymaster's coffers would put more heart into the common soldiers than a hundred great cannon.

'So, your Excellencies ... I raised better than I knew.'

The two senior officers laughed loud and Colonel Dundas patted my back. I had indeed raised more than I had suspected. It was common practice to ship cannon with their muzzles well plugged with oak tampions. I had neither thought, nor indeed had I had the chance, to unseal the bores of any of the guns. But I knew that in a weight of eight thousand pounds or so of bronze, a hundred or more pounds of gold pieces would have made little difference. It would be my pleasure to tell Ephraim Nellist that whatever feelings he had held 'in his watter' about the wreck of the *Gerda of Ems* had not been false. And I began to wonder too that Sylvanus Webster had taken my story that I could not find the fourth cannon so very lightly. The mystery was, I thought, partly solved ... but only partly.

The officer who had conducted me to the general's tent touched my arm and led me away. I had been given my orders, but it would be a poor foraging soldier who did not make the most of a captain's commission and the free run of a big encampment. My stomach rumbled for want of food and my mouth was dry.

I found a commissary officer and used the general's name and the story that I had just ridden in with despatches from Edinburgh to claim a small issue of week-old rye bread and wedge of sour-tasting white cheese. But he poured me a good dram of usquebaugh from a square black bottle. It may have been my thirst but I cannot recall ever having tasted better. Then I took my ease in the dusty late afternoon sunshine and watched the Scottish camp.

I found myself marvelling that so many of the Scots had come south armed only with the old fashioned broad sword and the round shield, or targe as they called them, made from oak board and thick enough to stop a musket ball. And there were archers among the ranks, hundreds of them, wild looking lads, recruited I fancied from among the poorer farmers, men who could afford nothing better than an elm stave longbow and a dirk. I wondered what the outcome of the afternoon's battle would have been if Lord Conway had thought to send the entire Newcastle garrison out to meet the Scots at Newburn.

A man's mind is a wondrous creation. I picked up the sonorous quality among all the hubbub of men and horses in the camp. My ears pricked. I had been aware of the murmur of talk in a tent to the left of where I sat but had not heeded it. Then there was a laugh that gripped at my innards like a spasm of the colic. It was a mellow enough noise, but I knew it only too well. I stirred and stood up and made my way towards the sound.

I moved gently and without haste, walking on the trampled grass and stopping to listen every few paces. There were hundred of troops wandering about the hillside, looking for firewood and using their sword blades to cut swathes of long grass to feed their horses. There may have been half a dozen men in the tent. One of them was the commissary officer who had given me the whisky. But it was the mellow voice, the one with the fruity tone that my ears were tuned to pick out from among the babble and the raucous Scots laughter.

'So, gentlemen, it is agreed. I undertake to provide the army of the Covenant with two hundred and fifty hundredweights of clean new harvested oats per day. The measure to be Scots measure ... that is to say ... sixteen pound to the stone and six stone four pounds to the hundredweight. The agreed price to be paid in sound English silver coin into the hands of Alexander McKee at the sign of the Goshawk and Throstle, near the Tolbooth at Edinburgh ... the monies to be rendered in full by the thirtieth day of October 1640.'

There was a murmur of assent, a pause and the clink of glasses. Then the flap of the tent was flung aside. I stepped back quickly and turned my head aside. I had not mistaken the voice. Surely enough it belonged to Master Nicholas Bronsard, Merchant Venturer of Newcastle upon Tyne.

Chapter 24

Cannon Royal for Newcastle

I stood by a tree and watched. Bronsard stepped out of the tent ahead of a small crowd of Scots officers. He looked every inch a prosperous Edinburgh merchant. His suit of dark grey broadcloth and the fine embroidered cloak with its silken tie cords and dull bronze clasps would not have looked amiss on Sylvanus Webster's shoulders. All was sombre and simple but of obvious quality – it was plain that the wearer was a rich man. To my eyes he needed only to have a little Rotterdam bible to clutch before his belly to conjure him into a Minister o' the Kirk.

Yet the face was not quite as I remembered it. There were still, I was pleased to see, signs of the scorching he had taken from my antics with the kraikie in the coffer. But even beyond that, all had not gone well for Master Nicholas in the last few days. Bronsard had suffered and, I fancied, fasted somewhat as well. The smooth shaven jowls had slackened, and it was plain that the man had slept badly for a night or two. In spite of myself, however, I marvelled that Nicholas Bronsard could summon up enough brass-faced gall to ride into the Scots camp and there dare to haggle over the delivery of oats. It seemed that no matter who held power in the North they would still have to call upon the House of Bronsard to supply the grain they needed. And this was the murdering bastard whose destruction I wanted to bring about. I watched, tight mouthed and grim, as he shook hands all round, smiling and nodding, and cracking jokes that set the Scots guffawing. Whatever else he might be there was no doubt that Nicholas Bronsard was a cunning merchant and a rare fellow for striking a good bargain. I recalled how he had me take a glass of strong drink when he had changed my letter of credit. He had done the same here today. The deal was bigger but the ploy was the same. The groom who brought Bronsard's horse also held the lead of a pack pony slung with empty pannier baskets. The way had been smoothed by good brandy.

A couple of dozen demi-john flasks would, I guessed, have set him back a few pounds – but that would all go in with the price that the Scots, and eventually the local English folk, would have to pay. That is unless I came upon the bastard first.

But it was soon all too clear that I would have little profit from following Nicholas Bronsard along the road back to Newcastle. An escort of a dozen Scots cavalry galloped up and stood ready. I heard the orders: 'Tak this guid man tae within sicht o' the walls o' the toun o' Newcastle. But mind ye dinna gaan sae close as to be speired y'r sells.'

I bit my lip hard. The impulse to shout, to challenge the man where he stood, died away. But in spite of all my caution I found that I had stood out from the tree. Almost against my will I found that I had unstrapped my helmet and stood there rubbing a hand over my shaved pate – and looking at Nicholas Bronsard. He rode past where I stood. For a moment I thought that he had not noticed me. Then, just for an instant, our eyes met.

He knew me well enough! The soft brown eyes darkened and then became hard. The flash of fury came, changed to a look of cold hatred, and was gone. His horse jumped and squealed as he rowelled it into a canter. I stood in the dust thrown up by his escort and looked after him. I waited, and, as I knew he would, he looked back over his shoulder. Though that was just the once.

My immediate thought was to return to General Leslie and tell him what I knew of the man but I quickly discarded that idea. In the general's eyes I would seem little better than a lad telling tales to the teacher. I knew that it would not matter at all to the Scots commander that Nicholas Bronsard had been, was, a supporter of Charles Stuart. So long as the heavy wains carrying those two hundred and fifty big sacks of oats arrived each and every day, Nicholas Bronsard could be the Devil himself. I knew that well enough, and David Leslie would know better than I that only the power that would chase the Scots out of the North of England now was starvation.

I thought about all that had happened during the last few days as I rode slowly through a golden summer's evening back towards Gateshead. The road was littered with discarded equipment and broken footwear. The very smell betrayed the fact that just a few hours before a fleeing army had passed by. Battlefields reek of powder smoke and human excrement. Men running for their lives purge their bowels like hunted beasts. I had learned that for myself when I ran from the defeat at Nordlingen! In the first few miles I rode past dead bodies: dark shapes lying in the long grass. Black flies clustered on the swollen faces. The carrion crows had smelled out the corpses first; already they were there, flapping over the shapes in the grass like black rags, ready to drop to the ground and begin their feast on the staring eyes. A dead man offers better feeding than a dead lamb. But like all carrion eaters, they would have to wait to feed. A battlefield corpse must rot for a week before a crow's beak can rend the flesh.

I had heard in the Scots camp that the losses on both sides had been almost unbelievably slight. A dozen Scots had been slain. Sixty English corpses had been left at Newburn when the army broke and ran away. That was close to miraculous in my reckoning. In Germany we had counted battlefield corpses in thousands, when we had bothered to count.

I was still thinking of the strange course of the battle at Newburn when my horse stopped at the wide ford across the river Derwent a little above where it joined the Tyne. I was not so deep in thought that I failed to see a sudden shake in the greenery of a clump of elder bushes close to the water's edge at the far side of the crossing. I bent to pat my horse's neck while l looked again. There was no doubt. I would have offered a fine target if I crossed that stream openly.

I waited, standing out of range. The safe way would have been to turn about and ride upstream looking for another crossing. The Derwent is no deep stream and even for the time of year the water was low. The bushes stirred again. I suppose that after all that had happened to me since I set foot ashore in England I had some right to be a touch uncertain in my temper. I hauled up my carbine, cocked the lock and loosed off a shot into the greenery at the other side of the river. I heard the clip of the ball as it sheered off twigs. Then I drew my sword and put my horse to cross the shallows at the canter.

The river bank offered a shallow slope up from the ford and my horse took it easily. I reined up and looked about. There was no ambush. But my nostrils caught the scent of woodsmoke. The fellow was well hidden. The roots of a wind torn tree lay to one side of the track. I could hear the crackle of dry twigs burning and now see the faint shimmer of blue smoke rising. I drew a pistol and advanced.

Will Blacket sat by a wood fire, grinning up at me from under a battered hat. I grinned back – I was damned glad to see the rogue. Without a word he chose three of the trout spitted on green withes from among the half dozen sizzling over the embers and stood up to offer them to me. Once again I could only marvel at fellow's skill in foraging. We might have been in Germany still. Two bulging sacks of what was obviously loot lay by the fire. The open neck of one of the sacks showed a patch of richly embroidered fabric and the edge of a silver plate. I had come upon him as he sorted his takings. All in all, Will had the look of a man who sat at ease with his world.

'How now, Will?' I dismounted and took the trout from his hand. He waited until I had nibbled one of the fish to the bones before he handed me a green glass flask. The drink was cider, good string cider. I wondered how far it had travelled to become part of Will's booty from Newburn battlefield.

'I stood at Amen Corner as y' bid me, Captain, and I saw y' sittin' there, rear man in the troop, gettin' blessed, handsome an' as holy as y' please, afore St Nicholas's steps. So I managed to get myself pressed into service with the English officers' baggage train, and followed on.' He winked at me. 'Never taken better pickins in all my days.'

'So you saw the battle … ?'

Will rolled his eyes back in his head. His derision at what he had witnessed was plain. He hawked sharply and spat into the fire.

'That wasn't any battle, Captain. That was a set piece rout! The whole army should have marched out. They sent one-in-three out o' the Newcastle garrison, and they sent the midden-sweepins of what they had. Did you see the state of the infantry!' He kicked at a burning log and sent the sparks flying. 'Them officers should ha' been paraded before their regiments and had their swords broke o'er their heads.'

'But you didn't do so badly out of it yourself, Will?' I kicked at one of the sacks. He gave me his curious scar-split grimace and patted the other sack. Then he pointed over my shoulder. I turned and saw two piebald sumpter ponies grazing among the bushes.

'Not so bad at all.' I added wryly.

'Y' see … it was like this, Captain, when them hymn-singin' heathen Scots bastards forced the passage across the ford, and the cavalry broke and ran, it was like a cat in a dovecote in that camp. I was just standin' there when up rides this officer, bleedin' about the head but still as haughty as you please, and he says to me: 'The army is retiring to Darlington, my good fellow. See you pack those two beasts with all you can carry and follow on at your best speed.' He shrugged and I found that I was laughing again.

It was dusk by the time we rode together into Gateshead. We needed no telling that things were not as they should have been in the town. Folk who on any other week-night would have been in their beds stood, sullen, and stared fearfully at us as we rode by. Little groups gathered at corners and talked in low voices. I could not help smiling when I saw a carpenter nailing stout planks across the windows of an empty house. Unless their luck changed these people would get some hard lessons to learn. Just the sight of a door or window barred with freshly sawn timber like that would draw looting troops like hounds to broth.

We found the shop of Elias Grant by the carved boot that hung over the door. It was a poor place, even for Gateshead. The street shutter was down but the door stood open. The place was silent. For a moment we stood in the gloom of the shop. A single rushlight flickered and smoked in its sconce over the cobbler's bench.

'Cobbler … I've a sole that needs a stitch!' My shout sprang back at me across the empty room. 'Elias Grant! Come, hear news o' y'r kin!'

'Be still! Be silent … i' the name of Providence let a man sleep.'

Sylvanus Webster lay on a palliasse on the floor under the cobbler's bench. He uncocked the pistol he was holding and rolled out of his blanket.

'John Ellyot … Will Blacket?' I would not swear to it but there was something that was close to relief in Webster's voice. 'God's good bounty, man, where have you been this last day?'

I told him of the English defeat at Newburn. It is a strange thing to see an Englishman rejoice at the news that an English army has been beaten off the field but that is what Sylvanus Webster did. I had never thought to see the man give vent to so hearty a laugh. And it was hearty laughter that rang through the shop.

There was the scrape and flap of a slipper sole on the grit of the floor. As ever, I thought, the cobbler is himself ill-shod. He was thin faced. The skin was as pale as cheese. But he was wearing the red flannel shirt that I had been told to look for. I had little doubt that he was indeed the man that General Leslie had described. He took a spill from the mantleshelf and began to light candles.

'You have news of John Martin?' The voice was mild but I sensed that there could be power in it if its owner had need.

'I spoke with him at Newburn not four hours since. He is in rare good fettle and has done a deal of business in his trade this day.'

I saluted. He gave me a short bend of his neck in return. He was dressed as a cobbler, and his wan cheeks were shadowed by a three-day's growth of dark beard, but the man's mien and stance told me that he was no shoe mender. Any lout with a lug to flap against a closed door can be a spy. But this man, my guts told me, had been David Leslie's own eyes. And I doubted not at all that he had long been over-looking Newcastle for his shrewd master.

Webster looked between us: 'Master Grant may I introduce to you Captain John Ellyot of ... ' he smiled, 'of our present business.'

'So you have come.' He did not offer me his hand but he looked at me keenly across the candle-flame. 'Not a minute before time. We have a pressing need for a master-gunner's skill here.' He looked me up and down and seemed to approve of what he saw.

'You can lay a piece of heavy ordnance against a target?' He leaned backward so that in the candlelight the hollows of his face were left in dark shadow. It was like being spoken to by a skull.

'I know my business as well or better than any man in the Scottish service. But I cannot do what you need me to do until you tell me what the service is. And I will need certain instruments.'

'To be sure.' He shook his head and in the half light I saw that his brow was heavily beaded with sweat. 'Ye maun forbear ... Ah've been on ma feet these three days and nights.' He sighed wearily and blew out his breath, making the candle flames flicker. 'If Newcastle does not yield it will be under tight siege by this time tomorrow. But the Scots army has no siege train with it. Nothing to speak of; leastways nothing heavy enough to breach the walls.'

I felt a curious twinge of pride. Newcastle's walls were said to be the strongest in Europe. But, I reminded myself, the mechanics of a siege were not always simple. I could see better than most that any siege of Newcastle could be a long drawn out affair. And that the odds were much against the Scots. The harvest had been gathered in. The chequer of fields all up and down the Tyne valley was now pale stubble and surplus grain would already be safe in the town's warehouses. So, I quickly saw, those precious oats promised by Nicholas Bronsard could only be had if Newcastle surrendered peaceably. But if there was to be a siege, and if that siege were long drawn out, the grain would surely be seized to be eaten by the townsfolk within the walls, while the Scots starved outside. Zeal for a cause fades fast in empty bellies. I spoke almost as though I been thinking aloud.

'So either the town surrenders straightway or the Scots army must leave?' To my surprise Grant nodded readily enough. I pressed: 'Yet the King's garrison is trapped in the town too. Or it will be when General Leslie's army reaches Gateshead to cut off the road to the south.'

'That difficulty solves itself.' Grant rubbed his hands and exchanged a quick bright-eyed glance with Webster. 'They're leaving. Some have already marched out. The main body will go at sunrise. The English garrison has pitched the town's cannon into the Tyne and is marching south to York ... out of harm's way.' He paused to see how I was taking the news.

'The orders were given ... privily ... ' The smile that gently creased Elias Grant's cheeks made him look thinner than ever. 'The day before yesterday, within an hour of the English troops marching away to Newburn.' His hands slapped down on to the table. 'That was told me at this very board by one of the waggonmasters who was to oversee the loading. The orders are that they are to take away all the powder that they can carry. Every heavy waggon in the town has been seized.' He laughed, low and heavy. 'That information cost me a gill of watered brandy and a pair of mended boots that had lain unclaimed for a year. And I had that intelligence within an hour of the order being given in the great hall of the Castle Keep.'

I was impressed. Boasting was not the custom in Elias Grant's trade – but on this occasion it was clear that he felt that he might allow himself a little triumph. And well he might.

'So Newcastle will be offered terms … terms that common folk will not groan under?' He was silent for a moment before he spoke. Then he splayed his hands before him so that he could use his fingers as an abacus to mark off his thoughts.

'We need Newcastle, John Ellyot. We need it as desperately as Charles Stuart will find that he needs it when he looks at his empty coffers.' He stifled a yawn and a little shudder of tiredness shook his frame. 'England needs Newcastle's coals; she needs them now and will need them the more in a few months time when the cold weather comes. Do you know much coal must be burned to boil the water that makes a ton of saltpetre pure enough for gunpowder?'

He broke off and we laughed together. It was a fair question to ask of a master-gunner. 'So Newcastle must surrender without a siege? Can perhaps only surrender without a siege,' I replied.

Elias Grant opened his hands as though to concede the point to me. 'And that is why you have been sent here.' He took my arm and steered me to a bench where there was a jug of ale and tankards. 'Listen … The royal troops will not be molested for twenty-four hours. They will be allowed to leave Newcastle, and Durham, and Tynemouth and anywhere else they hold … they can even save the tatters of their honour and take what guns they can haul away. General Leslie will remain at Newburn.' He folded his arms. 'But tomorrow morning he will send Sir William Douglas to Newcastle's southern gate under flag of truce to treat with the town, with the Council … not with the Military.'

I understood. By tomorrow Newcastle would be on its own. There would be no King's governor up in the Castle to rule the aldermen and the merchants.

'You are here to tip the balance of the scales in the right direction.' I looked at him, askance. His blue eyes became bright. 'Captain Ellyot, you are to fire on the town!'

The shock of what Elias Grant had said struck me and passed over and through me, and still I could not grasp the full import of his words. He seemed not to notice.

'Ten minutes before Sir William Douglas rides up to the town gates you will touch off a single shot from one of our great cannon.' I saw it all. I saw Webster's scheme. The three great guns that I had raised from the Wear had been dragged across country to Gateshead. The south bank of the Tyne above Gateshead looked across and down upon the town of Newcastle.

'But it's to be no more than a foretaste to encourage them to see sense. We could batter them!' Elias Grant was looking at me.

'If you had the guns ... ' I spoke too sharply.

'But we do have the guns, Captain. Three cannon royal would allow us to make a fair beginning at a bombardment. We can destroy the houses, aye and the warehouses, with ease; since there is no point in firing upon an empty castle. And in a week or two we can bring more. We can bring the great cannon from Edinburgh Castle ... '

'As you say, Master Grant, it were better for all if Newcastle surrenders without a fight.' I held up a hand as though to fend off his words. His argument was powerful. I would save my breath and bide my time. 'But before I can fire a cannon there are many things that I must have.'

If I had to fire on Newcastle then so be it. I had fired on more than a dozen other cities and towns, places with women and children in them. It was late in the day now to grow a conscience. I was a gunner. That was my trade, learned and well practised across the north of Europe during years of hard service. And many commanders had owned that I was good at what I did.

'I will look at your guns at first light, Master Grant. Meanwhile, I take it that you can provide rations for myself, my gunner's mate here, and our horses ... Master Webster!' I sought in my belt for the scrap of paper that Major Miniver had given me. 'Perhaps you can spare a moment to look upon this?' He could not have missed the hard edge I put on my words but he made no sign of it as he took the little slip of paper. 'I have read it a dozen times but there is no place of that name that I know of.'

Webster walked to a candle and held the paper to the light. I saw his brows come together and then clear. His mouth gave a little twitch.

'That is not surprising Captain, you have after all been overseas for a good many years. These are the names of two fine newly-built mansions near to the town. Indeed, they are houses well known to me … but not suspected.' He turned and handed the slip to Elias Grant. 'Is that not so Master Grant?'

'But are they truly places where Mistress Aphra may be being held prisoner?' I tried to keep the anxiety from my voice but I knew that I failed.

Sylvanus Webster stood up. 'That is something I shall know before this day has passed. Be assured of it!'

～

Windmills are not places that offer a soldier good lodgings. In my experience there never was a mill, wind or water, that wasn't so infested with rats and cockroaches as to make sleep nearly impossible. But it was in a windmill in Gateshead that I spent as comfortable a night as I could have wished. I had asked Grant to show me the guns and he had done so. Will Blacket spread my blanket that night on the piled wheat straw that hid the three cannon royal.

We slept soundly – but not for long. Dawn still comes early enough in late August. I sat up with a start. Somewhere, somewhere no great distance away, a solitary drummer was beating out a slow tattoo.

I had seen armies leave cities before. Mostly we left at the run, staggering under the weight of loot for which we had neither use nor market, and against a devil's canvas of the smoke and flames of burning. But I had seen a Swedish army march out with such wondrous solemn pomp and show as to bring a lump unbidden to a man's throat. The quitting of Newcastle came somewhere between the two.

They crossed the Tyne bridge in decent enough order. The drumbeat measured the pace and the narrowness of the way kept the ranks. But as soon as a troop or company was safely across the river the ranks began to break. As ever, the cavalry had little regard for any discipline but its own. Trumpets flashed in the sunlight as they were raised to give the calls. It was as though the Horse was anxious to be off, away from the black disgrace of Newburn.

It takes a dozen seasoned men to serve a cannon royal. I did the work with eight. Elias Grant and his craftsmen had worked hard to make a stout carriage to bear the recoil of so powerful a gun. But to look at it was indeed a makeshift affair. There was an axle and a pair of wheels that I was told had come off a timber-cutter's trug at Lambton; and two great baulks of seasoned oak had been waylaid on their way from Branspeth to the Bishop's Palace at Durham. The rest was stout rope and rawhide. It took much digging and the piling of great stones but inside an hour we had set the cannon firmly in its appointed place. Nor could I fault that position. Elias Grant had chosen well. The big gun was hidden behind the hedge of a cottage garden that over-looked the river a little below the bridge. We would not be seen until the piece had been touched off. Only then would our position be betrayed by a great flowering blos-som of white powder smoke.

I had worried somewhat about ammunition for the great gun. My concern was for the quality of powder that I was to use. Gunpowder is easy enough to come by – can-non powder is not. A cannon with a calibre of eight inches calls for large grained powder. Given time and a place to work I could have turned common musket powder into grains fit for a big gun – but not in the time I had left. My fear was allayed when Elias Grant and one of his fellows fetched a cowhide sack. He unlaced the sack to show me that it was full of black grains the size of big peas. I had my powder. Every trade has its secrets and gunnery has more than most. My eyes told me that the pow-der was sound enough. The large grains that had been made by squeezing damp pow-der paste through a parchment sieve were clean and unbroken. But I had to make some kind of show. I pinched up a grain, listened to it as I rolled it between finger and thumb, finally I licked it. The saltpetre tasted cold to my tongue. I rolled up a sleeve, plunged it into the sack and held it there. Then I kept a wise look on my face and frowned at Will Blacket who stood by sucking his teeth and looking doubtful. The powder was dry all through.

'Where has this come from, Master Grant?' I withdrew my arm. The hairs on it had collected almost no dust.

Grant looked a little worried for a few seconds. There was a distinct pause before he answered; then he decided to tell me.

'I had it off His Majesty's frigate, *Endymion*, she that was in the Tyne until the day before yesterday.'

I smiled and looked at him directly. 'More outlay for watered gin and old boots?'

Elias Grant shook is head ruefully. Clearly I had touched a sore point. 'Not this time, ma mannie. This trip it was good pressed Virginia tobacco leaf against the gunpowder – a pound for a measured pound, English weight, balanced on the ship's scales.' He drew breath. 'May that grasping English bastard writhe in the fires o' Hell!'

I smiled back at him faintly: 'Say only that you paid dear for it, Master Grant. And forbear to curse.' I raised a warning finger and narrowed my eyes at him. 'The powder you bought is as good as I could have wished for and will do our cause's work well enough.' My words pleased him, the reproach for his cursing almost as much as the news that he had done well to buy the powder. I had long since learned that these Presbyterian Scots wag their tails when you remind them that they are born damned. I let him enjoy himself for a short moment, then I thrust home a question that sounded like a comment. 'Aye ... it will be suitable for whatever target it is to be used to fire upon.'

I thought that he had stamped away in temper but he had not. He came back with a good big sea-glass. Then he pointed to the north across the river and focussed the glass.

'See ... ' he pointed. 'That merchant ship along the quayside.'

I took the glass from his hands and found the ship-rigged vessel. It was a big vessel to have risked a passage up the Tyne.

'But ... ' I was astonished. I had expected that he would point the finger at a public building, the Guildhall or the old Maison Dieu. Elias Grant was ordering me – wantonly it seemed – to fire so great a cannon at a moored merchant ship. I focussed again. The name across her stern was *Hepzibah*.

I heard Grant's soft laughter at my side. 'David Leslie has promised that he will do the town no harm – the town, mark you – if it surrenders to him. Nor shall he. But that vessel will sail when the tide makes enough water to bear her. You are only to shoot when she has cleared the quay and is fairly under way. Aim your gun out there into the river.' His arm described a slow arc. 'A great thundering from the blast in their stubborn, deaf papistical ears will serve to bring the Council to see the peril in which they stand. That is General Leslie's order.'

I took my eye from the glass and looked at Grant. He was smiling to himself now like a man that has been reminded of some pleasure to come.

'That vessel is the property of an accursed man. He is the enemy of us all.' Grant's hands came together as in prayer and he threw back his head and stood still like that, like a man in an ecstasy.

'But you must see that if I fire upon that ship there is every chance that the round-shot will strike the town walls. At this range no man could guarantee the accuracy of his shot.'

I had expected some protest from Grant but none came.

'His Excellence has a great wish for all Europe to know that Newcastle fell to him without a single shot being fired. That will be so. But a shot or two fired near the walls is neither here nor there. So I order you to set your aim to strike the ship when it is fairly under way. We are but officers of the Assembly preventing the escape of contraband.'

He looked at me. 'Be humble, Master Ellyot ... It is my belief that the Lord God Jehovah will guide your shot and that it will strike home.'

'So be it then, Master Grant.' I did not turn to look at him as I spoke. This whole business began to mean little to me. I was bonded, if by nothing else, by Leslie's written commission that was hidden in my shirt. I knew my target, and I was a master gunner. And for now that was much as I needed to know.

Chapter 25

The Sinking of the Hepzibah

In the handling of firearms it is not good practice to keep a cannon charged and ready for very long. Great ordnance should be loaded and touched off swiftly. But Elias Grant had warned me that I could expect little more help to move my gun – his lads wanted to be paid their wages, and to be away. They had not minded earning their silver groats by laying a cannon against the walls of Newcastle, but not a man among them was daft enough to stay close when the roundshot were about to fly.

So, except for Will Blacket, I was left alone to load the cannon. With borrowed scales and an alepot I had weighed out my charges of gunpowder, English measure, and fed the gun. For wadding I made good shift with a length of rope coiled tight and then wrapped round with a piece of felt.

Elias Grant had been proud when he had shifted straw in the windmill to uncover three cannon balls, but I quickly saw that none of them fitted the barrel well enough to allow me the hope of an accurate shot. It took an hour's work with a hammer to lap one of the granite roundshot tight and neat with a sheet of lead. The muffled thud that we heard when the shot was seated home on the charge was a sweet sound to us. We had a cannon royal loaded and its muzzle levelled across the river.

But the gunner's instruments that Elias Grant had promised were long in coming. I went up to his workshop to find him sitting before a green cloth spread on his cobbler's bench, paying out double handfuls of small coins to his labourers. If they were the men who had dragged the three guns all the way from the Wear then I reckoned that they had earned their money. He looked up for long enough to point to a big bundle lying in the corner. I recognised the cured reindeer skin at once. The last time I had touched it had been the morning I had left Karlskrona. After that it had been part of the baggage that Mouncey Bone had stolen when he left me for dead. Yet here it was now.

'I brought that from your farm, this morning, Ellyot.' Sylvanus Webster stood in the doorway with the sun behind him. He was dressed for riding. Someone had laboured long and hard at waxing his tall boots. His wide linen collar was washed and freshly ironed, while in his hands he held a handsome new black hat with a tall crown and a silken band with a bright silver buckle. And he was wearing a long sword. Doctor Sylvanus Webster had come into his own. For him such garb was court-dress; and it took no great intellect to know where that court would be. I could well see him among the grim faced men, the lawyers and scriveners who sat in the carved chairs of whatever High Council was now to govern Newcastle and indeed the whole of the North. His wink or nod, or the raising of his little finger, would now sway many outcomes.

'And have you news of Mistress Aphra?' My question was too eager. I knew that, but I did not care. Webster's expression became grave.

'The information we had from Major Miniver was valuable indeed. But it did not help me to find ...' Webster drew a breath, 'Mistress Aphra.'

I must have shown my dismay because Webster touched my arm. 'Be patient, John. I can tell you that I have good men scouring the town even now. The girl will be found.' Then, as though to offer me something other to think about, he said, 'take heart ... for at least now you have no need to fear about your property. It may lie in the path of the Scot's march towards Newcastle but nonetheless I have left a paper that will ensure that the place is not molested by foragers.'

'And have I some hope of gaining lawful possession of it? One that will stand in law even after our Scots friends have gone home? When I was in last Newcastle my legal position was, as you might say, a trifle uncertain. Written warrants tend not to disappear.' I looked straight into Webster's face. 'Can you truly make it so, Doctor Webster?'

'Be assured that I can, John.'

'Be assured!' Those were words that I had heard and swallowed before. In my time I have been a much-assured fellow – though I have not been a penny the richer for it. I said nothing but picked up the bundle of reindeer hide and began to unlace the thongs. That at least gave me some pleasure. It was like shaking the hand of an old friend. I took up my good boxwood quadrant with the copper plumb bob cast in the form of a skull; the brass angle pointers that I had picked up after the siege of Breisach. Nothing was missing. My fingers clutched the grease-blackened calf binding of Van Doorn's *Artilleriekunst, The Gunner's Art*. It was a manual that had seldom been out of my hand when I served in Germany. Damn me, I thought, a parson might know his scripture by heart – but not better than John Ellyot knows his Van Doorn.

'You have everything you need?' Webster asked quietly. 'You will be able to shoot when the signal is given? It has become important.'

'The signal? I don't yet know the signal, Master Webster. I have been told that there will be a signal but not what that signal is to be.'

Elias Grant was a tired man and I had no doubt that he had meant to tell me, but clearly he had forgotten. For once I saw annoyance in Webster's expression but he recovered almost before I had registered the emotion. I had met few such men in my time.

'I have a man in the bell tower of the church of All Hallows.' I looked across the river to where the smoke blackened tower poked up above the rooftops. There was no mistaking the deep clamour of All Hallows' great bells. One of them was flawed with a crack and had badly needed recasting for fifty years.

'When he gets a signal from the Guildhall that Sir William Douglas is with the Mayor and the Aldermen he will strike the great bell thrice with a hammer. You will hear that, make no mistake. But to make doubly sure he will unfurl a white bedsheet from the bell tower. When you hear or see either, you are free to fire at the *Hepzibah* as soon as she is away from the quayside.' He took a step towards me. 'Are you ready?'

I put a hand up as though to wipe my mouth. 'I have everything I need – save a light for my linstock ... '

'And Elias Grant has shown you the target?'

'He has shown me the target, the ship ... ' I paused for a second. 'But he has said no more than that.'

Sylvanus Webster closed his eyes and then he pinched the bridge of his nose with his gloved hand. He was going to indulge me. I was a servant who had done well – a tool that had served its purpose.

'General Leslie desires that all Europe shall know that Newcastle upon the Tyne fell to the army of the Covenant without a single shot being fired.' He pointed out of the open door. 'And so it shall be. Nor will the tale be lost upon Charles Stuart, but,' Webster's voice became low, guarded, 'you know as well as I that the Scots army is in parlous case for provisions. The sheep and cattle they drove down from Berwick are eaten long since, the only food they have is what lies in the men's haversacks. Yet they are bound by Leslie's promise that there will be no pillage. He has sworn to hang any man who steals so much as an egg. They must get into Newcastle without much fighting and they have to find food. And it is my task to help them do that. The shot you will fire has only one purpose, Ellyot, and that is to put a decent fear of the Lord God ... and the army of the Covenant into every last wavering soul in Newcastle. Once the army is here, in strength, that will matter less. But until tomorrow at noon there will be only five troops of Scots horse to control the entire town. Our sinews will be stretched thin and tight for a few hours. We cannot bite so we must bark all the louder!'

For a moment an orator's tone came into Webster's voice. He was declaiming, preaching, practising, I guessed for his new work. He went on. 'Many of the recusants ... the malignants ... will have quitted Newcastle. But the town still holds those who will make show of welcoming us, yet who in secret may do us great mischief. There are many such who sit on the town's council.' The smile was thin as gruel. 'I want the blast of that single great cannon shot to shake the rose window of the Guildhall just as they all sit down to sup their cock-o-leekie!'

'But the merchant ship? What profit to spend our only shot on such a target?'

For a moment Webster looked as though he was considering his answer. He waited until Elias Grant had gathered up his green cloth and gone into the back of the shop.

'Nineteen thousand pounds, John, about half of it in gold and most of the rest of it in shilling pieces.' He spoke in almost a whisper. 'The governor who fled Newcastle had received the money to pay his troops.' Webster's mouth twisted. 'Who pays soldiers who have run away?' The money was secretly put aboard the *Hepzibah* as soon as the news of the rout at Newburn reached the town.'

'But ... ' I got no further. Webster looked at me as though I was a simpleton to be humoured.

'The Scots have had their victory and they have been paid a handsome subsidy for it – in advance. It would be a sad thing indeed to spoil such good Christian men by exposing them to the evil influences of much gold!.'

Now I was sure that the man was laughing at me – though perhaps only a little.

'This is the case, Ellyot ... David Leslie desires that only a single shot shall be fired. He wants to make the folk of Newcastle tremble. Give him his wish. Elias Grant, poor fellow, has a desperate need to hurt the man who has ventured his entire fortune in one voyage of that ship.' Webster's look became distant for a moment. 'Vengeance is like a wildfire, Ellyot, but Grant has suffered grievously. Give him his wish ... use your skills to sink the ship *Hepzibah* as she tries to slip away.

'And you ... ?' I asked quietly.

'Why I want only to save the Parliament nineteen thousand pounds. And I do that just by denying the money to the King.' He almost laughed at the thought. 'And likewise, and in a way, I do that also if I can deny it to the Scots.' He moved closer to me. 'Put that money beyond any man's reach but your own for a year or two – let it lie on the river bed until we can reclaim it ... Sink me the *Hepzibah*, Ellyot, use your skill and do it! Is that not so, Master Grant?' Elias Grant had returned. But Webster's greeting went unanswered. Grant was looking at me.

'Davy Leslie has rewarded his servant. I look to you, Captain Ellyot, to fulfil the general's command. Your target however is my choice. It is the property of the man who, five years ago, helped to have me cast into the Thieves' Hole in the Edinburgh Tolbooth. Eighteen months in the darkness feeding on carlin peas and foul water is a long time to mull over a matter.' He put up his hands to his face and then lowered them to look at me. 'That man, the Reverend,' he spat the title, 'Sidrach Jorey, so-called Bachelor o' Divinity has fled the town, but once when I lay in chains I swore to his smirkin' English face that the hand of Divine Providence would strike down his pride. You are that hand this day, Captain Ellyot.' I clenched my teeth together and forced myself to nod gravely. I could do no other.

Webster touched his brow with his riding whip in sálute to us and turned about. I watched him mount a fine black horse and ride off, down towards the bridge. He was a strange man indeed. I felt that I owed him little loyalty, and his cause, whatever it was, none. And it was certain that I had not yet had so much as a penny's piece of money out of him for all the work I had done in raising the guns. Yet I felt that he was a man whose star was rising and who might yet better my fortunes for me – if we both lived.

Will Blacket and I stood by the gun and swigged at Elias Grant's warm, sour tasting beer while we watched the surrender of Newcastle to the Scots. Late in the morning, a little after eleven, we saw a dozen horsemen ride through Gateshead's silent streets. They came in from the west, at the Pipewellgate, at the fast gallop. I recognised the colours and the bay horses: the College of Justice troop, drawn, it was said, from among the younger lawyers of Edinburgh. I had seen them earn honour at the charge across the Tyne at the Newburn ford. The troop halted at the Gateshead side of the bridge. A short trumpet call sounded and echoed across the water. Then just three of the horsemen advanced across the bridge to Newcastle.

'Yon is auld Sir William Douglas.' Grant had followed me to the gun. He sat down heavily and fought to catch his breath. 'He's the Sheriff o' Teviotdale and a rare chiel for changin' a man's mind.' Grant's laugh was like an axe held hard to a slow turning grindstone. 'Be assured, the Scots army will tak its ale an' its bite o' beef in Newcastle this nicht!'

The entire ritual did not take more than ten minutes. I saw a small cluster of figures walk out of the gate to meet the Scottish herald. There was talk. Then I saw the figure of the Mayor, Sir Nicholas Cole, bow and stand aside. Sir William Douglas took off his hat and held it aloft. The curious gesture was more signal than salute, for I noted a stir among the cavalrymen left at the Gateshead side of the Bridge. The sound of cheering within the walls of the town carried across to where I stood. It was done.

So I laid the gun. No man can promise accuracy with a single cannon shot. Powder varies in its strength and goodness; nor will two roundshot weigh the same.

There are too many things that vary and influence the flight of the ball. Though to be sure I have never taken more than five shots to bring my shooting in on a fair target like a town gate or the chosen place along a wall to be breached. Nonetheless, I determined to try my very best. With Will I hammered a stake into the ground under the cannon muzzle, marked off a hundred yards with my measuring chain, and drove in another. That was to be the base of my great triangle. The target would be at the apex. Then I took a careful measure with my smaller brass traverse pointer of the angle that the new position made with a randomly chosen white stone standing downstream and across yon side of the river. I did the calculation carefully, working from the printed tables in my *Artilleriekunst*. I had the range. I would loose off the shot so that the ball would intercept the ship as it came almost abeam of the white stone.

I set the elevation of the cannon's barrel with stout wooden wedges. Again and again I used my quadrant to test that the angle was accurate. I knew the powder charge that I had loaded to an ounce and the weight of the ball to within a pound. All those things that a man could have power over in seeking accuracy, I had done.

I looked across at the ship that lay alongside the quay. Its form wavered in the shimmer rising off metal of the gun. The thirteen-foot-long barrel was taking heat from the sun. That was something for which I had not allowed. And then we waited – for close to three hours. The town clocks chimed out, the birds sang, and a breeze sprang up off the river. Twice Will cut fresh slow match and set it in the sapling he had cut for a linstock. Then suddenly it was there. The bell of All Hallows church did not chime out, but between one second and the next the white sheet unfurled from the belltower.

Elias Grant stood by the gun. The man had changed. He had hoisted his true covenanting colours. The dirty red sark had gone. In its place he had put on a suit of decent black worsted cloth, cut baggy and fastened with loops rather than buttons, the long skirted coat was topped with a linen collar that came down almost to his shoulders and had the laces showing.

I raised my linstock in salute and he acknowledged by taking off his hat and holding it across his chest. It entered my head that I might offer Grant the chance to touch off the cannon at my command himself. It was, after all, his vengeance. But I thought better of it. I stood-to, waving Will back out of the way. Now I was alone. I felt the tight little grin, half of it nerves, forming around my mouth. I stepped forward. The trick is to wave the linstock in the air so that the slow match is cleared of ash and glows bright. I did so, and it was a grand flourish too. Then I took two paces forward and bent a little at the shoulders. I could not help myself. It was a gunner's crouch.

Across the river at Newcastle the *Hepzibah* had cast off and was standing away from the quay. A single topsail on her foremast was all the canvas she carried. The falling tide was taking her down river. There was a maddening slowness to it all. I raised the linstock.

The triangle I had calculated was traced out in my mind's eye. I saw the ship moving to cross the distant apex of that triangle. I could visualise the granite cannon ball striking the target. Then, at the last instant, I threw away all of my science and fell back upon what a thousand cannon shots had taught me to know in my very bowels.

I stepped forward a pace, waited, judged, and then trailed the slow match across the priming. My body began to curl and half turn away in self-protection as I heard the soft 'whuft' of the little pile of gunpowder taking. I saw the straight plume of smoke blow upwards a yard into the air from the touch hole. I dropped the linstock, turned my face aside to shield it from the flash, and clamped my hands hard over my ears. The concussion struck me and I staggered. Then I was standing amidst a billowing cloud of smoke. The thunderclap of the shot was already echoing up and down the valley and through it I could just hear the low moan as the granite ball flew.

I had struck my target. Elias Grant's cry of 'Hallelujah!' told me that. He handed me the spyglass. The ship was still there and she was still moving out into the channel. But she looked lopsided and, even as I watched her, the foremast with its scrap of sail tilted forward. Her bows were deeper into the water. She drifted like that for a moment. Then I saw the splash as the cockboat was lowered and the scramble of men into it. They were just clear in time. For a moment the *Hepzibah* seemed to have lost way. Then, save for her masts, she was under. The Tyne is nowhere deep enough to sink a ship of that size completely; but as I watched she rolled on to her side. Then there was nothing to be seen except a single spar that stood clear with green water piling against it to mark the flow of the current.

'So, the matter of the great cannon is ended, Master Grant.' I would rather have spoken the words to Sylvanus Webster but I felt that I needed to tell someone of the fact. 'My work is done.'

'Y've done well … for an Englishman.'

I had anticipated the quip. There is always a little o' the whips and scorpions to Scot's humour. I inclined my head in a half bow.

'Aye, God has granted yet another great victory to the arms o' the Covenant.' As Grant spoke he raised his face to to look up at the sky. I turned away and winked at Will Blacket.

'A word!' He called after us like a man remembering something almost too late. 'The password in the town tonight is Tubal Cain, y' mind, the maker o' brass. You will need it. There will be a troop of horse at the head of every street in the town.' So it had started. A Scot's promise indeed! It was well to be seen that there were officers among the ranks of the army of the Covenant who had learned their trade in the Swedish service. They would be men who knew well how to make a town jig to their tune. It would be a foolish man who walked abroad after sunset tonight.

'You are to see Master Webster at the Scotch Inn at the top o' the Newgate, tomorrow at three o' the clock. The whiles, he says there's some auld wifie tae see in some hoose across in Blith's Nook.'

We entered Newcastle unchallenged. There was a rusty halberd set against the wall as we rode through the Bridge Gate but the Town Watch had made itself scarce. They would get no bribes of dressed chickens from the Scots cavalry when they came in.

The streets were not entirely deserted but such folk as we saw scuttled rather than walked. The stalls and booths were gone and the shops shuttered. I had twice to bark out 'Tubal Cain' to armoured horsemen on my way to the Three Crescents.

On the night I had been arrested by the Town Watch, Will Blacket had cleared all my gear from my room before the Sheriff's men could come back and make themselves free with it. But he had not known that I had hidden the fistful of gold coins that had been the bait in Bronsard's iron chest. The pieces lay in the thick dust along the top of the bed cupboard in my room. I badly wanted to feel the weight of them in my purse.

The inn's door was barred but we went round to the little close at the back. I let Will hammer on the door. There was shrieking and wailing inside for a few moments but then the landlord risked a look from an upstairs window and hurried down to let us in. Sight of the scrap of old plaid that I had worn over my shoulder since Newburn worked miracles. I went upstairs to my room and left Will to take advantage of the situation.

They were still there, the seventeen gold coins, thick, heavy, and neither clipped nor sweated. I threw myself down on to the bed and let them fall through my fingers on to the counterpane. I reckoned that I had close to a half pound of fine gold in my hands.

I lay for a moment. With the business of the guns ended I found that I could think. And the thoughts that came most readily to my mind were of Aphra Thornton. It was strange. Today was Saturday the twenty-ninth day of August in the year of our Lord sixteen hundred and forty. I had landed at South Shields on the twelfth of August, just seventeen days ago. It had been less than two weeks since I had met Aphra at my uncle's shop. I sat up sharply.

I was a fool! I had bound myself to serve Sylvanus Webster for three months. Yet tomorrow he could call me to follow him into some new hazards; and that might take me almost anywhere in the country. When he had left instructions that I was to wait upon him he had been giving me leave, a twenty four-hour furlough, a very little time in which I might try to find my Aphra.

Chapter 26

Find the Lady

Blith's Nook was as I remembered it: less a street than an alley. Even on a summer's day sunlight seldom warmed its dirty cobblestones. Steep pitched roofs on either side jutted out so that in places they almost touched. Yet around here the arrival of the Scots army seemed to have frightened folk far less than around the Castle and along the Side. It may be that there are times, a few, when being poor is a small advantage.

Certainly, the street was busy enough and it had a rare ripe stench from a tripe dresser's shop on one side and a fellmonger's on the other.

Elias Grant had said nothing about exactly where in the Nook I should find Hannah Thornton but that didn't worry me. There weren't more than a dozen houses on either side of the lane and the mere presence of two strangers, armed men, would be whispered about the place soon enough. After just twenty paces into the Nook I knew I was right: Hannah Thornton had been waiting for us.

A quick drumming of fingers against a grime caked window brought us up short. We slipped into a house through a door that winked open and was closed as quickly behind us. Hannah's maidservant led us up dirty wooden steps into a first floor room that overhung the street.

'Well then, Stella Carr's laddie … ' The old woman sat like a queen amidst filth. When I had seen Hannah Thornton at her house on the bridge she had been old and yet dignified, in her own way, even beautiful. The happenings of the last few days had sapped some of the spirit out of her. Now she was just an old woman, wiry and hard, but with the fire in her burning low. 'I heard that you raised the guns and that now y' stand in well wi' the new masters o' the town.'

'I did what I undertook to do, Mistress Hannah … and now that's done, I've come to seek the lass ... ' Boldness surged up within me. 'And I may tell you ... ' I knew that my face had flushed a little – and that shows up well when a man has a close shaven head. 'That my ... er ... affections are engaged by Mistress Aphra, and ... ' Damn me but I faltered. If there had been a time to act the dashing gallant with the old woman it was then. Back in her house, in her own parlour and wearing a silk gown she could play the great lady with me. Here, in a stinking kennel in Blith's Nook with fat bluebottles buzzing across the low ceiling, things could have, I had fancied, been different. Then I had wavered, my courage had faltered. But the old woman gave me cause to bless her. She looked up at me and there was something of the old twinkling brightness in her eyes: 'Get her back to me first m' son, then y' may talk to me o' courtin'.'

'So you have news of where Bronsard has her, Mistress Thornton?' My question was more abrupt than I had intended. 'There can be no charges against her in this town now.' I smiled grimly at the realisation. 'Since yesterday His Majesty's Special Commissioner has no power this side of York.'

'No power, y' say!' Old Hannah's face creased and her lips twisted with bitterness. 'He has the lass ... that's power enough. Give him a week, ten days at most, and he will stand as high with Leslie as ever he did with the King's party. The bastard has Satan's own cunning in him. To my certain knowledge Bronsard has bought up every spare sack of grain in the town and has it hidden away somewhere. So long as he can put himself forward as a good Protestant merchant, wi' friends in Edinburgh, he'll keep his property and prosper. I'm told that the Scots asked for a 'loan' o' twenty thousand pounds the minute they stepped in the gate. Who do you think will be the big man in the raisin' of such a loan?'

Hannah was right. I had seen the confidence with which Nicholas Bronsard had moved among the Scottish officers at Newburn. If he was able to organise the collection of the money for a forced loan, he had already become invaluable to the Scots. Bronsard would surely know how much his fellow merchants would have, cash on hand, to a bent halfpenny! Such a man would soon be able to act much as he had under the King's rule. Truly, power may shift, yet the same few men go on holding the reins.

'So there is no news as to where he is holding Mistress Aphra?' There was no spoken answer, but the old woman pulled her knitted shawl up around her shoulders and shook her head. I looked around the room. Thick dust lay everywhere and the fireplace was choked with dead ashes. 'But at least you can return to your house now, Mistress Thornton. I can get you a pass to move freely in the town. There's no need for you to sit in this rat hole.'

'There's every need, Jack Ellyot.' I exchanged glances with Hannah's young maid. The girl's eyes showed no understanding of her mistress's words.

'Every need … to stay here?' I was puzzled.

'Because of the starching … ' The old woman grabbed at my sleeve. 'And because today is Saturday.' I think it was the little sigh of exasperation that escaped me that angered her. Her grip tightened. 'I am not in my dotage yet, Master Ellyot!' The voice rose from deep inside her and seemed for an instant to take on strength of its own. It was almost as though a younger woman was speaking to me.

'Listen … m' Laddie!' Her eyes glowed with the intensity of her effort to concentrate. 'For three days and nights I walked the streets and chares of this town. I offered gold, I threatened some high and mighty folk; I pleaded and I begged for news of the bairn. Not a living soul has been able to give me one word of where young Aphra is being held. That was until last night.'

She turned away and leaned forward to peer out of the grimy window towards the patch of bright sunlight that marked the narrow entry to Blith's Nook.

'That's when I learned that m' Lady Daft has been missing since Thursday.'

'M'Lady Daft?' I knew that Hannah was talking about Margaret Ellyot as soon as I had mouthed the name. 'But what has that to do with Aphra?'

Hannah smiled a mirthless, secret smile that was aimed inward rather than at me.

'Your farm at Benwell stands i' the path of the Scottish army as it marches on Newcastle. The bastards will be there by now. And for certain Nicholas Bronsard would know the dangers that held for his beloved niece. So if he took her out of the way then it seems likely that he will have her in a safe place. Yet I have made certain sure that the poor addled bitch is not in his house on the Side.' She pursed her lips: 'Find where Margaret Bronsard is, and there we will find my Aphra!'

'But ... ' I got no further. A wave of Hannah's hand killed all argument.

'No man thinks to take heed of a woman's needs.' The double meaning of what she said touched upon her humour and she gave a raucous little laugh. 'But if Margaret Bronsard is being kept mewed-up somewhere she will not be still. There will be screams and fainting if she is thwarted.' Hannah looked at me directly and for an instant again she was something of her old self. 'And I know that the one soul on this earth that Nick Bronsard will humour – if he can – is his niece.' I remembered the letters that I had read in Bronsard's room. Did old Hannah know more than she would ever say?

'If she is like her mother she will call for a clean shift every other day and for the Sabbath she will need a her lace fresh starched.'

My disbelief must have showed, for Hannah Thornton tossed her head and gave what in a younger woman might have been called a flounce. She was an old woman not best-pleased.

'That is a perilous weak notion to sit in this place for three days to test, Mistress. And why here?'

'I sit here because across the street there is the house of Mistress Shafto. Mistress Shafto was for many years a maid in the service of Lady Isabelle Ogle.' I waited patiently for her to unravel her reasoning. 'And while she was in that lady's service she was taught the making of a fine white starch from potatoes. Also she owns a set of French flatirons to hot-crimp and smooth fine lawn and linen. The lass is much in demand and can charge as much as sixpence for making up a single ruff.'

I went to the window and looked out across the narrow lane. The house opposite was a trifle better kept than the others in the street. The windows were curtained with plain stuff and the street door had been painted green where the others had been brushed with tar.

'You'll see nothing from the street, John Ellyot. Ellen Shafto has a good mystery and she means to keep the secret of it to herself. She bars friends o' twenty years from the house when she's working.'

'And you expect ... What?' The antick logic of the old woman was beyond me.

'On Thursday morning the maid Bessie Carver came to Mistress Shafto's with a big basket. Tonight is the Sabbath eve. Somebody will collect that basket before this day is done. I believe that whoever it is will lead us to Aphra.'

My whistle of disbelief had come and gone before I could stop it. I tried to cover for it by taking up a tune, but I could see that the damage was done and that I had offended Hannah by it.

'Blacket!' I bellowed in spite of the fact that Will stood not two paces away. 'What can you be thinking of man! Get out of here and don't come back without vittles and wine, and get coals for a fire.' He winked at the maid and made for the door. 'And get a pack of unpricked playing cards, you rogue!'

I took Hannah's hand. It was ice cold.

'Mistress Hannah … ' I had not thought to see the bright tears that had come into the old woman's eyes. 'At this moment your plan is the only hope we have. We'll wait, and I hope to God that we shall see good come of it.' That afternoon was long. Hannah Thornton taught me a card game she called Jezebel and I allowed her, nay; say rather that I could not prevent her, from winning nearly seven shillings in small coin from me. Once we sat silent while the clatter of hooves marked the passage of a patrol of Scots cavalry past the end of the lane, but that was all. Mistress Shafto's business was slower than anyone else's in the Nook that day. It seemed starched linens and suchlike had gone quite out of fashion in Newcastle. Not a single soul came to the green door.

Will returned nearly empty handed and looking shamefaced. That astonished me. But it seemed that the good folk of Newcastle were unwilling to put fire into their ovens either to roast meat or to bake bread for fear that the smell would attract the Scottish soldiers. I suppose it was a wise precaution. All that Will had been able to scavenge was a small cut of cold roast beef and a square-faced bottle of raw Geneva that had been double dosed with juniper berries so that the taste of it rifted back on me, again and again.

But a glass of the gin, watered, and the warmth that came from the fire that Will had lit cheered Hannah. She played cards with a mixture of gusto and cunning that was deadly. And as I gathered from the weight of the oaths she let fly when she did not win, old Hannah had spent time in the company of hard-fisted men. Then a shadow caught my eye. A figure was coming down the lane. Silently we laid down our hands of cards and stood up. I had expected to see Bessie Carver, the servant girl from our farm. But it wasn't young Bessie. This woman was older, and she was dressed in a town serving-woman's garb, a blue linsey-woolsey dress and a plain linen cap. I heard the quickening wheeze of Hannah Thornton's breath.

'She's the one ... ' There was certainty in her words.

'But suppose ... ' I warned – and was cut off.

'Suppose be damned! No honest serving lass looks over her shoulder like that in broad daylight. Follow the shifty bitch. See where she goes.' Hannah was alert and spitting out orders like an angry wildcat.

We had a damned long walk of it. The lass came out of Blith's Nook carrying a basket and went to a tethered pony. I heard Will curse as she gathered her skirts about her so that she could mount up. She heeled the beast into a fast trot.

It is not easy to run fast or far in a trooper's boots and breastplate, even harder to run after a trotting pony and still keep yourself decently out of sight. I doubt we should have lost her had she turned up into the maze of lanes that make up the east ward of the town. But she didn't; she made for the Sand Gate. That would take her clear of the town. For a moment she was out of sight. Will and I pelted for the gate. Yet when we got to it there was sign of neither woman nor pony.

We stood panting for breath. Will held up a hand for me to be still. Then he pointed. From up the bank we could just hear the fast clip-clop of iron-shod hooves dying away. We ran again.

Thank God for the Sin of Eve and Will's sharp eyes. We had run uphill as fast as we could and had stopped again to listen. We stood at one of the town's conduit heads, a place where a public spring gushed from the hillside into a stone basin that in turn overflowed and let the water run down the street to find its way to the river. Will staggered over to the basin to splash cold spring water over his head. I stood still listening. I was about to shout a curse when I saw Will point.

There are gardens thereabouts. Most are cultivated but a few patches are left to run wild for years at a time. The pony stood cropping the grass in one of these. We heard them before we saw them. The reason the lass had ridden off at the gallop had nothing to do with keeping her mission to Blith's Nook a secret. All she was doing was stealing a little time to be with her lover. I saw the white flicker of a petticoat at the side of an elderberry bush and then a bare arse rose up and there was a flurry of pale limbs. The lad grunted like a rooting hog; the lassie gave a long low groan that broke into a little whimper.

I motioned Will not to go closer. We walked back a'ways and left them to commit the sin of fornication to their hearts' content. They frolicked for quite a while. We watched from a distance. Then they were quiet so that all we could hear was the snatch of the pony's teeth at the lush summer grass as it grazed. The woman sat up. Her cap was gone and her dark hair much tousled. Again I caught the white scut as she pulled down her petticoats. She was older than I had first thought, perhaps in her late twenties; but the lad was a great gangling, long limbed, tow-headed lout of maybe sixteen. I found myself wishing them well of it.

Thank the Lord. She led the pony up the bank again, her hips swaying and sometimes giving a little skip as she walked. We were trailing a happy woman, aye, and one very well sated!

The evening air had turned to smoke blue, and pools of white mist were beginning to form in hollows in the ground as we followed the pony's pale rump down the lane between high hedges towards the village of Jesmond.

'There!' Will Blacket growled. The pony had turned in between the two carved stone pillars of a gate. The front of the house was newly-built of the mottled brown-red brick that has come to be made in Newcastle these last years. But the building itself was older and ran far back from the road. We walked past the tall wrought iron gates. The lass was talking to a watchman and laughing at something he said.

'One man armed wi' a fowlin' piece an' another portin' a half-pike ... ' Will breathed rather than spoke the words; it was less than a whisper yet I heard it plainly. I had not seen the second man. We made a careful circuit of the house. The wall of mortared fieldstone was high but it was not yet complete. We found a place where a paling of cut saplings bound together with green withes filled the gap. Will pulled out a knife and began to slice at the interwoven willow branches. With no more than a half dozen slashes he was able to pull aside three of the sapling palings. We were in.

The house was locked up. The lower windows were shuttered and barred. But there was light upstairs. We saw the flickering of a candle being carried from room to room.

'It seems that the only way into this place is by the front door … ' I whispered to Will when we had come full circle around the house and still found no way that we could break in. I was beginning to doubt. We still had no more evidence that this was the place where Aphra was held than Hannah Thornton's fancy. We might have followed the wrong servant.

My doubts were put to flight almost at once. There was a burst of laughter from above our heads and the dance of candlelight. The laugh was long, too long, and even at that distance there was an edge of madness to it. At least I knew for sure that Margaret Ellyot, my sister-in-law, was in the house.

'It's the front door or nothin', Captain.' We had stood awhile. Will was only voicing what I had already thought. I nodded in the darkness. 'An' we'll have to fettle the man with the firelock first. A shot would raise the house.'

'Then let's do that, Will.' I punched at his broad shoulder. 'And let's do it in a soldierly fashion.' Will's smile gleamed in the moonlight.

The first watchman was easy. He came around the corner of the house with a horn lantern swinging in one hand and an ancient matchlock fowling piece over his shoulder. He was whistling a tune under his breath. Will stepped out. There was a swish and a hard thud that ended with a soft clink. The fellow went down like a poleaxed bullock. Which seemed apt when I saw what Will had hit him with. He had swung his purse. The bag was made from a bull's scrotum. Well filled with coin, it served better than any blackthorn club. The lantern and the watchman's hat gave us a stalking horse behind which we could get close to the gatekeeper. Will took up the whistling, kept his head down under the brim of the hat, and swung the lantern as he walked. As he held the man's attention I edged along his flank in the shadows. The watchman had just begun to frown with the beginnings of alarm when I rapped him hard along the jaw with the steel pommel of my sword hilt.

But silencing two scarecrow watchmen had not got us far. The front door of the house was closed. We seemed to be no further forward. But then that puzzle too solved itself. Though first it damned near did for us. There was a shout of drunken laughter from along the lane, the soft drum of horses' hooves and the flare of torches.

We might have bolted and been clean away before the horsemen had shaken the gate and shouted out for the watchmen to open up. But I was in a strange mood. I walked like a man possessed. I unbolted the tall gates and pulled them open just as the first horseman came up. Thank God that they were drunk. Five horses cantered past me into the courtyard. Those beasts had been ridden hard. Their sides heaved and their breath billowed out in white clouds into the damp night air. Will ran out and took the bridles. One of the riders cursed him for a lazy dog and cut a drunken blow at him. But Will dodged nimbly and led the horses away to the stables. I stood back in the shadows. Even an officer of the army of the Covenant can hardly be mistaken for a stabler when he is wearing a steel breastplate.

It was only when one of the riders held up his torch that I saw a face that I recognised. I had no name to fit to it but I had seen it at the Guildhall feast. The man was a merchant. Another of the company had managed to stay in the saddle but he was too drunk to stand up. He swayed on his feet. I heard the gurgle and spew of vomit and saw his friends leap aside, leaving him to fall on his face. There was laughter. And in the laughter I picked out the ripe fruity mellowness that could only have sprung from Nicholas Bronsard. I watched them go into the house. They were just five gentlemen returning from a dinner, an uncommonly good dinner by the looks of it. And they left the carved double doors ajar. We waited for a long few minutes – then we followed them in. The wide hallway was panelled with carved oak. There was a rush mat on the floor to save the rich wood from riding boots. I breathed softly and took in the smell of beeswax and turpentine, and brown soap. We were in a house that was well tended.

Will and I stood there in the bright moon glow that flooded in through the tall side windows. It was so quiet that the steady tick-tock of a Dutch clock standing in a corner sounded loud. We tried the doors at either side of the stairway. Everything was locked. Then Will found a door under the stairs that led to a short passageway. There was a bright seam of candlelight at the end. We stepped down into a steward's pantry and still-room. The air was heavy with the scent from wide glazed earthenware dishes filled with rose petals steeping in water. She was sitting close to the light, sewing a rent in her petticoat.

'Stand up for the gentleman, you fornicating slut!' Will barged past me and stood over the woman. She was pretty and had, as a girl, perhaps been darkly beautiful. Now she was terrified. Her sewing dropped from her fingers as she rose from her stool. Will's zeal as a counterfeit parish constable was wondrous to behold.

'This is the woman, Sir! I'd swear to it. We've had complaints before but this evenin' she was witnessed fairly and squarely to commit acts of gross and fleshly fornication with the lad whose mother laid the information.'

Every syllable was delivered in a hoarse low whisper but it was none the less effective for that. Will Blacket coughed gently into a big fist and stood aside waiting for me to act.

'Your name ... ' I too spoke very softly.

'May ... please ... Sarah ... Trotter ... ' The woman was close to fainting with terror.

'And your state?' I contrived to sound bleak. She goggled at me with staring eyes for a moment before she understood. Will placed a heavy hand on her shoulder.

'Married ... in a church ... or not?' His growl in her ear brought her head up sharply.

'I am the widow ... of Ernest Trotter,' she said, timorously.

'Ah ... ' I allowed her to make what she liked of the sound. 'A good, God-fearing man by all accounts.'

The widow Trotter's head fell and she began to sob. I was about to say something comforting but Will cut me off. He took the woman's chin between his thumb and his forefinger and raised her head again until he was looking full into her face.

'Save your tears m' lass.' His words grated like a surgeon's bonesaw. 'You'll need them when you're dancing down past the White Cross behind the cart's tail with the hangman's whip cuttin' bloody stripes into y'r pretty shoulders.'

The woman went into a half-faint. But Will caught her sagging body and set her down on the stool. He stood back. She was ready.

I poured a little water into a cup and put it to her lips. 'However, Mistress Trotter, it would not honour the memory of your late husband's name if you were lashed all around Newcastle's streets … would it?' I paused. 'You have children?' She shook her head and looked down at her hands folded in her lap. 'Let us say that I am prepared to hold out to you the chance, just the chance mark you, that you may escape the punishment that your fornication so richly merits.' She did not look up but I saw that she stiffened with a new alertness. I was offering her a way out.

'This house is under suspicion of the … Authorities. Help me, and I will try to help you.' I waited until she had looked up at me and then dropped her eyes again before I went on. 'Where is the lady who is being held captive in this house?'

I might have hit Sarah Trotter across the face. The woman all but jumped.

'Oh, but, Sir that's Sir Nicholas's business. We're forbidden that part of the house. We were told that the poor lady was smitten with a contagion, the Spanish flux or some such, that you could catch from a breath … '

'Where is she? Tell me, as you hope for Salvation, show me where she is!'

'I can take you to the top landin' but it's all locked up. Only Oswald Crozier, he's the steward, has the keys. We aren't even allowed up there to clean.'

'And where may we find this Master Crozier?'

'He's abed, Sir.' Sarah's dark eyes fell. Then her lips tightened with spite. She spat: 'You'll find him in Jessie Turner's bed!' It seemed Sarah was a woman scorned.

We followed the flickering rushlight. On the first landing we edged past a thin line of light escaping under a door. The gentlemen had come home drunk and were getting drunker. A single slurred voice was stumbling over his verse of a part-song but no one took him up on it.

'Here … ' There was a note of triumph in Mistress Trotter's voice as she held up the rushlight before the door. Will slipped into the room. After a moment there was a muffled little cry. Then Will came out carrying a bunch of keys. I raised my eyebrows in question. He grinned. 'He slept through it … pig stinkin' drunk by the smell of him. It was the woman ah had t' give a bit o' a tap to!'

The head of the stairs leading up to the top floor of the house had been closed off with a strong door that was fastened with an iron lock. But its very newness made it easy enough to find the key from among the dozen in Master Crozier's bunch.

We found Margaret Ellyot. She stirred as the light flickered briefly over her pale face. She had ended her day, it seemed, with a tantrum. There was smashed glass on the floor around her bed and the vapours of spilled perfume hung heavy on the still air. My brother's widow lay like a little girl. She moaned a little in her dreams and sucked at her thumb.

The last door was barred from the outside but it was not locked. I lifted the beam and went in. There was a four poster bed with no curtains, a table and a single chair. The bedclothes were thrown back. The bed was empty. I held up the rushlight. Aphra Thornton was there. She sat in a corner of the room, huddled, shaking. Her eyes stared at me, dazed, wild, reflecting back the pale flame of the rushlight like the startled gaze of some small animal. She was mother naked.

We got her on the bed. She made a little cry and struggled. Will found candles and lit them. Even by candlelight I could see that the girl had been beaten. One side of her face was swollen and discoloured, bruise upon bruise. As I bent over her to turn her face to the light I caught the faintest whiff I recognised at once – laudanum. I had paid a gold piece for a little vial of the brown tincture on the eve of the battle of Wittstock. The apothecary had sworn that it deadened the senses better than brandy. My foot set something rolling on the floor. I bent down and found it. It was a tin tube. I knew: the drug had been forced into the girl's throat. She had fought hard and they had hurt her for it.

'Find a clean shift and a cloak of some kind!' I grabbed Sarah Trotter and threw her towards the door. 'Will, we must get Mistress Thornton away from this place before we do anything else.'

Will flicked at his brow with his forefinger: 'There's good horses in the stable, Captain. If we can get back down the stairs without makin' a noise … why then we're away.' He pulled his dagger out and licked the blade. 'But we might do well to come back to this place in God's good daylight, for I tell you, Captain, that I can smell pickin's here the like o' which … '

There was a rustle of skirts and Sarah Trotter came back with an armful of clothes. Together we dressed Aphra. It is a strange thing. Had I seen just the calf of the lass's leg, or caught a sly glimpse down the forbidden vale between her bosoms at any other time I would have been as hot as a dog for a bitch. But I found that I had slipped the soft lawn shift over her head and guided her arms into the sleeves without a lecherous thought entering my head. She was a hurt child. Yet when she was halfway decent I was Devil-tempted. I looked. Aphra had a fine, fair body. Her legs were long and most shapely, the ankles were trim. I had never thought about it before, but in the Bible the Song of Solomon says that a woman's belly is like an heap of wheat; the moment I looked down at Aphra I knew what that meant. Then suddenly my lewd thoughts were cut off when Sarah gave a little quivering sob.

'Oh, Jesu! They've pricked her ... ' The horror in the woman's voice was manifest. We held the light close. They were there. Three dark marks on one thigh and two on the other. Dark bruises were already forming around the tiny wounds. Sarah Trotter pulled down the girl's skirts with a jerk.

I stood there and swore, cursing Bronsard, bowels and blood, for a heathen bastard. Will handed me a sheet of paper. I squinted at it in the candlelight for a moment before I could make out the written script. My hands crumpled it. It was all there in proper form:

'A Deposition of the Examination of one Aphra Thornton charged with Witchcraft at Newcastle on the twenty-eighth day of August in the Year of Our Lord, 1640 ... ' The unholy process was laid out in detail. 'Present at the pricking ... outcome of the first pricking ... prisoner's statement ... Findings.' I scanned the signatures. These were men whose names at least I knew. There was one signature that was so scribbled that I could not make it out.

'Burn it, Captain.' Will urged. 'Make an end of it.' He held put up the rushlight and I held the paper to the flame. Then I scoured every corner of the room looking for more papers. There were none, but I did find something else. I found the witchfinder's instruments. There was a Bible upon which lay a copper box with three needles fitted with handles like saddler's awls. The points were sharp and long.

I knew then what had been done. Aphra would have been deemed to have been a witch if she failed to bleed when she was pricked. My fingers felt the salt that still stuck to one of the points. I knew about that too. A wound would not bleed if dyer's alum was rubbed into it. I wet my finger and tasted. It was alum. Aphra had not bled. A charge of witchcraft does indeed make a pretty catch-all in political matters.

I carried Aphra myself. She lay in my arms. Her eyes were open but I think she saw little. We moved along the dark passageways in two pools of yellow candlelight. At night a house gives a thousand sounds that by day go unheeded. Each squeak of the floorboards had my jaw clenching. We were at the head of the main stair. The big front door of the house stood open. Then I heard Sarah give a little squeak of fright.

'Good evening, Master Ellyot.' Nicholas Bronsard stepped quietly out of a dark corner. 'I fear that my hospitality must fall short of allowing you to carry off a proven witch!'

Chapter 27

Flint and Steel

They slipped out of the shadows like wraiths, but the rub of their taffety silk breeks whispered to us softly as they moved, and the Oporto wine wafted strong on their breaths. All four of the men who had ridden in with Bronsard were there. And they were all armed. We stopped two steps down the stairway.

'Truly, Master Ellyot, I welcome you to my house. Pray set down your burden. There is much that we must talk about this night; much that could benefit us all, Captain.'

The words were civil enough but there was no mistaking the glass brittle edge to them and the rising note of triumph in the voice. Bronsard moved forward, deliberately, stepping into a patch of bright moonlight that threw enough light enough for me to see that he was holding a brace of pistols.

I had Bronsard standing where I would have wished. Where I would have wished had I not been burdened as I was. What a teasing old bitch is Fate. This was no time for me to settle my reckoning with him. I had to get the girl who lay in my arms to safety. That had become all that mattered to me.

We were in Bronsard's line of fire. Even with a pistol, at less than twenty feet he could hardly miss putting a ball into the pair of us. Something told me that he would not care greatly that he could well hit Aphra when he fired at me. Slowly, with a curiously light footed gait, he came forward to the foot of the staircase and stood, smiling, the twin muzzles of his pistols raised so that he was sighting at my head.

All manner of thing might have happened at that moment. But it was Will's move that saved us. I felt Will's hand at my back. I heard the slither of steel over oiled leather and sensed the weight ease on my belt as he drew my pistol. Then I felt the hard clutch of his great fist as he took a grip on a fold of my buff leather coat. I was barely ready for him. He jerked, and with one straight heave he lifted the pair of us. I was hoisted, bodily, backwards, and then he loosed his hold, letting me drop like a sack of coals. With my own weight and that of the lass I was carrying I went down, hitting a floor that was damned hard. But I knew that Will's move had pulled me back up the stairs and out of Bronsard's line of sight. For a second I lay in a heap with Aphra's body limp across my chest and the breath knocked out of me. But the ploy had worked. We were all out of the line of any volley from the hall below. And they did fire – but they shot too late. I heard the metallic clicks as pistol locks snapped to strike flakes of crimson spark off gunflints. Priming powder flashed. Then the house vibrated and echoed to the savage crash of three heavy pistol shots. Behind me the new oak panelling split as heavy calibre balls smashed into the carvings. At once there was an answering click and a heavy bang that set my ears ringing as Will loosed off my pistol down into the darkness. Two more shots answered almost at once.

Gunpowder flame, violet then dazzling white, lit the hall. And in that light I saw men, posed, stooped, frozen in the flash. Below us, in the white powder smoke that swirled in the moonlight, a man began to scream. The terrible wail rose to a screaming cry that sounded like the shriek of a lassie with a rat up her skirts. I had heard just such a cry before and knew the cause of it. Will Blacket's shot had smashed into a joint. I guessed a knee. I heard the man blunder about in the dark, blinded by his agony. His arms flailed and brought the Dutch clock down with a crazy reverberating crash of metal springs. No man born is hard enough to take a ball in the kneecap or to the wrist joint and not scream. It was no Christian thing for me to do but I found myself smiling in the darkness. And it was plain enough then that these fellows were no soldiers. I could hear them fussing over the wounded man. In a night skirmish a man shot lies where he falls. But we used the few seconds they gave us. I got to my feet and picked up Aphra again, hefting her limp body at Sarah Trotter, pushing the pair of them back into the shelter of the passageway. Will handed me a re-loaded pistol and we crouched behind the carved banisters – waiting.

They had taken cover. All save one man who ran out through the double doors and into the courtyard. But I could hear the others in the darkness below. And we were still trapped. There had to be another way out: these new fashions of house all had back staircases for the servants to come and go by. If I could find the servants' stair it might offer a way out. But I realised that Bronsard would know that better than I did. And he had enough men to cover all the ways out of the house. Yet I wondered about Bronsard's men. It is one thing to take up a brace of pistols when your head is spinning with the fumes of your host's wine. The game might not be so much to their tastes with one of their friends at their feet moaning with the agony of a shattered bone. Who were these men? One I had placed as a Newcastle merchant, what they called a boothman, a big dealer in grain. Another, I had fancied, was in holy orders. He was wearing white linen bands at his throat. Then it came to me. I had indeed seen him before. He was the canting bastard who had blessed my troop at St Nicholas's steps before we rode off to do battle at Newburn. Damned strange company to be sure!

And my recognition of the clergyman allowed me to make a strong guess at the link between Bronsard and his partners in the scheme to sell grain to the Scots army. They would all make a fat profit out of the town; and out of the Crown, and out of the Scots. It mattered naught to them. I felt my face twist with a sudden anger. So these were some few of few dozen or so of the knowing ones, the men who really ruled in Newcastle, the men who would have their profits no matter who triumphed or what misery befell our town.

There was another sharp clash of flint against steel and a spurt of white spark that lit the shadows below us for an instant. A flash in the pan – but it was followed by no crack of pistol shot. I saw Will's teeth gleam in the moonlight. We both knew that sheer fright had made a man forget to put a charge into his pistol. The flash betrayed his position to within a pin's point. Fear mixes ill with old Portugal wine. My guess was that the fellow had been unmanned by his drink and had sprung for cover when the fight began. Now he had found himself cut off from his friends. I shook Will's sleeve. In the far corner of the hall there was a tall chest of the kind the Scots call an awmrie. Its brass-bound lid caught the glimmer from a stray moonbeam seeping in through a window pane. The chest had been eased out, edged away from the wall. Someone was stirring behind it. The movement was slow; yet I could even pick out the soft creak of the bombast padding in his fine clothes as he moved.

'That man there! 'Ee is a fumblin' wi' his ramrod, Captain!'

Will's voice thundered out across the gloom. It was the age-old foul-mouthed banter of the sergeant of musketeers shouting out his filthy jokes along the line of battle to stay frightened men's courage. I took him up:

'Fumbling! Y'say fumbling, Sergeant?' I gave the wild boar grunt of a Swedish drill-master feigning his disgust at a company of green recruits.'

'With his ramrod!'

I simulated a tone of aghast disbelief. 'Then I do pray you ... shoot me the pandering catamite!' It was a threadbare piece of repartee but it saved a precious shot and it may well have started the retreat. A figure leaped from behind the chest and bolted for the door, the man's breath sobbed in terror. It was the curate from St Nicholas.

Bronsard's partners were not soldiers or even fighting men. But a firelock in the hands of even a dandiprat can rip your guts apart just as surely as a ball loosed off by a King's jaeger. So we were still trapped. And many minutes had gone by since I had seen or heard Bronsard.

'Mistress Trotter ... ' I whispered into the darkness. She was nearer to me than I had supposed. Her hand touched my knee. 'Tell me ... are there back stairs to this part of the house?'

'There's the servants' stairway ... but only to the second landing.'

I sensed where Sarah Trotter was pointing. I put out my hand to her face to feel the movement of her head. 'No other way?' Again the servant woman nodded against my touch. I felt Aphra stir beside me. She began to moan softly.

'She'll waken soon, Sir. I know the signs.' There was a hesitation. 'It's like that when we have to use the potion on Mistress Maggie.'

'The potion?' That told much. Though I could see that giving my sister-in-law a dose of laudanum sometimes might be the only way to make life tolerable for the servants who had to attend her.

'Captain! That hallway's empty. I reckon that the bastards have up and run.' Will was already halfway down the stairs. He had a cocked pistol in his hand but he was not moving like a man who expected to be fired at. And he was right. Bronsard's friends had drunk his wine but it seemed that they were no longer inclined to risk their necks for him. Will went down to the front door. For an instant he showed himself and then he stepped back. It was as well that he was nimble about it. There was a red flash and a blast louder than the harsh crack of a pistol. Birdshot rattled like spilled peas as it spent its force against the walls and fell to the floor. From outside beyond the courtyard there was a ragged cheer that broke into drunken laughter. Master Nicholas's friends may have faltered but the two watchmen that we had laid out looked to have come round and found a fowling piece. And by the sound of the cheer the company had come by more wine.

Our situation was still dangerous. I could feel that much in my guts. Whatever else he was Bronsard was not a fool. Nor was he a man who would give up an enterprise easily. If he was prepared to leave his own safety and the security of his venture in the hands of a few gentlemen roisterers then there had to be a reason for it. And where in hell was Bronsard? I had had no sight of him since Will's first pistol shot had sent them all scampering for cover. I could see no way that Bronsard would leave the house and run – unless he stood to gain by it. Nor, I was sure, would his friends stand fire if they thought for a moment that their leader had run away and left them to fight alone.

'The Steward's pantry, where you were sitting, is there a way out of it? Surely it leads to a yard.' I was impatient for Sarah Trotter's answer.

'It gives on to a yard, where the pump and the privies are; and that lets out by a little passage to the side of the house.' She touched her mouth with her hand as she remembered something. 'Oh, but that way's all locked up with an iron grille … ' Will jangled Oswald Crozier's bunch of keys in front of her face and grinned like a wolf.

We reached the steward's pantry. There was better light there. The walls were fresh whitewashed and two wax candles gleamed with a clear flame. We stopped. I laid Aphra down on the scrubbed tabletop and cradled her head in my arms. Sarah Trotter poured water and held the pot to Aphra's lips. She was able to drink. She opened her eyes. At first there was fear. Then she recognised Will, and then me. She smiled and for a moment closed her eyes again. But I could see that she was fighting for consciousness. She struggled to sit up.

'Breathe … Breathe deep.' I ordered rather than urged, putting my mouth to her ear. Sarah wet a cloth in one of the bowls of rose petals and bathed the bruised face. I touched the side of Aphra's cheek with my fingertip. She winced.

That made me angry in a way that I had not been before. I knew that I was going to kill Nicholas Bronsard this night. I was going to have full revenge for the murder of Luke Ellyot. That was the way thing were done in the North, both sides of the Border. It irked me that I could not kill the swine twice: once for my brother, and again for what he had done to Aphra.

'The buggers are at the yard gate, Captain ... ' Will stood to one side of the small window and held a candle. A pistol ball struck the stone of the sill and ricocheted away with a soft whine.

'The cellars?' A mansion would have cellars. There was bound to be a way out from the cellars. Ale casks and herring barrels had to be got in and out. There would be a place where that could be done. But Sarah shook her head.

'There's cellars, right enough, but the Master keeps the keys himself. Not even Oswald Crozier is allowed to get down there.'

I felt the tingle of hope. 'Which is good reason why we should go that way. Even if we have to break a door or two to get in.'

But there was need for us to smash a way in. The little door under the staircase stood open. Whoever had gone that way last had been in haste: the big iron key had been left in the lock. This was the way Bronsard had gone.

'You stay here, Will ... Take one of the pistols. Shield the light of the candles. I may be back in minutes or I may not. But if I am not back in an hour ... ' I stopped. What if I were indeed not to come back in an hour? Words fled. I could think of no order to give.

'If you're not back inside an hour, Captain, I do it the old soldier's way. I set a torch to the house. That should bring up a troop or two o' Leslie's cavalry up soon enough.' We laughed – but I knew that Will would really do it. I looked at Aphra. She was sitting up with her head against Sarah's shoulder. Our eyes met. She smiled at me. The brightness of life was coming back. I put my right hand across my chest and gave a slow little bow before I returned her smile. It was a rough soldier's salute and I wished that I had some better knowledge of gentle manners so that I could do things as she would expect them to be done. I moved to go.

'Captain!' Will grabbed hard me by the shoulder. 'The boots, for Christ's sake take off the boots. The bastard will hear you.'

Will was right. I leaned against the wall and raised a leg so that he could pull off the long cavalry boots. A man who pulls his legs free of a pair of quartermaster's issue cavalry boots could feel a good two stones lighter; even if he does stand a hand's breadth shorter. Will also handed me the long dagger that he had taken from the freelance's body on the road from Shields. He clicked his tongue gave me a villain's wink.

The cellar steps creaked at almost every step and at every creak I stopped in the darkness and listened hard. But there was no sound, not even the soft scamper of mice. I sniffed the still air. There was a dampness to it but the usual mustiness of cellars was missing. In its place there was the sharp fresh smell that I knew I had smelled before but that I could not put a name to. I was at the bottom step before I saw glimmer of light ahead.

I halted. A man standing out against the only light in the cellar would make a perfect target. For perhaps a minute I stood there in the darkness, trying to sense the presence of anyone lying in wait, trying to listen against the fast thump of my heart's pounding. Then I moved. I stepped softly across to the cellar wall, pressing myself against the damp mortar so that I could keep within the protection of the shadows yet still outflank the little glow of yellow light. Slowly I came abreast of the flame. It was a tallow candle stuck on the top of a firkin barrel. I was about to move on past it when I looked closer and realised what I was looking at.

Bronsard had not lost his taste for infernal devices. My trick with the trap I had set in the lid of his strongbox had taught him nothing. This one was more simple, nothing simpler, but I knew well enough that it stood to be far and away more deadly. A firkin gunpowder barrel had been broached and a handful of loose cannon powder had been piled around the bunghole. A short stub of candle had been set in the middle of the little pile of glistening sable grains. I stood at the barrel's head. The light flickered in a sudden draught. Melted tallow like fat tears trickled down and spread cooling back to white fat as I watched. The little wall of mutton fat stood high around the flame. But even as I watched the dam broke and the melted tallow ran down on to the sable grains. There is no accurate way of telling how long it will take a candle to burn down to a mark. But here it seemed that Bronsard had badly mistimed. The wick had curled down upon itself and the candle had burned down too fast. Grains of gunpowder heaped close around the candle stood no more than a knuckle joint's length from the drooping flame. The spittle on my thumb and forefinger fizzled loud as I put out my hand and firmly nipped out the flame.

I stumbled around in the dark for some precious minutes before I found the steep wooden steps, the twins of those I had come down by. At the head of the steps I came out into a narrow passage with bare stone walls. Here there was more light, bright summer's starlight coming in through an uncurtained window. The pine boards of the servants' stairway were quiet under my stockinged feet as I climbed. But as the maid Sarah had said, the servants' stairs stopped at the second landing. I passed through a felt hanging cloth and found myself back in the panelled gallery. I stood for a moment, listening to the sounds of the house. There was a soft thump from above me, upstairs. I forced myself to relax. To steady my nerve I hefted my pistol in my hand and held it on its side so that the lock lay uppermost. With the edge of my thumb I clicked open the pan and raised the pistol to my mouth to blow away the fine black priming powder. Fearful for the few seconds that the weapon was useless, I fumbled quickly for the little copper flask and primed the gun afresh. The soft tattoo of my finger as I tapped to settle the powder home in the pan sounded like a distant drum. Then, finally, forcing myself to it. I sought the turnscrew that kept the flint tight in the jaws of the hammer and tightened it hard. The exercise had cost me perhaps ten seconds. Yet when I had done it I was strangely calmed. It was as well – Bronsard's mellow voice sounded out softly at the head of the stairs.

My tactic was already decided. Bronsard would have two pistols, at least. I wanted to shout out a challenge, to bring him down those stairs. I even drew a breath and opened my mouth. But my hard-won battle-sense stopped me before I could make a fool of myself. The time for words with this bastard was long past. The man had ordered my brother killed. For that I would shoot him. And I knew how I would do it. I would put a shot into the bulk of his body. Then I would rush him and skewer him in the guts with my dagger.

There was the scrape of a boot and the flicker of a candle that made a square of pale light on the floor at the foot of the stairs. I aimed my pistol down the oak pan-elled gallery. The daft fancy that it would be like shooting the popinjay at a Midsummer's fair flitted across my mind. I heard the double snick-snack as I thumbed my pistol to full cock. Then for an instant a flash lit up the gallery. I sprang aside like a trodden cat. The shock of the bang made my finger tighten on the trigger. Jesu! Had my pistol not misfired on me I would have stood there caught, helpless. My lips worked silently as I cursed myself for a stupid, cack-handed ploughboy! My fingers fumbled clumsily with the steel mechanism as I struggled to re-cock my weapon. I was shaking. Cold sweat trickled down between my shirt and my skin. The sharp breath of air I snatched turned to a stifled half sob in my throat. I stood with my pistol crooked over my elbow and forced myself into some semblance of steadiness.

There had been two shots, two blasts from a brace of horse pistols. The whole house had shuddered. There was quiet again. Then I fancied that I heard a woman's voice, distant, softly humming a little tune, a spinning song, with a lilt to it. Still I stood in the darkness for a long time.

Chapter 28

Margaret's Revenge

Every soldier knows well that there is a cord strung tightly between caution and cowardice. I knew it. And after I had stared into the darkness at the end of the gallery until the white motes began to dance before my eyeballs I knew that I was standing astride that line. Nonetheless I was gnawed by the fear that the two shots were no more than a trap to lure me in. Then, again, I caught the softest drift of sound. I had not been mistaken – and yet I could hardly believe it. It was indeed a woman's voice, singing beautifully, then softly breaking away into a sweet hum. I even could recall the name of the tune. It was 'Shall I Bring Thee Silver? Shall I Bring Thee Gold?' My mother had often sung it as she sat at her spinning wheel. If this were a ruse then it was a strange one. I edged forward.

At first sight he looked like nothing so much as a man overcome by strong drink. He lay across the bed. His legs were splayed at an odd angle and his tongue lolled out. I have seen bloody death all over the north of Europe but never had I seen a man who had died with his eyes so wondrously crossed as Bronsard's were. I stepped into the room.

His hat of beaver felt with its fine cavalier plumes of ostrich had fallen on to his chest. I lifted it. A brace of horse pistols loosed off at close range does a deal of mischief to a man's mortal frame. He had been shot under the breast, twice. The entry of the balls was marked by two blackened patches like dirty hand marks on the pale blue embroidery work of his waistcoat. The muzzles must have been close: the fine embroidered camlet cloth of his coat was still smouldering. He would, I supposed, have lived just long enough to realise who it was had shot him.

'Luke, my dearest, is that you?' Margaret Ellyot sat before a Venetian mirror combing her hair with her fingers. I took her hands in mine and squeezed then together gently. She smiled and kissed them.

'We have to go … home.' I spoke quietly. 'This is not our place, Margaret. We have no business here. Come … m' love.' I bore my brother's widow no ill-will – I was as certain of that as I was of anything – but my teeth gritted a little at the hypocrisy. I was but acting a part to get her away from that room. There was no resistance in her. I found her cloak and draped it around her shoulders. She let me lead her gently downstairs.

Will was alert. I had to call out well in advance and show myself before he put up his gun.

'They're still out there.' He reported. 'Front and rear. Could they be just holdin' us here until they send for reinforcements … D'y think, Captain?'

I shook my head. 'There's no longer anyone to reinforce Will.' For a second Will looked puzzled. Then he understood. He licked his lips, just once.

Margaret Ellyot went willingly enough to Sarah and sat down like an obedient child. I looked at her for a moment. There was no doubting that this lass was indeed fey. Yet I fancied that even now the devil in the girl was dying. There was a curious look of peace about her. It was strange, I thought. I had sworn to kill Bronsard myself. But providence had decreed otherwise. I would try to draw together the threads of the story when I could, but for now there was too else much to do. Bronsard was dead but his enterprises would still writhe like a headless serpent. Yet I wondered how long his men would stay if they were told that their master was no longer there to direct their business.

I made plans as we went. Will burst into Oswald Crozier's room with a blazing torch in one hand and a cocked pistol in the other. I doused the drunkard with a jug of water and stepped back. The woman woke first and opened her mouth to scream. Will lifted her by her hair and snarled into her face. She shut her mouth and stayed silent, and wide-eyed. I had to slap the steward's black stubbled cheeks twice, hard, before he stirred. He opened his bleary eyes and stared, and then his jaw fell.

'Get up Crozier!' I waited until he had blinked. 'Get your arse out of that bed unless you want to dance at the end of a hangman's rope. There's a troop of Leslie's horse riding here now. We can see their torches at the end of the lane. Sir Nicholas has been riding hard for York these two hours and has left all of us here to swing!' I took him by the front of his nightshift and pulled hard. I could only guess what he made of my story but it served to make him leap. He was out of bed and in a great scramble with himself to pull on his clothes.

'There are some of Bronsard's fellows outside.' I spat the words at him. 'Warn them that the Scots will surely put the gelder's knife to the balls of every man jack o' them if one musket is so much as poked in their direction.'

We heard Crozier and his mistress running about downstairs for a few minutes. They were undoubtedly snatching up odd valuables, but we let them go to it. Then from the window I saw Crozier's shadow leaping large in the flame of torchlight as he ran out across the yard shouting the alarm.

Will came back from his round of the house and stables with a broad smile on his face. His arms were full of booty and I begrudged him not at all.

Bronsard's friends had fled. All except one of the watchmen, who still lay in the stable, too drunk to move.

We harnessed a horse to a cart and spread a couple of bales of new hay for bedding. Then we loaded the women on to the hay and tethered three spare horses from Bronsard's stable behind. I reckoned the beasts to be fair prizes of war.

'Take the lasses to ... ' I found myself to hesitate. 'Take them to my farm, Will. Go by the by-lanes. Keep well away from Newcastle. And if you do get stopped by a Scots patrol, tell the bastards that your master is Captain John Ellyot and that he undertakes to see that any man who offers you hindrance will answer to the wee crookit mannie himself for it.'

I looked down at Aphra. The power of the laudanum was still strong on her but she was awake.

'Mistress Thornton ... ' I began. She turned her head and smiled at me, softly. 'I ... ' The words failed to come. 'Go with Will ... you will be safe ... And, God willing, we shall talk ... you and I, tomorrow.'

I watched the swinging wink of the cart's lantern as Will drove off down the lane at a good pace. Then I reminded myself that I a deal of work to do and little of the night left ahead of me to do it in.

First, there was a corpse to be put where no one would find it. I worked without a qualm. Nicholas Bronsard's grasping business with this world was done. But I did not want to answer questions about him to anyone – ever.

My search of the corpse was perhaps not so thorough as Will's would have been, but I fancy that I missed little. The gold ring set with the big topaz stone that he had worn the first time I had met him was still on his finger. Even with a smear of tallow it would not be eased off. I reached for my knife and then stopped. My snort of laughter sounded eerie in the room. I left the ring.

Bronsard's own cloak served as his shroud. Good living makes for a heavy corpse. He was a weighty man to carry. It was a shame to waste the cloak but I knew better than to keep a garment like that, no matter how costly. Nor was I long in finding a place for him. There was a servants' privy, not long dug, beyond the vegetable garden at the back of the house. I tore up the seat plank and without pause tipped Sir Nicholas Bronsard head first into the stinking pit. He went in easily, and the hole was deep enough to take him. There was a pile of sieved earth readied to cover the daily *stercus humanum*. I shovelled in enough to cover him well. It would have been profane of me to have said any holy words over him. 'Let a great stench and contagion arise!' I did fight to keep the words from rising up into my thoughts, but they came nonetheless. And without thinking what I did I hawked into the grave. Privies are dug and filled, and the hut is moved when the hole is full. No one would find him. Every day men ride out on journeys and just disappear, for ever, even in England. Just as I might have done on the road from South Shields.

Upstairs again, I began to gather up Bronsard's baggage. It was clear enough that he had intended leaving the house that night. I think that he had gone to Margaret Ellyot's room with the intention of bringing her away with him. But no matter. I had his well-filled purse and a pocket timepiece of Nuremberg work that was truly a wonder. And I had the pistols that had killed him. Beyond that it looked much as though he had intended to travel light. There was a small oxhide trunk and a fat satchel. That was all. The trunk held clean linen, three boxes of the sweetmeat they call *eryngo*, and two bottles of good Bordeaux wine. I lit more candles and emptied the satchel out on to the bed.

There was a streak of pale grey light along the eastern horizon when I pushed the last folded sheet of stiff scrivener's paper back into the satchel. I had read everything, everything from the new granted patent of nobility to a bill from a town jeweller for the mending of a clasp. And I had sipped my way through most of one of the bottles of good wine and chewed my way through a whole box of the candied sea-holly.

I would give most of the papers to Sylvanus Webster. As a Commissary of the army of the Covenant he would doubtless be able to make something of them. I had the bones of it. It was a not even a swindle. Bronsard and his friends, the Boothman and the others named had simply engrossed to themselves the grain crop of the country far and wide around Tyneside. They had intended to sell wheat to the King's agents to feed the troops when they arrived in Newcastle. Documents had been countersigned by Major Miniver and a third of the cost had already been handed over to Bronsard. But the royal garrison had fled and good Sir Nicholas had been set to sell the grain a second time, to the Scots.

There were however five pieces of paper that would not go to Master Webster. They were fat letters of credit drawn on Mercantile houses, two in Paris and three in Amsterdam. By far the smallest value was my own note that Bronsard had discounted for me. I sighed loud, and finished the wine. It would be safest, I thought, to wait a while, a year or more, and then to present the bills directly at their houses of issue. Their value would make that trouble well worthwhile.

I went downstairs and stirred the coals of the kitchen fire. There were good smoked hams hanging from hooks in the rafters, so I fetched one down and filled a wide brass frying pan with thick slices. Then I wandered down to the fowl house and took up a dozen new laid eggs. There was a press in the kitchen with a keg of twice-brewed ale newly broached on it, and inside the kist I found fresh bread. I made a good breakfast.

I was filling a second pot of ale when I heard the sneck of the kitchen door creak, softly. I had the muzzle of my pistol against his jaw as soon as he stepped through the door. It was Sylvanus Webster.

'Good morning, Captain Ellyot.' He spoke with an uncommon pleasantry. Then he looked around very slowly. Satisfied with what he saw he sat down and helped himself very liberally to my ham and eggs. As he ate I told my tale.

'You have done well.' He wiped a smear of yolk from his lips.

'Say rather that I have done most excellently well.' I said dryly.

'You have indeed.' I was given one of his wintry smiles. I would have to settle for that.

'You knew that I was here?' I was more than a trifle irked that Sylvanus Webster had been able to lay his hands upon me so easily. I had thought that the enterprise of finding Aphra was my own affair. He paused with his mouth full of ham. I waited until he had chewed a space. He belched quietly and pointed to the window. I stepped across and looked out. There was no mistaking the stooped figure in the ragged cloak standing there with the morning mist swirling around him.

'You knew because you set the Blind Piper to spy upon me ... did you not know that it was Davy Turnbull who pointed the finger at me when I landed at Shields?'

'Master Turnbull has, since, proved a trustworthy and handy servant of the Covenant.' Webster held up a hand and gave me a sidelong look. 'And since it may well be that I shall soon have business where you must work alongside that man ... ' He let his voice trail away as he put the last egg onto his platter. I snorted and looked out of the window again. Damn my eyes but Blind Davy had disappeared.

'Calm yourself, Captain Ellyot.' Webster mopped up the egg from his plate with a crust of bread. For a moment he looked round as though he sought more food. 'Our friend's task was to follow and report. That is all.' He cut more bread, put a piece into his mouth, and spoke as he ate it. 'Now ... if you wish to thank any man for this night's work, it is the hand of Matthew Stobbs that you should shake.'

'Stobbs!' I would have to confess that I had not given that fellow a moment's thought since he had been taken from Sir Joseph Ord's house on the morning after the raid. Webster nodded gravely.

'Mattie Stobbs has been of more use to us than you, or indeed he, could imagine. As providence would have it, his wound was not fatal. But he was stricken by a great fever two nights after he had been stabbed. I spent many hours at his bedside.' Webster looked up at me and narrowed his eyes so for the moment he had the look of a hawk with sewn eyelids.

'A man may say things while he is in the toils of a fever that he could not recall even under torture when he is well. While Matthew Stobbs writhed in the fires he was able to take me by the hand, as it were, and guide me to all the places that Nicholas Bronsard had sent him as a messenger. There were only three places, three houses, where Aphra could have been kept. Two of them were named on the piece of paper that Major Miniver gave you. I have been to those two houses once more this night, this time with Leslie's troops. We found much – but we did not find Aphra Thornton.

As Sylvanus Webster supped at a pot of ale he had me sit across from him and tell him again every detail of what had happened. I did that, leaving out only the letters of credit that were now securely stuffed into the legs of my breeks. Only once did he make a move. It was when I told of Aphra being pricked for a witch. The hand that lay on the table before him clenched and then relaxed. I saw a red fire in his eyes. But after a minute or so he motioned for me to go on with my report. He made his ale last as long as my tale. Then he wiped his mouth with a linen kerchief and, I fancy, gave a little sigh of fatigue.

'Show me the cellars,' he said suddenly. 'I want to see this wondrous petard of Nicholas Bronsard's.

I was surprised that Webster should be interested in a barrel of gunpowder. Nonetheless I lit candles and took him down the stairs to the cellar. He stood for some moments looking at the barrel.

'So it seems that the enterprise turned stale on Bronsard when Newburn was lost. He tried to mend his case by dealing with the Scots. Then he began to feel my hot breath on his neck and so he decided to run.' Webster stopped for a moment and looked upwards. I could see that he was placing the last few chips into the mosaic of the story.

'He had invited his friends here last night, perhaps under the pretence that he was to pay them their share of the monies from their enterprise.' He looked at me in the golden candlelight. I think, indeed I knew, that Doctor Webster had already guessed that I had taken something of value from Bronsard's corpse. 'But in reality it was his plan to blow them all to hell and then to fly southwards to join his friends, with the King at York.' I could see that in his mind he was already drafting out the paragraphs of an official report for his own masters. He pointed to the beams and planks over-head. 'This room where he was entertaining his accomplices, it stands directly over this point.' He walked across to the barrel. His long fingers felt across the staves and as he did so the corners of his mouth went up a little.

'Good!' The cry echoed back from the walls. 'This barrel bears the broad arrow brand of the Tower of London. That means that the powder comes from the Castle magazine.' For a moment the man sounded as though he were presenting evidence before a court. Sylvanus Webster had the look of a truly happy man.

'But what else may we expect to find here?' He looked at me keenly. 'I had thought that a sharp intelligencer like yourself would have made use of his nose and well as his eyes.' Webster sniffed deeply and I found myself doing the same. 'Wet pargeter's work … plaster.' Now that he had named the smell I knew it instantly. 'That cannot have been done more than a day.' Webster spoke with a studied airiness. I held the light to the wall and ran my fingers over the surface. He was right. The par-geting was poorly smoothed and the cow hair in it had been insufficiently mixed with the plaster. 'And who spends good money in having a cellar plastered at all?'

He had brought back his leg and kicked before I had time to answer. The wall cracked and a piece of the plaster the size of a meat trencher broke away. There was neither brick nor stone under it. Webster's boot had uncovered a partition of green wattle, roughly woven willow branches. He took the candle from me and held it to the gap. An inch or two back from the wattle the tied ears of a coarse sack showed. My knife point snipped through the wisp of spun-yarn tying the neck. Wheat grains, yel-low gold in the candlelight began to trickle out. Behind me I heard Sylvanus Webster's hands clap together.

'So the adversary that could have brought the whole enterprise of the North to nothing is defeated.' Webster took off his hat and bowed his head. His lips moved. He was, indeed, saying his prayers.

'Without this grain the Scots army would have had to return to Scotland before the Autumn.' He spread his arms and then looked at me. 'Y'see, Ellyot, this is all con-traband. We found as much again in the two houses Miniver named. Every grain of it can – lawfully – be seized without payment. General Leslie has sworn an oath that he will not oppress the folk under his dominion. And he means to keep his word ... to all true Protestants.'

I kept my face as straight as I could – but I had to speak out.

'Master Webster, do you not realise that the common run of our Northumberland or Durham folk might have a deal of trouble in persuading your Presbyterian Scots that they are indeed any kind of Protestants at all. You must know as well as I do that most of your Scots commissaries learned their trade in Germany. Those bastards will skin a rat for hide and tallow. The Scots are here, Master Webster. But we are Englishmen.' I found my temper rising. 'It may be well enough for you to return to, where is it? Norfolk? London? But we in the North will have to live under what is for us foreign rule. Be assured, Sir, if that rule proves to be cruel and grasping then Charles Stuart may yet find plenty of true Protestants ready to fight for him.' Now it was my turn to smile and look sidelong at Webster.

I capped my argument: 'And then our Scots friends might find Newcastle lads making themselves free of folks' homes in Edinburgh and Dundee.'

For a moment I thought that Webster was going to give me a hot answer. But then he looked at me from under his eyebrows and said very quietly: 'I hear you, friend Ellyot ... I do hear you well. Your fears have been my own. That is why we must stay with the Scots while they bide in the North. Leslie has sworn a great oath that he will muzzle, tether and hobble his men. You have my word that it lies within my power to make him hold fast to that oath.'

We came out of the cellar to hear the jingle of harness at the front of the house. Outside we found a full troop of Scots horse drawn up in the morning mist. And as though to reinforce the power that Sylvanus Webster had spoken of, a sharp command was barked and swords were swung up in salute the moment that he appeared on the steps. Then I saw who was troop commander.

'Lieutenant Alexander McLeish at your service! Sir!' Pride hung about the lad like an aura. There was a swagger in his step as he dismounted and strode towards us. I understood his feelings well enough. It is indeed a great thing to be a young commissioned officer in an army that has just won a great victory.

'Mr McLeish.' Webster's voice carried and I knew that it was by design. 'You come here in good time. I welcome you. You shall have written orders in your hands by this evening but in the meantime billet your troop in this house.' At those words a little ripple passed along the ranks of cavalry. Something like a smirk passed across McLeish's face. It would do his reputation with his men no harm if he was able to get them billeted in a good comfortable place.

'You will find in the cellars a barrel holding a half hundredweight of good English gunpowder. Take it, and, without blasting yourself to Gateshead or Gehennah, get it shared out and into your men's powder flasks without delay.'

Webster half turned to me and said: 'Did you know, Captain Ellyot, that when they had driven the English from the field at Newburn there was scarcely a pound of gunpowder left in the entire Scottish army?'

McLeish had the satisfaction of seeing my sour look. But the thought of the fat letters of credit stuffed down my breeks cheered me considerably.

I rode with Webster back to Newcastle. I wanted to talk to him but it was plain that he wished to be silent as we rode along the lanes. Nonetheless, as we neared the town I coughed and waited until he had looked at me.

'The lass ... Mistress Thornton ... ' I was at a loss for words for a moment. I had wanted to ask Webster's advice. I thought he would know something of the Thorntons. They were an old Newcastle family, but I needed to know how they stood now. It was strange that there were no menfolk to whom I might address myself. There would be little to gain from my making my advances to the lass herself without permission from her family. But where was Aphra's family? Hannah had sons, she had said as much; though that did not mean that she had sons who were living. Dame Hannah could be all of eighty and might well have outlived all of her children and even her grandchildren.

'The child is comely.' Webster looked across at me as he reined up and sat back in the saddle. 'She has keen wits ... and, as I have learned, she has a tongue to match. That is something she has from her mother.'

'You knew her mother?' I asked eagerly. Webster's eyes opened wide and then his shoulders began to shake. 'Oh ... aye. I knew her mother well.'

'Then tell me, Master Webster ... ' I got no further. Sylvanus Webster put up the palm of his hand.

'Soldier, be still!' He sighed and shot a curiously whimsical look at me. 'If you can get Mistress Hannah's leave, then in God's name, you may ... '

'I may what, Sir?' I was truly bemused.

Without warning Sylvanus Webster spurred his horse into a gallop so that I was only just able to catch the words he tossed over his shoulder: 'You have my leave to pay court to my daughter, Master Ellyot ... and good luck to you!'

Chapter 29

Triumph for the Wee Crookit Mannie

The town had an odd feel to it. The day was hot and sunny, the sky blue with scarcely a cloud in it. Yet I could smell ill-omen. There was a tension in the air like that which foretold the breaking of a storm. We rode up through narrow streets that were nearly deserted. The few folk we saw drew aside from us or scurried for the shelter of alleyways until we had passed by. The silence was unnerving. The echo of our horses' hooves sent a strange tingle through me. Had I not known that it was impossible I would have wagered a gold maximilian that the smell of an ambush hung about the place. As we topped the bank at the head of the Side, I turned in my saddle and looked back, down over the red pantiles of the roofs. Smoke rose from no more than three or four chimneys. Yet it was a Sunday. I had expected to hear singing at least, and organ music from the churches. Then my face cracked into a smile. I remembered that the town's Church of England clergy, those who had not fled the town with the English army, would know only too well that the Scots Presbyterians did not hold with the playing of any 'kist o' whistles' in their churches.

But then that afternoon I saw Newcastle had truly submitted. I uncovered my head and bent my neck with all the others, Scots and English alike, as the 'wee crookit mannie' himself, General David Leslie, went meekly to his prayers in St Nicholas. Nor was His Excellence crowing at the surrender of the town. He limped, bare headed and stripped of his sword, flanked by four plainly dressed fellows. Everything about the ceremony had been contrived to make the Scots look as unlike conquerors as possible. Yet Leslie's humility seemed false. The man could not hide his personal vanity. I doubted that the suit of dark grey velvet, cunningly tailored to conceal his twisted shoulder and arm could have cost less than two hundred pounds, not including the many pearls sewn about it. But he might have saved himself the expense. The com-

284

mon folk of Newcastle, those too poor to flee the town, stayed behind their barred doors. There was indeed a good throng of men, women with bairns too, at St Nicholas steps. And there was a company of pikemen, helmets and breastplates all agleam with a fresh dressing of oil of linseed, drawn up to hold the crowd back from the solemn procession of worshippers who walked silently into the church. But it was as plain to me – as it was to others there – that from the numbers of blue bonnets in the crowd the men were for the most part Scots, coal-hewers drawn from among the hundreds who worked in the mines in and around the town.

I took good note of the dignitaries and merchants who filed past me. They had turned out, or more likely had been turned out, in good numbers. They stood together, the wolves for once like shorn lambs, whey-faced and tight-lipped, unsure. The silks that I had seen at the Guildhall just a few days before had gone. This Sabbath morning wardrobes had been rummaged for sombre cloth. And the faces grew longer still, and more pale yet. Alexander Henderson, a noted Presbyterian divine, had been fetched down from Edinburgh to preach in the fallen temple of Baal. So they were forced to sit, humbled, and listen while he ranted down his Hellfire upon their heads from the high pulpit. I think it may well have been the longest sermon that I have ever had to listen to. But I cared not at all. My thoughts were for Aphra Thornton and how I might begin to court her in proper fashion – and then win her.

A little after the town's clocks had struck two o' clock Sylvanus Webster made a sign that we might leave. We waited until the preacher's ravings had the congregation sitting with their mouths agape, then quietly we stood back from our places by the font and slipped out.

It was Webster's way, it seemed, to give me leave to court his daughter then to keep me too busy to go to her. I followed him down through the steep cobbled lanes to Sir Joseph Ord's house. There was near pandemonium there. Royal troops had been billeted in the place and had left it as any troops would. There is nothing quite like having a score of the soldiery pissing their way down your stairs and spewing into your linen closets for a week or two to give a house a rare spirit of its own. We squeezed past the rhythmically moving bums of kneeling servant women who scrubbed frantically at the floors and the stairs. The miasma of the stench shimmered breast high. Strong lye and brown soap was fighting the hard rearguard action offered by caked filth. Quickly we were ushered into an upper room.

Sir Joseph Ord sat with a well cleared platter and an empty ale pot before him. The Scots may have taken Newcastle but the old man still wore his rich old fashioned clothes. He was smoking a white clay pipe and looked content with himself. He took his pipe from his mouth and inclined a friendly eyebrow in the direction of the window. Ralph Carr, my uncle, stood there with a spy-glass trained across the Tyne at Gateshead Fell. I stood quietly at his shoulder for a moment without his being aware that I was there. He looked older, his hair had turned almost all white now; he looked smaller than I remembered him, but when he turned and saw me the eyes were as blue and as full of twinkle as they had ever been. Nor had the strength of his hug lessened. I loved the old man. He was now the only close kin I had. It had been Ralph Carr who had persuaded my mother to badger my father into letting me to go to the grammar school; it had been my uncle who had taken me into his shop and tempered the rough farmer's lad into ... well, into a lad o' parts. My heart was full. He cleared his throat noisily and handed me the spy-glass.

'The beggar's army is setting up camp across at Gateshead.' There was a wryness in Ralph's tone. Gentle fellow he was but he was no man's fool. I squinted down the glass. Across the river there was the orderly movement of men and horses. And there was no mistaking the line of men swinging picks. Already my cannon royal were being emplaced to command the town.

'So it may indeed be that David Leslie is going to keep his word. There won't be more than a couple of thousand men occupying the town.' I was baiting Sylvanus Webster. My uncle watched Webster's response with amusement wrinkling his face.

'The General thinks that fourteen hundred men should serve well enough to guard the hordes of clerks who will soon be here from Edinburgh to oversee the running of the coal trade!' Now it was Master Webster's turn to show that he could take a gibe in good part.

'Which would seem to show that there will be one Scots soldier to protect every two or three of the quill-riders that are to come!' The company laughed but there was a nervous edge to it. Sir Joseph Ord made a sound in the back of his throat and took his pipe from his mouth.

''Tis strange indeed that our Scottish allies should have thought so much about how to ensure that the coal is tallied and the profit counted,' he looked directly at Webster. 'Yet nothing at all on the winning of the coals from the earth, the paying of the miners; nor on who is to be offered coals to buy.' He stood up with his back to the empty fireplace and looked at us each in turn.

'Yesterday there were more than a hundred and twenty ships standing off the Tyne's mouth, all ready to come into the river to load coals. This morning the horizon is bare. There isn't an English merchant ship between the Tyne and Flamborough Head.' The old knight closed his eyes and stood, sucking in the fragrant tobacco smoke. There was silence. Webster brought his hands together as though he were about to offer up a prayer. Then his face broke into a curiously human smile. For a moment he was as a natural a being as I could have wished to know. The hawklike look softened. Sir Joseph filled a pipe and offered it to him. Webster took it and began to light it with a spill. I watched the man straighten himself, like a good steel blade that has been flexed.

'Gentlemen, this enterprise is done. We have fulfilled our commission. We have succeeded. Charles Stuart has been denied the great revenue he had from Newcastle's coal. With that I am content.' He looked keenly at Sir Joseph. 'And I think that the cause we have all sworn to support has been well served these last days.'

It was early evening before they had talked out their business. I listened and I learned the fine detail of much that I had been able only to guess at before. Enough to say that had His Majesty, King Charles the First of England, and of Scotland, have heard their deliberations he would perhaps have fallen to his prayers. But he could not, so I shall speak no more of it.

I wanted private words with Ralph Carr. And at last I had them. We took a flagon of wine and sat in the long gallery.

'So ... it is done, lad?' Blue eyes, eyes that might have been my mother's, settled on me, twinkling a little, yet searching hard too.

'This part of the business is finished.' I yawned, suddenly weary. 'The Scots will stay until they can no longer wring a profit. And the King has neither the seasoned troops nor the money to pay them. He'll not try to win the town back. That means that the Scots will get their pay. It is said that the town is going to make an 'amiable' loan of forty thousand pounds to the Scots army, and that the King will be asked to contribute eight hundred and fifty pounds every day to maintain their troops in the North.' I was sitting with my eyes shut; yet I knew that Ralph was still looking at me. I heard him stir in his seat. He spoke quietly.

'There will be a civil war within a year or so. Have no doubt about that!'

I looked across at Ralph. 'And I care about that ... not at all. I have promised service to Master Webster for a few months more. That much I shall do. I dare say that I will be called upon to raise the cannon that the English garrison put into the Tyne and to see what can be salvaged from the ship that I sank. But after that ... well, you must just see the mare that I fetched back from Sweden.' I was stopped in full flood by my uncle's soft laughter.

'Lad ... do you not know the nature of the man in whose service you find yourself? John, Master Webster is a power and has a power in this land that ... waxes.' He spread his hands. 'Though I fear that he is about to find the Scots a sore trial and a vexation if he hopes to rein them in. They have the whole of the North of England from Tees to Whitehaven and they are raiding beyond that. I fear that you will find that you must serve for as long as he wants you to serve.' I sat up ready to deny it. But Ralph laughed again. 'Besides,' his voice dropped almost to a whisper, 'Master Webster, or as I know him, and as he once was, Master Roger Thornton, could well be your father-in-law ... '

I was on my feet, alert, and almost hopping about the gallery, not knowing which question to ask first: the true identity of the man I knew as Sylvanus Webster, or the fact that my uncle had clearly taken a hand in my affairs.

'You mean to tell me that you have actually spoken with Master ... Thornton about such things?' I was amazed. I had asked Sylvanus Webster about Aphra Thornton only that morning. And to my certain knowledge he had not had a chance to talk to Ralph alone in that time. I heard myself snort. I began to pace the length of the gallery, while my uncle puffed at his tobacco and watched me.

'So ... what, Uncle Ralph, has the Great Council decided upon?' I stood over the old man, but he just sat back in his chair and smiled up at me.

'Thorntons are of as good a blood as you'll find in the North.' He gave the ghost of a wink. 'And their midwife tells me that their womenfolk birth their bairns like puddin's from a bag. It would be a very fair match. Times are uncertain and both of your fortunes are scant. But the pair of you might yet mend that with hard work. So I agreed with Mistress Hannah Thornton that we could do a lot worse.'

'We! By God!' I stepped backward and left my cry hanging in the air. Then I realised that I could not he angry and laugh at the same time. 'I do think, Sir, that you have ... disposed of me ... like a wall-eyed old spinster with bandy legs!'

'Well, John , since you are a lad without a mother to find for you, you'll have to make shift with what I can do.' He started to chuckle, but he sucked his pipe too hard and set himself coughing. I waited until he was right again.

'And what of the farm? As things are, does not half of it lie in the hands of Luke's widow?'

'Leave the business with me, John. I shall put the word around the town that when, in a season or two, the Bronsard family set its lawyers snarling at our heels they are to come to see me.' He tapped his nose with a finger and cocked his head on one side. 'What think you of the worth of land that now lies under the foul dominion of the Scots? Do you think that it will fetch a great price in ready money ... or a very small one?'

That was a thought that had not occurred to me. It was the work of a few seconds to get the sheaf of letters of credit out from my breeks and to hand Ralph the notes that I had fetched with me from Sweden. There was uncommon pleasure for me in the knowledge that I was to be paid twice for the same letter of credit, yet that it would still go to the House of Bronsard.

'Use that to redeem the land. If you need more you shall have it. But I fancy, uncle, that with the Scots about our ears that a sound letter of credit will fetch a better discount hereabouts that gold itself.'

Ralph Carr sought for his spectacle glasses. He scanned the note for a moment, his lips pursed tight. Then he nodded, and a keen knowing look came into his blue eyes. I waited until he had stowed the paper away in his clothes.

'And what of Mistress Aphra, does she know of these dealings in fine blood-stock?' I waited, half hoping that somehow, in some way, my way had been cleared for me. 'I mean … ' I began and then faltered.

'Stud bulls and stallions need help to mount. Men seldom do … Ellyot men never! This is something, bonny lad, which you must do for yourself!'

Chapter 30

For the Love of Aphra

B ut I still could not mount my horse and gallop off to Benwell to take Aphra Thornton in my arms. News about the town was that malignants, the King's supporters, had fired a warehouse and there was to be a strict curfew that night, so I had to bide where I was.

I was wakened next morning by a servant who gibbered with fright as he told me that there was a military escort waiting for me outside. The elderly lieutenant was a Lothian man and he was civil enough to me. And he was damned grateful when I called for ale and a breakfast for him. But he would not take a place at the table. I watched him wolf down a plate piled with black pudding and bacon where he stood. Then I caught and followed his gaze when he looked out of the window. His troopers were at both front and back of the house.

My horse was saddled for me and I rode between escorts from Sir Joseph Ord's house the short distance to the quayside. I was much relieved. Already there were a dozen fellows, young lads, stripped to the buff save for scant linen clouts to cover their private parts. They had already contrived to get two of the smaller ditched cannon out of the river. It began to look too as though the folk of the town had begun to get over their fear of the Scots. For I saw that there was a great throng, mostly of women, dames as well as maids, who had found that they had Monday morning business on the bridge and the quay.

And I did a fair day's work without having to shed a clout myself, nor even to get close to water. I ordered horses commandeered from a brewer. Then I watched the poor old bugger's face as he goggled at the promissory note that the commissary clerk handed him as payment. Heavy ship's ropes were fetched from a chandler's warehouse.

The tide did not fall as low as I would have wished. But the guns lay at no more than a man's height below the water at the deepest part and soon every one was found and the place marked. It was not difficult to get ropes around the trunnions and then to drag the cannon clear of the water by main force of horses and men. And the Scots troops made a great sport of the enterprise, whooping and jumping into the water, and contriving to come up without their breech clouts. Maybe it was for the best that the womenfolk, who shrieked so loudly and then peeped at the pale, naked bodies through splayed fingers, should see that their conquerors were – after all – mere mortal men. The whole atmosphere in the town was changed by it.

By three o'clock the last piece of Newcastle's ordnance was laid in straw on carts and on its way across the bridge to Gateshead. My small escort had disappeared. But I had not ridden far on my way back to Sir Joseph Ord's house when the prickle of my neck hair told me that I was being followed. I reminded myself that the Scots had learned their trade in the Swedish service. A newly taken town was always flooded with spies and informers. Nor did I forget that, although the King's men had fled Newcastle, many pairs of well-paid eyes and ears would have been left behind to keep York and London well informed. It did not take me long to pick my man out of the crowd. Who but a hired knave would wear a felt cloak on a sweltering afternoon? He was badly trained in his work. Our eyes even met at one point – and I touched two fingers to the brim of my hat in mock salute to him. Then I spurred my horse to a gallop up the Sandhill bank. He had either to run after me or give up his game. The incident gave me some amusement but I knew that I would be a fool to treat it lightly. I dallied with the idea of riding up to the Scotch House in Newgate Street to make a show of laying the information before the governor who resided at Sir Lionel Maddison's mansion; and as quickly I rejected the notion. Likely as not, the spy had been set on me by General Leslie himself. Clearly I needed to have talk with Sylvanus Webster – or Master Roger Thornton as I was beginning to think of him.

But when I rode into the stables of Sir Joseph Ord's house I saw that Webster's mare was gone from its stall. Sir Joseph's cook told me that he had been ordered to make up provisions of bread and meat to last for four days for Master Webster and that the saddle bags had been taken late that morning. At last I was in some measure free.

I found what I had half expected. Every one of the town's six gates was guarded by a full company of Scots musketeers. And there was no mistaking that David Leslie had given his governor William Kerr the best of his best troops to garrison the town. In spite of myself though, I could hardly help feeling a touch of pride when I watched a guard change at the Close Gate that would not have been out of place at the royal palace at Stockholm. But pride would not get me out of the town. I rode back and stabled my horse at Sir Joseph Ord's house. The Scots may well have had the gates held fast but I was easily able to whistle for a boatman at the Sandgate steps. For a handful of small silver he sculled me up river and through the arches of the bridge on the flood tide and put me ashore at the haughs above Clarence Island.

Will Blacket's Meg opened the door and bobbed a very pretty courtesy for me as I stepped over the threshold. I sniffed. As a lad, ever hungry, I had sniffed deeply whenever I had come in. There was the smell of newly baked bread through the house, my house, and somewhere I could hear the steady scritch-scratch of wool being carded and the treadle of a spinning wheel working.

'I bid you good afternoon, Master Ellyot ... and welcome home.'

I stopped and looked upwards. Aphra stood at the head of the stairs. My heart gave a leap. I wanted to blurt out nonsense words, words of affection, to say there and then that I loved the girl and that I wanted to marry her. Just in time my soldier's caution got a grip on my daft haverings.

'Thank you.' I heard myself speak and could scarcely believe that the voice was mine. She came down the stairs like a queen descending. The soft swish of her petticoats and the scent of verbena sent a small shiver through me.

'You are ... perhaps ... a little recovered ... after your ...' My voice trailed away. I did not want to remind her of the nightmare she had gone through at the house in Jesmond. She smiled. It was a smile that had something, at least, of Roger Thornton in it.

'I mend, Master Ellyot. I slept off the drug, and my wounds are ... ' Just the beginning of a blush came to her cheek. I turned away my gaze. 'The prickings were deep but they are not grievous.' There was a little toss of her head and a mischievous little smile began to flitter around her mouth. 'We women are made of firmer substance than you might suppose, Master Ellyot ... consider the travails of childbirth.'

I had not. But it was a line of thought not too far removed from what I had in my mind.

As I had walked up the bank to the farm I had devised in my mind a script of the things I would say, and the order in which I would say them, and the way I would speak. Suddenly the entire plan was swept away and like a stuttering schoolboy I said the first thing that came into my head.

'The ... deposition, the sworn testimony of the ... ' I sought for some gentler word and failed. 'Witch-finder ... I burned it to ashes.' Her hands reached out as though to touch me but at the last instant shrank away. She hung her head and whispered, 'Thank you ... John.'

'The Inquisitor?' It had come into my mind that I might yet have to make it certain that Aphra would be safe from ever being named a witch again – that I might have to seek out the bastard who had tortured her, and shut his perjuring mouth for good. I had seen four crazed old women burnt alive as witches at Leipzig. I never wanted to see the like again. And I knew well what Godless bastards these so-called witchfinders were. It was not a task I would fear to do – and truly it was the only way to render Aphra safe from the accusation.

'His name was Master Alvey Lamb ... ' Aphra's whisper died in her throat and a little tremor went through her body. That had been the signature that I had not been able to decipher.

'Lamb-of-the-Lord! Jesu!' I swore in spite of myself. We bear evil with uncommon patience in the North. Alvey Lamb had been busy about Northumberland having senile old dames pricked and hanged, or drowned for the sake of their half acre of land of land years before ever I had gone to Sweden.

'He will be found. I'll set Will to start looking this very day. He can not have gone too far.' Her hand touched me.

'Is Nicholas Bronsard ... dead?'

'Put all thought of Nicholas Bronsard out of your head ... He is gone.' I stepped forward and took up her hands in mine.

'But did you ... was it you who killed him?'

'No; I can swear my oath, Aphra, that I did not kill Nicholas Bronsard.' I looked into her eyes. The black flecks looked to have grown larger.

'Then Margaret ... '

'Nor have I any proof that my sister-in-law did her uncle any hurt ... I saw nothing.' It was a clever use of words but for the present it would have to serve. Her lips quivered. I touched them with my fingers.

'Be still, lass,' I whispered. 'It may be that I shall have more of this to tell ... but not today, nor any time soon. So be content.' I smiled and looked at her again. 'Besides, I did not come here to talk of the past. I came to talk of the future.'

Aphra let me take her arm and lead her gently to the kitchen hearth and the tall-backed settles that faced each other by the fire. I sat her down on one and I took a place opposite. It was not a way for any courting couple to sit but I had the sense to realise that the treatment that she had suffered at Nicholas Bronsard's hands would not be likely to make her eager for any man's embraces ... for a while, at least.

'Mistress Thornton,' I began and then my courage faded, withered. I rallied and tried again. 'I have spoken with your father.' Her head turned in the firelight. For a moment she looked away from me, into the flames. Then her gaze turned and she looked directly at me. For just an instant I could have sworn that she was about to give me a little smile. Again I was unmanned. 'And my uncle, Ralph Carr, has discussed certain matters with Mistress Hannah. And the upshot is ... '

'The upshot, John Ellyot is nothing! Nothing at all! I tell you now, Sir, that I shall not be sold off like a heifer. It will not do for you to make sheep's eyes at me and say, 'Mistress Aphra wilt thou ... ' For I tell you now John Ellyot that I no intention of being a farmer's wife ... nor indeed a soldier's woman. I will not be worked into an early grave, nor worn out by bearing a brat every nine-month and a ... ' She ran out of words and sat staring into the dancing flames in the hearth.

In the North we say that a body shocked speechless has been gobsmacked. Truly I was gobsmacked. But Aphra Thornton sat with her hands folded demurely in her lap like a little maid in church and she had on her face a look of thrice-distilled innocence.

'I do not ask you to become a farmer's wife ... nor a soldier's woman ... ' I took a deep breath and then spoke, softly and with restraint, and, I admit, through half clenched teeth. 'My fortunes ... ' I stopped. Like father like daughter. She may have been able to stem the tiny ripple of a smile that almost escaped to flit across her face; but she had not guile enough to suppress the little tremor that made her shoulders give a little shake. I stood up and took a step towards her.

'My fortunes are uncertain ... ' I let my voice rise, 'But I ask you to share them. And I tell you that I am no farmer and that I have quit soldiering for good. So, Aphra Thornton, will you be my wife? Will you wed me and share my life and my fortune what ever they be, and love me and bear our bairns ...' I stopped for I could think of naught else.

'Upon certain conditions ... ' This time there was no trace of amusement. I heard myself give a long drawn out sigh. If this was courting then I was glad that I had been spared it for so long. How much easier it had been to wink at a doxie and show her that you had a flask of akvavit and owned a few ready groschen to pay her in the morning.

'What conditions?' I began to think that perhaps I had come back to Newcastle to find the place stricken by a veritable plague of mad women.

'If we are to be married ... and I do say if ... it must be in the Auld Kirk at Edinburgh.'

Surely this was some game. I clenched my fists by my side and looked down into her face.

'I have never loved the Scots, Aphra. It is true that duty has made me serve with them sometimes ... But why, my love, must we go to Edinburgh before we can be wed?' I had forced myself to let a note of sweet reason enter my speech. And she replied in the same tone.

'We must go to Edinburgh so that my father can perform the ceremony. There is also the matter of a dispensation for the time. For if we are to be married at Edinburgh then it must be by next Friday morning.'

I think that I swore, not quite under my breath, and I think that she heard me. What devilry was Doctor Webster ... Roger Thornton ... up to now?

'And why by next Friday, my dearest? I have led a wild life but I had hoped that when I married I should do it properly. I would have had the banns called at St Andrew's church, and a wedding feast for the neighbours here afterwards.'

'We would have to be married by next Friday because it would be unseemly for me to share a cabin on shipboard with a man who is not my lawful husband.'

Now it was my turn to take Aphra by surprise. She gave a little scream of alarm as I took her by the arms and lifted her bodily from her seat.

'Shipboard! Lassie, explain yourself before you have me as daft as yourself!' I allowed her to slide down so that I was holding her in my arms. She let her head drop against my chest. I liked that feeling a lot.

'My father wishes us to be aboard Ephraim Nellist's new ship, the *Hannie*, at Leith Walk, ready to sail for Amsterdam on Saturday morning's tide.'

There was no point in my protesting so I gave her a little squeeze to urge her on.

'You were right. The loving cup that the Parliamentary party has shared with the Scots Covenanters is beginning to sour. Leslie's army has control of the country. Their arrogance grows. They would like to forget the promises that they made. The prize is in their hands and they know that neither the King nor the Parliament has the power to curb what they do. General Leslie has tried to keep his word – but with Newcastle taken he has not the power he had. It is the commissioners and clerks come down from Edinburgh who hold sway now. And they mean to squeeze what they can while they may.'

'But why does that call for us to flee to Edinburgh, to Edinburgh of all places?'

'Because of the gold ... '

'Gold?' I made a huge effort to stay silent and waited for her go on.

'There was supposed to be more than eight thousand pounds worth of gold aboard the ship you sank. It was rumoured to be all the ready money that the Newcastle merchants had left. It was said that it was being sent to Norwich for safe keeping.'

'And was there ... was there eight thousand pounds in gold?'

Aphra raised her face. I looked into it. No, she was not beautiful. But by God she was as near to it as made not a whit of difference to me.

'I don't know ... '

297

'Nor, I think, does your father. The story was just another one put about to … to encourage the Scots to fight hard to take the town.' Aphra bit her lip a little and nodded slowly. She was worried.

I found that I was smiling a bitter little smile. Sylvanus Webster seemed to have been caught by his own devious ways.

'So it was a story like the one about the guns lying off the Farne Islands. It was just another cunning tale to beguile the wits of simple fellows. But did not Master Thornton realise that such as story would not die once it had been told? Did he not know that the Scots will believe the money as good as got!'

Then I realised … 'And of course they will want daft John Ellyot to rig his diving bell and … ' The cold chain of consequences clanked, like manacles, link by link, through my brain. I might sit in my butter tub on the bottom of the Tyne river until Kingdom Come but I doubted very much that I would be able to convince the grim faced servants of the Covenant that there was no gold to be found. I knew the Scots. If there was no profit to be had out of the Tyne then there would doubtless be other wrecks to rummage. They would use me. I was a prize of war.

'Aye … all of which may well be.' I looked up at the rafters of the kitchen ceiling as I spoke. The house was welcoming. 'But what of this place? I have suffered a deal of trouble to get it and I am loath to leave now that I have it.'

Aphra put up her hands and held them to my face. Her fingers were cool.

'Come away, John. This will be no place for you for a year or more.'

'But … ' I began to protest. Yet even as I did I knew that it was no use, that she was right.

'Listen. My grandmother offers you a plan. Take her advice. Leave this place. We must ride to Edinburgh tonight. Leave Will Blacket to see to things here. Make him your tenant.' There was a sudden urgency in Aphra's voice. 'Will wants to marry his Meg. As your tenant he will have a fair place here and he is the one man you could trust to see that you precious mare is well looked after. And you should allow Margaret Ellyot to stay here. Let folk think that she is still the mistress of the house. She is much better now, and Sarah Trotter has agreed to look after her. Your uncle Ralph will oversee everything while you are away.'

I looked into her face and sighed deeply. Then I nodded my agreement.

'Anything you say, my love.' We looked at each other. 'But you should know, Mistress Aphra, that it had been my plan to court properly for at least half of a year.' She smiled at me softly. 'Also that I can pick a tune on the mandolin and play the recorder well – and hold my place in a part song and at that sing a little more sweetly than a tomcat.' Now she put a hand to her lips to hold back a giggle. 'I can frame a sonnet, of sorts, and could have brought you candied peel by the keel load ... '

Suddenly the tears welled up into those wonderful eyes. To kiss her was the most natural thing in the world ... a gentle kiss and then another. I took a handful of her soft brown tresses and held her face to me. 'All these things would I have done ... '

'And I will take them as being done, John Ellyot,' she said softly.